Praise for
Death at Glamis Castle

"Gypsy prophecies, sing-alongs at the pub, a possible ghost or two: There's something for everyone. And if you don't fall in love with Glamis Castle, you haven't a wee dram o' romance in your soul." —*Kirkus Reviews*

Death at Dartmoor

"A fantasia on themes from *The Hound of the Baskervilles* whose focus on the Sheridans shows an altogether more lighthearted side of the moors than Doyle ever revealed." —*Kirkus Reviews*

Death at Epsom Downs

"Enough danger and intrigue to keep readers turning the pages, which are filled with vivid historical detail." —*Booklist*

"Readers who like their historical mysteries on the lighter side will find much to enjoy here." —*Publishers Weekly*

More praise for
Robin Paige's Victorian Mysteries

"I read it with enjoyment . . . I found myself burning for the injustices of it, and caring what happened to the people."
—Anne Perry

"Wonderfully gothic . . . A bright and lively re-creation of late-Victorian society." —Sharan Newman

"An original and intelligent sleuth . . . a vivid re-creation of Victorian England." —Jean Ha[illegible] *Murder*

"Robin Paige's de[illegible]chnol-
ogy and detection [illegible] Emer-
son have done for V[illegible] *Journal*

C[illegible]

The Victorian and Edwardian Mysteries by Robin Paige

DEATH AT BISHOP'S KEEP
DEATH AT GALLOWS GREEN
DEATH AT DAISY'S FOLLY
DEATH AT DEVIL'S BRIDGE
DEATH AT ROTTINGDEAN
DEATH AT WHITECHAPEL
DEATH AT EPSOM DOWNS
DEATH AT DARTMOOR
DEATH AT GLAMIS CASTLE
DEATH IN HYDE PARK
DEATH AT BLENHEIM PALACE
DEATH ON THE LIZARD

China Bayles Mysteries by Susan Wittig Albert

THYME OF DEATH
WITCHES' BANE
HANGMAN'S ROOT
ROSEMARY REMEMBERED
RUEFUL DEATH
LOVE LIES BLEEDING
CHILE DEATH
LAVENDER LIES

MISTLETOE MAN
BLOODROOT
INDIGO DYING
A DILLY OF A DEATH
DEAD MAN'S BONES
BLEEDING HEARTS
SPANISH DAGGER
NIGHTSHADE

AN UNTHYMELY DEATH
CHINA BAYLES' BOOK OF DAYS

The Cottage Tales of Beatrix Potter by Susan Wittig Albert

THE TALE OF HILL TOP FARM
THE TALE OF HOLLY HOW
THE TALE OF CUCKOO BROW WOOD
THE TALE OF HAWTHORN HOUSE
THE TALE OF BRIAR BANK

Nonfiction books by Susan Wittig Albert

WRITING FROM LIFE
WORK OF HER OWN

Death in
Hyde Park

ROBIN PAIGE

BERKLEY PRIME CRIME, NEW YORK

THE BERKLEY PUBLISHING GROUP
Published by the Penguin Group
Penguin Group (USA) Inc.
375 Hudson Street, New York, New York 10014, USA
Penguin Group (Canada), 90 Eglinton Avenue East, Suite 700, Toronto, Ontario M4P 2Y3, Canada
(a division of Pearson Penguin Canada Inc.)
Penguin Books Ltd., 80 Strand, London WC2R 0RL, England
Penguin Group Ireland, 25 St. Stephen's Green, Dublin 2, Ireland (a division of Penguin Books Ltd.)
Penguin Group (Australia), 250 Camberwell Road, Camberwell, Victoria 3124, Australia
(a division of Pearson Australia Group Pty. Ltd.)
Penguin Books India Pvt. Ltd., 11 Community Centre, Panchsheel Park, New Delhi—110 017, India
Penguin Group (NZ), 67 Apollo Drive, Rosedale, North Shore 0632, New Zealand
(a division of Pearson New Zealand Ltd.)
Penguin Books (South Africa) (Pty.) Ltd., 24 Sturdee Avenue, Rosebank, Johannesburg 2196,
South Africa

Penguin Books Ltd., Registered Offices: 80 Strand, London WC2R 0RL, England

DEATH IN HYDE PARK

A Berkley Prime Crime Book / published by arrangement with the authors

PRINTING HISTORY
Berkley Prime Crime hardcover edition / March 2004
Berkley Prime Crime mass-market edition / February 2005

Copyright © 2004 by Susan Wittig Albert and William J. Albert.
Cover design by Pamela Jaber.
Cover illustration by Teresa Fasolino.

ISBN: 978-0-425-20113-8

BERKLEY® PRIME CRIME
Berkley Prime Crime Books are published by The Berkley Publishing Group,
a division of Penguin Group (USA) Inc.,
375 Hudson Street, New York, New York 10014.
The name BERKLEY PRIME CRIME and the BERKLEY PRIME CRIME design are trademarks
belonging to Penguin Group (USA) Inc.

PRINTED IN THE UNITED STATES OF AMERICA

12 11 10 9 8 7 6 5 4

CAST OF MAJOR CHARACTERS
* indicates historical persons

Charles, Lord Sheridan, Baron Somersworth

Lady Kathryn Ardleigh Sheridan, aka Beryl Bardwell

*Jack London, American adventure writer

Nellie Lovelace (Ellie Wurtz), actress

Bradford Marsden, investment promoter

Officials, Police, and Agents

Inspector Earnest Ashcraft, Special Branch, Scotland Yard

*Sergeant Charles Collins, fingerprint expert, Scotland Yard

*Fredrick Ponsonby, assistant secretary to King Edward VII

Dmitri Tropov, alias Vladimir Rasnokov, member of Russia Ochrana (Czar's secret police)

Captain Steven Wells, Intelligence Branch, War Office

Anarchists, Trade Unionists

Charlotte Conway, editor of the *Anarchist Clarion*

Sybil Conway, Charlotte Conway's mother

Adam Gould, Amalgamated Society of Railway Servants

Ivan Kopinski, Russian Anarchist

Yuri Messenko, Hyde Park bomber

Pierre Mouffetard, French Anarchist

*Helen Rossetti, coauthor of *A Girl Among the Anarchists*

It was the best of times, it was the worst of times, it was the age of wisdom, it was the age of foolishness, it was the epoch of belief, it was the epoch of incredulity, it was the season of Light, it was the season of Darkness, it was the spring of hope, it was the winter of despair, we had everything before us, we had nothing before us, we were all going direct to Heaven, we were all going direct the other way. . . .

Charles Dickens,
A Tale of Two Cities

CHAPTER ONE

With this sword do justice, stop the growth of iniquity, protect the Holy Church of God, help and defend widows and orphans, restore the things that are gone to decay, maintain the things that are restored, punish and reform what is amiss, and confirm what is in good order.

The Archbishop of Canterbury,
presenting the Sword of State to King Edward VII
at his coronation, 9 August 1902

Edward VII almost missed his coronation.

The great event had already been postponed some eighteen months after Edward ascended Queen Victoria's empty throne, primarily because of the ugly debacle of the Boer War. But at last the war dragged to its conclusion, and plans were made to crown the King and Queen on 26 June 1902. Heads of state from around the world began to converge on London; twenty-five hundred quail and three hundred legs of mutton were ordered for the Coronation banquet; the Peers took their Coronation robes out of storage and had them cleaned and aired; and the cavalry who were to participate in the parade polished their swords and buffed their golden buttons. The Empire was preparing for a grand exhibition of its power and glory.

The difficulty began some two weeks before the great event, when the King began to suffer severe nausea and abdominal pain. After a few days, his worried physicians brought Sir Frederick Treves into the case. Treves, perhaps best known for his association with the Elephant Man, had written and lectured on the difficult topic of appendicitis, or "perityphilitis," as it was called. The first appendectomy had been performed in the United States some fifteen years earlier, but the operation was still considered novel, radical, and dangerous. Treves recommended surgery. Edward refused.

"I have a coronation on hand," the King said testily.

Treves frowned at his sovereign. "It will be a funeral if you don't have the operation, sir."

At last, the King gave in, and the surgery, which required less than an hour, was carried out at Buckingham Palace. Since Edward was sixty-one, obese, a heavy drinker and smoker with a family history of gastric cancer, the prognosis was not particularly good. An anxious Empire waited in nail-biting suspense for the dreaded announcement that the King had died under the knife.

But Edward had a strong constitution and an even stronger will to live—after all, he had waited a great many years to ascend his mother's throne—and he survived. His Coronation was rescheduled for August 9. And while some saw the King's narrow escape as a dark omen for a reign already marred by a war that could not be won, others understood that it merely proved (as if proof were necessary) that Englishmen lived in the very best of all possible times, in the very best of all possible circumstances, and in the very best of all possible worlds.

* * *

It rained on August 9. The heavy gray skies wept over the great, gray city, and frequent showers chilled the August day. But the rain did nothing at all to quench the giddy exuberance of the vast throngs gathered to watch King Edward and Queen Alexandra make their triumphal progress, at last, to Westminster Abbey. The people had waited a long time for this day, and they did not intend to let a few showers spoil their celebration. And while the ceremonies were shorn of the glitter and glamor of foreign heads of state, most of whom had already gone home, the great day was still perfectly splendid—better, many said, because it was a family event rather than an Imperial gala. Thousands of British prelates, princes, and peers gathered to witness the crowning, while hundreds of thousands of British citizens noisily thronged the streets and filled windows along the route of the parade.

At eleven-fifteen in the morning, Edward and Alexandra were passing up St. James Street and through Trafalgar Square, their crystal and gilt coach drawn by eight superbly matched cream-colored horses preceded by an escort of the Royal Horse Guards. The crowd in the square roared when the coach came into sight, followed by ranks of glittering cavalry and foot soldiers, a broad stream of scarlet and gold flowing through the wet, gray streets. It was a demonstration of the Empire's military prowess, perhaps designed to ease the sting of the recent military disgrace in South Africa, where England's finest had been hard put to it to suppress a rabble of sixty thousand Boer farmers. But that humiliation was forgotten now. The people had come to see and to cheer the King and Queen, and cheer they did, at the tops of their lungs and with all their hearts.

Jack London, an American writer recently arrived in England, joined the throng. He couldn't see much except for the backs of the double line of soldiers walling off the line of march, but between their shoulders he saw the gold coach bearing a man and a woman, both in the regal splendor of coronation robes.

"Gaw' blimey, wot a splendid ol' chap," exclaimed a ragged, dirty man leaning on a stick. He dug his elbow blithely into Jack's ribs and blew his beery breath into Jack's face. "Ain't 'e a rum un, eh? As fine a king as ever wore crown, is wot I sez. Too bad 'is ol' mum kept 'im waitin' so long to put it on 'is head."

"An' there be 'is Queen," sighed the woman on Jack's right, whose tattered gray shawl did nothing to shield her disheveled hair against the spitting rain. "A rare beauty, an' 'er pushin' sixty, if ye'd b'lieve it." She heaved a gusty sigh. "Wisht I 'ad a few of 'er diamonds to put in me 'air. I'd glitter, I would."

Jack London, gloomily calculating that just one of the Queen's glittering jewels could provide enough to feed the one million subjects who would receive poor-law relief on that day, shook his head in disgust as the Royal coach clattered past. He had never witnessed such mumbo-jumbo tomfoolery, he would write later, except maybe in a Yankee circus. He shoved his chapped hands into the pockets of his ragged coat, lowered his capped head against the rain, and made off through the crowd.

Nearer Westminster, another group of spectators enjoyed a somewhat wider view. Bradford Marsden, his pretty wife Edith, and a dozen guests watched the procession from a high window, sipping champagne and eating fresh oysters. They applauded the crimson-and-gold tide, the ponies prancing, the drums drumming, the bugles bugling, all in a cacophonous celebration of wealth and power. The coronation, Marsden reflected with immense satisfaction, was an inspiring statement of the Empire's indisputable authority and undeniable magnificence: Long might the Empire endure and prosper, and long might Bradford Marsden prosper with it. He smiled as he thought that the vantage point his guests were enjoying with such careless gaity would have put a hundred guineas a head into his pocket, had he been as hard up for a bit of ready as he'd been in the past—when he'd had to pawn his mother's emeralds, for instance.

But time and tide had changed for the better, and Marsden was feeling happily flush. His family property and wealth, like that of many of the aristocracy, had vanished in the national decline of agricultural income, and Bradford, the last scion of the family branch, had been forced to fend for himself. Like other young aristocrats—Charles Rolls, for instance, the younger son of Lord Llangattock, was selling expensive motorcars; and Sir Harley Dalrymple-Hay, a baronet, was building underground lines in London—Bradford Marsden had turned his hand to commercial enterprises. He had formed a fortunate association with Cecil Rhodes's gold mining enterprise in Rhodesia, married Rhodes's goddaughter, and managed to come out of the war with a substantial profit in his pocket. In fact, his new investment business was doing well enough to allow him to purchase a house and furnish it stylishly, to dress his wife in a Worth gown, and to grace her elegant throat with several fine strands of matched pearls.

Bradford slipped his arm around Edith's waist and nuzzled her neck as the King's coach came into view. For him, the Coronation was a celebration of all that was right with the world, and a promise of even better things to come.

Within Westminster Abbey, the spectacle was much more intimate and immediate, many of the spectators themselves a part of the pageant. In the transept, Kate Sheridan fidgeted on her hard wooden chair. Her coronation robe, last worn by a previous Baroness Somersworth at the crowning of Queen Victoria in 1838, was trimmed in two inches of miniver and two bars of ermine, with a yard-long train that she had found almost impossible to manage gracefully. Like the robes of the ladies around her, it smelt faintly of the camphor-chest, in spite of being aired. The bevy of duchesses, marchionesses, countesses, viscountessess, and baronesses were seated in strict order of precedence, their ranks signified by the quantity of miniver and ermine on their robes, the length of their trains, and the style of the coronets they would don upon the crowning of the Queen. They all, however, wore identical white elbow-length gloves. Later, when the King was asked what had impressed him most about the ceremony, he would answer with a glint in his eye that the simultaneous lifting of those graceful white arms as the ladies put on their coronets had reminded him of a scene from a beautiful ballet.

Kate, feeling very much an imposter among this exalted assembly, wished fervently that she could have been seated with her husband Charles. But Lord Sheridan, Baron Somersworth, sat among the other peers in the transept on the opposite side of the throne, where she could not even catch a glimpse of him. She suspected, though, that he was every bit as uncomfortable as she. Charles had attended the ceremony not because he wanted to, but solely out of a sense of duty and as a testimony to his respect for the King who had finally come into his own.

Left to her own devices, Kate found herself surveying her imposing surroundings with something like an awed disbelief, astonished that an American woman who had grown up among the Irish of New York's Lower East Side had managed to find her way to the Coronation of King Edward VII of England. Other American women were there, of course: Consuelo Vanderbilt, now the Duchess of Marlborough, had a featured role as bearer of the Queen's canopy; Mary Leiter Curzon, a baroness and wife of the Viceroy of India, occupied a place of honor; and Jennie Jerome Churchill was elsewhere in the audience. But Consuelo and Mary had brought their British husbands a great deal of money, while Kate was dowered only with intelligence, determination, and a certain beauty (or so Charles asserted), and she had never forgot the poverty of her early life. Like Jack London, Kate Sheridan saw the Coronation through the spectacles of her American experience, and although she would not have described it as a Yankee circus, nothing about it seemed real, especially her part in it.

Then the trumpets sounded a fanfare, the organ pealed majestically, and the Royal procession entered through the West Door and began to make its way down the long aisle, past rows of invited guests—mostly members of the five hundred hereditary families who owned one-fifth of England— who were seated on tiers specially built for the occasion. The audience included those in what some irreverently called the "King's Loose Box," arranged by His Majesty to accommodate some of his former and current lovers: Sarah Bernhardt, Mrs. Hartmann, Lady Kilmorey, Mrs. Arthur Paget, and the reigning favorite, Mrs. George Keppel.

As the choir sang an anthem, the officials of the Court came first down the red-carpeted aisle, carrying white wands; the Church dignitaries followed in magnificent miters and vestments, and then the bearers of the Royal regalia: the Sword of State, the Great Spurs, the staff of St. Edward, and St. Edward's crown. Queen Alexandra was next, her maids of honor carrying her purple velvet train. Finally came the King, solemn, stately, and regal. At the sight of Alexandra and Edward, a collective sigh swept the spectators and Kate felt her throat tighten. She might have become more British than she knew.

The ceremonies had been shortened because of the King's recent illness. Everybody agreed that Edward bore up handsomely under the strain, although the old Archbishop of

Canterbury was wobbly throughout and had to be prompted in his lines. He got the King's crown on back to front and managed to anoint the Queen's nose, rather than the Royal forehead, with holy oil. But finally the ceremony was over and the Royal party returned to their coaches. They were cheered enthusiastically by the multitudes of loyal subjects along the route back to Buckingham Palace, where the Royal chef had managed to keep in cold storage some of the quail and mutton that had been destined for the earlier celebration, and there was enough champagne and fine wines, as one guest put it, to float an entire fleet of the Empire's battleships.

Kate and Charles, however, did not attend this gala banquet. Shedding their heavy robes and uncomfortable coronets, they climbed into Charles's Panhard and motored down to their home in Essex, where Kate put on a cotton smock and a pair of corduroy trousers and went straight out to dig in her garden.

Not everyone witnessed the parade or the ceremonies, of course. Many sensible people (among them Socialists, Democrats, and Laborites) rejected the revels, taking advantage of the holiday to escape to the countryside for a breath of fresher air. A multitude of others, less privileged, remained at their posts, performing their usual duties—cooking and cleaning, sweeping streets, carting coal, manning fire brigades, unloading ships in the docks along the Thames—scarcely mindful of the glories being paraded through their city. And there were those, particularly among the homeless who had flooded into the City desperate for work, who were too drained by lack of food and sleep to care about the festivities, however grand. As Jack London observed when he wrote about the scene in *People of the Abyss,* almost the whole of the East End stayed in the East

End and got colossally drunk, the public houses awash in ale and thunderous waves of song:

Oh, on Coronation Day, on Coronation Day,
We'll have a spree, a jubilee, and shout Hip, hip, hooray.
For we'll all be merry, drinking whiskey, wine, and sherry,
We'll all be merrily drunk on Coronation Day.

Walking through Green Park, London came across an old man on a bench and asked him how he had liked the procession.

" 'Ow did I like it?" the old man replied scornfully. "A bloody good chawnce, sez I to myself, for a sleep, wi' all the coppers aw'y, so I turned into the corner there, along wi' fifty others. But I couldn't sleep, a-lyin' there 'ungry an' thinkin' 'ow I'd worked all the years o' my life an' now 'ad no plyce to rest my 'ead; an' the music comin' to me, an' the cheers an' cannon, till I got almost a hanarchist an' wanted to blow out the brains o' the Lord Chamberlain."

There were others who planned to attend the pageant and were, for various reasons, prevented. Perhaps the most notable of these was a certain Yuri Messenko, a tall, well-built young man, slightly stooped, with a fair complexion, a blond beard and moustache, and fervent eyes. Wearing an old black woolen overcoat with a frayed velvet collar and carrying a satchel, he was striding swiftly through Hyde Park in the direction of Hyde Park Corner, beyond which lay Buckingham Palace, where crowds awaited the return of their newly-crowned King.

Hyde Park occupies 615 acres taken by Henry VIII from Westminster Abbey, to use as his hunting grounds. It was opened to the public in the seventeenth century, and it quickly became a popular site for horse-racing, duels, games, and fairs. By the mid-nineteenth century, it was also the site of gatherings of dissenters of various stripes, with as many as 150,000 people thronging the Park to protest such things as the Sunday Trading Bill, the high price of food, and the violation of the people's rights, and to demand the right of access to the Park itself. After the riots there in the summer of 1866, Parliament began to debate the issue of free speech, and in 1872 set aside a space in the northeastern corner of the Park for the open expression of dissent. By now, the area around Speakers' Corner was hallowed ground to Yuri Messenko and his comrades, and fiery orators cried their views on every subject, free of interference by the authorities, although they might be, and often were, hissed and booed by their audiences.

Ignoring the rain that dripped down his collar, Yuri smiled to himself at the thought of the heroic deed he was about to perform, with the assistance of a new friend named Rasnokov, who had helped him gather and assemble the materials. He, Yuri Messenko, was about to send King Edward of England to join the elite group that had gone before: the premier of Spain, Empress Elizabeth of Austria, King Umberto of Italy, and President McKinley of the United States, all four of whom had been assassinated in the past four years.

And who better than he? Yuri thought jubilantly. He had come to London from the slums of Manchester three years before, his father a Ukranian refugee who worked as a bootmaker, his English mother long since worn down by the twin devils of pregnancy and poverty. He had worked diligently, doing his part to keep the *Anarchist Clarion* alive and thriving, helping to print and distribute the newspaper throughout London, taking leaflets to meetings, and working among the filthy warrens of the poor, where a dozen hungry men, women, and children crowded together in a single fetid room, desperate for work, sickened by the unsanitary conditions, with no hope for a better future. Assassination was a moral response to the immoral institutions and governments that spawned such horrors.

Yuri glanced across the crowded park, but he did not see the many celebrants gathered there, or the heroic statue of Achilles, erected in honor of the Duke of Wellington and cast from cannon captured at Waterloo, where the Iron Duke had defeated the Emperor Napoleon. He did not see, either, the watchful man, thickset and wearing brown tweeds and a brown derby hat, who had followed him through the park since he had entered at Speakers' Corner. Instead, he was gazing into a future when there would be no more coronations and no more emperors and dukes, when the yoke of capitalist oppression had been thrown off and the downtrodden peoples of the world had risen up, glorious and free.

Of course, Yuri did not work just for the Cause, although that was uppermost in his loyalties. He also worked for love, for the love of a female comrade named Charlotte Conway, who was the editor of the *Clarion* and, in everyone's estimation, the most dedicated member of the group. As he strode purposefully through the Park, he thought with pleasure of the look on Lottie's face when she learned that it had been he, Yuri, who had carried out this momentous work, who had rid the world of—

But Yuri Messenko did not finish his thought, or his task, either. He had barely reached Hyde Park Corner when it seemed that someone called his name. He turned, tripped over a stone, and pitched forward upon his satchel. Instantly, it exploded, the blast ripping Yuri into little pieces and scattering them across the ground, under the triumphant sword and victorious gaze of the bronze Achilles.

CHAPTER TWO

I felt a strong desire to free myself from all the ideas, customs, and prejudices which usually influence my class, to throw myself into the life and the work of the masses. Thus it was that I worked hard to learn how to compose and print, that I might be of use to the Cause of Anarchism in the most practical manner of all—the actual production of its literature.

Isabel Meredith,
A Girl Among the Anarchists, 1903

Charlotte Conway pulled the sheet of paper out of her typewriter, put it on the desk in front of her, and reached for her pencil to make revisions. It was nearly 10 A.M. on Wednesday morning, and she needed to finish the article—the story of Yuri Messenko's funeral the day before—in time for Ivan to set up and print it. The *Anarchist Clarion* was scheduled to come out on Friday, although things were always in such chaos in the newspaper's office that to get it out at all seemed a miracle.

Charlotte reached for a loose hairpin and pinned it through the mop of dark hair piled carelessly on top of her head. She had been astonished when she heard what had happened in Hyde Park on the previous Saturday. She had not known Yuri especially well—no better, that is, than she knew Ivan and Pierre, who also worked for the *Clarion*, or any of the other comrades in their Hampstead Road cell. Since the upheavals in Spain and France, attendance at meetings had been irregular and people kept to themselves, fearing that they might be turned in by one of the police spies that swarmed everywhere. But the Yuri who had run errands and helped Ivan with the press had seemed far more idealistic than militant, and while he might not have been very bright, he had always seemed much more interested in changing people's lives for the better than in blowing things up. But one never knew what lay hidden in another's heart. Obviously, there had been a streak of dark violence somewhere within Yuri's depths that she had never glimpsed.

Charlotte took out a cigarette, lit it, and leaned back in the rickety wooden chair, turning to glance out the grimy dormer window of the loft she used for her office, overlooking Hampstead Road. If those who had encouraged the boy—and she felt sure that trusting, dim-witted Yuri had not conceived or carried out the plot on his own—had imagined that an explosion on Coronation Day would encourage the workers to rise up against the rich and powerful, they had been very wrong. Two days after Yuri's death, *The Times* had written, "Everywhere, the Anarchists are hated. To step out on the street is to encounter a storm of abuse heaped on Anarchist heads. Terrorism is not the way to a brave new world, and those who practice it only damage themselves and their cause."

Charlotte rose and went to the window, gazing down at the stream of horse-drawn vehicles and motorcars passing along rainy Hampstead Road, nearly three stories below. She had joined the Anarchist movement some ten years before, when she was still in her teens and full of fury against the suffering and injustice she saw around her. Now, halfway through her twenties and with a decade's experience behind her, she still believed in the movement's purposes and was committed to doing all that she could to achieve them, but she knew in her heart that *The Times* was right. Terrorism was not the way to a brave new world. Attempting to blow up the King and Queen had been a terrible idea, and was bound to turn all London—all England, for that matter—against them.

Yet despite her cautions, Ivan and Pierre had insisted on trying to transform poor Yuri into a martyr. What few bits of his body the police had found and scooped up had been placed in a coffin, which was sealed shut and balanced across two chairs draped with red and black in the parlor of the meeting house a few blocks down Hampstead. But when Adam, Ivan, and the others carried the coffin out to the hearse, they had been met by an unruly crowd, booing and throwing rotten vegetables, scarcely restrained by a few policemen, who obviously had orders to let the crowd do all the damage it would. Another hostile crowd waited at St. John's Wood, where Yuri was to be buried. Stepping forward to make a speech, Ivan had got no further than "Fellow Anarchists, we are here today to bury a brave man," when he was rushed. A cordon of police pushed the crowd back, and the small group of mourners saw Yuri's remains lowered into the grave without even the comfort of a revolutionary song. Charlotte, her eyes swimming with tears for the poor lad who had died in such a terrible way, had whispered a few words of farewell, and then made her way through the jeering crowd. She had long ago learned to keep on the lookout for police, but she was too upset to notice the stocky, bowler-hatted man with his hands in his pockets, his glance sharply predatory, his thin lips pressed tight together.

"Well, there you are," Adam said, poking his blond head through the opening in the floor, where a wooden ladder led up from the second-floor print shop below. "How soon will the article be ready? Ivan has almost finished setting up the forms." His pale blue eyes were serious. "You know how nervous Ivan can be—and today he's worse than usual. He says somebody's been watching him. Pierre says he's being watched, too—but of course, Pierre always seems to feel a certain paranoia." He paused, frowning. "What about you, Lottie? Have you been followed?"

Charlotte gave a small nod, not wanting to worry Adam, who had a tendency to be protective. Being dogged by the police wasn't new to her—and it wasn't just the British police, either. French and Russian agents swarmed all over London, and because the *Clarion* attracted the most radical of the Anarchists, it often attracted their attention, too. Since Ivan and Pierre were also being followed, perhaps someone thought that the three of them had something to do with Yuri's bomb—that they were all involved in a plot. It was a sobering thought.

But Charlotte didn't have time to worry about that now. "Tell Ivan I'll be finished in fifteen minutes," she said, going back to her desk.

"And then we'll go out and get some lunch," Adam said. "I have to be back at the union office at one." He lifted his hand, gave her an affectionate smile, and went back down the ladder.

Charlotte sat down and pulled on her cigarette, thinking that if it were not for Adam, her world would be rather bleak. He wasn't an Anarchist—in fact, his work for the railway union made him what Pierre sneeringly called a "reformist"—and he lacked Ivan's disciplined hatred of the ruling class. But he believed that the way forward was to put as much power as possible into the hands of the laboring man, and he saw no contradiction between his work for the railway union and her work for the *Clarion*. He supported her, and worried about her, and was always there to lend a hand when the newspaper was going to press. If she had believed in marriage, Adam would have made a wonderful husband, but she felt that marriage was part of the bourgeois plot to confine women to their homes and keep them under control, and—

But that wouldn't get the article corrected. Charlotte stubbed out her cigarette, picked up her pencil, and within ten minutes had finished the piece. She had been only a few days past her twentieth birthday when she became editor of the *Clarion,* and in the intervening five years, she had grown quite competent as a working journalist, able to crank out stories quickly. Of course, her work involved more than just writing. She'd had to learn how to set type, manage the small handpress, and deal with the many odd people—mostly men, many of them foreigners, and all of them revolutionaries of one stripe or another—who found their way to the Clarion's office at the rear of Mrs. Battle's green-grocer's shop. She had also learned to make sense of the impassioned but irrational rhetoric that poured in a constant flood across her desk, submitted by any revolutionary who thought he could persuade the masses to overthrow the world's governments. It was her skillful pen that refashioned these often indecipherable diatribes into something that might actually be accessible to the ordinary reader.

It was hard work, damned hard work, if she were honest with herself, and required her to do a great many things that a bourgeois woman, safe-harbored by husband and household, could never think of doing. She traveled frequently alone by rail and bus and bicycle, often at late hours, to attend meetings of political organizations, some of whose members, like Pierre, were more than a little mad. She had no time to pay attention to her hair or dress, and she slept many nights—when she slept at all—on a pallet on the floor of her loft-office, Ivan and the others working, drinking, and singing in the print shop below. And in addition to printing and distributing two thousand copies of the *Clarion* each month, she wrote and printed leaflets and booklets, helped to organize meetings, and occasionally found food and lodging for visiting foreigners. In this way, she felt, she was doing practical work for the Anarchist cause, work that might otherwise not be done, or done well.

Charlotte picked up the article and was heading for the ladder when she was startled by the sudden rattling thud of a door and the sound of glass breaking. "Where is your warrant?" she heard Adam demand angrily. "What gives you the right to—" And then there was a deafening metallic crash.

Charlotte caught her breath. She knew that sound, for this wasn't the first time she'd heard it. The *Clarion* was being raided by the police, and someone had sent the heavy type form crashing to the floor, the loose lead type spilling everywhere. In a matter of seconds, a detective's head and shoulders would pop through the opening in the floor, and Charlotte would be placed under arrest. It wouldn't be the first time for that, either, and she had the awful suspicion that, given the violent anti-Anarchist mood sweeping the city, she wouldn't get off with a fine and a stern lecture from the Police Court magistrate, as she had on other occasions. This time, she would go to jail, and her keepers would probably throw away the key.

There was another, muffled shout from Adam and a string of violent French curses from Pierre, and Charlotte knew instinctively what she had to do. Without hesitation, she stepped to the dormer window and pushed up the sash. Ignoring the rain that stung her face, she swung her left leg over the sill. On either side of the window, the slate roof sloped sharply downward for several feet, until it ended at a copper gutter. She gathered her bulky woolen skirt with a muttered curse (this would have been *so* much easier in trousers), swung her right leg nimbly over the sill, and eased herself onto the gutter, facing the roof. She could feel it give slightly, but it seemed firm enough to bear her weight—at least, that's what she had thought when she'd watched the workmen putting it up the year before and decided that it might provide an escape if there was ever a fire in the building.

Now, balanced precariously, she moved carefully to the left, leaning forward at the waist, her left hand flat against the roof. With her right hand, she managed to yank the window sash down far enough so that it would not be apparent that she had escaped through it—although she seriously doubted that a man with as little imagination as a Scotland Yard detective would dream that a mere woman would clamber onto a roof three floors above the street.

Three floors. Giddily, Charlotte pushed the thought out of her mind. If she gave in to womanish fears, she'd be lost. Her mind carefully blank, her lower lip pinched tightly between her teeth and her palms flat against the wet and sooty slate, she inched awkwardly along the gutter. She had gone only a few feet when she heard a brusque shout from within, the sash was flung up, and a head popped out. Fearing discovery, Charlotte held her breath and pressed herself tight against the roof, her heart pounding like a trip-hammer.

"Well, she didn't jump," a disgusted male voice said. "Leastwise, I don't see 'er down there. She must've sneaked out."

"Don't see 'ow," a second man said, puzzled. "We've 'ad the entrances watched all morning. Inspector Ashcraft was most partic'lar about that. She came in at seven and 'asn't come out since."

"Well, she ain't 'ere," the first man said roughly, "unless she's learnt 'ow to make 'erself invis'ble. Or maybe she's learnt to fly. Ashcraft'll be in a ravin' paddy-wack about losin' 'er." Furiously, he slammed the window.

Pulling in her breath and willing herself not to look down to the street so dizzyingly far below, Charlotte began to move toward the corner of the building, sliding one foot at a time along the gutter, first her left, then her right, then her right again. It was hard going, made even more difficult by the rain that slicked the slate and the wet hair that fell across her eyes and—

Her foot struck an obstruction. There was a fierce squawk and a wild flurry, and suddenly something with beak and claws flew into her face, beating at her with hard wings. Terrified by the unexpected attack, she raised her arm to ward it off, almost losing her balance and pitching over backward. But as she swallowed a scream, she realized what had happened. A pigeon had built its nest in the gutter and she had dislodged it with her foot, sending nest and eggs hurtling down to smash in the street—as she would have smashed, if she had fallen, too.

For another moment she clung to the roof, breathless and giddy, the sour taste of fear in her mouth. But since she couldn't go back, she had to go on. One foot, another foot, another—and in a few minutes she had reached the corner of the building. She looked to her left and saw, with a vast relief, that she had remembered correctly. This building and its four-story neighbor were only a few feet apart, and she was almost within arm's reach of the iron fire-ladder that was bolted to the other building's brick wall. Almost. All she had to do was lean out across that horrid, empty space, reach for the ladder, and . . .

Charlotte squeezed her eyes shut, her breath coming hard, the blood pulsing in her throat. The ladder was a full yard away, at least a foot out of reach. Only a foot, she thought, paralyzed with fright, but it might as well be a mile. She couldn't reach the ladder unless she let go of the roof. And no matter how hard she willed herself to relinquish her grip, her fingers clung to—

From the street below, she heard the shrill of a police whistle and more loud shouting, and saw two uniformed

policemen wrestling Adam out of the building and into a
police van. *Now!* she thought. *It's now, or not at all!* Closing
her mind to her fear, she turned toward the ladder and
launched herself across the void, her right hand grasping the
rusty iron, her right foot reaching, slipping, leaving her
swinging like a circus wire-artist above the emptiness.

And then her right foot found a rung, and then her left,
and she was clinging to the ladder, then stepping smartly
down, praying that her foot would not catch in the hem of
her blasted skirt. A few moments later, she was safely on the
sidewalk, to the delight of a strongly-built, dark-haired
young man in a coal stoker's singlet, worn trousers, and a
green cloth cap, who had apparently been watching her
descend. As she dropped lightly to the ground from the last
rung of the ladder, the man gave her a look that seemed full
of recognition, and she saw that he had very blue eyes,
deeply fringed with black lashes. Then, his eyes still fastened on hers, he grinned engagingly and tipped his cap.
His hair was dark, too, tousled and rakish.

Charlotte felt the immediate attraction between them as
if it were an electrical charge. But this was no time for such
things. She threw him a dazzling smile, put a warning finger to her lips, and disappeared into the crowd.

CHAPTER THREE

"GETTING INTO PRINT:
ADVICE TO YOUNG WRITERS"

Don't quit your job in order to write unless there is no one
dependent on you. Fiction pays best of all, and when it is of fair
quality is more easily sold. . . . Avoid the unhappy ending, the
harsh, the brutal, the tragic, the horrible—if you care to see in
print the things you write. . . . And keep a notebook. Travel with
it, sleep with it. Slap into it every stray thought that flutters up
into your brain. Cheap paper is less perishable than grey matter,
and lead pencil marking endures longer than memory.

Jack London,
The Editor Magazine, 1903

Jack London stripped off his coal-smudged stoker's jacket
and splashed water from the basin over his face. Then he
put on a clean white shirt and exchanged the clumsy leather
brogans for his own soft leather shoes. With a sigh of relief,
he pulled out a flask of gin, took a swig, and dropped down
on one of the two narrow beds, surveying his surroundings.

The small upstairs room was rudely furnished and uncomfortable, but adequate for his purposes. It had been found for
him by members of the Social Democratic Federation in the

home of an East End police detective, an irony that was not
lost on Jack, who during his vagabond days had developed an
intense dislike of all policemen. But he was in something of
a dilemma, for his research—he was conducting what he
thought of as a sociological study—required him to go about
the East End dressed in ragged, dirty clothes, while other
business would take him out in his ordinary clothing. A
decent landlady would be apt to be suspicious of a gentleman
leading a double life, while lodgings in a house where nobody
gave a damn might not be entirely safe. And Jack needed a
safe house, a refuge where he could sleep comfortably, work
on his book, and go and come as he pleased.

So when the S.D.F. had found him a lodging in the home
of Detective John Palmer, known to East Enders as Johnny
Upright, Jack had jumped at it. The room—which contained two beds, a table, and two chairs—was at the back of
the house and had its own private stair. It was, of course, a
far cry from his country home in the Piedmont Hills of
California, a large redwood bungalow with a panoramic view
of San Francisco Bay, the Golden Gate, and the Pacific Ocean.
There, he entertained his artistic friends and lived the lavishly
hedonistic life that was entirely suited to a successful writer.
If this luxury seemed at odds with his rough, rugged stories of
life-and-death adventure in the wilds of the Yukon Territory
or his well-known stance as a Socialist who advocated the abo-
lition of the class system—well, so be it. Jack had left school
to work in a cannery at fourteen, and had known a decade of
poverty since. Now that his writing had begun to bring in
money, he deserved (he felt) to revel in his prosperity,
although he somehow managed to spend more than he earned
and was continually in debt.

But the household in the Piedmont Hills also included
Jack's mother, his pregnant wife Bess, and their infant
daughter, a stifling, suffocating responsibility. For a time—
wondrous, but far too brief—it had also included the woman

he loved, Anna Strunsky, she of the lustrous black hair and black eyes, a radical Socialist from a Russian Jewish family with Anarchist leanings. When Bess discovered Anna and Jack in each other's arms, however, Anna had packed up and gone to New York, leaving Jack beside himself with lonely desolation.

Feeling trapped in a marriage to a woman he didn't love, his writing mired in the lucrative but tedious Klondike rut, and (as always) in dire need of money to fund his extravagant life, Jack had jumped at an offer that came in late July from the American Press Association. The Boer War had just ended, and the APA wanted America's foremost adventure writer to go to South Africa and report on the postwar situation. With enormous relief, he telegraphed his acceptance, packed his bags, and caught a train for New York—only to learn when he got there that the APA had canceled the project.

Having already bought a steamer ticket and not eager to return to Bess and his mother, Jack came up with another idea. An admirer of Jacob Riis's graphic indictment of the New York slums, *How the Other Half Lives,* he proposed to capitalize on the best-selling book's success by writing a similar exposé of London's infamous East End. He would disguise himself as a tramp so he could travel unobserved through the notorious slums. "I shall sink down out of sight," he had written to Anna during his crossing on the steamer *Majestic,* "in order to view the Coronation from the standpoint of the London beasts. That's all they are—beasts—if they are anything like the slum people of New York—beasts, shot through with starry flashes of divinity." He would call his book *The People of the Abyss.*

Of course, the East End wasn't the only allure. For one thing, Jack had never traveled to England or Europe, and there were sights he wanted to see. For another, the British publishing company Isbister had recently brought out a collection of his short stories, *The God of His Fathers*, and would soon publish *The Son of the Wolf*. Perry Robinson, Isbister's director, assured Jack that he had many British admirers and seemed anxious to introduce him to the literary community.

Well, Robinson's introduction—a first-rate champagne supper in one of the best hotels—was over. Isbister had done well by him, inviting a posse of literary critics and several dozen of Britain's literary lights to meet him. Jack knew the work of several, and particularly admired that of Beryl Bardwell, whose strong women characters reminded him of what he liked to call the "Mate Woman," women who were filled to the brim with life and refused to be bound by conventional moral codes. Jack had told Miss Bardwell about his plan to go incognito into the East End, and learned to his surprise that she was familiar with the district and had gone there more than once herself, unaccompanied.* Jack's pleasure in meeting the striking Miss Bardwell and her husband (a baron) was offset, unfortunately, by his disappointment that Rudyard Kipling had declined Isbister's invitation. That little slight had caused him to sulk all evening.

The Coronation was over, too, several days ago, and Jack had already made two or three extended safaris into the wilds of the East End. A dirty face and a knockabout costume gave him a marvelous sense of anonymity and freedom, while the coins in his pocket and the gold sovereign stitched into the armpit of his jacket made him feel secure. It was true that he wanted to sink down out of sight, but he certainly didn't want to lose himself in the wretched hellhole. If he got into a situation that was too dangerous for him to handle, he wanted to be able to buy his way out.

Jack had spent the afternoon in the company of a fiery young Socialist from the S.D.F. and a beaten-down sweat-shop

*Kate's expeditions into the East End are described in *Death at Whitechapel*.

worker who had taken them to Frying-pan Alley to visit the hole in which he worked, an eight-by-seven room that housed five men who spent fourteen hours a day attaching the uppers of shoes to the soles. Outside in the street, a spawn of children cluttered the slimy pavement, like tadpoles (Jack thought) just turned frogs on the bottom of a dry pond. He reached for a pen and his notebook. He had a hundred impressions to jot down before he forgot them: images of hungry men, damned women, and doomed children, their plight making them stupid and heavy, without hope, without (worse) imagination. There was no question that the East End situation was a bad one, although he had occasionally glimpsed a determined resilience that would not allow these people to be kept down long, given half a chance to better themselves, and to be honest, it was hardly worse than the New York slums. But he had made a reputation as an adventure writer by focusing on the dark and dangerous side of things, on brutishness and inhuman savagery, the more brutish and inhuman the better. Readers expected brutality from Jack London, and that was what *People of the Abyss* would be about: people who had been so inhumanly, so pitilessly brutalized that they had no hope.

But there was one impression that wouldn't appear in his book. Jack had been walking on Hampstead Road when a police van drew up to the curb in front of a green-grocer's shop and a half-dozen policemen charged into the building. From the crowd of onlookers he had learned that the raiders' target was an Anarchist newspaper on the second floor, the employer of the wretched boy who had blown himself to bits on Coronation Day. He watched, interested, as the policemen dragged three handcuffed men out of the door and shoved them roughly into the van. They were in for it, he thought—sympathetically, for he had been roughed up by the police himself, and had spent some months in jail.

At that moment, a bird's nest fell at Jack's feet, the eggs smashing on the pavement. He stepped out into the street and looked up to see a remarkable sight: a woman making her precarious way across the wet roof, then leaping nimbly across the gap between buildings to a rusty iron fire-ladder. While he watched, this lithe, strong young woman, her hair loose and wet, swiftly descended the ladder and dropped to the pavement right in front of him, dazzling him with her sudden smile. It was a smile of intrigue and mystery. It reminded him somehow of Anna's smile, and yet it promised a greater excitement, for the girl seemed to hold nothing back, seemed easy in her body and eager for any challenge, for every adventure that the world might offer. In the long, intimate look they shared (longer and more intimate, perhaps, in Jack's recollection than in the reality of it) he felt he had found exactly the woman he had been looking for all of his life.

But in the next instant, she had vanished, swallowed up by the noisy, milling crowd. He started to follow her, but she was fleet-footed, and he quickly gave it up as a bad job. He returned to the crowd and learned her name by the simple expedient of asking. Suspecting that she may have been attempting to escape from the police, he inquired of a male bystander whether a woman was connected somehow with the Anarchist paper.

"Connected, is she?" The man gave a snort. "I'd say she's connected. She's the bloody editor. Been raided more than onct, too. Damn persistent lot, those Anarchists. Knock 'em down and they come back for more."

"And her name?"

"Conway," the man said. "Charlotte Conway."

Jack had just written that name in his notebook and drawn a double circle around it when there was a tap at the door.

"Teatime, sir," Mrs. Palmer called.

Jack sighed. He wanted—he *needed*—to write, and his typewriter waited invitingly on the table under the window.

He was not getting anything like his daily quota of a thousand words, and he would have to write fast if he intended to take the manuscript back to New York at the end of October. But he was also hungry, and he always wrote better when his belly was full. He put down his pencil and raised his voice. "Thank you, Mrs. Palmer. I'll be down in a moment."

Later, when Jack thought back over what happened during his stay in England, he would recall this occasion as vitally important, because it would lead him to Charlotte Conway. When he went downstairs to eat bread and marmalade and drink tea with Mrs. Palmer and her two pretty and flirtatious young daughters, he found that an even prettier and more flirtatious young woman had been invited especially to meet the famous American adventure writer. Her name was Nellie Lovelace, a former resident of the East End and now an actress of some fame. She was starring in a musical at the Royal Strand Theater, and before they had finished their first cup of tea, she had invited him to attend her Saturday night performance.

CHAPTER FOUR

DEATH IN HYDE PARK
BOMBER MEANT TO KILL KING & QUEEN!
NARROW ESCAPE ON CORONATION DAY!!

London Anarchist Yuri Messenko was killed yesterday when a bomb apparently intended for King Edward and Queen Alexandra exploded in Hyde Park. Witnesses say that the assassin, who was employed at the Anarchist newspaper, *The Clarion*, dropped the satchel he was carrying, causing it to explode. It is thought that Messenko, and several others in the cell to which he belonged, have been the target of a Scotland Yard inquiry for the past several weeks.

This threat to the Royal lives, coming only eleven months after the assassination of the American president, William McKinley, raised new fears. . . .

The Times,
10 August 1902

Charles Sheridan poured a glass of after-dinner port and handed it to his friend, Bradford Marsden. "Sit down, Marsden," he said, gesturing to a chair in the smoking room at Sibley House, the Sheridans' London home. "I want to hear more about this new business enterprise of yours."

But Bradford Marsden had picked up the Sunday *Times* from the table and was reading the front-page headline. "One wonders where this will lead," he said grimly. "Sounds like a repetition of the bombing at Greenwich Park seven or eight years ago, but with a clearer intent." He dropped the paper onto the table and sat down in the leather chair opposite Charles. "This sort of thing simply cannot be tolerated, Charles. The Yard must put an end to it, once and for all."

Charles Sheridan pulled thoughtfully on his after-dinner pipe. "Well," he said, "as to this particular incident, it would appear that the bomber has put an end to it—although not quite the end that he anticipated."

Charles and Bradford had been friends from childhood, but they hadn't been close since Bradford had involved himself with Cecil Rhodes and his Rhodesian enterprises. That connection had ended with Rhodes's death the previous March, and Bradford had created a new investment brokerage business, which was doing quite well, it seemed. His marriage to Rhodes's goddaughter appeared to be progressing smoothly, too—at least, if one could judge by the way they had behaved at dinner that evening. Edith was intelligent and pretty and had produced a male heir within the first year. No wonder Bradford looked so smugly pleased with things, although Charles had to admit that his friend's self-assured conviction that this was the best of all possible times grated a bit. He himself saw the world rather differently.

Bradford, a fair-haired man, rather heavily handsome, put his feet on a leather hassock and lit his cigar. "A pity the idiotic fellow blew himself up, if you ask me. It would have been better if an example could have been made of him—and sweet revenge, as well."

"I rather think," Charles said quietly, "that revenge is not the best course of action. The Anarchists believe that if the police and the courts can be provoked to harsh reactions,

they will awaken the anger of the dispossessed and bring on
the revolution. And they may be right." He raised his glass
in a mute salute. "After all, it's happened before; in France
and in America."

Bradford lifted his glass. "And just how do you know
what's in the Anarchist mind, old chap?" he asked jokingly.
"Haven't gone over to their side, have you?"

This question, had it been meant seriously, would not
have perturbed Charles, for it had been put to him any
number of times by his colleagues in the House of Lords,
who did not take it kindly when he supported the trade
unions or advocated the removal of public education from
ecclesiastic control. It did not ruffle him because he knew
that his fellow Peers were as heedless of the need for social
change as they were of the conditions that propelled it.

But the landed aristocracy took comfort in their igno-
rance at the peril of their way of life. England had been
changing in very fundamental ways for seventy years now,
and the longer this fact was ignored, the harder would be the
lesson, when it came. The triumphant rise of science and
technology had brought the nation unimaginable riches, but
had also shredded the fabric of its closely-knit society. Not
only had machines eliminated the need for unskilled manual
labor, but they were also rapidly displacing the skilled
wheelwrights, coopers, cabinetmakers, smiths, weavers, and
others, once the proud flowering of the English laboring
class, now tossed on the scrap heap of the unemployed. At
the same time, technology had flooded the English agricultural markets with cheap food from around the world, displacing farm workers and undermining the economic
foundation of the old aristocracy: the production of their vast
lands. Charles saw the crisis looming, and knew that if it
came, it would be catastrophic.

Bradford and his sort, on the other hand, with their keen
sense of business and nose for opportunity, represented the

promise of England's future—but only if they recognized that while controlled capitalism would strengthen the entire country, uncontrolled capitalism would surely destroy it. Could they not see that everyone, rich and poor, must have a share in the future, or there would be no future for anyone? Could not some sort of compromise be found which allowed all to share in the opportunities of business and technology, or would the anger and frustration of the dispossessed ignite a final, terrible conflagration?

So in answer to Bradford's question, he reached under *The Times* and retrieved another newspaper, much thinner, scarcely a half-dozen pages. The banner declared it to be the *Clarion*.

Bradford frowned. "What are you doing with that garbage?"

"Better the enemy you know than the one you don't," Charles replied mildly, putting the newspaper down again. "The *Clarion* is sometimes strident, but most of it is quite well written, and it offers some interesting insights into the way these people think. This last issue suggested some ways that the fortune lavished on the Coronation might have been better spent to help those in need. It bears reading, Bradford."

Bradford sat forward, frowning. "Answer me this, then, Charles. How is this lot to be dealt with, if not by the police and the courts?"

"Perhaps by addressing the underlying grievances," Charles replied. "Wider suffrage, more employment, a more equitable distribution of wealth—"

"But that would mean the end of the rights of private property!" Bradford exclaimed heatedly. "Is that what you're after?"

Charles shrugged. "Perhaps it would only be the end of the monopoly of privilege. Perhaps—"

There was a knock at the door and the butler entered. "Mr. Frederick Ponsonby to see you, m'lord."

Charles and Bradford exchanged glances. Ponsonby was Assistant Personal Secretary and Equerry to His Majesty King Edward VII—in effect, a Royal messenger. Charles sighed and rose from his chair. A visit from this man, particularly at this hour of the evening, did not bode well. "Thank you, Richards. Show him in."

The man entered the room. A few years younger than Charles, with a finely-modeled face and a broad forehead, he was graceful and dignified, a courtier to his fingertips. He bowed.

"Good evening, Sheridan. I'm sorry to trouble you so late. I hope I'm not interrupting anything."

Charles smiled. "Ah, Ponsonby," he said, with as much cordiality as he could muster—although it was not Ponsonby himself that he regretted, but that he had doubtless come on an errand. "Good to see you. You know Bradford Marsden, I believe."

Ponsonby bowed slightly. "My congratulations on your successful ventures in South Africa, sir."

"And my congratulations on your safe return, Ponsonby," Bradford said, standing as well. "One day the Boers will thank us." He stroked his blond moustache. "A pity we had to knock sense into them. All so unnecessary."

"A pity indeed," Ponsonby agreed dryly, his eyes darkening.

Charles knew that Ponsonby had seen a great deal of rough action during his nearly ten months with the Grenediers and had only recently been invalided home, a newly promoted lieutenant colonel—while Bradford had waited out the war in Rhodesia, a safe distance from the front. Covering the awkwardness, he said, "You'll have a glass of port, Ponsonby?"

"Thank you, yes," Ponsonby replied.

"Has His Majesty recovered from the excitement of his Coronation?" Charles asked, handing the glass.

"Quite," Ponsonby replied, as they all sat down. "He endured the strain very well, although the ceremony must have been physically trying." He cleared his throat. "And there was that unfortunate incident, which rather marred the day."

"You're referring to the death in Hyde Park, I suppose," Charles said. "As a matter of fact, Marsden and I were just discussing it."

"I was saying that we must put an end to this sort of nonsense," Bradford put in, getting up to help himself to more port.

"Yes. Well, the thing of it is," Ponsonby said, "this incident has caused Their Majesties some considerable distress. Of course, the Queen does not like to show it to the public, but since the incident in Brussels, she has been rather nervous. It seems to have affected her strongly."

That near miss would have affected anyone, Charles thought. On 4 April 1900, Edward and Alexandra were passengers on a train to Copenhagen. When it stopped in Brussels, a fifteen-year-old boy dashed forward, thrust a revolver through the window of the Royal coach, and fired two shots before being wrestled to the platform by guards. One of the bullets had whizzed between the two Royal heads, but by a miracle, neither Bertie or Alexandra were hit. To make things worse, this was not an isolated event. Only eleven months before, William McKinley, President of the United States, had been shot at point-blank range by a self-proclaimed Anarchist named Leon Czolgosz, who was put to death less than sixty days later. As he was being strapped into the electric chair, Czolgosz had said, "I killed the President because he was the enemy of the good people. I did it for the good people, the working men of all countries!"

Ponsonby cleared his throat and said, half-apologetically, "In regard to the Hyde Park event, Sheridan, I wonder if we might have a word alone."

Bradford glanced at Charles, his eyebrows raised, and then made for the door, glass in hand. "I'll just tell the ladies that you'll join them in a few moments," he said, and went out.

Charles felt his heart sink. "What is it?" he asked.

Ponsonby regarded him thoughtfully. In a quiet voice, he said, "His Majesty regrets having to ask your assistance again, but he would like you to look into the matter. The Hyde Park affair, that is."

Charles frowned. "But the bomber is dead. Isn't that an end to it?"

"The incident might have been the work of one insane mind," Ponsonby agreed. "But without some investigation, we cannot be sure. The bomber's fellow Anarchists attempted to make a show of his funeral. What if one of them hopes to succeed where Messenko failed?" He paused and added, rather more delicately, "His Majesty is also interested in the . . . shall we say, underlying causes of the matter."

This assertion took Charles by surprise. He had long known that, while military matters held the Royal interest and foreign affairs were of great importance, social issues scarcely merited a passing thought. The King was quite aware, of course, that there were poor people in London and elsewhere, but he found discussion of the topic rather boring. How the poor lived and died, what they ate or wore, what illnesses afflicted them, what they hoped and feared—these matters were of as little interest to Edward as they had been to his mother Victoria, during the years of her long reign.

Charles's skepticism must have shown in his face for Ponsonby added, in an apologetic tone, "I did not make myself clear, I'm afraid. I mean that there may be a foreign angle in all this."

"A foreign angle?"

Ponsonby gave a little shrug. "Our English Anarchists have been a relatively peaceable lot, as I'm sure you know. Marches, demonstrations, speeches, newspapers." He dropped his glance to the *Clarion* and raised it again, with just the barest hint of a smile. "French Anarchists, of course, are rather more excitable, as are the Spanish and Russians. They prefer deeds—bombs, arson, assassination—to words. Owing to our leniency in the matter of immigration, a great many of these foreign Anarchists have taken refuge here, and some of their governments would like very much to get them back. We must walk a very fine line between protecting the rights and liberties of the people we have allowed to settle here, and alienating certain foreign powers." He cleared his throat. "At the same time, we must make certain that these radicals are not infecting our own people with their militant ideas."

Charles got up and began to pace. All of this was true. The East End was full of Russians, Poles, Italians, and Jewish immigrants, each group with its own political and social agenda, and all covertly watched by agents of foreign governments. The Foreign Office and the Home Office had the devil of a time dealing with the complex situation, and he had no desire to become entangled in it. What was more, he had conducted one or two personal investigations for the King and he preferred not to conduct any others, if he could help it. But he couldn't tell Ponsonby this, of course. He had to think of something else.

He put down his glass and turned back to Ponsonby. "But surely now that Edward is King, he has the unlimited resources of the government to pursue such inquiries. What could I possibly offer?"

Ponsonby sighed. "Ah, yes, therein lies the problem. Now that he is King, His Majesty knows that a great many persons will tell him only what they think he wishes to hear." He pursed his lips and regarded Charles thoughtfully. "He is sure that this is not the case with you. And of course, there

are many in his government with reasons to conceal important matters from him, particularly when it comes to foreign
affairs. I speak confidentially, of course, but you may be
aware that there is a great deal of strain at the moment. His
Majesty is not anxious to involve Lord Landsdowne in this
matter, for instance, or Mr. Balfour. And as far as the Home
Office goes——" He paused. "I'm sure you take my meaning."

Charles did. Arthur Balfour, the new Prime Minister, was
not an admirer of the King, while Lansdowne, the Minister
for Foreign Affairs, was, according to all reports, ready to
resign over the King's refusal to grant the Order of the Garter
to the Shah of Persia. Clearly, some of Edward's ministers held
the same low opinion that Queen Victoria had held of her old-
est son's ability to be trusted with matters of state.

"The King does not expect you to handle this matter
entirely on your own," Ponsonby continued. "Rather, he has
asked me to arrange for your introduction wherever you
think it might be useful, particularly in the Intelligence
departments." He lowered his voice. "I *am* sorry to have to
ask you to do this, Sheridan. But I am also aware that you
have a . . . certain sympathy with the cause of the people and
a knowledge of some of the parties who may be involved."
His glance fell once again to the *Clarion.* "You're simply the
best man for the job. In fact," he added ruefully, "I'm afraid
that you may be the only man for the job."

Charles stopped pacing. "And what does he wish me to
accomplish?" he asked testily.

"Merely to look into the incident and the circumstances
and conditions surrounding it and report back to him what
you find. No more, no less than that." Ponsonby smiled. "It
is not all that difficult, really. He is not asking you to crack
the case, as our friend Sherlock Holmes might put it."

Charles sighed. "Well, then, I suppose I shall do my best.
Lady Sheridan and I had arranged to go down to Bishop's
Keep at the weekend, however. I'm seeing Marconi on

Saturday, and I hadn't planned to come back to London before the beginning of next week."

"Splendid." Ponsonby put down his empty glass. "The beginning of the week will do very well; I don't think there is a great hurry." He stood, his tone lightening. "Do give my regards to your wife, Sheridan, and tell her that I very much enjoyed Beryl Bardwell's novel about Dartmoor, which I read while I was in hospital. I must say, I felt it to be more realistic than Doyle's *Hound of the Baskervilles,* which was rather more Gothic than I would have liked. Lady Sheridan exactly caught the spirit of the moors and the people there."

Charles smiled. "She'll enjoy hearing that. Funnily enough, Doyle was at the Princetown hotel, writing, while I was carrying out a project at the prison and Kate was doing the research for her book."*

"Is that right? Odd how these things happen." Ponsonby took Charles's hand and shook it. "Well, good night, then, Sheridan. Let me know how I can aid your inquiry."

"I shall," Charles said. "Good night." He watched Ponsonby leave the room and then, with a long sigh, went to join Kate and their guests.

---

*For the full story of Kate and Charles's encounter with Conan Doyle in Devonshire, read *Death at Dartmoor.*

CHAPTER FIVE

❦

In the decade between 1903 and 1913, Scotland Yard faced a difficult challenge with regard to the Russians who sought refuge in London's infamous End. There were two different revolutionary groups, the Anarchists and the Bolsheviks, and Scotland Yard frequently confused the two. To complicate matters still further, the Czar's Secret Police, the Ochrana, hired spies to infiltrate both groups. These spies employed agent-provocateur tactics, inducing the revolutionaries to commit illegal or terrorist acts, then betraying them to the police. When the informants employed by the Yard were added to the mix, it was sometimes very difficult to know who belonged to one side or the other.

Albert J. Williams,
"A Brief History of British Anarchism"

The Metropolitan Police, founded by Sir Robert Peel in 1829, was headquartered in an area of Whitehall known as Scotland Yard, a term that (owing to the English habit of naming buildings and agencies after their location) became synonymous with the force itself. Scotland Yard grew rapidly, from 1,000 in 1829 to 10,000 in 1870, to 15,763 on the eve of the new century. But new technologies and new kinds of crime required a new kind of thinking and a different sort of training. For instance, when the streets and roads began to fill up with motorcars, the work of the Public Carriage Office changed from monitoring horse-drawn lorries and brewers' drays to dealing with speeders (motorized vehicles traveling faster than twenty miles an hour) and issuing licenses to drivers; and a new "Fraud Squad" had to be formed to investigate the escalating numbers of embezzlements, swindles, and con games, some of which involved some rather important personages who had lost (or had made) significant amounts of money.

Other challenges required the Yard to branch out in other ways. In the early 1880s, a Special Irish Branch of the Criminal Investigation Department was staffed with Irish officers and organized to deal with the Fenians, the Irish Dynamiters who blew up *The Times* office and a government office in Whitehall and set dynamite bombs in Scotland Yard, Trafalgar Square, and Westminster Hall. By the 1890s, however, the Fenian threat was replaced by the Anarchist threat, and the Special Irish Branch became simply the Special Branch. The Continental terrorists making their way to England—Italian, French, Spanish, and Russian— seemed to believe that a few bombs were neither here nor there, and through the nineties, members of the Special Branch were kept busy hunting for bomb factories, pursuing accused bombers and their accomplices, and keeping a wary eye on those they suspected of plotting terrorist activity. There were Anarchists in Walsall and a botched explosion in Greenwich Park (which Joseph Conrad used as the inspiration for his novel *The Secret Agent*), followed by bomb bursts in Mayfair and in the Underground, together with a half-dozen other minor skirmishes.

All this uproar was followed by silence, an uneasy, fear-inducing silence that went on from the last three years of Victoria's reign and into the first two years of Edward's.

Abroad, assassins were spreading terror among heads of state, while in England, Special Branch became increasingly anxious that a storm was brewing in the East End. But frustratingly, the police were left with little to do, except to keep a close watch on known and suspected Anarchists in the hope that they might commit a crime under the noses of the police. The Branch were assisted in this effort by the growing number of counterrevolutionary *agents provocateurs* who had begun to appear in London, sent by the Russian Secret Police to entrap Russian émigrés who posed a threat to the Czar's life and regime.

Inspector Earnest Ashcraft of the Special Branch was perhaps more frustrated than any of his colleagues, for he had a very strong sense of duty, and every day that passed without his being called upon to perform that duty was a day that he felt he had somehow failed. Ashcraft was a man in his early thirties, broad-shouldered and thickset. He deeply regretted having missed the excitement of the Fenians and the Walsall terrorists and that bang-up Greenwich affair, all of which had occurred while he was still a youth.

In fact, almost everything of note, Inspector Ashcraft often thought sadly, seemed to have happened before he joined the force in '98—except for the Boer War, of course. He had done his duty there, not waiting to be called up but enlisting as soon as the trumpets sounded and shipping out on the very first transport to South Africa. But he had been struck by dysentery before he could fire a shot at the enemy, and had come back wasted, in what he felt in his soul to be a kind of mortal disgrace. The fact that Scotland Yard welcomed him back without question and even promoted him to the rank of Inspector made no difference to him. In his mind, his promotion had no redemptive qualities; he could only hope to redeem himself by some sort of significant action.

While others in the Special Branch may have been lulled

by the seeming quiet on the Anarchist front, Inspector Ashcraft was convinced that these dangerous people were only biding their time. The times themselves were dangerous, for the end of the war threw thousands of men into the labor market, and large throngs of the unemployed marched through the streets of London, disrupting traffic and frightening law-abiding citizens. And even the employed were dangerous, for membership in the trade unions was rising and the unions held the cudgel of the strike in their hands. In this restive, rebellious climate, Ashcraft felt, any little spark might flame up into an uncontrollable conflagration. All hell would break loose, and unholy chaos would reign over law and order. But Ashcraft knew this could not be allowed to happen. When the peace and stability of society were threatened, Special Branch would be there to protect it. And Earnest Ashcraft, at last, would have the chance to do his duty.

To that end, over the past few months, Ashcraft had paid special attention to the half-dozen Anarchist groups in the East End. He was most interested in the *Clarion,* an Anarchist newspaper that had begun publication a decade ago under the editorship of a woman named Sybil Conway, whose daughter was now the editor. Ashcraft had studied the *Clarion* diligently, and in his opinion it was among the most inflammatory of all those published in the country; it stood to reason, therefore, that if a plot was brewing, the *Clarion* would be somehow involved.

Inspector Ashcraft's interest in the newspaper had been further fueled by a man calling himself Dmitri Tropov, although Ashcraft had reason to believe that this was not his real name. At Tropov's invitation, Ashcraft had met him in a dirty, crowded café near the docks. Tropov was a thin man, rather tall and dressed as an ordinary seaman, although his fingers were long and delicate, the fingers of a musician, perhaps, but hardly the hands of a sailor. There was something about his eyes, too—something watchful and wary, as if he were always on the lookout.

After some initial conversation, Tropov identified himself as a member of the Ochrana, the Russian Secret Police. He was especially interested, he said, in a man called Ivan Kopinski, who worked as a printer at the Anarchist newspaper, the *Clarion*. If Special Branch ever had occasion to detain or arrest Kopinski, Tropov would be glad to be notified, for Kopinski's name was on his list of dangerous individuals. In fact, if the opportunity arose, Tropov would be delighted to take Kopinski off Ashcraft's hands and arrange his clandestine deportation to Russia.

"One less Anarchist to trouble the Yard," he had said with a chummy laugh, in perfect, unaccented English. "Right, Inspector?"

Ashcraft was not surprised by Tropov's fluency or easy manner. That was the way of it with these Ochrana chaps— they spoke any number of languages, could assume any number of disguises, carry off any number of masquerades. The next time he saw Tropov, he might be an aristocrat, or a race-course tout, or (with those hands) even a woman. Of course, he couldn't be trusted; those fellows would sell their mothers if they could make a profit thereby. But that was of little importance to Ashcraft, since Tropov was not in his employ. The man made him uneasy, however. It was those eyes, he thought, those endlessly watching eyes.

In the event, Ashcraft had agreed that one less Anarchist would indeed be a good thing, and had gone back to the Yard to inform Chief Inspector Mattingly about his conversation with the Russian agent. The press had been full of stories about the thaw in Anglo-Russian relations and the eventuality of an Anglo-Russian alliance, and Ashcraft was not surprised when the chief inspector suggested that he keep in close touch with Tropov, to learn what the man was up to.

"I shouldn't wonder if the Foreign Office would be interested in hearing about this particular contact," Mattingly said with a deliberative air. He was a round-faced, white-haired man with the look of a genial Father Christmas but a reputation that was a great deal more sinister. "And especially about Tropov's interest in the *Clarion*'s printer—that fellow Kopinski." He paused, his eyes narrowing under bushy white brows. "One never knows about these things, Inspector. It could be that Kopinski is a nothing. On the other hand, he might be a something." He stroked his white beard. "If you take my meaning."

Ashcraft clasped his hands behind his back and said that he certainly took the chief inspector's meaning.

"Well, then." Mattingly picked up a sheaf of papers to signal the end of the interview. "I leave it to you, Inspector, to determine how to deal with the situation." He would see to it, he added, that Tropov's name was handed up to the assistant commissioner. If Ashcraft felt that he needed additional personnel to conduct surveillance or other activities, he might choose two or three Special Branch officers to assist him. If noses—informants—were needed, why, that would be no problem, either.

So Inspector Ashcraft, feeling that this was a significant assignment, through which he might at last be called upon to do his duty, had begun to watch the offices of the *Clarion*. He paid special attention to the comings and goings of Ivan Kopinski, of course, but he also kept his eye on Pierre Mouffetard, a Frenchman with a strong propensity to violent expression. There was a third employee, a boy named Messenko, but he did not seem of much importance. The editor, however, the attractive, free-spirited Charlotte Conway, was clearly dangerous, since hers was the hand and the brain behind the pen.

Indeed, as the days went on, Ashcraft's attentions to Miss Conway gradually intensified. He was not the sort of man who would search his soul for the reasons for his growing interest in this female Anarchist, although if he had, he would have had to acknowledge a serious conflict, for Ashcraft was happily married and believed that he loved his wife and two children. Nevertheless, he frequently watched the lighted window of Miss Conway's bedroom as she prepared to go to bed at night, standing on the street until long after the lamp had been extinguished, and he assigned to himself the task of following her from her mother's house to the newspaper offices in Hampstead Road.

But however entranced Ashcraft may have become by the intriguing Miss Conway, he did not allow her to distract him from other important aspects of the investigation. He spent the day in the neighborhood of the *Clarion*'s office, and assigned to two associates the jobs of trailing Kopinski and Mouffetard from their rooms to the newspaper. And he purchased several noses.

From its beginnings, Special Branch had employed informants to help with investigations. In fact, while the Yard itself might modestly explain that a certain crime was solved by a good police work or a lucky chance of some kind— information offered by a disgruntled employee, a jealous lover, or a good-doing informant—the truth was that most often the information was purchased, and often at a very good price. This practice had been hotly debated for decades, for it certainly smacked of entrapment, and worse. Noses were known to sell unreliable information, and (when hard up for a guinea) to implicate innocent people. But Special Branch—and Scotland Yard in general—could not have done without noses, and continued, surreptitiously, to employ them. And Ashcraft himself would have dealt with the devil, if that's what it took to do his duty.

But that was not necessary in this instance. The inspector procured the services of Mrs. Georgiana Battle, the owner of the green-grocer's shop in the front of the building, as a nose—or in this case, perhaps she might perhaps rather have been called an *ear*. There was an opening in the wall at the back of the shop where, when the presses were not operating, voices could be distinctly heard, and Mrs. Battle was more than happy to keep Inspector Ashcraft apprised of what she heard when she applied her ear to the opening.

In addition to Mrs. Battle, Ashcraft had taken the precaution of obtaining the services of a young Russian émigré named Nicholas Petrovich, whom he paid to infiltrate the Anarchist cell in Hampstead Road. This group met each Sunday night in the grimy basement room of a bookseller's shop a few doors down from the *Clarion*. Petrovich represented himself to the group as having just arrived from Munich, eager to carry out any duties to which he might be assigned. Anarchists, by and large, were a naive lot, and they readily accepted Petrovich's offer, and he quickly became an indispensable member of the group.

In addition to these strategies, the inspector took the precaution of developing certain evidentiary contingencies that might make conviction more reliable, should he be called upon to make arrests in this case. He had once seen an Anarchist snatched from the clutches of the law, so to say, when a zealous barrister pointed out in the course of his client's defense that there was no physical evidence of his guilt and that the informant upon whose word the police had acted had disappeared. The jury aquitted. Inspector Ashcraft did not intend that to happen in this case.

Given all these careful measures, then, it was certainly unfortunate that the inspector had neglected to monitor the movements of Yuri Messenko. But the young man had seemed a vague, gentle sort, not in the same class with the dangerous Kopinski, the inscrutable Mouffetard, or the clever, comely Miss Conway, and it did not seem useful to expend funds or footwork to watch a half-wit. It was only the greatest good luck, therefore, that had taken Inspector Ashcraft through Hyde Park on Coronation Day, at the precise moment that young Yuri blew himself into little pieces with the bomb that had obviously been meant for the King.

For once in his life, Earnest Ashcraft thought exultantly, he had been at the right place at the right time, and fully prepared to do his duty. Of course, it was altogether unfortunate that, in the subsequent raid on the offices of the *Clarion,* the tantalizing Miss Conway had been allowed to escape—how, he still did not quite understand. But that was of no great concern. He knew he would find her.

CHAPTER SIX

❖❖◎❖❖

I WANTS T' BE A LIDY

> I wants to 'ave an evening dress that opens down to 'ere,
> And wear a great big di'mond ti-a-ra in me 'air;
> And when I to the playhouse go, I wants to play the grand
> With a wreath of flowers on me breast and a basket in me 'and.
> I wants t' be a lidy through an' through!

> George Dance,
> *A Chinese Honeymoon,*
> A Musical Play in Two Acts, 1901

"No!" Nellie Lovelace exclaimed, raising a hand to her mouth and stifing a disbelieving gasp. "Across the *roof* and down the fire-ladder? You couldn't have, Lottie!"

"Afraid I did," Charlotte Conway replied with a rueful look. "It was rather a daredevil trick, and certainly ill-advised. I'm lucky I didn't kill myself. But I was desperate, Nellie." She bit her lip, looking anguished. "Adam and the others—I feel as if I abandoned them. It was a rotten thing to do."

"But you had to," Nellie said practically. "You couldn't go to jail." She knew that Lottie had been hauled before the magistrates on several previous occasions. She'd be in for it this time. Political radicals of all persuasions were increasingly targeted by the police, and since Lottie's name was on the masthead of the *Clarion*, she was a perfect quarry. The newspapers would trumpet her arrest, the courtroom would be jammed at her trial, and the magistrate would be harsh.

Lottie sighed, glancing around Nellie's bedroom. "I suppose I shouldn't have come here, but I honestly couldn't think of anywhere else to go. I can't impose on any of the comrades—if I do, and I'm caught there, they'll go to jail, too." She lowered her head and glanced obliquely at Nellie. "I thought . . . well, you're not a sympathizer. I didn't think their spies would be watching you."

"You did the right thing, Lottie." Nellie opened her gold cigarette case—a gift from an admirer—and offered her friend a cigarette. "Good Lord, you *are* in a dreadful corner, aren't you, old girl? Where did you sleep last night?"

"In Green Park." Charlotte took the cigarette, wrinkling her nose. "I didn't sleep, actually. A copper came along about midnight to roust out the vagabonds, and I slipped away before he collared me." She bent to Nellie's light and puffed, blowing out smoke. "The question is, Nellie, what the devil do I do now? I can't go home, because that devil Ashcraft is no doubt watching Mum's house. And I can't go to the newspaper—from all the crashing and bashing I heard, I'm sure they wrecked the place. Last time, it took us a couple of months to put everything right and start printing again. This time, they've closed us down for keeps." She closed her eyes and added, reflectively, "A damned shame, too. Without us, the movement has no voice." Her own voice became bitter. "But that's their aim, of course—to stifle anyone who doesn't agree with the government. So much for the right of free speech."

Nellie Lovelace sat back on her velvet sofa and regarded her friend. She had met Charlotte several years before, at the very beginning of her acting career. At the time, Nellie was still taking whatever parts she could find, mostly as a bit player at Henry Irving's Lyceum Theater. She had gone to a meeting of the Fabian Society, the foremost Socialist group in England, to hear a lecture by the drama critic for the *Saturday Review*, George Bernard Shaw. She and Charlotte had sat next to one another. Nellie was only marginally interested in Socialism, and Charlotte was a committed Anarchist—a rather idealistic one, in Nellie's view—but the two women quickly became fast friends and saw one another as often as their other commitments allowed.

"Yes, that is certainly the question," Nellie said thoughtfully. "What are you to do now?" She surveyed her friend's disheveled appearance with a critical eye. Never very tidy, Lottie certainly looked much the worse for wear: her boots were muddied, her skirt was torn, her blouse was stained, and her hair was a matted mess. "When did you last have something to eat?"

Lottie screwed up her forehead as if she were trying to remember. "An old lady gave me half of her sticky bun—this morning, I think it was."

Nellie frowned, thinking that half a bun since morning wasn't enough to keep body and soul together, even if you were a stick like Lottie and used to missing meals while you pecked away all day at the typewriter. "And you're sure you can't go home?" she asked. "You need a change of clothing, at least."

"I don't dare," Lottie replied. "If Ashcraft so much as catches a glimpse of me, he'll have me in Police Court by morning. I need to get out of London for a while, Nellie, but I'm sure the filthy beast is watching the railway stations." She made a wry face. "I have no money for a ticket, anyway. And nowhere to go. I'm afraid I'm a dreadful nuisance."

"Well, money is not a problem," Nellie said, considering. "I certainly have more than enough." The year before, she had taken on her first important role, as Princess Soo-Soo in *A Chinese Honeymoon*, at the Royal Strand Theater. Musical theater had not been her goal when she had declared to herself that she wanted to be an actress—a serious Shakespearean actress. But Nellie was nothing if not practical, and she had quickly discovered that there was a great deal more money to be made in musical comedy, which was more respectable than music hall and more appealingly light-hearted than serious theater. She'd had some incredible luck along the way, of course—meeting Lady Sheridan, for instance, who had introduced her to Henry Irving and Bram Stoker at the *Lyceum*, and then to Frank Curzon, who managed the Royal Strand. It was Lady Sheridan who had persuaded Mr. Curzon to give her a part as one of the bridesmaids in *A Chinese Honeymoon*, and he had suggested that she understudy the leading lady. When Beatrice Edward got into a tiff and left the play, Nellie had stepped into her role.

And from there on, it had been roses all the way. It looked as if the musical might enjoy a very long run, and Nellie was so much admired as Princess Soo-Soo that her dressing room was banked with fresh flowers every night and she was bombarded with invitations from men who wanted to make her acquaintance. Her photograph was in all the shops, her name was in all the newspapers, and she had a dozen admirers on her string, such as the charming American adventure writer she had met at the home of the Palmers the day before. Jack London was quite the man, she thought, and his rough-hewn American ways made him seem more rugged and virile than the foppish young men who usually courted her.

But that was all by the way. More important than attention, success brought money. Nellie was earning forty pounds a week—an unimaginable amount for a young woman who four years before had lived on one of the worst streets in Whitechapel and could only dream of somehow, someday becoming a lady, with beautiful dresses in her closet and clean sheets on her bed. Her earnings had enabled her to find this absolutely topping West End house with a bathroom with piped-in hot water and a garden and furnish it exactly as she'd always wanted, with a golden velvet sofa in her bedroom and yellow silk bed curtains, and a Persian carpet thick enough to curl her toes in. But her money and her newfound fame hadn't separated her from her old friends—like the Palmer girls, who still lived with their policeman father in the East End, and Lottie Conway—and Nellie vowed that it never would. Whenever necessary, she was there to help.

Lottie lifted her chin with a proud look. "I'm not going to take any of your hard-earned money, Nellie. I can manage for myself."

"Rubbish," Nellie said, with a careless wave of her hand. "Don't push your ridiculous Anarchist principles onto me, Lottie Conway. I know you're a staunch comrade and all that, but everybody needs a helping hand every now and then, and you're in a bit of a fix, if you ask me." She frowned at her friend. "Let's see, now. When exactly was it that you did your mad daylight flit across the roof?"

"Yesterday morning," Lottie replied unhappily, looking down at the cuts and scrapes on her capable hands.

"It might be yesterday week, from the look of you," Nellie said in a crisp tone. When Lottie looked up, her eyebrows raised, she added imperiously, "Well, take a peek at yourself, then." She took Lottie's hand and pulled her up, turning her around to face the cheval mirror in the corner of the bedroom.

"Oh, dear," Lottie said, with an embarrassed little laugh. "My face is rather dirty, isn't it? And my hair—" She turned away from the mirror. "I shouldn't have come here," she said quietly. "You can't have me hanging about, Nellie—I'm too simply awful. I'll go straightaway. You don't need to see me to the door."

"You *are* simply awful." Nellie rolled her eyes in a theatrical gesture. "Your face is unspeakably dirty, your hair needs a wash and a curl, your boots are positively done for, and every stitch of your clothing ought to be burned. You are definitely going straightaway—for a bath." She steered her friend toward one of the doors off her bedroom. "I think I can find something that might fit you."

"But what—" Lottie spluttered, resisting. "What are you—"

"Don't 'but what' me, Comrade Conway." Nellie pushed her into the bathroom and closed the door firmly. She raised her voice. "If you turn the tap on the tub, you'll get three gallons of hot water a minute. If you want more, it'll be hot again in ten minutes. There are towels in the cupboard, and soap in the dish. I'll get you something clean to wear. And after that, we're having ourselves a nice tea."

"But, Nellie—" Lottie protested.

"I don't want to hear another word," Nellie said smartly, "unless it's *pass the jam.*" And with that, she went to her closet and pulled out a pretty cotton frock with embroidered lace on the bodice, singing under her breath the first verse of "I Wants to Be a Lidy."

CHAPTER SEVEN

Despite the long-standing prejudice against women farmers in England, a number of women owned and managed their own farms, and quite capably, too. In Berkshire, in the 1880s, Mary Bobart ran a farm of 250 acres, employing eight men and five boys. After Mary Ann Pullen was widowed, she expanded her husband's farm from 340 to 450 acres. In Lincolnshire, in the 1890s, Mrs. Watson of Market Deeping owned and managed a hundred-acre farm and a retail shop where she sold farm produce. "I could certainly not have brought up my four children without the aid of the business," she said. By 1911, the British census reported 4,043 unmarried women farmers in England and Wales.

Lenore Penmore,
"Women Farmers in Victorian England"

Kate Sheridan folded her gloves and tucked them into the belt of the linen smock she wore over coarse canvas trousers to work around the grounds. "Well, what do you think, Mrs. Bryan?" She frowned down at the sickly-looking calf lying in the hay. "Should we ask the veterinary to stop round?"

"I'm afraid so, m'lady," Alice Bryan said, sounding vexed

and regretful. "If we could only get the poor creature on its feet, I feel sure we could save it. But nothing I've tried seems to help."

Mrs. Bryan was the new matron of the School for the Useful Arts, which Kate had begun several years before at Bishop's Keep, the Essex estate she had inherited from her aunts. The school now enrolled nearly two dozen women—half who came daily from the neighboring villages, half boarders—for a year-long scientific and practical course in horticulture, dairying, bee-keeping, and orchard management, organized after a plan for scientific education in rural districts developed by the Countess of Warwick, near Dunmow. Mr. Humphries, Kate's head gardener, taught horticulture (including glass-house growing and orchards); while Mrs. Bryan handled the dairying, poultry, and bee-keeping courses; Mrs. Grieve came in regularly to teach a course in the cultivation and use of herbs; and Kate herself taught the fundamentals of financial management—a subject in which she had some practical experience.

Kate had put a great deal of effort into this ambitious project during the past several years, for she felt it would give women the skills and confidence that would enable them to earn an independent living in rural areas, where land was rapidly going out of cultivation. Since the Corn Laws had been repealed, traditional crops such as wheat and oats could no longer compete with cheap foreign imports, and many farm workers were forced to desert their fields for factory jobs in the industrial cities. But there were still women in the villages, young women desperate for work and willing to take on the most poorly-paid pursuits. These deserted acres and unproductive lives could be turned to good account—if not by growing traditional crops, then by raising flowers, fruit, and vegetables for the inexhaustible new markets in the towns and cities. But this could happen only if young women learned how, at an early age, before they were driven into service or factory work.

Kate knew, despairingly, that her small effort wasn't nearly enough. There were thousands, no *tens* of thousands, of women who needed help in finding good work for themselves and their families. And there was strong opposition from neighboring gentry, who were upset at the idea that women who might have gone into their service were instead hoping to become independent farmers, and from certain local clergy, who felt that education might encourage the village women to aspire to goals beyond those appropriate to their class. But at least it was a start, she consoled herself, and several small efforts might, collectively, turn the tide of townward migration. And even if only a few of her graduates succeeded in creating smallholdings and market gardens, they would show the way to others. They would—

"Two guests, m'lady. Miss Lovelace, and a young gentleman."

Kate turned around to see the butler. Hodge's tone was dryly correct, but the muscles knotted in his jaw reflected his belief that no self-respecting butler should have to summon her ladyship from a dirty byre, where she clearly did not belong.

Kate smiled. Nellie Lovelace was her young friend from the theater, whom she had not seen in months. "Thank you, Hodge. Tell Miss Lovelace that I'll be there in a moment." To Mrs. Bryan, she said, "Let's send one of the girls to the surgery on a bicycle. Perhaps the vet can stop in this evening. And do let me know when he comes—I'd very much like to hear what he thinks."

"Very good, m'lady," Mrs. Bryan replied. She turned, raising her voice. "Polly!" she bawled. "Polly, ye're needed. Come 'ere." At her strident summons, the calf, startled, clambered clumsily to its feet.

* * *

"I've shown Miss Lovelace to the library, m'lady," Hodge said stiffly, his eyebrows registering his disapproval of the lady in question, whom he had known when she worked at Bishop's Keep a few years earlier, as a kitchen maid.

"Thank you, Hodge," Kate said. "Please be so good as to send in some tea, would you?"

"Certainly, ma'am." The butler opened the heavy oak library door and stepped back to allow Kate to enter.

"Nellie!" Kate exclaimed, holding out both hands. "What a delight it is to see you!"

"Good afternoon, m'lady." The young woman who rose eagerly from the plum-colored settee was tall and dark-haired, with flashing dark eyes and a coquettish expression. She wore a stylish cream-colored flannel suit with a pink velvet sash, the jacket trimmed in silk soutache braid. Her wide-brimmed hat was made of braided straw and heaped with pink silk ribbons, and her cheeks and mouth were unmistakably rouged. No wonder Hodge disapproved, Kate thought. He was not used to seeing women who painted—although to her, Nellie looked splendid, in a theatrical sort of way.

"I thought," Kate said, putting her cheek to Nellie's, "that we had settled that m'lady business long ago. You must call me Kate, or I shall call you Ellie Wurtz, as you were when we met, and you won't like that." She turned to Nellie's companion, a thin young man, finely-featured and rather effeminate. He wore a white linen suit with a puff of beige silk handkerchief in the breast pocket and a gold watch chain draped elegantly across an embroidered cream waistcoat. "And who is this friend you've brought for a visit?"

Nellie's slanted glance, Kate thought, was more than a little uncomfortable. "This is Charles Conway. My . . . my cousin. From Brighton."

"Welcome to Bishop's Keep, Mr. Conway," Kate said

with a smile, as the young man made a graceful bow over her hand. With half a smile, she added, "I wasn't aware that Nellie had any cousins, in Brighton or elsewhere, so I am even more glad to know you."

Kate had discovered Nellie Lovelace some four years before, when she was still thin, pale Ellie Wurtz, a seventeen-year-old orphan waif living in Miller's Court, off one of the worst streets in the East End.* She had brought the girl to Bishop's Keep, where Ellie had worked as Mrs. Pratt's kitchen maid for nearly a year, eating regular meals and spending her spare time reading with Kate until her gaunt frame had filled out and her confidence had begun to bloom. Then, because the girl wanted more than anything else to become an actress, Kate had introduced her to those she knew in the theater: Bram Stoker, at the Lyceum, and Frank Curzon, who managed the Royal Strand. Now Nellie Lovelace, hers was one of the brightest stars in the firmament of the newly popular musical theater, and Kate read frequently of her in the London papers.

Nellie cleared her throat uncomfortably. "Charles isn't exactly a . . . a cousin," she said, her cheeks glowing under her rouge.

Kate smiled, thinking that perhaps Nellie was about to tell her that there was an engagement in the offing—although this slight, rather pretty young man did not strike her as the sort who would steal Nellie's heart. She would expect her to be attracted to a man's man, someone with more energy and self-confidence.

"Nor from Brighton," Nellie added. She raised and lowered an apologetic shoulder and glanced at her friend. "I'm sorry, Lottie," she said with a dramatic sigh. "I tried, but I just can't lie to Lady Sheridan."

---

*Kate met Ellie in *Death at Whitechapel*, when she was helping Charles to trace out the secrets of the decade-old Ripper murders.

"I didn't really expect you could," the other said in a practical tone. The voice was low and throaty, but it was not a man's voice. "I'm very sorry, Lady Sheridan. Please forgive us for trying to deceive you. My name is Charlotte Conway—Lottie."

Kate looked at the speaker sharply, realizing that he was really *she*. "My goodness," she said, startled. "It's a very effective disguise. I was completely fooled."

"I've learned a trick or two when it comes to costume," Nellie said smugly. "But really, the only thing we did was cut Lottie's hair and beg a suit of clothes at the theater. She makes a very handsome young man, don't you think?"

"I do indeed," Kate said, "although it was a pity, Miss Conway, that you had to sacrifice your hair."

"Not a bit of it." Charlotte tossed her head. "To tell the truth, Lady Sheridan, it's topping. I feel light as a feather!"

The library door opened and a maid appeared with a tea tray. She set it down, curtsied quickly, and disappeared.

"Now, then," Kate said, sitting down in front of the tray and picking up the silver teapot. "Why don't we have a cup of tea while you two tell me what this is all about?"

"Thank you," Nellie said. She sat back down on the plum-colored settee, her friend beside her. "I do hope we haven't interrupted your work."

Kate chuckled, looking down at her smudged tunic and trousers and brushing off a straw. "I was attending to a sick calf. As you can see, I'm not dressed for callers, but since Miss Conway is in trousers, too, I don't feel a bit awkward." Filling a cup and handing it to Nellie, she added, "Now, then. Let's hear the story."

The narrative took only a few moments, and by the time their cups had been emptied once and then refilled, Kate had heard the whole narrative, from Yuri Messenko's death in Hyde Park to the raid on the *Clarion* and Charlotte's narrow escape across the roof, to Nellie's decision to bring her friend to Bishop's Keep.

Not all of this was news to Kate, of course. She had read of the young Anarchist's death in *The Times*, and Charles had told her about the raid on the *Clarion* and the arrest of everyone in the office, except for the editor, who had got away. He had also told her that he wanted to talk with the editor, as part of his inquiry into the Hyde Park explosion. Since he had only consented to investigate and report back to Ponsonby, it occurred to her now that Miss Conway might be willing to help him—although she would probably refuse if she were afraid of implicating any of her friends.

Kate didn't reveal these thoughts, however. Instead, she merely remarked, in a mild tone, "My goodness, Miss Conway. You *have* had an adventure."

"Worthy of one of Beryl Bardwell's heroines," Nellie put in. She gestured to a row of red leather-bound books on a shelf, "That's who she is, Lottie. Lady Sheridan, I mean. She's Beryl Bardwell. The famous novelist." She turned to Kate. "I simply adore your most recent one—*Death on the Moor*. So realistic, in every detail. One would almost think you were on Dartmoor when that man broke out of that horrible prison!"

Kate suppressed a smile. As a matter of fact, she *had* been on Dartmoor when the man escaped, she and Charles and Conan Doyle. As a writer, she found it best to work from her own experience, although that sometimes got her into trouble with acquaintances who did not fancy meeting their own fictional counterparts in one of her books. Just now, she was at work on a book set at Glamis Castle in Scotland, where Charles had been summoned to find one of the Royal Family's lost black sheep.* Of course, she didn't dare reveal the details of what had happened while they were there— the whole episode was, as Charles kept reminding her, a State Secret. But Glamis Castle had proved a splendid setting for a ghost story, with echoes of Macbeth and Bonnie

*The true story may be read in *Death at Glamis Castle*.

Prince Charlie, and she would be taking the finished manuscript to her publisher in a few weeks.

Charlotte frowned. "Beryl Bardwell? I don't think I've read—" She glanced at the bookshelf, hesitated, then added awkwardly, "I don't have much time for novels, I'm afraid, Lady Sheridan."

"I can't think that you would," Kate said, seeing her discomfort and wanting to ease it. "My novels are meant to fill idle moments, and I doubt that you have many of those." She smiled at Nellie, who wore an embarrassed look. "It does seem as if we all have our secret identities, doesn't it? Nellie has adopted a stage name, I write novels under a pseudonym, and you—"

"And I'm hiding from the police," Miss Conway said. She put down her cup. "But I'm not under arrest," she added earnestly. "I haven't done anything wrong or against the law, so you wouldn't be harboring a criminal." She looked flustered. "That is, if you—"

"So you want me to take Miss Conway in?" Kate asked, with a questioning look at Nellie. "Is that why you've come?"

"In a word, yes," Nellie said, "and thank you for putting it so simply. It's all very unfortunate, of course, but that awful fellow has staked out his spies everywhere. Lottie's disguise got her out of London, but—"

"Who?" Kate interrupted. "What 'awful fellow'?"

"Inspector Ashcraft, from New Scotland Yard," Miss Conway replied. Her mouth tightened. "He thinks I don't know his name, or even that he is a police officer, for he always goes in plain clothes—brown tweeds, and a brown bowler hat. But all of us know him, for he has made himself an infernal nuisance. He thinks it's his duty to harass us, even though we've not broken the law. It is *not* a crime to speak and write about the wrongs the people must endure and to say how we believe they can be righted." A grim smile touched her lips. "At least, it isn't a crime yet, although the government may make it so." She looked down, her hands twisting in her lap. "I have no idea what Adam and Ivan and Pierre have been charged with, or whether they have been charged at all."

"Who are they?" Kate asked.

"Ivan Kopinski and Pierre Mouffetard are employed at the *Clarion*," Miss Conway replied, her voice thin and tense. "Adam Gould is a friend of mine. He doesn't work at the paper—he was only there so we could go to lunch together. But the police put all three of them into a van and took them off. They're still being held, as far as I know."

"The important thing is that these men haven't *done* anything against the law," Nellie said urgently. "And neither has Lottie. But she must be kept out of sight." She extended her hand with a melodramatic gesture. "Please, Kate, please help us!"

Kate thought swiftly. "Why don't you both plan to stay overnight, at least," she suggested. "I believe that my husband will be interested in meeting Miss Conway and hearing her story. But he's driven over to Chelmsford this morning to visit Mr. Marconi's wireless laboratory. When he comes back—certainly by teatime—we can all discuss the situation."

Miss Conway bit her lip nervously. "Your husband— Lord Sheridan?"

"He's not what you think, Lottie," Nellie said. "His lordship isn't an Anarchist by any stretch, but he's always on about free speech and the rights of workers. And he was interested in that union case that Adam was involved with a couple of years ago. In fact, he and Adam must know each other." She patted her friend's hand. "Anyway, there's nothing in the least frightening about him, so don't you be worried."

Kate laughed. "If you have the courage to cross a roof three stories above the street, Miss Conway, I'm sure that Lord Sheridan should not cause you any difficulty."

Miss Conway seemed not to know what to say, but Nellie consulted the gold watch pinned to her lapel, and rose. "I'm afraid I can't stay to tea," she said. "I have a performance tonight, and afterward, I'm going to supper with a visiting American author." She glanced at Kate, her eyebrows raised. "His name is Jack London. I wonder if you know him."

"As it happens, Charles and I met him just last week," Kate said, "at a party given by his British publisher." She smiled at Nellie's excitement. "He's certainly a charming man, and extraordinarily good-looking."

"He's a Greek god," Nellie said, rolling her eyes. "Sent from heaven."

Kate wasn't quite sure of that. She had certainly felt the magnetism of London's charismatic charm—not a woman at the party could have escaped the allure of his personality—but she couldn't help feeling that there was something of the rogue about him. She wondered if Nellie knew that he had a wife and young child back in California, but she didn't like to interfere. Whatever lessons about life and love Nellie was to learn through her attraction to Jack London, they would have to be *her* lessons.

Kate stood. "Ask Hodge to bring the pony cart round to take you to the station," she said. She put her arms around the girl in a warm embrace. "I wish you would visit more often, Nellie. It's always a great pleasure to see you, and to hear about all your success."

"It's all due to you, Kate," Nellie said simply, returning Kate's embrace. She put out her hand to her friend. "I hope things work out, Lottie. You must let me know if I can help further."

When Nellie had gone, Miss Conway stood too. "Thank you, Lady Sheridan," she said soberly. "If I'm to stay, I'll try my best not to be any trouble. I'm afraid I don't have any money to give you, but I'll be glad to work for my room and board."

"There's always plenty of work to be done around here," Kate replied. She smiled. "Do you happen to know anything about doctoring sick calves?" When the girl shook her head, she said briskly, "Not to worry. But do come upstairs and I'll find you something to wear. We don't want to spoil that delicious white linen suit."

Charlotte Conway's father had been an engineer and her mother the daughter of a wealthy Lancaster button manufacturer. Her father had died when she was quite young, her mother had never taken much notice of her, and Charlotte had grown up in a large, well-appointed house in Fitzroy Square with all the comforts that money could buy and a squad of servants to maintain them. She found nothing intimidating, then, about Bishop's Keep, either the imposing house and staff of servants, or the fine furnishings, or the surrounding park. And of course, a true Anarchist would never be at all impressed by the trappings of wealth, no matter how grand.

She was, however, reluctantly impressed by Lady Sheridan herself, for the woman was both self-confident and unselfconscious, seemingly without regard for her own wealth and possessions. Although she was not conventionally beautiful, she had a strong, striking Pre-Raphaelite face, with a resolute mouth, heavy brows, and decisive chin. Her eyes were an intense hazel-green that seemed to take nothing for granted, her thick auburn hair straggled untidily out of its knot on top of her head, and her hands were square cut and capable-looking, the nails rather the worse for wear—certainly not the hands of a titled lady or a famous writer. To tell the truth, they looked very much like the hands of a farmer.

And then there was the surprising business of Lady Sheridan's School for the Useful Arts. For one thing, Charlotte had assumed that Bishop's Keep, so convenient to the city, was merely a weekend country home, and she was taken aback to discover that it was a working farm, an extensive one, at that—and entirely under Lady Sheridan's management. For another thing, she had no idea that a woman of such a high social standing would have any interest at all in the plight of the working woman. But there were more surprises in store.

After Charlotte had been outfitted in what her ladyship called a "working costume"—a simple, short-skirted blue dress topped with a smock, and a pair of leather brogans—the two of them went out for a tour. A little later, they were walking through the poultry yard, where a group of women was building a new chicken coop, and Lady Sheridan was explaining the purpose of her school and the idea behind it: to help young women acquire skills that they could put to work on the land, to create both productive lives and productive smallholdings.

And now, Charlotte *was* impressed, in spite of all her Anarchist learnings. Her fellow comrades had dinned it into her that no wealthy landowner cared a fig for those who worked the land, or cared only to keep them oppressed. But while Pierre would probably sneer at Lady Sheridan's "reformist" notions and argue that her efforts were merely palliative, Charlotte could not but feel that the school was accomplishing something important, and said as much.

"It's not enough, of course," Lady Sheridan replied. "There are too many thousands who need help. But if what we're doing here can keep even one young woman out of the factories and the slums, it will have been worthwhile." Her smile became rueful. "I know about slums firsthand, you see, because I grew up in New York, in a tenement. I was an orphan, and my aunt and uncle O'Malley took me in and raised me. Uncle was a policeman, and Irish, and there were a great many mouths to feed." She shook her head. "I sometimes wonder that we all survived. But we did, actually. Survived and thrived."

Lottie stared, her surprise turning to a complete and utter astonishment. "You . . . you grew up in a tenement?"

Lady Sheridan's hazel eyes regarded her thoughtfully, and her mouth softened. She took Charlotte's arm and they began to walk toward the orchard, where three women were picking fruit from the heavily-laden trees. "I certainly did. I remember almost every day of it, both the good and the bad. And it wasn't all bad," she added after a moment. "Sometimes I think that adversity teaches us to be strong and resourceful. If I had grown up under different circumstances, with more privilege and fewer responsibilities, I might not have the strength and resilience I have now." Her tone was reflective and matter of fact.

"But how did you—" Charlotte was puzzled. "New York is so far away and—" She stopped, unable to think of a polite way to frame the question.

Lady Sheridan paused at the edge of the orchard and leaned her elbows on the old stone wall. "How did I get from there to here? With my pen, I suppose you might say. You see, I was already earning my living as a writer when I discovered that my father's sisters, my Ardleigh aunts—of whom I had no knowledge at all—lived here at Bishop's Keep. I was invited to come to England and work as a secretary to my Aunt Sabrina Ardleigh, with time from my duties to do my own writing. When she and my aunt Bernice both died, I inherited this place."* She raised her head and gazed at the neat rows of trees and the field beyond, where a group was stacking hay. "Sometimes I find it difficult to credit my good fortune, Miss Conway. Perhaps that's why I try to do what I can to change things."

"I see," Charlotte said, thinking that while her Anarchist

---

*Kate's story is related in detail in *Death at Bishop's Keep.*

friends would doubtless charge Lady Sheridan with the hypocrisy of the wealthy, her heart certainly seemed to be in the right place.

"And you, Miss Conway?" Lady Sheridan turned to face her. "How did you come to be doing what you're doing now?"

Charlotte clasped her hands, hesitating. She liked Lady Sheridan and wanted to tell her the whole story, but it all seemed so complicated. She settled for a sketchy outline. "It was my mother," she said finally. "She joined the Fabian Society in the 1880s, but she was more interested in Anarchism than in Socialism. So she left the Fabians and started the *Clarion* in 1891 and carried it on until five years ago. Then she . . . fell ill." She looked away, thinking how difficult it was to describe what had happened to her mother, and to herself, over the past few years. "There was no one else to continue the *Clarion,* so I took it on. I felt it my . . . duty, you see. Both to my mother and to the cause."

Lady Sheridan paused, seeming to think about what she had said. Charlotte was afraid she might question her more closely, but she only said: "And you live at home still, with your mother?"

Charlotte nodded. That part of it, too, was difficult to describe. But Lady Sheridan seemed concerned about something else.

"Does your mother know where you are? Would you like to send her a message, telling her that you're safe? If you're concerned that her house is being watched, I'm sure we can arrange—"

"No," Charlotte said. She might have added, *My mother doesn't care,* but it wouldn't have explained anything. Best just to leave it all unsaid. "It's all right, really, Lady Sheridan. Mum won't worry." She turned to look at the orchard, where a woman was loading baskets of fruit onto a wagon, and thought an Anarchist thought. "You have rather a large crop, don't you?" she asked archly. "It must bring in quite a lot of money."

Lady Sheridan was silent for a moment. "Yes," she said at last. She turned to look steadily at Charlotte. "Each of the workers earns a share of the profits from our venture, based upon her contribution to it. We are organized as a cooperative, you see. In that way, it is possible for a woman to earn her living while she is gaining the skills she needs for her future."

It was Charlotte's turn to fall silent.

CHAPTER EIGHT

Since the advent of mass communications (the radio, television, and the Internet), it is no longer possible for any government to control the flow of information and the power it represents. This is true anarchy.

Albert J. Williams,
"A Brief History of British Anarchism," 2002

Early that morning, Charles had driven the Panhard to Chelmsford to spend the day with Guglielmo Marconi, whose Wireless Telegraph Company was located in an old silk factory in Hall Street. It wasn't Charles's first trip to the wireless telegraphy laboratory. He was much impressed by Marconi's innovative work, especially his patented system for tuned coupled circuits, which increased signal range and permitted adjacent stations to operate without interference by allowing simultaneous transmissions on different frequencies.

To Charles's mind, Marconi was a genius, although most scientists thought the man was more than a little mad. Until last December, it was believed that wireless waves could travel only in straight lines from the transmitter, and that signals could be sent and received only as long as the transmitters were within the line of sight. But Charles had watched as Marconi confounded all the scientists and proved that the curvature of the earth was not a barrier to wireless transmission. At his wireless station in Cornwall, Marconi had received a signal—the letter *S* in Morse code—transmitted from St. John's, Newfoundland, eighteen hundred stormy miles away, across the Atlantic. Charles had heard it himself, and to him it had seemed almost a miracle. But if what he had seen in the laboratory today was any indication, there were still more miracles to come. As he drove back to Bishop's Keep, his head was full of exciting possibilities for wireless transmission, using Marconi's new system. Someday it might even be possible to transmit the human voice over the air waves, just as was now done over the telephone wire.

He was still preoccupied with these ideas as he walked into the library at Bishop's Keep, to join Kate for tea. He bent to drop a kiss on her auburn hair, thinking as he always did how pleasant it was to come home to a woman who was not only a pleasure to look at, dressed as she was in a simple ivory afternoon gown, but clever. Yes, exceedingly clever. Kate could always be counted on to listen intelligently to his visionary thoughts—although she might accuse him of being a dreamer like H. G. Wells, with his fantastic visions of the future. But they weren't so fantastic, were they? Not when men like Marconi could turn science on its head, and make it possible for every ship at sea to communicate with stations on the shore. He turned on the electric light beside his favorite chair. The petrol-powered generator he had installed several years ago had given good service, and he had extended the circuitry throughout the first floor of the old house. So far as he knew, Bishop's Keep was the only estate in the area to enjoy the luxury of electric light, and he thought that it might not be many years before he and Kate would also enjoy the luxury of listening to the human voice over the airwaves.

Charles sat down and took the cup of tea she had poured for him. "It's been quite a day, Kate," he said excitedly. "Wait until you hear what Guglielmo is working on now. He has built a device that—"

"In a moment, Charles," Kate said, interrupting. "Our guest will be downstairs very soon, and I think you'd better hear the story before she puts in an appearance."

"A guest?" Charles stirred sugar into his cup and sat back. "I didn't know we were expecting company this weekend."

Kate buttered a scone and put it on a plate for him. "Her name is Charlotte Conway. She is—"

"Charlotte Conway?" Charles nearly spilled his tea. Charlotte Conway was the editor of the *Clarion*—the only staff member Special Branch had not placed under arrest, and only because she had not been found. He stared at Kate, who sat calmly buttering another scone. He was continually amazed by his wife's inventiveness and her ability to anticipate his interests, but she had outdone herself this time.

"You are a witch, Kate," he said emphatically. "How under the sun did you manage to get Charlotte Conway here?"

"I didn't do a thing," Kate said with a little smile. "It was Nellie Lovelace who brought her, dressed as a young man. It was quite a convincing disguise, actually. I was totally fooled. Nellie has taken the train back to town, but I've invited Miss Conway to stay the night, and longer, if you approve." She shifted uncomfortably. "I know that you planned to go up to London to find and talk with her, but she is after all a fugitive, and I'm not sure you'll want to have her here. You should also know that it was only by determination and luck that she managed to elude the police, and she's convinced that if she goes back to the city, she'll be snatched up by the Scotland Yard detective who engineered the raid."

"I don't doubt it," Charles said, settling back in his chair again. It was an odd but fortuitous coincidence, Miss Conway coming here, since he had planned to attempt to locate and question her about the *Clarion* employee who had blown himself up in Hyde Park. With any luck, she might have information that would fill in the many blanks in the story, as he knew it now. He sipped his tea. "Did she mention the men who were arrested during the raid—Adam Gould and the other two?"

Kate nodded. "She's terribly concerned about them." She gave Charles a slantwise look. "If Miss Conway thinks you are genuinely willing to help her friends, I'm sure she'll tell you whatever you ask." There was a sharp, cautionary undertone in her voice. "But if you feel you must convey her information to the Crown as part of this assignment you've taken on, I'm equally sure that she'll refuse to cooperate. If it were me, I shouldn't like to tell you something that you might turn around and use against my friends."

Charles chuckled. "I think I can tell whose side you're on." He paused. "Now that I've had time to think about what Ponsonby asked me to do, Kate, I've found plenty of my own reasons for wanting to know what really happened in Hyde Park. It's possible that the bombing was planned by one of the foreign agents who have been so active in the last few months—and we certainly have to think about the possibility of another attack. So far, though, no definite clues have emerged."

Kate refilled his cup and handed it to him. Lightly, she said, "And you think you'll have better luck than Scotland Yard at turning up a clue or two?"

"Oh, I just might," he replied, grinning. "They have their noses, I have mine." He paused, the smile fading. "But that raid on the newspaper and the arrests of the men—it's troublesome, Kate. So far, at least, Special Branch hasn't alleged a conspiracy, or specified any crimes. It's not even clear on what charges the men are being held."

"What about Miss Conway?" Kate asked, frowning. "Can she be charged with sedition?"

"The *Clarion*'s rhetoric may be a bit overheated," Charles replied, "but other Socialist newspapers—*Freedom*, for instance—are equally vociferous, if not more. And if it is sedition for one to speak out, it must be sedition for all." He shook his head. "The men ought to be freed, for there is no merit in stifling dissent. If the *Clarion* can be closed and its staff arrested, who's to say that the same thing won't happen to anyone else who ventures to speak freely, or to any other newspaper that dares to print something at odds with the general view?"

"If you really mean that, Lord Sheridan," a quiet voice said from the doorway, "I would welcome whatever help you are able to offer."

Charles set his cup aside and stood as Kate made introductions. Charlotte Conway was thin and angular and her dark curly hair was cut startlingly short, but there was a lively intelligence in her face and she moved with confidence across the room. She was wearing one of Kate's dresses, of a pewter color that made her dark hair and eyes seem even more lustrous and gave her a feminine appearance that was somewhat at odds with her assured manner. She sat down, accepted a cup of tea from Kate, and said, without prompting, "I expect you want to know what happened when the newspaper was raided."

"I do, yes," Charles said, and listened as she related the story of her narrow escape from the *Clarion* office. He concealed his surprise at the idea of this slight, fragile-looking young woman scrambling adventurously across a roof, and went instead to the thing that concerned him most. "Was there any warning of the raid?" he asked. "Did the police present a warrant?"

"A warrant?" Miss Conway frowned. "I heard Adam ask about it—he was quite insistent, actually—but I didn't hear an answer. And I'm sure there was no warning." The corners of her mouth quirked upward in a ghost of a smile. "If there had been, I shouldn't have had to take to the roof, now, should I?"

Kate passed around a plate of buttered scones. "On what basis could the police obtain a warrant, Charles? If no laws were broken—"

There was no amusement in Miss Conway's short, brusque laugh. "I doubt that Inspector Ashcraft would worry his head with such niceties, Lady Sheridan. But if he did, he wouldn't have any difficult finding a magistrate to issue a warrant for the arrest of an Anarchist. Any Anarchist, it doesn't matter who, or that he's done nothing illegal." Her voice became bitter. "The name itself is proof of our criminal deeds."

"Inspector Ashcraft?" Charles asked.

"Special Branch," Miss Conway said dispiritedly. "Most of the police are at least civil, but not that one. He's aggressive and arrogant. He's out to make a name for himself, whatever it takes."

"I see," Charles said, thinking that it might be good to have a conversation with this Inspector Ashcraft.

Miss Conway gave him a long, straight look. "As I came into the room, I heard you say that you thought the men ought to be freed. Do you mean to offer any help to make that happen?"

"I will do what I can," Charles said. "One of them, Adam Gould, is an acquaintance of mine. I supported the union in a case that came up on appeal last year—the Taff-Vale case. You may have heard of it."

Miss Conway's eyes widened in surprise. "You took the union's side in the Taff-Vale case?"

"Yes," Charles said. He smiled slightly. "For what little good it did." It had been an ugly matter, a suit by the Taff-Vale Railroad against the Amalgamated Society of Railway Servants, seeking reparation for losses suffered during a strike. The case had come up to the Lords of Appeal, who had found the union liable to the tune of twenty-three thousand pounds. The decision had annulled the long immunity that protected British labor unions against acts carried out by their members and exposed every union to crippling financial penalties each time its members were involved in a labor dispute. All but the most conservative newspapers had decried it as another instance of the power of the Lords being exerted on behalf of large industrialists and against the people.

Miss Conway tilted her head to one side and regarded him thoughtfully. "I had no idea," she said. She gave a little laugh. "I supposed that all the Lords were against the unions."

"Most are," Charles said, "but there are a few of us who count ourselves Liberals—and worse." He picked up his pipe and tobacco pouch. "I must say, I came away from the debate with a great admiration for Adam Gould's courage. I should hate to see him brought to trial on a trumped-up charge."

"If you sided with Adam on the Taff-Vale case, I can have no reason not to trust you," Miss Conway said. She paused and, with a glance at Kate, added guiltily, "To tell the truth, I'm beginning to feel more than a little ashamed of myself. When I first escaped from the police, I was so frightened that I could think only of getting away. That's why I went to Nellie and begged her to help me get out of London." Her face darkened. "But the more I think about what I've done—coming here, I mean—the more I believe that I was wrong. I should have stayed in the City, where I might have been of some service to Adam and the others. They're all alone, with no one to stand up for them." She shook her head despairingly. "I don't even know if they've been able to find a barrister to handle their defense."

"I may know someone who might be willing to help," Charles said, tamping tobacco into his pipe. "He is certainly more than competent. I'm planning to go up to London on

Monday, and I'll see him then. I'll try to see Adam, as well, and find out exactly what the charges are."

"I'll go with you," Miss Conway said vehemently, putting her cup down.

Charles shook his head. "Not unless you want to be jailed yourself. I don't see how you can help Adam and the others if you are behind bars."

"Lord Sheridan is right," Kate said firmly. "You're safe here, Miss Conway. If anything can be done, his lordship will do it. He'll get at the truth, and within a few days, your friends will be out of jail."

Miss Conway's mouth hardened. "I hope you will pardon my skepticism, Lady Sheridan. Now that the men are in the hands of the law, the courts will never release them—not after what happened in Hyde Park. Scapegoats are wanted, and since Yuri is dead, others will have to do, the more the better." She bit her lip. "Adam and the others will be lucky to get off with ten years' penal servitude, like the comrades at Walsall."

Charles put a match to his pipe. He had followed the Walsall case closely, and while he did not like to admit it, he suspected that Miss Conway might very well be right. Some years before, six Anarchists living in the village of Walsall had been charged with the unlawful possession of explosives with the intent to manufacture bombs. No explosives were ever found; in fact, the only evidence the police were able to produce was a length of fuse taken from one man's house, a sketch of a bomb found in another's, and a stack of Anarchist pamphlets discovered in the flat belonging to a third. On this flimsy evidence, the prosecution based its assertion that the men were "a dangerous new class of revolutionist," part of a vast and frightening conspiracy that threatened the peace and stability of the entire country, and argued that it was not what these Anarchists had done that mattered, it was what they were prepared to do. The newspapers quickly took up the battle cry and a kind of mass hysteria began to prevail, for it seemed that unless the Walsall Anarchists were convicted and sentenced, all England would be at the mercy of terrorists with their dynamite.

Had the prosecution's case been based solely on the evidence, it could not have held up against a vigorous defense in court. But fortunately for the Crown (the Attorney-General himself conducted the case for the prosecution), one of the conspirators, a man named Deakin, was persuaded to turn nose and supply a confession that implicated three of the others. Also fortunately for the Crown, several bombs exploded in France the week before the trial began, which increased the hysteria in Britain. It took the jury less than two hours to find Deakin and three others guilty and sentence them to five- and ten-year prison terms. Upon learning the verdict, the *Commonweal*, the Socialist League newspaper, printed an angry, impassioned editorial, pleading for justice. Shortly thereafter, the paper was raided, and both its editor and publisher jailed.

Charles pulled on his pipe. "This man Yuri Messenko," he said. "The bomber. I read that he was employed at the *Clarion*. Did you know him well?"

Miss Conway sighed. "I knew him a little. His father was Ukrainian, his mother English, I believe. They lived in Manchester, although they are both dead now. Yuri seemed a soft-spoken, kind young man, always willing to run errands or do what he could to help. He was especially good with children and with people who were in trouble; he always knew what to say to comfort them." She smiled a little, crookedly. "He wasn't very bright, though. And his views were not threatening—at least, not as threatening as those of others, Pierre, for instance."

"Did he have any expertise in chemistry?"

"In chemistry? I should say not!" Miss Conway gave a sad little laugh. "Yuri was no more able to build a bomb than to construct a flying-machine. He wouldn't even know where to obtain explosive material."

"But he was obviously carrying explosives," Charles pointed out. "He might not have known exactly what was in the satchel, but someone did. Someone had to obtain the materials, construct the explosive device, put it into the satchel, and hand it to Messenko—all which suggests a conspiracy of some kind. Equally obviously, Yuri Messenko did not succeed in killing anyone else but himself." Casually, he spoke around his pipe, not seeming to look at her. "Was that by accident, do you think, or by design?"

Kate frowned. "You're suggesting that the explosion was not meant to kill the King?"

"I'm not sure what I'm suggesting," Charles replied. "Miss Conway? Was it by accident?"

"How could I possibly know the answer to that question," Miss Conway said defiantly, "unless I were a party to the conspiracy. And I was not." Then, more tentatively, she added, "You are thinking that someone deliberately set out to kill Yuri?"

"At this point, it's as likely an explanation as anything else," Charles replied. "Do you know where he lived? Who his friends were?"

Miss Conway seemed wary, but she answered nonetheless. "He lived in Telson Street, Number 17, I think, or Number 19—not far from the *Clarion* office. As to his friends, I'm afraid I have no idea. Ivan might know. I've occasionally seen the two of them leaving the newspaper together in the evenings. Sometimes they went to meetings, sometimes they just went out for something to eat." She pulled her brows together. "As for a conspiracy, all I can tell you is that different people who come to the newspaper—the Spaniards or the Italians, mostly—sometimes make threats or skulk around as though they are planning some violent action. But there isn't as much of that as the authorities and the newspapers lead one to believe." Her lips curved in what might have been a smile. "Most of the people in our cell—the Hampstead Road cell—prefer propaganda by word to propaganda by deed."

At Kate's puzzled look, Charles translated. "Miss Conway means that they prefer to educate people to the need for change, rather than try to bring about change through violent action."

"Thank you," Miss Conway said. Now she did smile. "Some, less charitably, say that the *Clarion* is a call to talk, rather than to fight." She pulled a face. "I'm sorry. I'm not a very helpful informant."

Charles puffed on his pipe. "After I've talked to Adam and the others and done a little more digging, I may have other questions to ask you, if you don't mind."

"I don't mind. I just wish I could *do* something." Miss Conway sighed despondently. "Something more helpful than trying to answer questions."

CHAPTER NINE

❖═◉═❖

I never saw a man in all my life with more magnetism, beautiful magnetism . . . . When he talked, he was marvelous. His eyes were big and his mouth was just as sensitive and full of expression, and his words came out of him just rippling . . . . He talked better than he wrote.

Finn Frollich,
quoted in Alex Kershaw, *Jack London: A Life*

Nellie Lovelace always felt a special energy sweeping through her at the close of an evening's performance. It was as if the audience's laughter and delighted applause were a kind of electricity, jolting her awake and making her feel like dancing, a boost that was almost always strong enough to keep her going until the next performance. In fact, it had begun to seem to Nellie that she pretty much lived from one performance to another, the time in between a monotonous stretch of gray humdrum when nothing of interest happened. Her life was on the stage and the stage was what she lived for.

Tonight, however, she had the feeling that her life was about to change, for as she took her final curtain, a little brown-skinned boy, dressed in red satin and wearing the turban of an Indian potentate, leapt lightly onto the stage and thrust a gigantic bouquet of roses into her arms. "Compl'ments of Mr. London," he lisped, bowing so deeply that his turban touched the stage.

And then, returning to her dressing room, she found it actually banked with flowers, their scent so strong that she could scarcely catch her breath. And there was Mr. London himself lounging in the open door, dressed in smart formal attire, a silk hat under one arm. She pulled in her breath at the sight of the flowers and at the sight of him, for he was even more striking than she had remembered, and there was a crooked smile on his lips and an admiring glint in his daring dark eyes, fringed by marvelous long lashes.

"You were magnificent, Miss Lovelace." He grinned and waved expansively at the flowers. "A small thanks for the sheer pleasure of watching you perform." He paused. "I should very much like to invite you to dinner."

"And I should be pleased to accept," Nellie said eagerly, although some of her gaiety evaporated, as she realized from his flushed face and the easiness of his gesture that Mr. London was already a little drunk. But just a little, she told herself, as she slipped behind a screen and quickly exchanged her costume for a close-fitting, low-cut gown of garnet velvet that showed her voluptuous figure and smooth white shoulders to advantage, adding a matching fur-trimmed velvet cape. Anyway, men who drank too much were among the hazards of the acting profession, and one learned to manage them, if one wanted to be invited to dinner.

Nellie's gaiety was fully restored by the time they got into the waiting four-wheeler, for they were going, Mr. London told her with a certain careless flair, to the Carlton. The Carlton! Nellie's admirers had taken her to some of the best restaurants in the City, but not yet to the Carlton, and the anticipation made her breath come faster. She settled into the leather seat with a shiver of delight and gave herself over to the pleasure of a late-night ride through the streets of London.

The daytime city might be gritty and grimy, but at night it became a glittering fairyland. A misty fog hung like a diaphanous curtain over the streets, the starry gaslights shimmered on the damp pavement, and the arc lamps shone like haloed moons. The uncurtained windows of brilliantly-lit salons gave glimpses of handsomely-dressed high-spirited pleasure-seekers of all ranks, and strains of music floated through the open doors. Heedless of the misty damp, men in silk hats and women in evening gowns tripped lightly along the sidewalks in front of gaily-decked shop windows, and the streets were crowded curb to curb with bustling black carriages and sleek hansom cabs, with here and there a shiny motorcar.

"Quite a city," Mr. London remarked, pursing his lips. "Not up to New York's mark, of course," he added judiciously, "or even Frisco, which is still a bit raw. But quite a city nevertheless."

Nellie felt at a disadvantage, since she had not been to New York or San Francisco. But she was stung by the condescension in his tone and observed tartly that many people seemed to prefer London to any city in the world. She softened her remark with a sideways smile, though, and the comment, "From the East End to the Carleton—you're seeing quite a good deal of the City, Mr. London. The writing is going well, I hope?"

They talked about Mr. London's new book, then, which he had described to her at length the other afternoon at tea at the Palmers'. He said he had spent the day doing research—tramping the docks, talking to dockworkers, and taking notes about their awful working conditions, as well as any number of photographs—and he gave her a detailed description of the dens and dives, as he called them, that he had explored. He had been glad to return to the Palmers', where he could get a hot bath and change out of what he called his "slum costume" before coming out for the evening. He was writing steadily, he added with a conscious pride, working from notes he took on his expeditions into the East End and from some documents the Socialists had provided him, figures and statistics and the like. He expected to finish the book, which he was calling *People of the Abyss,* before he returned to New York.

"*People of the Abyss?*" Nellie repeated, not sure that she liked the sound of the title.

"People of the pit," Mr. London said. He shrugged, his dark eyes glinting. "Hell, if you like that better."

"Well, of course, some of Whitechapel is very bad," Nellie conceded. "There's no denying that. But I lived there myself for a time, and I—"

"Then you understand exactly what I'm talking about," London said. He slipped an arm around her shoulders. "Now, Miss Lovelace, let's talk about pleasanter things. You were a vision tonight, up there on that stage. The way you moved, I couldn't keep my eyes off you." His glance dropped to her breasts, and his lips to her mouth, forcibly. Nellie was decidedly relieved when the carriage jolted to a stop in front of the Carleton. Mr. London pulled back as a liveried valet opened the door.

And then they were entering the Carleton, and Nellie found herself surrounded by a wonderland of plush carpets, soft lights and music, sweet-scented flowers on the tables, and green palms in every corner. They were shown to a table covered by snowy damask linen and set with sparkling crystal and elegant china, where they quickly agreed to call each other Jack and Nellie, then lingered for a very long time over a lavish supper of rare roast duck (Jack's favorite) and several bottles of Liebfraumilch (another of his favorites). Afterward, they floated (at least, that's how Nellie remembered it) into a private lounge, where they sat together on a velvet settee with their coffees and liqueurs and cigarettes.

Jack was a marvelous conversationalist, as one might expect of a famous adventure writer, and the words flowed out of him in a wild torrent. He had sailed before the mast on the last of the seal-hunters to leave San Francisco Bay, he said, and felt "absolutely exalted" when he stood at the wheel of the wildly careering schooner, guiding it through a maelstrom of waves. "When I have done such a thing," he said expansively, "I glow all over. Every fiber of me thrills with it."

Nellie started to say that she felt exactly the same way when she was on the stage, but he was hurrying on to tell her about how he had nearly lost his life among the icebergs of the Bering Sea, and while she was still gasping at the brutal dangers of that desolate scene, he began to describe the harrowing winters he had spent searching for gold in the Klondike, where he had learned to love the loud, clear call of wolves in the echoing wilderness. She had barely transformed him in her mind from sailor and seal-hunter to goldseeker, when he was describing how he had hitched his way right across the United States in a railway boxcar, and then had only just missed being elected Mayor of Oakland, California—in fact, he would have been elected if he hadn't run on the Socialist ticket, because Socialists weren't quite the thing in America just yet.

But they would be, he insisted, stubbing out his cigarette in his coffee cup. There would be a revolution, it was absolutely inevitable, and then the millions of people (like himself) whose birthrights had been denied would rise up and reclaim them from the capitalists who had stolen them. That Jack London was a Socialist and spoke so warmly against the destructive powers of capitalism was somewhat surprising to Nellie, because she had thought—naively, it seemed—that only capitalists could afford to eat roast duck at the Carlton.

Over their liqueurs, the conversation turned to another event that seemed to have caught Jack's fancy, for he told the story with an amusing panache. He was walking down Hampstead Road when a bird's nest fell out of the sky and onto the pavement in front of him. Looking up, he saw to his great surprise a woman scrambling across a roof, and then, to his delight, descending straight down an iron fire-ladder and practically into his arms, while on the street at his very elbow, the police were bustling three men into a police van. Questioning those around him, he learned that the woman who jumped off the ladder and disappeared into the crowd was none other than the editor of the *Clarion,* an Anarchist newspaper, and that she was escaping from a raid. He seemed to find this whole affair wonderfully amusing and stimulating.

"That would be Charlotte Conway," Nellie said, glad that she was at last able to contribute something to the conversation, which up to that point had been mainly his. "I know her quite well, actually. In fact, I've already heard all about her narrow escape. She told me herself."

Jack's dark eyes glinted with excitement. "She *told* you? You mean, you know where she is?"

Nellie frowned. Things might be a bit blurry from everything she'd had to drink, but she still had her wits about her. "I know where she *was,*" she said cautiously. "She's not there now."

"Then where is she?"

Feeling that there was an odd urgency about the question, Nellie put on a mysterious smile. "Why, she could be anywhere," she said lightly. "Those Anarchists, you know. Always so independent, never wanting to ask for anything."

"Somehow I guessed that about her," Jack said, half to himself. "A free spirit, nothing held back, nothing denied. Mate woman."

Nellie frowned, puzzled by the phrase *mate woman*. In her experience, men (especially sailors and Aussies) considered one another as mates, and animal pairs were thought of as mates, and sometimes married people spoke of their spouses as mates. *Mate woman* didn't make much sense, if Jack was thinking of Lottie.

Still, she didn't want him to suspect that she herself was withholding something, so she only smiled and said, "That's Lottie, a free spirit," adding, "The last time I saw her, she had cut her hair short and disguised herself as a young man."

"The hell you say!" Jack exploded into a raucous laugh. "A man, huh? What a woman!" Catching her curious glance, he said, still chuckling, "Well, then, if you see her, let her know I'm looking for her. I'm dying to interview her—get her opinion about the East End and what's going on there. I'll wager she knows more than most about what I'm interested in. As an Anarchist, that is."

With a twinge of jealousy, Nellie thought that there might be more to it than that, but she just shrugged. "I'm sure she does," she said, tossing her head carelessly. "Well, if I happen to run into her again, I'll see if she wants to talk to you."

His face darkened, and for an instant, she thought he was going to say something. But then he smiled, glanced at his watch, and hoisted himself off the settee. "Say, it's still early, Nell. I've been hearing about Earl's Court, and I want to see it. Let's go have some fun." And without waiting for her to reply that she was actually a little tired and would prefer to end the evening now, he was striding toward the door.

The rest of the evening—the night, really—was a blur. Nellie was more tired than she had thought, but she tried to put her weariness aside and match Jack's boundless, boisterous energy. She had been many times to Earl's Court, but always found it most enticing in the evening, when darkness threw a mysterious cloak of illusion and fantasy over the scene. In the center of the Court was a lake rimmed with colored lights that cast shimmering pools of color across the surface. There was an exotic stone grotto at one end and a bridge across the middle, where one could stand and watch little electric launches designed to look like gliding swans. At one side of the lake, boats full of people swept down a tall water-chute and into the water with a giant splash. From beyond the bridge Nellie could hear the sprightly sound of a German band playing a polka, and a Chinese dragon railway puffed real steam as it ran around the lake, its miniature cars filled with squealing passengers. And then there was the Exhibition Court, in which all sorts of side-shows were offered, and there was champagne to drink.

During the day Earl's Court was always crowded with children and their nannies, but at night it attracted people of all classes: wide-eyed servant girls in their Sunday best strolling on the arms of their gawking beaux; and top-hatted men of the world squiring velvet-clad ladies decked with glittering jewelry. If any of these lovely ladies were no better than they should be, it would have been exceedingly difficult to pick them out from the others, for the multi-hued gaslights cast a shimmering veil over all, softening sharp features, sweetening sour tempers, and disguising illicit intentions.

With so many other well-dressed ladies around her, Nellie did not feel at all out of place in her velvet finery, although she was not entirely comfortable when Jack insisted that they tour the India Exhibit. This was a circus-like coterie of snake-charmers, jugglers, exotic (and smelly) leopards, and veiled women dancers with bare navels and bare feet, the latter much applauded by a great crowd of drunken men. In fact, by now Nellie had rather got the idea that Jack preferred the gaudy excitement and bawdy silliness of Earl's Court to the earlier elegance of the Carlton. But perhaps that was simply the American in him. She had not known many Americans, but she had the idea that they thrived on excitement, as Jack certainly seemed to do.

She decided that this was definitely the case when he bought more champagne, and then tickets on the Big Wheel, and they found themselves sailing up and up into the cool dark night, the bright lights and sparkling music wafting eerily up out of the fog below.

"Not as tall as the Ferris wheel in Chicago," Jack said critically, and began to rock their carriage to see how far he could make it swing, until Nellie squealed with fear. "But I guess it'll do." He smiled down at her and slipped his arm around her shoulder. "Hell," he said. "I *know* it'll do."

Nellie shivered with pleasure, and when Jack bent to kiss her, it was easy to kiss him back, gently at first and then fiercely, with a passion she had not realized was in her. And when the ride was over, he took her hand and led her to the exit, and into a cab, and there was more kissing, far more than Nellie (for she did not have nearly the experience she pretended) had ever before allowed. And within a very short while they were at her door and she was clinging giddily to his arm and fumbling for her key, and he was taking it from her and letting them both into the little house.

And then he was pulling her dress off her shoulders, not at all gently, and yanking off his shirt and trousers. As his intention became clear, she tried to push him away, crying "No, no, please, no!" with a mounting fright, as much at the urgency of her own whirling desire as at the brutal roughness of his hands and mouth. But he pulled her to him as if her resistance only fueled his passion, and as he pushed her onto the bed, still crying out in protest, she realized how incredibly strong he was. There was no use in fighting, for he would do just as he willed. He would take what he wanted, without restraint.

Everything became very blurry after that, and when Nellie

woke in the gray light of an early morning, she had a savage headache, her mouth was as dry as a desert, and her body ached as if it had been assaulted—as, to tell truth, it had. She lay for a moment, not quite remembering what had happened, and then sat up in bed, clutching the rumpled sheets around her nakedness.

Jack was gone, but there was a pencilled note on the dresser, in a sprawling, careless script. "Dear Nell," it said. "Thanks for the evening. Remember, if you happen to see Miss Conway, let her know I'd give anything to talk to her. Yrs, JL"

Pressing her lips together to keep them from trembling, Nellie, still naked, stood for a very long time with the note in her hand. Then she took it to the fireplace, where she knelt down and put a match to it, watching as it flared into an orange flame, then fell into a heap of black ash. By the time the last spark had died, there was a hard ache in her throat and her eyes were swimming with tears. She had the feeling that something very precious had been taken from her, and she had received nothing in return.

CHAPTER TEN

Anarchism dramatized the war between the two divisions of society, between the world of privilege and the world of protest .... It was the last cry of individual man, the last movement among the masses on behalf of individual liberty, the last hope of living unregulated, the last fist shaken against the encroaching State, before the State, the party, the union, the organization closed in.

Barbara Tuchman,
The Proud Tower

A dam Gould sat on a wooden chair in a dark cage in a small room in the depths of Holloway Prison. Across from him, on another wooden chair on the other side of the wire barricade, sat Mr. Morley, of Masters, Morley, and Dunderston, the solicitor sent to him by the Amalgamated Society of Railway Servants. Morley was thin as a broom-straw, stiff-necked and nearly bald, and with a dour and depressed demeanor. He felt—no, he *knew,* and gloomily asserted as much—that nothing short of a miracle could save Adam from the retributive power of the law.

"If I've said it once, I've said it a hundred times," he added in a sour whisper, as if he did not wish to be overheard by the guard, who stood not ten paces away. "Anarchists are trouble. And, sir, you have asked for it. Hanging about the offices of the *Clarion,* consorting with known Anarchists. Nothing good can come from the Anarchist principle, I say, and that's the short and the long of it." He sniffed contemptuously. "Nothing, to put it in the fewest possible words."

Adam sighed, for Morley had never been a man to put anything into the fewest possible words, and his political persuasions were already very well known. Like most of those involved with the trade unions, he felt that the Anarchists were nothing but inept bunglers, and dangerous in their ineptitude. "What I want to know," Adam said patiently, "is whether you've heard anything from Miss Conway."

"No, and not likely to, either," Morley rejoined, in a low, dispirited tone, as if oppressed and deadened by the burden of his gloom. He took out a large white handkerchief and blew his nose with a loud honk. "Infernal places, prisons," he muttered. "Dank and musty. Not good for the lungs, nor for the heart, nor for the spirit. In short, not good at all. In fact, I do truly believe that each time I am forced to come here, I—"

"I hope that Miss Conway will attempt to contact me," Adam said crisply, attempting to stem the flow of words, "if only to let me know that she is safe. You will give me her message, I trust."

"Safe!" harrumphed Morley with an ill grace, pocketing his handkerchief and straightening his cuffs. "Took to her heels like a common vagabond, did she not? Disappeared into the crowd without a thought for anyone's safety and welfare but her own, as I heard the tale. Anarchists!" he hissed. "Nothing but trouble from them, especially the women. And that's what got you into this difficulty in the first place, isn't it, Gould? Hanging about with that Anarchist woman? You might have had better sense."

Adam sighed. He had worked with Morley on the

Taff-Vale matter, and knew that the man was a solicitor, not a barrister, and thus could not represent him in court. Instead, Morley would consult a barrister, present his instructions for the handling of Adam's case, and pay the barrister's fee, which would be charged, along with his own, to the ASRS. He straightened his shoulders and took a different, more professional tack. "Well, then, Morley, p'rhaps we should get down to business. Have you learnt the charge? What do they say I've done?"

"Have I learnt the charge, he asks. Have I learnt the charge?" Mr. Morley rolled his eyes heavenward in mute appeal to a higher power, then pulled his brows into a stern frown and focused his gaze upon Adam. "Very well, sir," he growled. "The charge against you, sir, is made under the Explosive Substances Act of 1883. You are accused of the possession of explosives with intent to endanger life. If you are convicted, you are likely to be sentenced to fifteen to twenty years of penal servitude." He waggled his finger at Adam. "Little good you will do the Amalgamated Society of Railway Servants if you should be found guilty. Precious little good you are doing them *now*."

Possession of explosives? Adam felt a great surge of relief at this news. He had expected to be charged, if at all, with something vague and difficult to refute—conspiracy or consorting with known criminals or some such. But this? He chuckled.

"Possession of explosives," he said carelessly. "Well, that's easy, Morley. I've never possessed an explosive of any sort in my entire life."

"Not at all 'easy,' sir," Morley said with a darkly sarcastic emphasis, "when they have the evidence. The *evidence*, sir, which I have seen with my own eyes." He looked down, pursuing something on his sleeve, a flea, probably. "Ah!" he cried, catching it. He held up his fingers, pinching hard. "Ah-ha!" he cried again, triumphantly. "Got you, you little fiend!"

"Evidence?" Adam asked, frowning. "They can have no evidence, unless—" He stopped. The police could have no evidence unless they had themselves manufactured and planted it, something to which they had been known to resort, although they were rarely called to account for the deception. His heart sank down into his boots. "What is this evidence, Morley?"

Morley paused, fixing him with a long and penetrating stare. Into the silence intruded the sound of a woman's heartbroken weeping—a visitor, she must be, since women were confined in another part of the prison. Somewhere a chain clanked, and a rusty hinge squeaked. To Adam, they seemed the sounds of doom.

Morley cleared his throat and, giving each word a sternly judicial weight, said, "The evidence, sir, as you know very well, is the ginger-beer bottle containing nitric acid—according to the chemist's report—which was found in your rooms, and which I myself have seen."

"Know very well!" Adam exclaimed angrily, half-rising from his seat. "Know very well, you say? I know nothing of the kind. An explosive bottle may have been found in my rooms, but *I* did not put it there!"

Morley pulled his mouth down. "Nothing short of a miracle," he said in a funereal voice. "That, sir, is what it will take to gain you your freedom. Therefore, I counsel you to pray for a—"

"It was put there by the police, I tell you!" Adam cried hoarsely. "And I depend on *you,* Morley, to find me a barrister who will prove that I am innocent of this trumped-up charge."

"Depend on me, sir?" Morley's expression became even more ominously funereal, and he once more dropped his voice to a whisper. "I will certainly do my utmost on your behalf, since the Amalgamated Society of Railway Servants has employed my firm to assist in your case. But you must not expect miracles, not at all. In fact, I should say that the chances for your acquittal, under the present circumstances, are virtually—"

"By God, you *will* do your utmost!" Adam shouted, now on his feet and pushing his face against the wire barricade. "I am innocent, Morley. You know it, and you'll prove it, or I'll—"

A guard emerged out of the darkness behind him. "Here," he said severely. "We can't 'ave this." He seized Adam by the collar of his prison shirt and yanked him backward. "This interview is done. Back to yer cell wi' ye."

Morley straightened his lapels, as if he had been physically assaulted. "I will do my utmost," he said, speaking with gravely offended dignity. "In the meantime, sir, I most heartily counsel you to pray. You should depend not upon the power of earthly men, who must all certainly fall short of perfection, but upon the mercy of the Almighty. You must—" The rest, thankfully, was lost in the clanging of the cage door and the vituperative mutterings of the guard as he roughly escorted Adam down the passageway and back to the prison block.

A few minutes later, Adam was alone in the damp darkness of his cell, sitting on the wooden plank that served as a bed, his face in his hands, thinking despairingly of what Morley had told him.

He had been seized in the Anarchist newspaper where the Hyde Park bomber had been employed, in the company of the bomber's comrades. Some sort of bomb had been discovered in his rooms, and he had been charged with the possession of explosives. In the current climate, in the aftermath of what must have been a plot to assassinate the King, such a charge was tantamount to a charge of treason. Furthermore, his persecutors would draw no distinction between an Anarchist and a trade unionist; both would be tarred alike with the same awful brush. And that incompetent fool of a solicitor, who believed the police lies, would be of no help at all. He had been given a certain ticket to doom.

And he was not the only one. In a cell down the passageway sat Ivan, and some little distance away, Pierre. No doubt explosives had been found in their rooms, as well, and they were charged as he was. When they came to court, they would all three share the same miserable fate.

And this was not the only thing that tore at Adam's heart. Somewhere out there in the great, gray inhospitable city was Lottie, alone, a fugitive from the police. She couldn't go home to her mother, or to any of her comrades, for no doubt the police had planted spies at every place she was known to frequent. Where would she go? How would she survive? Adam shivered as he thought of the ugly things that could happen to a woman, the terrible things that happened every day to women who were alone and undefended on the streets of London.

But then he took heart, and smiled a little. He could not believe that Lottie would allow herself to become a victim. She was far too clever and too resourceful to come to serious harm, and he wouldn't be surprised if she was even now attempting to find a way to help him. The image of her dark, dancing eyes, the dazzling impudence of her smile, seemed almost to lighten the darkness of his cell. He had no idea how she had managed to escape from her little loft office—across the roof perhaps, although that seemed impossible. But Lottie was never constrained by what others considered impossible. Lottie had the heart of a man, and the courage of a man, and a man's daring.

And the body and soul of a woman, he thought with a little smile. He lay back on the wooden plank and let himself dream of Lottie.

* * *

A few paces down the passageway, Ivan Kopinski was also lying on his wooden plank. Jails were not new to him, and he had long ago learned that a man who exercised both his body and his mind during his imprisonment was far likelier to survive it than one who did not. Consequently, he allocated his time, alternately, between stretching exercises and running in place, and mental exercise. Just now, he was rigorously reviewing a certain period of his past, casting his mind month by month over the five years he had spent studying the writings and work of his mentor, Prince Peter Kropotkin. He found that he could name all of Kropotkin's many writings, in the order of their publication, and could mentally compose a brief synopsis of each, including its major arguments. He could also recall where he had been when he read these, and what he had been doing, and how they had changed his thinking. It was an excellent exertion, and he smiled with satisfaction. During his next period of mental exercise, he would review the works of Bakunin, another of his teachers.

Ivan had lived in France while he was studying Kropotkin's work. He had been employed as a printer's apprentice and had spent all his spare time perusing Anarchist books and pamphlets with the passion of a zealot—and a zealot he was. As a very young man, Ivan had been seized by the Russian police for refusing to serve in the Czar's army; imprisoned, he had refused to recognize the authority of his judges and jailers, and had been brutally beaten for his resolute naysaying. The way out of prison had involved taking as hostage Georgi Fedorov—an important official, the son of Princess Fedorovna and the nephew of Grand Duke Gerasimov, a favorite of the Czar—and when Fedorov was shot by prison guards during the escape, a price was laid on Ivan's head. He had fled to his village for a last farewell before leaving Russia forever, but there he discovered that his parents had been brutally executed by the police, in retribution for their son's escape. Until then, he had been genuinely remorseful at Fedorov's death, but this pitiless murder of innocents hardened him. There was nothing left for Ivan, as there was nothing left for so many dispossessed, dispersed Russians, but to stoke the flaming fires of hatred in his heart and vow to find a way to bring down the hated regime of the Czar.

And Anarchism seemed to offer that way. Living on his luck and by his wits in some of the filthiest slums of Paris, Munich, and Brussels, he had met many other comrades who shared his passionate views, his hatred of corrupt regimes, his fury at the ruling class. And at last, he met Kropotkin, a Russian nobleman who had repudiated rank and riches and become an uncompromising apostle of the necessity of violence as a means of destroying the old world and clearing the way for the new. This should be done, Kropotkin urged, "by speech and written word, by dagger, gun, and dynamite," and when the revolution had come (Kropotkin calculated that it would take no more than three to five years), all governments would be destroyed, and all property would become the property of all the people. Each person would draw upon the community warehouses for food and goods according to his needs, and each person would work according to his talents, for the good of all. In such a world, there would be no greed, no oppression, no slums, no prisons—and no murder of innocents.

Ivan's hungry soul had been fed by Kropotkin's shining, inspiring dream. He knew that he was strong and dedicated enough to answer the stirring summons to "men of courage willing not only to speak but to act, men who prefer prison, exile, and death to a life that contradicts their principles." These men of courage—and Ivan knew that he was one— would make up the advance guard of the revolution, prepared to act long before the masses were awake to the possibility of a new future. Men of strength like himself and Pierre and even Adam (although he was a trade unionist, and a reformer, and not an Anarchist). Women of strength, like Lottie, lovely Lottie, whom Ivan would have loved with all the fierce passion of his Slavic soul, had he allowed himself to do so. Lottie, whose mischievous smile and gay laugh so belied her firm will, her dedication to all that was right and just and noble. And then there was Yuri.

Still on his back, Ivan raised his right leg and began to flex it rhythmically. It was ironic, wasn't it? He had considered himself in the advance guard, laboring to spread the Anarchist word through the pages of the *Clarion,* when all the time, unbeknownst to anyone, Yuri Messenko—affectionate, gentle, Yuri, a boy to whom no one had paid any special regard—had been plotting a revolutionary deed so bravely violent and so startlingly audacious as to bring credit to them all.

Ivan had been astonished when he heard what Yuri had done; he had been utterly dumbfounded, and he was dumbfounded still, as he thought about it. That Yuri would have the courage, the cleverness, the extraordinary *commitment* required to carry out such a singular act made him feel enormously proud, even as he shook his head over the amazing improbability of such a thing. He felt a sharp sense of loss, as well (although he reminded himself that this was unforgivably bourgeois), for he had allowed himself to love Yuri (to the extent that an Anarchist could feel love) for his gentleness and compassion. Ivan feared that he had never fully understood the boy, for at times Yuri seemed remarkably dim-witted and yet at other times exhibited a deeply intuitive vision. And he had certainly neither understood nor shared Yuri's devotion to Pierre, that inflammatory firebrand of a fellow who seemed to Ivan to be manipulative and devious in the extreme. But this had not changed Ivan's fondness for Yuri, and while he saluted Yuri's heroic act, he mourned the lost young hero.

But there were other problems upon which Ivan must

exercise his mind. His defense, for instance. Mr. Morley, the solicitor who had been sent by the Amalgamated Society of Railway Servants to defend Adam, had refused to take Ivan's and Pierre's case, on the grounds that the ASRS was paying him to arrange the defense of one man, not three. Nicholas Petrovich, one of the few comrades brave enough to acknowledge any connection with their jailed colleages, had paid Ivan a visit the day before, bringing some cheese and apples—which were promptly confiscated by the guard. Nikki had come to let Ivan know that a solicitation was being conducted among the members of the Hampstead Road cell to collect the eight guineas required by Mr. Brownlow, a barrister who had defended other Anarchists on occasion.

"Brownlow is very sharp, we understand," Nikki had said, in his thick Slavic accent. "If anyone can get you two off the charge, he's the man."

"*If* the eight guineas can be found," Ivan said dispiritedly. "That seems high."

"I'm afraid it's the charge," Nikki replied in an apologetic tone. "If it had been anything else but explosives with intent, he would've come cheaper. But explosives—"

"Explosives?" Ivan had interrupted sharply. "How do explosives come into it?"

Nikki gazed at him as if he didn't quite understand. "Why, the bombs," he said. "In your room, and Pierre's. Ginger-beer bottles with something in them—nitric acid, they say. Not to mention the Anarchist literature, and the bomb-making instructions found in Pierre's pocket." Admiration and pride were mixed with exasperation in his look. "The comrades said to tell you that they didn't know that you were a Dynamitard, or that you and Yuri and Pierre were planning to blow up the King. If they'd known, they'd have said it wasn't a good idea. Too dangerous all 'round."

"It was Yuri's plan, not mine," Ivan said. "I had nothing

to do with it." He was about to add that he had no idea how a bomb had come to be found in his room, but held his tongue. The comrades could think as they liked about him. And if they liked to think that he was a man of deeds, rather than words only, well, that was their choice. He stood no chance before the British bench, anyway, with or without the aid of the eight-guinea Brownlow. He was a Russian and an Anarchist, and when he was found guilty and had served his sentence, he would be handed over to the Ochrana, the Czar's secret police, who would arrange for his deportation. Once in Russia, he was a dead man.

And this opened another vast panorama of problems upon which Ivan must exercise his mental faculties. For the past three weeks, he had suspected that he was being trailed by one of the Russian secret agents who prowled London, keeping a watch on the Russian émigrés, many of whom had sought refuge in the teeming East End. Ivan had done his best to avoid the man—a tall, thin fellow with a black Vandyke beard, wearing a dark overcoat with a fur collar— but he knew it was a futile effort. Whatever he did, he could not get away from the man. And even if he did, it would be of no use, for now that the Ochrana had located him, they would merely assign another agent to trail him.

In fact, now that he thought about it, it seemed to him quite likely that the explosives found in his room had been put there by a Russian agent, immediately after he was seen to be seized in the raid on the *Clarion*. The agent would know that Special Branch police would search his rooms and would want to ensure that they find something incriminating. Of course, the Ochrana would prefer to get their hands on him immediately, so it was possible that they might make some sort of arrangement with the British authorities to hand him over—a trade for another prisoner, or even an arranged escape. One had heard of that sort of thing.

Ivan ran his hands through his lanky, dirty hair. Of

course, this didn't explain why a bomb had also been placed in Pierre's room, since an Ochrana agent was not likely to have any special animosity toward a French Anarchist. Ivan smiled bleakly. Especially an ineffectual French Anarchist, all fierce words and no deeds, whose passion for the Cause blinded him to any real possibility for vigorous action. But there were French secret agents in the City as well (not to mention German and Spanish and Italian and American) and perhaps there had been some sort of collaboration.

However, Ivan did not intend to expend his mental energies on Pierre and his fate. He had to think how best to manage to free himself from this unimaginably tangled web and from the agent who would be waiting to lay hands on him when the Court found him guilty—which would happen, he was sure of it, whatever the efforts of Mr. Eight-Guinea Brownlow.

B ut Brownlow was to make no such efforts on their behalf, as Pierre Mouffetard learned the next day.

Pierre, a dingy, hard-faced man, his jaw patchily smudged with a meager whisker, had also been in jails before, usually on a charge of picking pockets, for that was his criminal trade. But he had never stayed for long, since he or his associates had always managed some early means of egress. He therefore remained unconcerned about his current situation and continued to carry himself with his customary air of blustery self-confidence, even when Nicholas Petrovich came to tell him that Brownlow would not be hired, after all.

The conversation had taken place just an hour ago, in the visiting cage. Nikki said that he had been sent to inform both Pierre and Ivan that the Hampstead Road Anarchists had changed their minds. Instead of helping to procure a defense, they had decided that it would be best for them to disassociate themselves from their jailed comrades. As a messenger, Nikki was clearly uncomfortable with this announcement, and stammered as he said it.

"They . . . we want to express solidarity with militant action, of course, but we . . . the group, that is, feels it can't be reckless." He colored. "You must take it as you like, Pierre, but they . . . we have decided to disclaim all connection with you and Ivan. And Adam Gould, too, of course—he's not a member, anyway. It's the explosives, you see. Everyone's nervous."

Pierre frowned, not so much at the way the comrades had abandoned him, but at the charge itself, which he had heard from Nikki the day before, for the first time. "But I had no explosives in my room," he said. "I told you that yesterday."

"That does not alter the fact," Nikki replied somberly, "that the police say they found a bomb there. And there were the instructions for bomb-making in your pocket."

"Instructions?" Pierre gave a hard laugh. "That was merely a letter—a French compatriot writing to tell me about a Spanish comrade who built an explosive device of some sort."

"Doesn't matter." Nikki pressed his lips together. "The comrades said that they are sorry, but they know that you, of all people, will appreciate that they must act in their own self-interest."

Of course they must act in their own self-interest, Pierre thought scornfully, and *he* would act—as he always did—in his. That was what it meant to be an Anarchist, and whatever else he was (and he was many things), he was an Anarchist at heart. He stared down for a moment at the knot of his long, thin fingers, thinking about the bomb that had been put in his room by—by whom? He frowned, for while his impulsive actions and inflammatory temper had made him many enemies, he could think of none who would have chosen this route to revenge. But Pierre had been in difficult straits before, and things had come right in the end. Things seemed dark indeed, but there would be a way out. And if he could not find one, why, then, he would make one.

So Pierre had merely smiled tightly, asked Nikki to tell the comrades that he appreciated their position, and retired to his cell to consider the matter further. In his considerations, of course, his mind went to Ivan and Adam, in whose rooms the police had also found bombs. Pierre had no special liking for Adam, who was a reformist, not a revolutionary. But he was truly sorry for Ivan, whom he especially admired, for Ivan was both passionate and dedicated and had suffered through many trials, always showing himself worthy. With his training as a printer, Ivan was well on his way to making important contributions to the Cause—far more than he, Pierre, could ever hope to make. Pierre did not possess a great deal of self-knowledge, but he knew enough about himself to recognize that he had made very little of his life, and of the opportunities that had come his way. If he had to do it over again, he would do what Ivan had done: study more diligently, learn a trade, and find a way to do something significant for the Cause.

But there was no use in regret. The past was past, and neither here nor there. For now, there was nothing to do but wait and see what might happen.

CHAPTER ELEVEN

The first thing we do, let's kill all the lawyers.

William Shakespeare,
Henry VI, Part 2

Charles took the train up to London early on Monday morning. He disembarked when it reached the Liverpool Street Terminus and found a cab to take him to Sibley House, the Mayfair mansion that had been purchased by his great-grandfather for the family's use when in London. Charles did not enjoy the pleasures of the City and much preferred his wife's home at Bishop's Keep to the London house—or to Somersworth, for that matter, his family estate in Norfolk. Now that his mother was dead, he went less often to Somersworth; at some point, and perhaps very soon, he ought to come to some conclusions about how best to deal with the estate, which was far too large to be conveniently managed. He did not like the idea of breaking it up for sale, for there were the tenants and estate staff to be considered, and besides, he had no need for the money. While he was in town, he planned to talk with his old friend Canon Rawnsley, who had created a new organization he was calling the National Trust. Perhaps the Trust would be the best way to deal with Somersworth.

But that question did not have to be settled this morning. When Charles reached Sibley House, he handed his hat and coat to Richards, the butler, inquired about messages, and then went into his study, where he lit his pipe, accepted Richards's offer of a cup of coffee, and made a few telephone calls. After several brief inquiries, he learned that Adam Gould's employer, the Amalgamated Society of Railway Servants, had handed over the matter of his defense to Mr. Morley of Masters, Morley, and Dunderston.

Charles sat back in his chair, frowning over his coffee. He was already acquainted with the firm through its representation of the ASRS in the Taff-Vale matter, and had not been especially impressed by either the competency or the passion of Masters, Morley, or Dunderston—cold fish, the lot of them. But there was no barrister in the firm, as far as he knew, so Gould's defense would have to be turned over to someone who was admitted to plead at the Bar. And he thought he knew just the man for the job, if Mr. Morley could be persuaded to agree.

He drained his cup, tapped his pipe into the ashtray, and stood. It seemed to him that Adam Gould definitely required a bit of extra help to save him from his lawyers.

Mr. Malachi Morley was deep in *The Times* when there was a deferential tap at his office door. He frowned. He had given explicit instructions that he was working on a case and was not to be disturbed. And he was working, of course, for every solicitor needed to be well-informed, and *The Times* was full of snippets of important information. Ignoring the tap, he turned the page, but when it came again, he dropped the paper and cried irritably, "I told you I was busy. Now go away and——"

The door opened and the slender, red-haired clerk appeared. "I'm very sorry, sir," the boy said contritely, "but his lordship says the matter is urgent and—"

A tall, brown-bearded, brown-moustached gentleman in morning coat and gray-striped trousers stepped forward. "Charles Sheridan, Mr. Morley. I am a friend of Adam Gould, and I feel it is most urgent that we talk about his case."

Morley frowned down at his newspaper. "I'm actually rather busy with some research just now. Perhaps we could—"

"Then I shall try to take as little of your time as possible," his lordship said. He was a handsome man, with an imposing demeanor and an air of command. He placed his hat on Morley's desk and seated himself comfortably, waving at Morley's empty chair. "Please, sir. Do sit down. We shan't stand on ceremony here."

Feeling a little confused at being invited to sit in his own chair, Morley did as he was bid. He recognized Lord Sheridan, of course; he was one of the few Liberal Peers who had supported Amalgamated in the Taff-Vale matter. But he had not known that Adam Gould was connected with—

"Now, then," his lordship said in a genial tone. He took his pipe out of his pocket and prepared to light it. "Perhaps you can tell me what charge our young friend faces."

Morley tented his fingers. "A very serious charge, I'm afraid," he said dolefully. "Possession of explosives with intent to endanger life."

"Well, then." His lordship drew on his pipe. "And I suppose you have already given considerable thought to the nature of Mr. Gould's defense."

Morley hesitated. He had indeed given thought to the matter, and the end to which he had arrived was not at all satisfactory. It would not satisfy Masters and Dunderston; it would not satisfy Adam Gould; and it would most certainly not satisfy Amalgamated, since it would mean the loss of a valued employee. Nonetheless, he could think of nothing else to do.

"I'm afraid," he said, "that I must direct Mr. Delderfield—he has agreed to take the case—to enter a guilty plea on behalf of Mr. Gould." He was not happy with the choice of Delderfield, but he was the barrister with whom the firm usually did business, and anyway, it did not matter who handled the defense, for there was only one likely outcome. In a somewhat more diffident tone, he added, "Gould hasn't a chance, of course. Defense is a waste of time and money. I can't in good conscience advise Amalgamated of any course other than a guilty plea."

"A waste of time?" His lordship's eyebrows went up. "And what makes you say that?"

"The evidence." Morley cleared his throat. "The bomb that was found in his flat. I've seen it with my own eyes. Mr. Gould denies any knowledge of it, of course," he added hastily.

"Of course," his lordship said with an indignant air. He frowned. "The authorities were good enough to show this . . . bomb to you, then? What did it look like?"

"It was a ginger-beer bottle. Similar bombs were found in the rooms of the two accused with Mr. Gould." He shook his head sorrowfully, as if at the folly of such unlawful activity.

"Ginger-beer bottles?" his lordship asked in an interested tone. "What sort of detonators did they have?"

Mr. Morley frowned. "Detonators?"

"In order to have a bomb," Lord Sheridan said patiently, "one must have a means of detonating it. Of making it explode," he added, as Mr. Morley's frown deepened.

"I don't know about that," Mr. Morley replied irritably. "But all three of the bottles contained explosives, according to Inspector Ashcraft. Some sort of acid, I think he said."

His lordship's eyebrows went up. "What sort of acid? Picric acid? Nitric acid? Sulphuric acid?"

"Nitric acid, I believe," Mr. Morley said doubtfully, although the truth was that he had not paid a great deal of attention to the details.

"So it was bomb-making material, not bombs, that the men are said to have possessed."

"It is all the same under the law." Mr. Morley could feel himself growing defensive. This was not the sort of affair that Masters, Morley, and Dunderston usually found themselves engaged with. It was—

"It is not the same under the law," his lordship objected mildly. He paused, drew on his pipe, and expelled a stream of fragrant smoke. "The inspector seems to have been unusually forthcoming. Did you not find that a trifle . . . suspicious?"

Morley adjusted his cuffs. "I suppose I did," he admitted. In fact, it had occurred to him that Inspector Ashcraft might have shown him the evidence with the aim of inspiring a guilty plea. But Morley was not familiar with the conduct of criminal cases, and for all he knew, the entire procedure might have been quite normal. Of course, had it not been for the insistence of their largest client, the firm would not have taken the case at all and Amalgamated was certainly not going to like the idea of a guilty plea. He shifted uneasily. He was in rather a spot, and he knew it.

"And you saw no reason to question the official explanation, I suppose, or the charge?" His lordship's question was sharply put, and Morley winced.

"I did not," he replied, conscious that his answer left something to be desired. "I have never pretended, sir, to be a Sherlock Holmes. I am a solicitor, sir, and if there is some mystery here, it shall have to be left to the police to solve. Trial is scheduled for next week—August twenty-sixth, to be precise—which does not allow a great deal of time for preparation."

"August twenty-sixth?" his lordship asked with a frown. "Isn't that rather precipitous?"

Morley shrugged. "It seems that the docket was clear, and the authorities——"

"The authorities want to get it over with."

"I suppose." Morley sighed. "It is a difficult case, if I may be permitted to say so, and there is a great deal of public opinion against the accused men. Although," he added deferentially, "Mr. Gould is fortunate in having a gentleman like yourself in his corner." He gave a nervous laugh. "As it were. So to speak."

"I suppose," Lord Sheridan said, pursing his lips in a judicious manner, "that this is not quite the sort of case that Masters, Morley, and Dunderston usually take. It is not the sort of thing that Delderfield handles, either." He chuckled dryly. "Getting rather old, I should say."

"It is not our usual case," Morley replied, attempting to suggest by his tone just how far beneath the firm's usual notice this case lay. "My partners and I should not have accepted it at all if Amalgamated had not insisted quite so . . . strenuously." In fact, Masters and Dunderston had preferred to reject Amalgamated's request. It had only been his insistence that carried the day, and now he was faced with the unpleasant task of telling them that Delderfield would be entering a guilty plea.

"I say, old chap," his lordship said, interrupting Morley's thoughts. "It seems to me that you're in a bit of a bind here. It's not the sort of case you normally undertake, and not the sort of case you'd like to see associated with the firm's name, either——especially since you anticipate a conviction. And Delderfield isn't your man, either, from what I know of him. P'rhaps I might suggest another barrister with a bit more experience along . . . shall we say, criminal lines. A bit more drive, too. He would not be so quick to plead Gould guilty."

Morley eyed him speculatively, wondering if his lordship's suggestion might help him avoid what promised to be an uncomfortable situation with Amalgamated. "Who did you have in mind?" he asked finally.

"Chap named Edward Savidge. Good man, quite competent in his line. I thought perhaps . . ." His lordship let the pause lengthen.

"I suppose we might be able to work something out," Morley said, affecting reluctance. "But Amalgamated should have to agree."

"I will undertake to obtain their consent," his lordship said. He picked up his hat and stood. "We are agreed, then, that Masters, Morley, and Dunderston will request the services of Edward Savidge for Mr. Gould's defense?"

"With pleasure, sir," Morley replied with great alacrity, and took his lordship's hand. "With pleasure."

CHAPTER TWELVE

❖❖❖❖❖❖❖

*While women were recognized as superior gardeners,
there was a distinct prejudice against women farmers.
That is, women were encouraged to garden for enjoyment and to feed their families, but discouraged from
doing it as a source of income.*

Susan Blake,
"Women in Victorian Agriculture," 2002

Kate always found it easiest and most pleasant to do her
writing in the morning, beside the window in the
library of Bishop's Keep. It was her favorite room, the pan-
eled walls lined with old leather-bound books, generations
of her Ardleigh ancestors looking down from the wall, and
Charles's leather chair placed near the fireplace, her own
upholstered one opposite. But perhaps it was Charles's lingering presence in the room that made these surroundings
so pleasant, and the recollection of their enjoyable teatime
and evening conversations here. For Kate had discovered,
much to her delight, that marriage to Charles Sheridan
included a great many hours in lively conversation.

But the library was also a private retreat, for it contained
Kate's oak writing desk, placed in the small, green-curtained

alcove in front of the casement window. This forenoon, Kate was seated there at her Royal typewriter, typing the final page of Beryl Bardwell's latest fictional effort, a ghost story set at Glamis Castle, in Scotland. Several of Sir Walter Scott's novels were stacked at her elbow for inspiration, and she had, for reference, a number of photographs that she had taken when she and Charles visited the castle the year before.

Usually, Kate had no trouble keeping her attention focused on Beryl's current fiction, especially when it was as gripping as this ghost story. But she was distracted this morning by a group of students who were being instructed, just outside her window, in the fine art of pruning rose bushes. She was watching them and thinking with satisfaction that they were an attentive and diligent group, when she was interrupted by a knock at the library door.

"Come in," she called, and Mrs. Bryan entered. She was dressed in her matron's uniform of neat gray dress and white smock, and her brown hair was twisted up at the back of her head. She carried a sheaf of papers, the report that she made each Monday morning on the activities of the school. But she was not smiling.

"Good morning, your ladyship," she said gloomily.

"Good morning, Mrs. Bryan," Kate returned. She raised her eyebrows. "You don't look entirely happy. Is something wrong?"

"The calf's dead," Mrs. Bryan said shortly. "The veterinary came again early this morning, but couldn't do anything for him."

"I'm so sorry, Mrs. Bryan," Kate said. The matron always took such things to heart, as if the death of an animal were her own fault, or the fault of a malevolent Providence set on thwarting her best efforts to save it. "But I'm sure you did everything you could to save the poor creature. These things will happen."

"Aye," Mrs. Bryan acknowledged. "But it was a blow." She

put her papers on the desk. "Egg production's up, though, I'm glad t' say. And the apple harvest is done, all but the late trees. Murchison's taken it off to the fruit buyer and expects a good price." She was still not smiling, although the successful completion of the fruit harvest was always a happy event.

"I see," Kate said. "It sounds as if things are going well." She picked up the papers and thumbed through them, waiting to hear what else Mrs. Bryan had on her mind.

The matron folded her arms. "Mary Murchison's gone down with the measles. I sent her home yesterday morning, but some others may get it too, them as missed it when they were young. Better now than later, though."

Kate felt a stab of pain. Several years earlier, in the first few months of pregnancy, she had contracted the measles. She had lost the baby—a loss she still mourned—and the doctors had told her that there would be no others. Of course, there was Patrick, the boy, now nearly sixteen, whom she and Charles had taken as their own. She loved Patrick very much, but he could not quite fill the void.

"You're right, of course," she said. "Better measles now than later. But do send a basket of fruit and cheese to Mary and her family, please, and some extra eggs."

"Yes, mum." Mrs. Bryan stood stolidly, obviously not finished with her report.

"And what else?" Kate asked.

Mrs. Bryan gave her a dark look. "Conway's gone."

"Conway's . . . gone?" Kate asked blankly.

"The new girl. The one who came from London on Saturday."

"Yes, I know. Charlotte Conway." Kate frowned. "But I don't understand. How can she be . . . gone?"

"By shank's mares, I s'pose," Mrs. Bryan said shortly. "She must've left after prayers last night—after I told her that I was puttin' her to the pigs today." She tossed her head. "Anyways, she didn't appear at breakfast. I sent Portia to fetch her, and she come back with the news that Conway had made up her bed with a roll of blankets, so it seemed she was in it—but she wasn't. She's gone."

"Oh, dear," Kate said softly. "I expect she's gone back to London."

"Well, if you ask me, that one wasn't cut out to be a farmer," Mrs. Bryan said tartly. "Too independent. And too clever by half, but not clever enough to learn. Thought it was beneath her. Didn't fancy workin' with the pigs, I s'pose. Beggin' your ladyship's pardon."

"You don't need to beg my pardon," Kate said in a mild tone. "It wasn't my idea to bring her here, and it might not have been her idea to come. I don't suppose we should be surprised that she's gone." She paused, thinking that it might be a good idea to telegraph Nellie that her friend had decamped, and to send a telegram to Sibley House as well. Charles had had quite an interest in the young woman and in her Anarchist associations; he would not be pleased to learn that she was on the loose in London, where she was sure to be picked up by the police.

Or would she? Kate smiled a little, remembering the dashing figure the young woman had cut upon her arrival. At the thought of the disguise, she said, "I wonder—did Miss Conway leave her work costume behind?"

Alice nodded. " 'T was laid on her bed, so Portia said, and her brogans was on the floor."

Which meant, Kate thought, that if anyone should want to look for the elusive Miss Conway, they would be looking for a young man in a white linen suit. She frowned, wondering what to say in her telegram to Nellie, who might be watched by the police. If the telegram were intercepted—

She glanced up at the clock, which showed that it was nearly time for luncheon, then sat back in her chair for a moment, thinking. No, a telegram was not the answer, after all.

She would have to go to London.

CHAPTER THIRTEEN

[Pudd'nhead Wilson] made fine and accurate reproductions of a number of his [fingerprint] records, and then enlarged them on a scale of ten to one with his pantograph. He did these pantograph enlargements on sheets of white cardboard, and made each individual line of the bewildering maze of whorls or curves or loops . . . stand out bold and black by reinforcing it with ink. To the untrained eye the collection of delicate originals made by the human finger on the glass plates looked about alike, but when enlarged ten times . . . the dullest eye could detect at a glance, and at a distance of many feet, that no two of the patterns were alike.

Mark Twain,
The Tragedy of Puddn'head Wilson, 1893

Charles had a busy morning. Having left Mr. Morley, he went immediately to Holloway Prison in Parkhust Road, where he sat in a visiting cage and met briefly and sequentially with Adam Gould, Ivan Kopinski, and Pierre Mouffetard. Adam was glad to see him. He listened with gratitude to Charles's report of his conversation with Mr. Morley and accepted the suggestion that a barrister be found who would make the effort to put up a real defense.

He also insisted that he knew nothing of the bomb, if that's what it was, that had been found in his flat. He suspected, he said, that the police had put it there.

"For the past few weeks, Special Branch was dogging Ivan and Pierre—and Miss Conway, too," he said. "Yuri's bomb must have tipped the balance and they decided they had to arrest somebody." He eyed Charles anxiously. "I don't suppose you've any news of Miss Conway."

"As a matter of fact, I have," Charles said, and told him that the young lady was staying at Bishop's Keep.

"Thank God," Adam said fervently. "I was afraid she might be out on the streets. How did she come to you?"

"Her friend Nellie Lovelace brought her," Charles said, and smiled. "You can stop worrying, Adam. She is in good hands with Lady Sheridan. And I believe that you will be in good hands with Edward Savidge. I can't promise that he will get you off, of course. But I can promise that he will try."

"What about the others?" Adam asked. "Will he defend them, as well?"

"They have no barrister?"

Adam shook his head. "The comrades in Hampstead Road had agreed to obtain one, but decided against it. They've been abandoned, or so it seems to me."

"I'll talk with them," Charles said.

Charles's interviews with Kopinski and Mouffetard were much briefer. As he learned from Kopinski—a stocky man with high Slavic cheekbones and dirty brown hair that hung around his shoulders—the two had not yet arranged for their defense. If Adam's barrister would take on their case as well, Kopinski supposed he would be grateful. He seemed to accept his situation with a stoic detachment, answering Charles's questions briefly and dispassionately. He disavowed any knowledge of the Hyde Park bomber's plot, and his face clouded when he talked about Yuri Messenko, giving Charles the idea that he had genuinely cared for the boy. His chief worry seemed to be the Russian agent he was convinced was on his trail, and who (he said) had probably hidden the bomb in his room. He seemed convinced that the man would be waiting for him the minute the trial was over.

"I would prefer," he added, with a dry, humorless laugh, "to stay in jail. Here, at least, I am safe from being seized and sent back to Russia, where I will certainly be killed."

"The man who is trailing you," Charles said. "What does he look like?"

Kopinski gave a resigned shrug. "Tall and thin. Stooped a little. But he looks different each day. That is the way of these agents—they could fool their grandmothers with their disguises."

Pierre Mouffetard carried himself with an air of nonchalance that barely hid his suppressed anger. He seemed not at all surprised to hear that a total stranger was proposing to obtain his defense. He provided a careless answer or two in response to Charles's questions and denied all knowledge of explosives, explosive devices, and instructions for making bombs.

"I am a complete—how do you say?—dunce when it comes to things of a chemical nature," he said with a shrug and a thin-lipped, indifferent smile. "Although I suppose that will not matter," he added fatalistically. "We will no doubt be convicted. Your Scotland Yard, they are looking for Anarchists. They mean to make scapegoats of us."

"And the bomb-making instructions the police found in your pocket?" Charles asked.

Pierre turned his head. "A letter, merely. A friend writing from France to tell me about an explosive device made by a Spanish acquaintance."

Charles left the prison after a brief visit to the administrative office, where he discussed a certain matter of custodial procedure with one of the clerks. Feeling relieved to be out of Holloway's chill, damp gloom, he stopped in a noisy café across from St. Andrews in Thornhill Square, where he lunched on a shepherd's pie, washed down with a glass of ale. As it was still an hour to the time he and Savidge had set for their meeting, he decided to walk the two-mile distance to Gray's Inn, down Caledonian Road to King's Cross and into Bloomsbury. As he walked down Gray's Inn Road, he noticed how many more motorcars were taking to the roads these days, and what a havoc they were wreaking among the horse-drawn hansons and four-wheelers that already jammed London's streets.

As he passed Coram's Fields, a seven-acre expanse of grass and trees that softened the press of crowded buildings, he took out his watch. It was a fine August day, the early fog had lifted, and he still had time to spare, so he sat down on a wooden bench. The fields were part of the grounds of the Foundling's Hospital, established by Thomas Coran and endowed by George Frederick Handel, and they were full of nannies taking their young charges for an airing. The sight of children playing was pleasant, and he sat back to watch and think.

There was a great deal to sort out. Hearing Adam's vigorous denial and the less convincing but still persuasive stories of the other two accused men, he believed that the bomb-making material had been put in their rooms, but by whom, it was not yet clear. The Russian agent who was following Ivan? The police? Both of these were obvious possibilities, but there had been something in Mouffetard's denial that had made Charles doubt his complete candor. Perhaps that was the place to start a more intensive investigation. And he needed to inquire about Yuri. He took out his wallet and looked again at the address he had written down. Telson Street was off Hampstead Road, a mile to the west. He would go there after he had seen Savidge.

* * *

Edward Savidge kept chambers in the South Square of Gray's Inn, in a suite of second-floor rooms that included a large conference room and library lavishly appointed with maroon leather chairs, polished oaken tables, and Oriental carpets. The whole was a mute testimony to Savidge's success at the Bar—or at least, it gave the impression of success, which was equally likely to achieve the purpose.

One of Savidge's several clerks, dressed in a natty gray suit and cravat, glanced up from the telephone when Charles entered. He gave his name and was rewarded with a welcoming smile. "I believe Mr. Savidge is ready for you, Lord Sheridan," the clerk said crisply, and Charles was shown in. A second clerk followed with a silver tray on which were a pot of coffee and two cups. He poured the coffee and disappeared.

Edward Savidge was seated at an enormous desk, completely clear except for the paper on which he was making notes. Behind him was a window that looked out over the pleasant walks and green lawns of the inner court of Gray's Inn. He stood and extended a hand, smiling broadly.

"Sheridan, old fellow!" he said, in a deep, booming voice that could reach to the farthest seat in the courtroom. "Very good to see you."

"Indeed," Charles said, grasping the heavy hand. "What has it been? A year or better?"

Savidge was a large and powerful man, well over six feet and weighing some fifteen stone, well-featured, with an enormous head of curling black hair. His eyes were dark and deepset under heavy brows and a thick black moustache did not hide his mobile mouth or ironic half-smile; in court, he carried himself like an accomplished actor, playing with deliberate effect to the judge and jury.

Charles knew him to be a brilliant advocate and relentless cross-examiner.

They exchanged pleasantries—Charles asked after Mrs. Savidge, a well-known beauty who had disappointed half of the eligible bachelors of London when she married Savidge some five years before; and Savidge asked after Kate, whom he called "that splendid American treasure of yours." He passed Charles a cup of coffee and then opened a box of fine Cuban cigars, from which Charles chose one.

Proffering a light, Savidge said, "Well, now, Sheridan, suppose you tell me what this is all about. You haven't let your liberal views lead you into difficulties, have you?"

"Not yet," Charles said with a small smile, putting his cup on the table beside him. "At least, not directly." He pulled on his cigar, sat back in the massive leather chair, and went straight to the point. "The firm of Masters, Morley, and Dunderston has decided to ask you to represent a client of theirs named Adam Gould. I hope you will agree to defend the two men who are accused with him."

"The charge?" Savidge asked.

"Possessing explosives with intent to harm."

"Ah," Savidge said judiciously. "Those Anarchist fellows picked up at the *Clarion,* eh? The ones who worked with the young chap who blew himself up in Hyde Park?"

"Yes," Charles replied. He eyed his friend, wondering if he had promised something he could not deliver. Savidge was the right advocate, but would he take the case? "It's not going to be an easy charge to defend," he said. "But as I recall, you have always enjoyed a challenge."

Savidge had for some years worked in the offices of Mr. George Lewis, the lawyer who represented the affairs— of the purse and the heart—of half the aristocracy. But after a few years as a solicitor, Savidge had been admitted to the Bar and now specialized in representing people who had gotten themselves into serious difficulties, in one way or another. Since most of his clients were quite wealthy, his practice was a lucrative one, as was readily evident from his well-appointed office.

"Tell me about it," Savidge commanded, and Charles complied. He concluded his narrative with, "I very much doubt that a man of Adam Gould's stature with Amalgamated would put himself and his future at risk by possessing explosives." He paused. "Gould is a friend to Anarchists, there is no doubt about that, and he is an admirer and, I suspect, would-be lover of the *Clarion*'s editor, Miss Conway. But he denies any knowledge of the explosive material found in his rooms, and I believe him."

"These others—Kopinski and Mouffetard—they also deny possession?"

Charles nodded. "I cannot vouch for them, of course. One or the other of them may have been involved in the Hyde Park bombing. At this point, it is difficult to say, although I hope to have more information along those lines soon." He paused, half-tempted to tell Savidge of Ponsonby's visit and the Crown's interest in the affair. But he decided against it, since it had little to do with the task of defending the men, and Savidge might find it distracting.

Lounging in his chair, Savidge regarded the glowing tip of his cigar. "You think Special Branch may have wanted some extra insurance against their targets?" he asked dryly.

"Perhaps," Charles said. "All of the staff at the *Clarion* believe they were followed by the police for a period of some weeks before the Hyde Park incident, although Kopinski seems to think that a Russian agent is after him. I gather that he is considered to be an enemy of the Romanov regime, although I can't yet tell you why."

"An *agent provocateur*, eh?" Savidge said, raising his heavy eyebrows. "There seem to be a great many of those chaps wandering about the East End these days, all trying to dislodge refugees of one nationality or another, or otherwise cause trouble. I imagine that the Yard would like to be rid of the whole lot. Those foreign agents take up far too much of Special Branch's attention."

"Special Branch is in a difficult position just now," Charles said. "The City has been swarming with heads of state and visiting dignitaries—almost like a plague of locusts—since before the first scheduled date of the Coronation. Ensuring their safety no doubt required a monumental effort, and the explosion in Hyde Park must have rattled the Yard all the way up to the commissioner. But that does not permit them to—"

"To manufacture evidence, mistreat members of the Press, and arrest émigrés who have sought refuge in London, et cetera et cetera." With a bored expression, Savidge flicked the ash from his cigar. "I don't like to disappoint you, Sheridan, but there must be a more compelling reason why I should become involved with this affair. I am of course interested in the possibility of laying hands on a policeman who manufactures evidence, but such a thing is deucedly hard to prove, even when one knows it is true. And Anarchists are hardly my dish of tea."

"There is a compelling reason," Charles said. He pursed his lips. "The case may involve the use of fingerprints."

Savidge's eyebrows went up again. "You're saying—"

"I'm saying that if the police are telling the truth about those ginger-beer bottles, the defendants' fingerprints should be all over them. If, however, the only prints belong to the police, or to some unidentified party—"

"I see," Savidge said thoughtfully. "I must say, that changes things, doesn't it, old chap?"

Charles knew exactly what lay behind Savidge's sudden interest. It had to do with the fingerprints of a man named

Harry Jackson, whose trial for burglary was scheduled at Old
Bailey a fortnight hence. If the Crown's prosecution was successful, the case would certainly become a forensic landmark,
a vindication of a new system of criminal identification, and
a proud feather in the cap of Scotland Yard's new head of the
Criminal Investigation Department and Assistant Police
Commissioner of London, Edward Henry.

Henry had begun his work with fingerprints in the
1890s, when he was in charge of the Bengali police in British
India. An intelligent and cultivated man, he had a mathe-
matical bent and strong organizational abilities. Having
become acquainted with the fingerprint studies of Sir Francis
Galton, Henry developed a system that included not only
taking the fingerprints, but classifying, indexing, filing, and
retrieving them, and in 1906, implemented it in Bengal,
where it replaced the current anthropometrical identification
system called *bertillonage,* after the Frenchman who had
developed it twenty years before. Henry thereupon proposed
the new method to the Governor General of India. It was
quickly adopted, proving to be a faster and more reliable
method of identification than the slower, more complicated
bertillonage.

It was a long way from India to England, and revolutionary
ideas do not flow swiftly or smoothly through bureaucratic
channels. But Charles had brought Henry's program to the
attention of the Home Office, and in 1900, he was appointed
to a committee under Lord Belper, to look into what was being
done in British India. The committee recommended the aban-
donment of anthropometry—the measurement of the skull,
the length of arms, hands, and feet—and the creation of a new
system of criminal identification based on Henry's fingerprint
system. In March 1901, Edward Henry himself was appointed
to the post of Assistant Police Commissioner of London and
head of the Criminal Investigation Department.

Henry had not found it easy to convince the Yard that

fingerprints represented a more reliable means of identification than anthropometry, in which a great deal of time and effort had been invested and which some still held to be superior. Henry persevered, however, and soon the first Scotland Yard fingerprint department was in full operation. Within the year, nearly two thousand convicted persons were fingerprinted. Charles himself had directed the fingerprinting of prisoners at Dartmoor, and similar programs were conducted in prisons and jails across England.

Mark Twain had introduced the first fingerprint evidence into a fictional American courtroom in 1893, but the first real vindication of Henry's new method did not occur in England until the month before Edward's Coronation. On Derby Day at Epsom Downs, a team from the Yard fingerprinted fifty-four men who were arrested for various offenses, from public drunkenness to picking pockets. When the prints were checked against the new criminal records, over half of the men were found to have a history of arrests and convictions, thereby enabling the magistrate of the Petty Sessional Court to impose sentences twice as long as would otherwise have been awarded.

An even more important test was waiting in the wings, however, and both Charles and Savidge knew it. A house in Denmark Hill had been burgled and seven billiard balls stolen. The investigating officer noticed a dirty fingerprint on a newly-painted windowsill. The print was photographed, compared to those in the Yard's files, and found to match the left thumbprint of a convicted burglar named Harry Jackson. Jackson had been apprehended, charged with the burglary, and was awaiting trial on September 2 at the Old Bailey. If the jury found him guilty, the case would make news all over the country—all over the world, perhaps.

"The first thing to do, of course," Savidge said thoughtfully, "is to obtain the fingerprints of the men you wish me to defend. Then—"

"The men were fingerprinted when they were jailed, and their prints are in the custody of the administrator of Holloway Prison," Charles said. "I confirmed that this morning."

"Ah," Savidge said. "Then we must obtain a competent expert who can examine the bottles held by the police and determine whether there is any fingerprint evidence to be found."

"I think," Charles said, "that I can serve in that capacity."

"Of course," Savidge said approvingly. "I had forgotten your expertise in that business." He paused. "I don't suppose that the police have studied the bottles for fingerprint evidence."

"If they have," Charles said, "no mention was made of it to Morley, Adam Gould's solicitor. I rather doubt it, actually. Fingerprinting is not an investigative technique that Special Branch would have readily adopted."

"Well, then," Savidge said, "if you find the men's fingerprints on those bombs, the best course would be a guilty plea. If not—"

"If not," Charles said, "I suggest that we move for a continuance until after the Jackson trial is concluded. The chance for prevailing upon fingerprint evidence might be greater."

Savidge looked at Charles. "You've been following the case, I take it. Is it likely that Jackson will be convicted?"

"On the evidence," Charles said, "the Crown has a strong case. I should think he'll be found guilty." He paused. "I am afraid, however, that a jury will be less inclined to release three Anarchists on fingerprint testimony."

"Agreed. But juries don't like to see the police tamper with evidence. If that has happened here, and if it can be proved—" Savidge smiled maliciously around his cigar. "You present an interesting case, Sheridan. I don't see how I can refuse." He paused, narrowing his eyes. "But there is the little matter of the fee. Amalgamated is taking care of Gould, but what of the others?"

"I'm good for it." Charles rose. "You will be hearing from Morley. If we are agreed, then I must be off. I have one or two other matters to look into today, but I'll see what can be done about getting a look at that evidence."

CHAPTER FOURTEEN

The initial excitement and appeal of this novel (A Girl Among the Anarchists) reside in its entertaining account of an innocent, middle-class Victorian girl provocatively committing herself to an apparently fanatical, even dangerous group of subversives. The heroine's unchaperoned idealism enables an emancipatory narrative that provides a marvelously sustained vision of the New Woman. Indeed, the novel's central, implicit assumption that a woman can, in fact, be politically effective challenges powerful nineteenth-century injunctions confining the middle-class woman to the privacy of the home.

Jennifer Shaddock,
Introduction to the Bison Book Edition, 1992, of
Isabel Meredith, *A Girl Among the Anarchists*, 1902

"Good afternoon, Richards," Kate said, as the startled Sibley House butler opened the heavy door that led into the entrance foyer. She turned to the cabbie who had brought up her bags and put several coins into his hand. "Thank you," she said, and went inside with the same shiver of melancholy and shadowy foreboding that she usually felt when she entered the grim old house, even on the brightest of days.

"Good afternoon, m'lady," Richards said stiffly, taking

her coat. He paused and added, in a tone of subtle rebuke, "I'm afraid his lordship failed to mention that you would be coming up to town."

Kate took the bull by the horns. "I know it will be an enormous bother to Mrs. Hall to prepare dinner for the both of us," she said. "Present my apologies, please." Of course, dinner for two was no more bother than dinner for one, but the cook liked to pretend that it was, and Kate always played along with the game.

Richards sniffed. "Perhaps his lordship did not inform you. Canon Rawnsley is joining him for dinner here tonight."

Kate ignored the sniff and the delicate jibe. "How delightful," she said. She glanced in the mirror, patted her hair, and added, "I'll have tea, please. In the library."

"Of course, madam," Richards said, with another sniff, and went off to give Mrs. Hall the unwelcome news that her ladyship had come, unannounced, and that there would be three to dinner.

Kate did not enjoy London, and she did not like the house in Grosvenor Square. It was a mausoleum, chilly and uninviting, with large, overdecorated rooms, echoing passageways, and scarcely a scrap of garden. Worse, its staff had been selected and trained by Charles's deceased mother, the Dowager Baroness Somersworth, and it was impossible to change their habits or attitudes. And to compound Kate's discomfort, it was here that she and Charles had been staying when she lost the baby, which had only added to her aversion to the place. She came as infrequently as she could.

But today's trip to London had been unavoidable. When Kate learned that Charlotte had left Bishop's Keep, she had first thought of sending telegrams to Charles and Nellie, to let them know that the young woman had probably returned to London. But she had discarded that plan and decided to come up to town herself, on the train.

Now, going into the library (one of the few agreeable

rooms in the house), Kate poked up the fire in the grate, then sat down at the writing desk and jotted a quick note to Nellie. She put it into an envelope, addressed and sealed it, and when Richards came in with the tea tray—a silver pot, a pair of cups, and a plate of tea cakes—she gave it to him.

"Please ask Tommy to take this around to the Royal Strand and deliver it personally to Miss Lovelace," she said. "If she is not there, he is to wait until she arrives. I have asked her to return an answer."

"Yes, madam," Richards replied. The sniff was titanic. Richards did not approve of theatrical people.

Kate glanced at the clock on the ornate mantlepiece. It was nearly five-thirty. "Did his lordship say what time he planned to return this evening?"

"No, madam," Richards said, "only that he expected Canon Rawnsley at eight." He bowed slightly and left the room with her note, holding it at arm's length.

Kate had just poured herself a cup of tea and settled down in front of the fire with *The Times* and one of Mrs. Hall's excellent apricot tea cakes, when Charles came into the room.

"Kate!" he exclaimed, coming over to drop a kiss on her hair. "I had no idea you were coming up to town today. Why—"

"Because Miss Conway—Charlotte—has run away," Kate said. She put down the newspaper. "Sometime during the night, according to Mrs. Bryan. She didn't appear at breakfast this morning."

"Blast," Charles said softly. "She's come back to town, I suppose."

"To help her comrades, perhaps," Kate said. "I was going to send Nellie a telegram and thought better of it." She poured Charles's tea and handed him the cup. "It's important that we find Miss Conway, Charles. If the police get to her first . . ." She didn't finish her sentence.

"You've let Nellie know that the girl has disappeared?"

Kate nodded. "I've sent Tommy round with a note, and asked for a reply. I'm hoping that she knows Mrs. Conway's address. I should like to go there and see her." She regarded Charles thoughtfully. "Were you able to see Adam Gould and the others?"

"And Morley, as well." Charles sat in the wing chair on the other side of the fireplace, putting his cup on the mahogany table beside the chair. "He agreed to handing the case to Savidge." He gave her a wry smile. "And Savidge is delighted to take it, with the hope of becoming the first to win an acquittal through fingerprint evidence." He picked up his cup, settling back. "I also called round to the Yard to have a look at those so-called bombs that Special Branch claims to have found in the men's rooms."

"Oh?" Kate asked with interest. From the tone of Charles's voice, she judged that he had not been impressed by what he saw. "And what did you discover?"

"That the 'bombs' are stoneware bottles which contain traces of a substance purported to be nitric acid. He paused. "Savidge and I will go back tomorrow, for a closer examination. Meanwhile, I have sent a note to Edward Henry at the Yard, asking him to see to it personally that the evidence is protected from handling. At the moment, it's sitting on the shelf."

"You'd think that the police would do a better job of preserving evidence," Kate said warmly, "especially when so much depends upon it."

Charles's laugh was ironic. "The proper handling of evidence is not something the ordinary policeman thinks much about, I'm afraid—not, at least, at the moment. If Harry Jackson's left thumb convicts him of burglary next month, things will change. In the meantime—" He shrugged. "We'll see what can be discovered tomorrow, when Savidge and I study the fingerprints on those bottles."

"You've certainly covered a great deal of territory since this morning," Kate said.

"I did something else, too," Charles replied. "I took a cab to Telson Street, where Yuri Messenko lived. Number 17, upper floor rear." He grimaced. "A sad little room, with only a bed and a chair. The boy kept his clothes in a pasteboard box under the bed. The landlady had already let the room and was anxious for someone to take the box away, so I've brought it with me. I'll go through his things later tonight." He glanced at the clock on the mantle. "Did Richards tell you that Hardwicke Rawnsley is coming to dinner tonight?"

Kate nodded. "I take it, then, that you've decided to talk with him about Somersworth and the National Trust."

"Mother would hate me," Charles said wearily, "but the estate is much too large to be managed as it should be, especially in the current economic situation. It's beautiful, though, with all those open meadows and wooded lanes, and it's convenient to the people of Great Yarmouth, who like to picnic at the weekends. The Trust might find some parts of it of interest—as a gift, of course."

"And the house itself?" Kate had liked the great house's aspect, overlooking the Norfolk Broads, the shallow lakes and vast fens and marshes of the meandering River Yare. But the place was enormous, its upkeep a burden, and neither she nor Charles had any wish to spend a great deal of time there. And if they did, the keeper's lodge would be far more suited to the two of them. There were the tenants, of course, but Charles had closed down most of the house and kept only a skeleton staff.

"I don't know that the Trust will be any better able than I to deal with that medieval monstrosity," Charles said with a rueful chuckle. "But we can ask Rawnsley what he thinks." He glanced at her. "You will join us at dinner, won't you, my dear?"

"Of course," Kate said, "with pleasure." She paused. "I wonder if Hardwicke has heard from Beatrix. She told me that he brought her Peter Rabbit book to the attention of Frederick Warne, and they are to publish it—quite soon, I think." Canon Rawnsley was a friend of Beatrix Potter, with whom Kate usually kept in close touch. But Beatrix and her parents had gone to the Lake District for the summer, and Kate had not heard the latest news. She sighed. "I do hope the book does well, for Bea's sake—and because it is so delightfully original. But it is difficult to predict these things. How many children will be interested in reading the adventures of a rabbit?"

Dinner featured Mrs. Hall's usual splendid rack of lamb, preceded by a julienne soup, salmon with caper sauce, and chicken fillets with mushrooms, and followed by a greengage tart, iced pudding, and a plate of fruit and cheese. The elegant array might easily have fed a dozen guests, so three for dinner (rather than two) had clearly presented no difficulties to the able Mrs. Hall.

Canon Rawnsley was an affable, handsome man with regular features and a graying beard and moustache. He looked remarkably like King Edward, if substantially slimmer and more energetic, and was full of lively conversation. To Kate's delight, he told her that Beatrix's little book was to be published the first week of October in an edition of about eight thousand copies. And he was indeed interested in acquiring part of the Somersworth estate for the Trust, which he had helped to create in 1895 and which was already beginning to enjoy significant approval as a means of preserving some of England's most scenic and unique areas, which might otherwise have been broken up and sold to the affluent as housing sites. Already, as the Canon eloquently pointed out, far too much of the shoreline of the lakes in the Lake District had been purchased by wealthy people and closed off from public access. And the fens and marshes and ancient peat diggings of the Norfolk Broads were home to a vast variety of birds and wildlife. A gift of unspoiled property would be most welcome.

They had just finished dessert—one of Mrs. Hall's splendid trifles—when a maid came in and whispered to Richards. In turn, Richards came to the table and whispered to Kate, who put down her napkin and rose.

"I must leave you gentlemen now," she said. "I've received a message to which I must respond—from our theatrical friend, Charles." She smiled at their guest. "Canon Rawnsley, so lovely to see you again, as always. I hope you will visit us at Bishop's Keep."

The men stood. "Oh, I shall," Canon Rawnsley replied, with a genial enthusiasm. "You may depend upon it, Lady Sheridan."

In the hall, the maid dropped a curtsy and pressed a note into Kate's hand. "Tommy brought it," she said. " 'E's waitin' in the kitchen, if yer ladyship wants t' answer."

Kate carried the envelope into the library, turned up the lamp, and sat down at the desk to open it. Nellie's brief note was written in a sprawling hand and smelled strongly of lilac perfume. She wrote with distress that she could not imagine why Lottie would leave the safe haven of Bishop's Keep. She had not yet heard from her and promised to let Kate know the minute she got any word; she did, however, know that Mrs. Conway and Lottie lived at Number 12, Brantwood Street. In a post-script, she added that she would be very glad to meet Kate for supper the next evening. Kate rang the bell and, when the maid appeared, told her to tell Tommy that there was no reply, and that he might go on to bed.

Kate went upstairs, put on her dressing gown, and settled into a chair by the bedroom fire with a typescript she had been given to read by an editor at Duckworth, who wanted her opinion of it. The short novel was called *A Girl Among the Anarchists* and was written in the first person by Isabel Meredith—a pseudonym, the editor had told her, for Helen and Olivia Rossetti, the young nieces of the artist Dante Gabriel Rossetti and his sister Christina, the poet. The book was a fictionalized account of their actual experiences as editors of the Anarchist newspaper, *The Torch*, some seven or eight years before, which the girls, then teenagers, had published. Kate found the novel deeply engrossing, for it explored an aspect of women's activities—the political aspect—that was almost never written about. She admired Isabel's rebellion against the traditional female codes of behavior that confined women to the domestic world and promoted their submission to others. There was a great deal about the book that reminded her of Charlotte Conway, who seemed to be exactly the same sort of young rebel as Isabel. If the liberation of women was what Anarchism was about, she thought with a smile, there certainly ought to be more of it! She should like very much to meet the young Rossetti sisters and discover if they were as unconventional as their heroine.

An hour or two later, when Canon Rawnsley had left and Charles had come up to bed, Kate asked if anything had been decided about the fate of Somersworth.

"Only in part," Charles replied, taking off his shoes. "The land is not a problem for them, of course. They are especially glad to have the marshes, and that can be arranged straightaway. But the house and gardens are another matter, unfortunately. Rawnsley says that the Trust is in the midst of raising funds to purchase a property in the Lake District. Once that is done, he hopes to put a bill through Parliament to give the Trust a stronger management authority. Rawnsley thinks we should postpone any discussion of the house until then." He unfastened his collar stays and turned to Kate. "What's that you're reading?"

"A novel that Mr. Perry, at Duckworth, has asked me to look at. I've just finished it and am going to recommend it for publication." She gave Charles a mischievous look. "It is entirely subversive, and explains a great deal about our friend Miss Conway and her Anarchist connections."

"Speaking of Anarchist connections," Charles said, sitting down to take off his shoes, "I went through Messenko's box after Rawnsley left."

Kate put down the typescript. "Did you find anything of interest?"

"I'm not sure," Charles said. "I've found something I want to investigate, but it may not turn out to be of much consequence." He dropped his shoe and put out his hand, his eyes glinting with desire. "I have something else in mind that *is* of consequence, though."

Kate put her hand in his and let him pull her into his familiar embrace, and for the next little while there were no sounds except for their own soft sighing and the easy fall of embers in the grate.

CHAPTER FIFTEEN

Whereas the French and Russians had come to regard any form of intelligence as a commercial commodity that must be bought, Britain had once again reverted to her traditional amateur status, never officially spending too much on what was looked upon as something foreign to British instincts, but contradictorily and quixotically allowing full play to any amateur who lusted after information for information's sake.

Richard Deacon,
A History of the British Secret Service

The item that Charles had found in Yuri Messenko's box was a torn and much-folded scrap of yellow paper, tucked into the pocket of a ragged shirt. On it was printed an address in Church Lane and a man's name: Vladimir Rasnokov. Charles pondered the matter as he breakfasted with Kate, then put on his hat, picked up his umbrella, and went out into Grosvenor Square. He walked the few blocks up to Oxford and, when the drizzle turned into rain, hailed a cab.

The Intelligence Branch of the War Office was housed in a residence in Queen Anne's Gate, the shuttered building hidden behind a high wall and an unkempt garden—a fitting metaphor, Charles thought as he approached the building, for espionage work.

For nearly the whole of the previous century, polite society had regarded spying as indecently devious and completely out of character with the British gentleman's code of sportsmanship and fair play, something to be ignored, even actively thwarted where necessary. But the situation began to change in the 1850s, when the debacles of the Crimean War spotlighted the inadequacies of Britain's intelligence in the Middle East and it became clear that most of the military blunders of that ruinous war had resulted from an almost complete lack of information about the enemy. Disastrous as the Crimea had been, however, it was essentially a sideshow, for what really threatened John Bull was the predatory shadow of the Russian bear falling inexorably across Central Asia, Afghanistan, and the northwest region of India. To counter this threat to the Empire's "Jewel in the Crown," the War Office began to increase its effort to develop a more effective espionage program, including mapping explorations in remote Central Asia, contacts with foreign agents across the Continent, and networks of native spies, some of whom Rudyard Kipling had recently immortalized in *Kim* as players in the "Great Game."

But Whitehall still did not give military intelligence the support it deserved, and the Intellligence Branch continued to labor under the long-standing constraints of insufficient funding and staffing. One section, made up of only two officers and a clerk, had the task of covering the entire Russian empire and almost the whole of Asia, including China, India, and Japan. Despite the scale of its responsibilities, however, it was probably the most efficient and effective of all the sections, for Britain's history of confrontations with Russia in Central Asia had resulted in an increasing pool of knowledge about the Romanov regime and its military and political espionage activites.

It was this section that Charles intended to visit, for he had known one of its officers, Captain Steven Wells, during his military service in India during the eighties. Wells was a veteran of the Second Afghan War and had gone on to play the Great Game in the northern border region of India until he was summoned to England in '99 to join Intelligence. But Wells's interests were no longer exclusively focused on the far reaches of the Empire. Since joining Intelligence, he had begun to pay special attention to the activities of certain Russians in the East End, and Charles knew it.

"Sheridan!" Wells exclaimed, unfolding his long legs and standing behind his desk, on which were stacked a number of files with red caution notices on the covers. "Hullo, old chap. What brings you here?" His monocle dropped out of his eye and swung across his uniformed chest on its black ribbon. The third son of an earl, he had the unmistakable look of an aristocrat.

"Thought I should come and see what you've been digging up these days," Charles said with a grin. He looked around at the piles of papers on the shelves and floor, and the large maps laid flat on a table and rolled and stored in bins. The draperies were drawn and the room was lit, glaringly, with electric light. "Quite a change for you, Wells. Gone the days of mountain peaks and open plains, eh?"

"Afraid so, blast it," Wells said, grimacing. He raised his voice and bellowed, "Dinsmore! Tea, chop-chop!"

"Still the same voice," Charles remarked. "I've always thought that roar could move mountains. And it did, a time or two."

"All I move these days are mountains of paper," Wells said in a disgruntled tone. "Chaps here complain when I roar, as well. Don't know what the Service is coming to." He lowered himself into his chair as an orderly brought in a tray, placed it on the desk, and poured two cups of tea. When the young man had left the room, Wells eyed Charles.

"What brings you here?" he asked again, stirring in sugar. "I doubt it's idle curiosity."

Charles put his hand into his pocket and pulled out his pipe. "I wonder," he said quietly, "whether Intelligence has any special interest in the incident in Hyde Park involving Yuri Messenko."

Without answering, Wells sipped his tea, then put his cup down and took out a pack of cigarettes. He cupped his hands around the flame of his match as if there were a high wind, then leaned back. His face had become less open, his voice more guarded. "We were interested initially. But the Yard expressed a wish to pursue the case, and we turned to more pressing matters. We do not have staff to waste on wild-goose chases." He smiled dryly, a smile that did not reach his eyes. "There are far too many wild geese. We concluded that the Yard should do the chasing."

Charles set down his cup and rested his elbows on the arms of his chair, tenting his fingers. He was aware that there was an almost total lack of communication between the Yard and War Office Intelligence, for which Intelligence was mostly responsible. During the past decade, Intelligence agents had heavily infiltrated the Russian East End, in some cases paying Russian Anarchists to serve as British agents. Intelligence was naturally not anxious to share information about its activities with anyone, not even the police. As a result, the Yard could scarcely tell the difference between an ordinary Russian émigré, an Anarchist, a Czarist *agent provocateur,* and an British agent. And then, of course, there were the double agents, those in the pay of more than one government, France and Russia, for instance, or Russia and Britain. The situation could hardly be more confusing.

Charles put his pipe back in his pocket, unlit. "And how about Vladimir Rasnokov?" he asked. "Is he one of yours?"

Wells blew out a stream of smoke. "Now, Charles," he said in a tone of mild rebuke. "You know the rules as well as

I do. I can't discuss personnel matters, even with you, old boy."

Charles coughed apologetically. "Perhaps you wouldn't mind putting in a call to Fritz Ponsonby, then. He offered to make introductions, but I didn't like to trouble him." He gestured at the telephone on Wells's desk. "He may be reached directly. His number is—"

"Damn," Wells said under his breath. "It's like that, is it?"

"Yes," Charles said regretfully, "it is like that, I'm afraid. I did not choose the assignment, as you might guess, but having been handed it, I am doing what I can. Special Branch has not made my job easier, I fear. An inspector named Ashcraft has complicated things quite unnecessarily. Bombs, it would seem, have been found everywhere, and three men are being held on explosives charges."

Wells raised both eyebrows. "Ah, Ashcraft has been sticking his finger in it, has he? A rather obsessive fellow." He made an elaborate gesture. "I suppose, then, that I had best answer your questions. What was it you wanted to know?"

"Rasnokov," Charles repeated. "Is he one of yours?"

Wells sighed. "It's a long story," he said. "Will you have another cup?" Without waiting for an answer, he raised his voice in a bellow. "Dinsmore, more tea!"

A half-hour later, Charles was back in a cab and on his way to Sibley House.

CHAPTER SIXTEEN

Nature never deceives us; it is we who deceive ourselves.

Jean-Jacques Rousseau,
Emile

Around eleven that same morning, Kate asked Richards to obtain a hansom for her. It was raining, and she wore a dark serge dress that would not show the splashes, a matching jacket and close-fitting hat, and carried with her an umbrella. She had at least two errands in mind, perhaps others, and planned to be out for most of the day.

Brantwood Street, as Kate soon discovered, lay to the south of Regent's Park, in a decaying residential neighborhood, once quite fine, that had been invaded by pawnshops, markets, and the roving wooden push-barrows of fishmongers, butchers, and booksellers. She left the cab at the corner, put up her umbrella against the rain, and walked down the block until she found Number 12, a narrow, three-story house wedged between two identical houses. Its red-brick facade was blackened with a century of soot and grime, and there was a square of weed-grown garden behind a rusty metal fence that served mostly to catch the rubbish that blew across the sidewalk. The sky was dark and a fine mist

dampened the pavements, adding to the pervasive gloom
that seemed to have settled over the street.

Kate lowered her black umbrella, climbed the stone
steps, and confronted a door inset with a large oval of
beveled glass, curtained on the inside to screen the view
from the street. To the right of the door was a painted
wooden sign that announced that CLEAN ROOMS TO LET
were AVAILABLE WITHIN, GENTLEMEN ONLY. Kate knocked
on the door then, hearing no answer, knocked again, with a
greater authority. She was rewarded with the sight of the
tattered curtain slightly pulled to one side, and a large
brown eye peering out.

A bolt was drawn, a chain rattled, and the door opened
an inch. "Can't yer read the sign?" a woman demanded in a
high, cracked voice. "Gentlemen only."

"I've not come about a room," Kate said quickly, insert-
ing her umbrella into the opening to keep the woman from
shutting the door.

"Then wot're ye 'ere fer?" the woman asked.

Kate straightened her shoulders and said, "I've come to
see Mrs. Conway, on a matter of some importance."

"What matter?" the woman shrilled.

"It's about her daughter, Charlotte." Kate took a breath.
"She was staying with me for a few days, but she's disappeared. It's important that I find her."

"Move yer 'brella," the woman said, "an' I'll go an' see."

Kate removed her umbrella and the door was shut. She
stood quietly, while behind her on the street, a delivery boy
on an old-fashioned penny-farthing bicycle pedaled past,
whistling shrilly, while a small dog yapped ferociously at
the wheels. On the other side of the street, a pot-hatted man
in heavy gray tweeds loitered in the doorway of a small
tobacconist shop. Kate turned to find him watching her, but
when she returned his stare, he tipped his hat onto the back
of his head, thrust his hands into his pockets, and sauntered

nonchalantly down the street. Kate couldn't help smiling, for the man looked so exactly like a Scotland Yard plain-clothes detective that he was almost a parody of himself.

The door opened again, and the old woman, now revealed to be short and leather-faced, her hunched shoulders draped with an old black lace shawl, beckoned Kate in. Taking the umbrella and poking it into an umbrella stand, she closed the door and locked it. Then, still saying nothing, she padded silently down a dusky hall, lit only by a flickering gas jet. The air was stale and stuffy, as if the place had not been aired in a decade, and a distinct odor of boiled cabbage seemed to arise like a malodorous fog out of some nether region.

Kate followed through the shadows, her curiosity mounting by the minute. She remembered that Mrs. Conway had published the *Clarion* until five years ago, when she fell ill and her daughter had taken it over—out of a sense of duty, Miss Conway had said. Kate frowned at that, thinking that Anarchists were not supposed to act out of a sense of duty, since they owed no obligation to anyone but themselves—at least, that's how they were presented in *A Girl Among the Anarchists*. There was a puzzle here.

At the back of the house, Kate's guide took a narrow, uncarpeted stair to the second floor. The odor of cabbage was overtaken by the odor of cigars, and Kate guessed that this floor contained the CLEAN ROOMS let to GENTLEMEN ONLY. They traversed the long hallway again, this time to the front of the house, until they came to a closed door. The old woman knocked three times, slowly, as if the knocks were a signal. At a brusque, "Come in," she pushed the door open, shoved Kate into the room, and closed the door behind her.

Inside the room, Kate stood stock-still. The rest of the house had been dark and gloomy, the rooms she had glimpsed through open doors uncarpeted and sparsely furnished, with only the most utilitarian furniture. It had been chilly, too, so cold that despite her jacket, Kate had shivered. But this room, this *boudoir,* was suffocatingly hot and lavishly opulent, the walls hung with embroidered draperies, the floor covered with carpets, the canopied bed draped in billowy white gauze, the windows covered with blinds of the thinnest bamboo and draped with some exotic fabric in an Oriental pattern of pinks and golds. The air was heavy with the musky scent of sandalwood incense, and a canary spilled a melody from a gilded cage beside the window, which was banked with palms and exotic plants. Arranged in front of a fire in an ornate fireplace were two chairs upholstered in the same patterned fabric of pinks and golds, and a mauve-velvet divan. And seated on the divan, looking like some Oriental empress, was the largest woman Kate had ever seen.

"Well, don't just stand and stare," the woman snapped. Her voice was low and hoarse. "Come here and let me see you. What's your name?"

Kate went to stand before the divan. "Kate Sheridan," she said, trying to conceal her astonished consternation. The woman was grotesquely, preposterously obese, like the Japanese sumo wrestlers whose photographs Kate had seen. Her pale flesh ballooned shapelessly, her arms were like stuffed pillows, and her puffed cheeks squeezed her eyes into narrow slits. But in those eyes there was a sharp, shrewd look, more than a little mad in its focused intensity, that made Kate shiver. The woman's scanty reddish-brown hair hung in limp, old-fashioned curls around her ears, and she was draped from her chin to her ankles in a sort of Turkish caftan. She wore Moorish sandals on the swollen feet that were propped on a velvet footstool in front of her. She was smoking a cigarette in a long ivory holder, and daintily picking chocolates out of a box with fat fingers, each one of which bore a flashing ring. Kate knew that the woman must be Charlotte Conway's mother, although whatever physical resemblance there might have been between the two was buried in a mountain of flesh.

"Well?" the woman demanded. "What is it?"

Recovering herself, Kate began, "I've come to ask you whether—"

"I know, I know," Mrs. Conway growled impatiently. She gestured peremptorily to one of the chairs, her several chins waggling with the effort. "Sit down. It hurts my neck to look up at you. Where is she?"

"I have no idea," Kate said, sitting on the edge of one of the upholstered armchairs. She felt very much like Alice in the presence of the Red Queen, and the room was so hot and stuffy that she could scarcely get her breath. "I hoped that you might suggest—"

"Why should I?" Mrs. Conway asked, drawing on her cigarette and blowing the smoke out of both nostrils like a maniacal dragon. "The girl never tells me a thing. Just comes and goes, back and forth to that silly newspaper." Her voice became whiny. "The ungrateful child never pays her mother a minute's attention, doesn't even do me the courtesy of putting in her head to say good morning, or drop in for tea, or—"

"I understand," Kate interrupted hastily, feeling that she was in danger of being swamped by the woman's massive self-pity, "that you published the *Clarion* before Charlotte took it over."

"Yes, and I did a far better job of it, too." Mrs. Conway picked up the newspaper that lay on the divan beside her and waved it in the air with an expression of great disdain. "Just look at this, will you? Such namby-pamby, mealy-mouth porridge as I've never seen. When I published this paper, we printed strong stuff, I tell you. We were the voice of the revolution!" As she spoke, her own voice grew louder and more ringing, as if she were addressing a multitude. "We stirred men's souls, I say. We struck their hearts as if they were gongs. We got them out on the streets with revolution on their lips and dynamite in their hands!"

Kate cleared her throat, feeling uneasy. There was something almost electric in the woman's voice, something commanding. Perhaps Mrs. Conway had indeed stirred men to revolution, although if she had, things did not seem to have been greatly changed by it. "But you are no longer the editor?" she asked.

"Sadly, my health does not permit it." With a melancholy sigh, Mrs. Conway put out a fat hand and plucked a chocolate out of the box, popping it, whole, into her mouth. "There are my lodgers to look after, of course—quite a demanding lot they are, too, always needing this and that and the other thing. I can hardly keep up with them. And I am otherwise engaged just now, on an important literary project." She gestured toward a table pushed against the wall under a gas lamp, piled with stacks of papers. "I am writing the story of my life, which is quite extraordinary, really. I have known a great many fascinating revolutionists—Lenin, Kropotkin, Bakunin, Emma Goldman. My book will be of enormous significance."

"I am sure," Kate said in a tactful tone, although she felt that Mrs. Conway suffered from too great a sense of her own importance. "But I am deeply concerned about Charlotte." She took out a calling card with the Sibley House address on it and handed it to Mrs. Conway. "I would very much appreciate it if you could send a note around to this address if you hear from her. Do you have any idea where she might be just now?"

"None at all," Mrs. Conway said, carelessly dropping the card on the table. "I told the police as much, too, when they came around, pestering me about her. The girl is an adult, and not my concern. A true Anarchist—I consider myself such, of course—refuses to acknowledge any responsibility to family or comrades. A true Anarchist lives entirely for himself." She paused, delicately searching with her fat fingers among the chocolates. Finding what she wanted, she dropped it into her mouth. "Although there is one person I might have mentioned to that detective," she said, around the mouthful of chocolate, "if I had thought of her at the time."

Kate stared at the woman, astonished by her glaring inconsistencies. But she only said, in the calmest voice she could manage, "And who is that?"

"One of those Rossetti girls. I've no idea which one, and anyway, I can never remember their names. They published that wretched little paper, the *Torch*, they called it." She made a disgusted noise. "Such silly creatures. I could never see why Emma Goldman found them so interesting. Insipid, in my view. Not a breath of revolutionary spirit in them. It's not surprising that they have abandoned the movement."

The Rossetti girls, Kate thought with rising excitement. They were the authors of the manuscript she was reading, *A Girl Among the Anarchists*. If they were friends of Miss Conway, she just might have tried to make contact with them. "Do you happen to know," she said, concealing her interest, "where I might find these young women?"

"Oh, one never knows things like that," Mrs. Conway said carelessly. She fitted another cigarette into the holder and lit it. "Anyway, the *Torch* was put out some years ago, while the *Clarion* lives on—such as it is, of course. I will say this for Lottie: The child is persistent. Not a scrap of talent or gift, mind you, and no revolutionary boldness. But doggedly persistent, nonetheless. There's something in that, I suppose."

Kate could hardly decide whether she should feel pity for a woman who had so entirely deceived herself, or anger at a mother who had so little respect for her daughter. She rose. "Thank you for your time," she said through clenched teeth, and turned toward the door.

"But I'm not finished yet!" Mrs. Conway exclaimed, her

voice becoming shrill. "I haven't told you about my publishing plans. I have been in contact with the editors at Duckworth, who have assured me that my memoir—"

"I think you *are* finished," Kate said distinctly. "Quite finished." And with that, she went out the door, closing it behind her as if to make sure that nothing from the room would escape into the outer air.

CHAPTER SEVENTEEN

Now and again it happens that the (Russian) colony misses one or more of its prominent members, perhaps a man and a woman, or two women by themselves. They have disappeared suddenly, leaving no trace behind them. No one makes any enquiries, but these fugitives are not forgotten. Presently a newcomer brings tidings. Elzelina Kralchenskaya is in a Russian prison; Vera Ivanovna is in Siberia; Dmitry Konstantinovitch is dead.

Count E. Armfelt,
"Russia in East London," in *Edwardian London*,
Volume 1, 1902

When Charles arrived back at Sibley House, he spoke immediately to Richards, who just managed not to sniff at his lordship's unconventional request. He murmured a polite, "As your lordship wishes." Such things had never been asked for in the days of his lordship's brother and father, but those days were gone forever. So, after some consultation with the male members of the household staff, Richards at last produced a pair of brown trousers with traces of mud on the knees, a dark overcoat, a soft cap, and a knitted scarf, and handed them over with a look of restrained distaste. Charles dressed and combed his hair straight back from his forehead without a parting, in the Slavic manner, turned up the collar of the overcoat, rammed the cap down on his head, and made for Euston Station.

London had for centuries been a vigorously cosmopolitan city, but during the sixty years of Victoria's reign it had attracted increasingly large numbers of exiles seeking safe harbor from the totalitarian governments of the Continent. Among these London refugee colonies, the largest and fastest-growing were the Russian and Polish, populated by men and women and children who had fled the tyrannies of the Romanov regime. Pursuing as far as they could the crafts and trades they had learned in their native land, living on black rye bread, potatoes, turnips, and onions, they crowded together in tenements along the by-streets and back alleys of East India Dock Road, Commercial Road, and Whitechapel. But while their living conditions might be difficult and luxuries few, these people—many of whom were Jewish—possessed what was to them the greatest luxury of all: the freedom to work and talk and think as they pleased, without being harassed by the authorities.

The difficulty, however, as Charles well knew, was that not all of these people had come to settle down as peaceful, hardworking citizens of their adopted country. Most European governments had already passed severe repressive measures against Anarchists and others who aimed to disturb the social order, but tolerant Britain had taken no such action, and London's East End had become the safest refuge that the revolutionaries could find, as well as a sheltering haven for the Czarist counterrevolutionaries who aimed to discredit and unmask them. It made for an extraordinarily volatile and confusing situation.

Charles left the Underground at Liverpool Street Station and walked for some distance, past Spitalfields Market and the Ghetto Bank of Whitechapel. The bank was one of the busiest in London, for every Russian refugee managed, through sheer industry and determined economy, to send money to family and friends in Russia and Poland—a million rubles a year, it was said. As Charles walked along Commercial Road, he was struck by the vibrant energy and liveliness of the place: the remarkable variety of Yiddish and Hebrew and Russian dialects spoken on the street; the astonishing range of crafts—cabinetmakers, tailors, bootmakers, seamstresses, milliners, upholsterers, bookbinders, watchmakers, icon painters—represented in the shops along the way; and the fascinating spectrum of restaurants and cafés, serving such exotic delicacies as smoked goose, reindeer tongue, and pickled lampreys, along with the more usual caviar, smoked salmon, strong cheeses, black bread, and vodka. Someone else walking these streets—a Jack London, for instance, looking for the downtrodden and desperate—might see stooped shoulders, weary faces, and forlorn spirits. But Charles caught scraps of song drifting from open doorways and heard the pleasure in the greetings of old *babushkas* in aprons and shawls as they passed on the streets. These people might not have much, but their spirits were indomitable, their hopes invincible, and their dreams of freedom unconquerable.

The address on the torn scrap of paper in Yuri Messenko's shirt pocket proved to be that of a library located on the second floor of a small building in Church Lane, a block off Commercial Road. The first floor was occupied by a cigar shop that displayed tins of Russian tobacco and wooden boxes of Russian cigars in its square-paned, fly-specked window, along with hand-colored photographs of chubby-cheeked girls in native Russian costume and stacks of Russian newspapers and books. The entrance to the library was in a little alcove. There was a sign on the door; underneath a Russian inscription, in English, Charles read, "Free Russian Library. Open daily from 11 A.M. to 10 P.M." The door was plastered with dozens of other notes and notices, also in Russian.

The door gave onto a dark, steep stair. Climbing to the top, Charles opened another door and stepped into a crowded, stuffy room, lit by several hanging gas lamps. The walls were lined with shelves of paperbound books and journals, the air was filled with the distinct perfume of tobacco and sweat and unwashed bodies, and almost every chair at the two long wooden tables was occupied. Some of the men were reading books and newspapers, others were writing, and still others—those who could not write, Charles guessed—appeared to be dictating letters to scribes. The men were of all ages, from beardless students to elders with long gray beards neatly tucked inside their coats, and the muted murmurs of their conversations were sibilant and foreign.

The librarian, or so Charles thought he must be, was seated behind a small wooden table. "Might I help you find something?" he asked, in heavily accented English. He was a very young man with dark, anxious eyes, clean-shaven, and neatly dressed in coat and cravat.

Charles took off his cap and held it respectfully against his chest. "I'm looking for Yuri Messenko," he said. "Is he here, please?"

The librarian's eyes widened. "You haven't heard? Or read in the newspapers?"

"Heard what?" Charles asked innocently. "I've been traveling on the Continent for the last several weeks."

"Messenko was . . . killed." With an uneasy glance, the librarian took in Charles's worn overcoat and baggy trousers, seeming to be reassured by the unassuming costume. "It was an accident, or so I was told."

"I'm very sorry to hear that," Charles said. "It must have been a terrible shock to his friends. He came here frequently, I understand."

"Occasionally," the librarian replied, his tone becoming guarded, his eyes more anxious. "Why do you ask?"

"I need to contact someone, and I was told that Yuri Messenko could tell me how." Charles gave a discouraged sigh. "Now I suppose I'll have to find a different way."

The librarian moved some papers on his desk. "Who did you want to contact?"

"His name is Vladimir Rasnokov," Charles replied. He bent forward, adding eagerly, and in a louder voice, "Do you know Rasnokov? I should very much like to reach him."

The librarian's mouth tightened at the corners. "Rasnokov is not here."

Charles let out his breath. "Do you know where I might find him?"

A bearded man wearing a dirty gray jerkin and a black knitted cap rose from his seat at the nearby table, returned his newspaper to a rack beside the window, and brushed past Charles on his way out the door. Another man, on the opposite side of the table, looked up and caught the librarian's eye with a warning glance and an almost imperceptible shake of the head.

The librarian turned back to Charles. "Regrettably," he said, in a formal tone, "I cannot help you. Rasnokov is not here. I do not know where he is to be found."

Charles bowed his head. "Thank you," he said humbly. He put on his cap and went out the door and down the steps. He was not surprised to see the man in the black knitted cap and gray jerkin waiting on the pavement in front of the cigar shop.

The man approached Charles. "Ye're lookin' fer Rasnokov, eh?" His voice was low and gravelly and his breath smelled of onions and garlic.

"I am," Charles said. He straightened his shoulders.

"Wot's yer business with 'im?"

Charles, no longer humble, gave the man a long, hard look. "That is between Rasnokov and myself. Do you know where to find him?"

"Wot's in it fer me?"

Charles felt in his pocket and took out a shilling. "I have nothing else."

The man took the coin with a hard look. "Ye might try the Little Moscow Café, in the cellar next t' the Post Office. 'E has 'is lunch there most ev'ry day."

"Thank you," Charles said, and turned away. A few paces on, he paused and stood before the window of a tailor's shop, his hands in the pockets of his coat. In the reflecting glass, he caught a glimpse of the man in the gray jerkin. He had mounted a rusty bicycle and was pedaling swiftly down Church Lane—on his way, no doubt, to the Little Moscow Café.

CHAPTER EIGHTEEN

❖═◉═❖

Unfortunately, the Rossettis (Helen and Olivia) could not sustain such a narrative of female emancipation. In the conclusion to their novel, Isabel retracts her belief in anarchism and instead forcefully reinscribes the traditional feminine myth of hearth and home.

Jennifer Shaddock, Introduction to the
Bison Book Edition, 1992, of Isabel Meredith,
A Girl Among the Anarchists, 1902

Olivia Rossetti was now married and with her husband in Italy, but after a call to Mr. Perry at Duckworth, Kate had no difficulty finding Helen Rossetti, who was living with her father in a small, comfortable house with an ivy-draped porch in a street in Chelsea. Kate had no difficulty introducing herself, either, since she had finished reading the manuscript of *A Girl Among the Anarchists* the night before and could tell Miss Rossetti that she had heartily enjoyed the adventures of Isabel Meredith and was recommending the novel to her editors for publication.

"I admired it very much," she added, with genuine enthusiasm, when they were seated in the parlor. "It showed me an aspect of an Englishwoman's life that I would otherwise have found difficult to imagine."

Helen Rossetti, a small, plump young woman with dark eyes and dark hair pulled snugly back into a bun, sat back in her chair and gave a little cry of delight. "My dear Lady Sheridan!" she exclaimed. "How kind of you to come and tell me!" She flashed a mischievous smile that showed the dimples in her round cheeks. "And you are *truly* Beryl Bardwell?"

"Really, truly," Kate said with a smile, glancing around the parlor. Miss Rossetti's young years may have been unconventional, but her radical past could not be seen in this thoroughly conventional Victorian parlor: the tables skirted to conceal their legs, the windows heavily draped and closed to keep out the air, the souvenir knickknacks displayed on the fireplace mantle. But one wall displayed a large print of Dante Gabriel Rossetti's "Proserpine," and on a table lay a leather-bound copy of Christina Rossetti's book, *New Poems,* which had been published two years after the famous poet's death. Helen's uncle was perhaps the best known of the Pre-Raphaelite artists, while her aunt's poetry was widely admired.

"You've read some of my work?" Kate added, seeing two of her novels on the bookshelf.

"With great pleasure," Miss Rossetti replied. "In fact, Olivia—my sister—and I have often read your books aloud. Our Isabel is a little like your Fanny, don't you think, in *The Adventure at Devil's Bridge*? Fanny is such an unconventional woman! Olivia and I loved the scene in which she drives the motorcar in pursuit of the balloon."

"Your Isabel has an even greater sense of independence than my Fanny, I should say," Kate replied, wanting to lead the conversation away from herself. "I understand that her adventures as the publisher of the *Tocsin* were inspired by your own experience with the *Torch*."

"You know about that, then," Miss Rossetti said, half-ruefully. "I suppose the editor at Duckworth must have told you. Yes, Olivia and I printed the newspaper on an old hand-press, and it was distributed by the local Anarchist group. We were very young—I was only thirteen when we brought out the first issue, and Oliva was sixteen—but we were quite in earnest about it."

"If you don't mind my saying so," Kate ventured, "it seems an odd occupation for two young girls."

"It was indeed," Miss Rossetti agreed cheerfully. "But it may be that Anarchism—as we understood it, at least— chiefly attracts the rebellious young, or those who never mature. Olive and I both came to believe that Anarchism, as a philosophy, does not allow for the ties of love and family, or permit the Anarchist to accept responsibility for anyone but himself. That is why Isabel gives it up, in the end. She is disillusioned with Anarchism's self-centeredness." She smiled reminiscently. "In some ways, I'm sorry the *Torch* is gone. It was a remarkable education for a young woman, to be accepted in such militant circles. And I had more freedoms then than I do now that I am older—freedom to go about the city alone, freedom to say and write exactly as I thought. I doubt that many girls are granted such opportunities."

Kate was sure of that. The English girls she knew were kept at home, where the reading of newspapers and the discussion of political topics was thought to be unladylike. "You say that the newspaper is gone," she said. "You discontinued publication?"

Miss Rossetti nodded. "My sister married in '96 and went to Florence. I was not well, and Father took me abroad soon after. The *Torch* survived our departure by only a year or so." She gave Kate a slanting glance. "That kind of existence is chaotic, actually. There was always some turmoil or another—we did not much exaggerate Isabel's experience. Life is much more peaceable now. Father and I live here very quietly. I am helping him write the life of my Aunt Christina."

Kate smiled. "I know of another young woman like your Isabel, who edits an Anarchist newspaper. She also speaks of chaos—although she clearly values the independence her work affords her."

"You must be speaking of Charlotte Conway," Miss Rossetti replied. Her face darkened. "I understand that the *Clarion* was raided by Scotland Yard last week, and is now closed down. The men were arrested and jailed—something to do with that appalling Hyde Park business—but Lottie got away."

"Oh," Kate said, leaning forward eagerly, "you've talked to her, then?" Perhaps her search was over.

"No," Miss Rossetti said, and Kate felt immediately disappointed. "I read about it in *The Times*. I haven't seen Lottie for some time, I'm afraid." Her expression was regretful. "We write very often, however. Mrs. Conway—Lottie lives with her mother—is not well. She does not permit her daughter to have visitors."

"I've met Mrs. Conway," Kate said carefully. "She edited the *Clarion* before her daughter took it on, I understand."

Helen gave a short, hard laugh. "Yes, she edited it. But speak of anarchy! Mrs. Conway was completely disorganized, and the newspaper was always on the brink of total disaster. It didn't come out at all half the time, and when it finally did appear, it might be one page, merely, or two." She pulled her brows together. "And it was always full of the wildest rantings and ravings. Some people said that the editor must be mad, and I do think so."

"I see," Kate said thoughtfully. Yes, it had seemed to her that Mrs. Conway might be mad, and she was sorry, for her daughter's sake.

"Lottie was very reluctant to take over her mother's job," Miss Rossetti went on, "but it was a good thing for the *Clarion* that she did. She takes her work seriously, and others have taken her seriously—unlike Mrs. Conway, I must say, who was always the butt of jokes. No one could take her with any seriousness."

Kate looked at her. "Miss Conway did not want to become the editor of the newspaper?" The girl had said that she did it out of a sense of duty, but she had not said that she did not want to do it.

"Oh, my goodness, no," Miss Rossetti replied. "Oh, she supported the Cause, of course. But her heart was set on entering Girton College at Cambridge and becoming a teacher, and she had even won a scholarship. When her mother suffered what was thought to be a nervous collapse, however, Lottie felt there was nothing for it but to continue the work. The *Clarion* brought in almost no money, but even so, it was Lottie's and Mrs. Conway's only source of support. Now, under Lottie's management, the paper has begun to yield a little money. And the rooms Lottie lets in that big old house bring in some additional money." Her voice took on a darker edge. "Enough to keep Mrs. Conway in chocolates and incense, anyway."

"I see," Kate said quietly. So it was the daughter's industry that supported the mother's household in Brantwood Street. The young woman had taken on quite a large responsibility.

Miss Rossetti's mouth hardened. "You may think I am being unkind, but really, Mrs. Conway has made things so very difficult. And in spite of all, I do believe that Lottie loves her mother. She is not doing her duty, but is rather doing what her heart tells her to do." Her voice became softer, her smile sentimental. "I understand this, I suppose, because I choose to live with my father, who needs me to see to his welfare. Father's writing is important, and I am his secretary, as well as keeping his house."

"But what of your writing?" Kate asked in some wonderment. "Are you planning another book?"

"No," Miss Rossetti said, pulling herself up straighter. "It gets in the way of helping my father, and his writing is so much more important than mine. I imagine that Lottie has something of that feeling about the *Clarion,* which was her mother's work."

"Oh, dear," Kate said ambiguously. "I had no idea."

Miss Rossetti seemed to construe her remark to refer to Miss Conway. "Lottie is one of the bravest young women I know. She is not in the least bit conventional. She has the true Anarchist spirit; she believes in the freedom of the individual. She argues that marriage is a bourgeois tool to restrict a woman's freedom, and she believes in free love." She smiled slightly. "Yet she insists on taking care of her mother."

Feeling that the implicit contradictions defied every logic, Kate went back to the question she had come to ask. "Have you heard from Miss Conway since the paper was raided?"

"Not a word," Miss Rossetti said with a troubled look, "and I'm very anxious about her. It is not like her to be out of touch. I can only think that she is afraid that the police might be following her. I'm sure that she is reluctant to involve her friends, for fear the police might attempt to implicate them in the Hyde Park explosion."

Kate took a calling card out of her bag and handed it to Miss Rossetti. "I will be going back to the country this week," she said, rising. "The address is that of our town house, where my husband is staying. If you should hear from Miss Conway, I would very much appreciate it if you could send a note. If I am not there, it will be forwarded." She paused. "I would like to help Miss Conway, if she will allow it. I am sure there is something I can do."

"I doubt that she will accept help," Miss Rossetti said, getting to her feet. "She is so fiercely independent. But I shall certainly send word if I hear from her." She smiled. "And thank you for your recommendation to Duckworth. I'll write immediately and let Olivia know. She'll be delighted. And my father will be pleased, too." She added, diffidently, "The money from the book is of some importance to us, as you might guess."

As Kate put up her umbrella and walked to the corner to look for a cab, she wondered at the multiple ironies of what she had learned, not just about Charlotte Conway and her relationship to her mother, but about the woman she had just left. In her teens, Helen Rossetti had been the rebellious and free-spirited editor of an Anarchist newspaper; now in her twenties, she appeared to be a conventional and rather bourgeois young woman who worked as her father's secretary. Perhaps, somehow or another, it seemed to Miss Rossetti that while a young woman might be free to explore the possibilities of a self-governing life, an adult woman must give in to the definitions imposed upon her by her family and by society. Perhaps she could live free and unfettered only in her imagination, or in her recollection of her younger, more adventuresome years.

Kate squared her shoulders and quickened her step. She, too, felt the allure of the comfortable domestic life, but she knew that she could never give in to it. She loved Charles, but she could never use him as a safe haven, for that would be false to the passion she felt for him. And she would never use her writing as a means of retreat, either. She would live in the world, explore every corner of it as freely as she could, and do her best to help other women free themselves from the constraints of their family's and society's expectations. There had to be some midway point between the self-centeredness of Mrs. Conway and the self-abnegation of Helen Rossetti.

CHAPTER NINETEEN

Sed quis custodiet ipsos custodes?
(Who guards the guardians?)

Juvenal

*There has always been a question of oversight. Who
polices the police? Who spies on the spies?*

Albert J. Williams,
"A Brief History of British Anarchism," 2002

It was well past the lunch hour when Charles found the
Little Moscow Café. It was entered from a rear alley off
Whitechapel Road, next to the Post Office. Six narrow
cement steps led down to a basement, a large, windowless
room filled with diners seated at oilcloth-covered tables and
in wooden booths around the walls. Painted pillars supported a low wooden ceiling, and gas jets illuminated the
crowded room with a dusky glow. The walls and pillars were
plastered with Russian posters, playbills, and newspaper
clippings. In one corner, a balalaika player entertained with
traditional Russian music. A menu board at the entrance
announced in both Russian and English that diners today
would be enjoying borscht, *pirozhki* (meat pie), *golubtsi*

(stuffed steamed cabbage rolls), and *yablochny rulet* (apples, walnuts, and raisins wrapped in pastry).

A waiter bustled up. "Table for one, sir?"

"I am meeting Rasnokov," Charles replied. "Is he here?"

"His usual corner," the waiter said with a careless gesture. "You will have lunch?"

"Yes," Charles said. "And I'll have beer, please. Kars, if you have it."

Rasnokov had finished his lunch and was smoking a Turkish cigarette over a cup of coffee. He looked up inquiringly as Charles approached. He was a tall man of indeterminate age, thin, with slightly stooped shoulders, and clean-shaven. He wore a rusty black suit and round steel-framed eyeglasses that gave him a studious look.

"My name is Sheridan," Charles said. "I recently met a gentleman who suggested I look you up and ask if you had received a message from Smersk."

Rasnokov tapped his cigarette into the ashtray with a long, delicate finger. His hands might have been the hands of a surgeon. "Sit down," he said, in unaccented, expressionless English.

The waiter appeared at the booth with a bottle of beer. "Your lunch will be ready in a few moments," he said to Charles. Rasnokov pushed his cup forward. The waiter put down the beer, produced a pot of coffee, and poured.

The balalaika player swung into a soft rendition of "Moscow Nights," obviously a familiar favorite, since several of the diners began to sing the Russian words. Rasnokov stubbed out his cigarette. "What do you want?" he asked indifferently, under the music. "I don't know you."

"We have a mutual friend," Charles replied. He raised his beer bottle as if in salute. "In Queen Anne's Gate."

"Ah." Rasnokov's face became regretful, as if Charles had said that a friend had died, or that Rasnokov should have to do something he didn't want to do. "You have a proposition for me, then?"

"A question," Charles said, and got right to it. "What do you know of the Hyde Park affair?"

There was a slight hesitation, and when Rasnokov spoke, there was a defensive edge in his voice. "I've already given that report."

"You said, I understand, that two were involved in the business."

"Yes, two. The boy and a Russian named Kopinski. Both of them worked at the *Clarion*. Kopinski instigated the bombing and provided the materials." Rasnokov frowned, as if he were offended. "It's all in my report, if you'd taken the trouble to read it."

"Only the two? What about Gould and Mouffetard?"

Rasnokov blinked behind his glasses, but was delayed in answering while the waiter set down in front of Charles a bowl of borscht and a plate with a fragrant meat pie and two thick cabbage rolls.

Charles picked up his soup spoon. "You were saying?"

"I know nothing of Gould," Rasnokov replied sulkily. "Mouffetard was not involved, to my knowledge, although he appeared to be on friendly terms with the boy."

"Then how did it happen that a bomb and bomb-making instructions were found in Mouffetard's possession? The Yard has arrested him, you know. And Gould as well. Both are charged with making bombs, along with Kopinski. Why did you not include their names in your report?"

Rasnokov shrugged. He still wore no expression, and his spectacled eyes were guarded, the eyes of a physician who is withholding bad news from a patient. "Perhaps my information was not as complete as I thought. Or perhaps the Yard has its own reasons for implicating the others." His dry chuckle held no humor. "That inspector, that Ashcraft. He is a wily one. He does not always play straight."

Charles thought it ironic that a secret agent would accuse a Yard detective of underhanded dealings, although in this case, Rasnokov was almost certainly right. It was more curious, however, that the man seemed acquainted with Ashcraft, and familiar with his ways. Charles wondered if Wells was aware of this, and what it might suggest about Rasnokov's way of doing business.

"But Kopinski is the one who managed Messenko?" Charles persisted. "The *only* one?" He fixed Rasnokov with his gaze. "You're sure of that?"

"Kopinski is the one," Rasnokov repeated positively, as if offering a prescription for a medicine that would somehow fix things up. "The whole affair was his idea, start to finish. He is a most dangerous man, though he may not seem so." He reached into his pocket, took out several small coins, and laid them beside his unfinished coffee. "Is that all?"

"For the moment," Charles replied, digging into his meat pie. The savory fragrance of hot beef and pastry rose up temptingly. "They make a fine *pirozhki* here, don't you think?"

For answer, Rasnokov slid out of the booth. "If that's all, I'll take my leave." Standing, he bent over and said in a low voice, "Tell our friend in Queen Anne's Gate that I will be unavailable for a fortnight. Business is taking me out of the country."

Charles, watching him go, felt disturbed. Either Wells had not told him all he knew about Rasnokov, or there was more to the man than Wells knew. And it was the latter, Charles felt, that was more likely.

CHAPTER TWENTY

❖

*Not many years ago ladies' clubs were comparatively
unknown; now-a-days, almost every up-to-date London
woman belongs to one, butterfly of fashion and working
bee alike. . . . But what do the members do at their
clubs? This is what we are about to investigate.*

Sheila E. Braine,
"London's Clubs for Women," in *Edwardian London*, 1902

It is said that the fluffers—the people who clean the tunnels and Underground stations in London—were often frightened by the spectral figure of a woman in flowing white robes who appeared on the tracks at night at the site of the Aldwych Underground Station. The ghost was believed to be that of an actress who died before she could take her final curtain call, for the Aldwych Station (now closed except for use as a film and television set and for trendy opening-night parties) was built on the site of the old Royal Strand Theater. This venerable institution was erected in 1832, condemned and rebuilt in 1886, and finally razed in 1905, three years after Nellie Lovelace starred in the record-breaking musical comedy, *The Chinese Honeymoon*. The fact that it ran for 1,075 performances did not, unfortunately, preserve the theater from demolition.

But Aldwych Station was yet to be built, the Royal Strand had not yet been violated by the wreckers, and on this particular rainy August afternoon, as Kate's cab drew to a stop in Aldwych, Nellie had already finished rehearsal and was waiting outside, under the shelter of her umbrella. She didn't have to be back to the theater for the night's performance until seven-thirty, so Kate would be able to enjoy her company for several hours, at least.

"Hello, Nellie," Kate called, opening the door of the cab and motioning to her friend.

Nellie lowered her umbrella and dashed through the splashing rain. "Thank you for coming to get me," she said, settling herself beside Kate. "It's so difficult to find a cab on a rainy afternoon." Her smile came and went. "Has there been any word from Lottie Conway?"

Kate patted Nellie's gloved hand. "No, I'm sorry to say. I'll tell you all about my search over our supper, though. For the moment, just catch your breath."

In her note to Nellie, Kate had invited the actress to meet her for an early supper at the Pioneer Club, which was located in the West End, in a three-story house in Grafton Street, just off New Bond. Kate could as easily have invited Nellie to Sibley House, but she could not be sure whether Charles would be home or what time he might want dinner, and she knew that Richards would find it impossible not to sniff each time he served Nellie. The club was pleasant, the meals very nice, and their waiter would not sniff.

The last decade had seen a remarkable growth in women's social clubs, and by the turn of the century a woman might belong to one or even more, depending on her social class, her means, and her interests. A titled lady would join the magnificent Empress Club in Dover Street, where an orchestra played nightly in the ornate dining room, the *salon* was available for chatting and writing letters, the drawing room was reserved for concerts and dances, and luxurious guest rooms might be had for overnight stays. An employed woman might join the St. Mary's Working Girls' Club in the East End, at Stepney; the Honor Club in Fitzroy Square, which boasted a circulating library, a gymnasium, and a lady doctor who was available on Monday nights; or the Jewish Working Girls' Club in Soho, which offered lace-making and cooking lessons and classes in Hebrew. Professional women had several options: the University Club, which catered to the academic and intellectual woman; the Writers' Club, to the woman journalist; and the Rehearsal Club in Leicester Square, to the theatrical woman, providing rooms, board, and laundry service. There was even a Ladies Automobile Club, which was headquartered in the Claridge Hotel.

Given Charles's peerage and social position, Kate could have chosen to be a member of the Empress, or of the Green Park or Alexandra, for that matter. Instead, she had joined the Pioneer Club, whose members were committed to women's issues, social reform, and political affairs, and were far less interested in parties and balls. When she was in town, she often visited the club's library, which subscribed to all the leading periodicals, and attended the Thursday evening debates. This evening, Kate felt that the Pioneer was exactly the right place to have a quiet conversation with Nellie, who would be much more at her ease here than in the stuffy, stately dining room at Sibley House.

For her part, Nellie was simply glad to sit down to a nice supper in a pleasant room with a friendly face smiling over the bowl of white roses in the center of the table. It had been a long day, for she had spent the morning dropping in on several friends who, she thought, might have heard something from Lottie. But they had not, and she had gone on to the theater discouraged and more than a little angry at Lottie for spurning the refuge she had taken so much trouble to secure for her.

Unfortunately, the afternoon rehearsal had not gone well, either; whether it was because Nellie was upset or simply inattentive, she had missed even more cues and bungled even more lines than she had during the matinee and evening performances on Sunday, and the director had taken her aside for a firm talk afterward. Nellie knew that the man had no animosity toward her; it was simply his job to remind her that there was a particularly promising understudy who would be delighted to take her place if she found she could no longer play the role she was being paid—and paid very handsomely—to perform. She could feel the ax hanging over her head by the slenderest of threads, and it frightened her more than she could say. Another missed cue, another bungled line, and she was out, as quick and easy as a snap of the fingers. One night, a successful musical comedy star; the next, an out-of-work actress.

With this ominous black cloud looming on her professional horizon, Nellie said little as she ate her supper—a very good mock turtle soup, curried lobster, roast lamb, and vegetables. She didn't have to say much, for Kate had plenty to tell her about her visits to Mrs. Conway and to Helen Rossetti. Nellie wasn't surprised that Kate was making such an effort to find Lottie, for she knew her to be sympathetic, especially when it came to women who were in some sort of difficulty. She was a little surprised, though, to hear that Lord Sheridan had also involved himself in the case, to the extent of obtaining a lawyer to represent Adam Gould and the two men arrested with him, and that he had reason to hope that they might be acquitted of the bomb-making charge.

"That would be wonderful!" Nellie exclaimed. "Now, if we could only find Lottie." She fell silent. Her feelings about Lottie, now, were definitely mixed. On the one hand, they were still friends, and she wanted to help; on the other—

Across the table, Kate was looking at her with concern. "You don't seem yourself tonight, Nellie," she said quietly. "Is there something wrong? Apart from Lottie's disappearance, I mean."

"No, nothing," Nellie said. She looked down at her plate, then up again, meeting Kate's eyes. "Actually, there is," she blurted out, and to her surprise, she found herself confessing the whole story. The Saturday night she and Jack London had spent together. The dinner at the Carleton and the excursion afterward to Earl's Court. And then the brutal lovemaking and waking on Sunday morning to his terse note, which had made her feel used and tawdry.

Kate stared at her, eyes wide. "You don't mean to say that the man *forced* you!" she exclaimed in horror.

"Yes," Nellie said, in a low voice, "although it might be my fault." She bit her lip. "That's what makes me feel so awful, Kate! To think that I brought it on myself."

"Brought it on yourself?" Kate asked, frowning.

"I drank too much champagne," Nellie said guiltily, "and when we arrived at my house and he asked to come in, I let him. I did not intend—" She closed her eyes and swallowed painfully. "I didn't mean for anything to happen, honestly, Kate. I thought perhaps we'd have a kiss or two and a romantic cuddle, and I confess I was looking forward to it. But then he—" She shook her head. "I tried to say no, but maybe . . . maybe I didn't say it hard enough. Maybe I should have—"

"That's nonsense," Kate said decidedly. "A kiss is not meant to be an invitation to—" She broke off. "If you made it clear that you wanted nothing more than a kiss or two, Nellie, the man was honor-bound to respect your wishes, whatever his own might have been."

"I wanted . . . I wanted . . . Oh, Kate, I can't be sure what I wanted!" Nellie exclaimed. "But surely it wasn't *that*. And then to wake up and find that note the next morning—" She bit her lip, the tears welling up in her eyes. Nellie had enough experience of the world to know that many women suffered far worse at the hands of men than the loss of their virtue. She had often slept in close quarters with adults and was not naive about what went on in a woman's bed when a man got into it. But she had read too many romantic novels and cherished too many romantic dreams, and she felt humiliated at the recollection of the cruel reality. And complicating her feelings (although she didn't want to share this with Kate) was the thought that Jack London was far more interested in Lottie than in her. *Mate woman,* he had called her, as if they shared some sort of mystical romantic connection, even though he'd no more than laid eyes on her when she came down that ladder.

"What a dreadful experience," Kate said, reaching across the table and taking Nellie's hand. "I am so sorry, so *very* sorry, that it happened. And that I did not warn you. Perhaps if you had known—"

"Known what?" Nellie asked, startled.

"That Jack London is married," Kate said, her eyes full of compassion. "His wife Bess is in California, with their little girl. I learned this at the party his publisher gave for him when he arrived in London."

For a long moment, Nellie stared at her, the words echoing over and over again in her mind. *Married married married married.* Then, in spite of the fact that they were seated in a public dining room, she burst into tears, hot and harsh with bitter self-recrimination.

CHAPTER TWENTY-ONE

"When did you love me?" she whispered.
"From the first, the very first, the first moment I laid eyes
on you. I was mad for love of you then, and in all the
time that has passed since then I have only grown the
madder. I am maddest, now, dear. I am almost a lunatic,
my head is so turned with joy."

Jack London,
Martin Edin

It was nearly eleven on Tuesday morning when Jack London donned his slum costume and locked the door of his room on his typewriter and pile of manuscript pages. His room might be small and lack important amenties, but he could lock the door and know it would not be disturbed. Putting the key in his pocket, he went down the private stair and into the alley at the back of the garden, his Brownie in a canvas bag slung over his shoulder. The camera had cost him all of two dollars in New York City, and the film was cheap enough, twenty cents for six exposures. He planned to take pictures for his book—a great many pictures, since he was an amateur and couldn't know how the photographs would turn out until he had them developed back in America.

But it wasn't a very nice day for taking photographs. The gray fog that drifted through the streets was streaked with yellow, and the air had a sharply sulphurous smell. *The smell of the pit,* London thought dourly, glancing with loathing at the grim, smoke-smudged brick buildings that rose on either side of the street. He had spent the morning reading about that poisonous smoke in a report he had obtained from the Socialists. The curator at Kew Gardens, a fellow named Sir William Thistelton-Dyer, had studied smoke deposits on vegetation, concluding that each week no fewer than six tons of soot and tarry hydrocarbons fell out of the sky onto every quarter of every square mile in and around the City.

Six tons! It was no wonder, London thought, trudging in the direction of the East India docks, that the children were growing up into rotten adults, without virility or stamina or any energy for work. The Abyss was a huge, smoldering, sulphurous fire that smoked the juices of joy and spirit out of everyone, as if they were sides of beef hung to cure in some country smokehouse. Why, not a soul had any look of pleasure or delight or spontaneity or—

His eye was caught by a slender figure sauntering up the street ahead of him, a young gypsy woman in a gay red shawl, with a red flounce on her ragged dress and a red bandana tied over the mop of thick dark hair that swung loosely around her shoulders. He could not see her face, but her hips had a provocative sway and she carried herself with a confident defiance that made her stand out like a Romany princess among the weary multitudes on the dirty, crowded street. Now, there was a woman whose vital juices had not yet been smoked out of her, London thought with a sense of surprised pleasure, and when she turned into an eating-house, he went in after her.

She leaned her elbows on the dirty wooden counter, looked up at the fly-specked menu board, and ordered a two-penny pie and a bottle of lemonade. She was untying the money out of a knotted handkerchief at her belt when London slid several coins across the counter.

"Permit me," he said with a smile.

The woman turned toward him, and he was struck dumb. She was no gypsy, but the very same Charlotte Conway whom he had last seen jumping down from the rusty iron ladder in Hampstead Street. Now, as then, she seemed to him easy and free in her body, unconstrained and open and frank in herself, ready to meet any peril or opportunity that the world might offer. Stunned, he realized that this Anarchist gypsy was the woman he had been looking for all his life.

It took a moment—it felt like a lifetime—to shape her name. "Lottie!" he whispered. "Lottie Conway!"

Her eyes met his with an astonishing boldness, widening and then narrowing, taking in his seafaring clothes and his green cloth cap. "Do I know you?" she asked.

The huskiness of her voice, the artlessness of her greeting, delighted him. "Jack London," he said. "I'm an American journalist here to do a story. We met in an alley off Hampstead, when you shinnied down that ladder the day the cops raided the *Clarion*." He grinned. "That was swell, the way you ditched those John Laws. A second more or less, you'd'a been pinched and hauled off to the calaboose."

She looked at him as if he were speaking a foreign language, but at that moment, the meat pie and lemonade were passed across the counter. He picked them up and, in a proprietary way, led the girl to a wooden table in the farthest corner. She sat down and dove into the pie as if she were starving, saying not a word.

"You're on the lam, are you?" he asked, when she was finished.

She frowned and pushed back the empty plate. "On the lam?"

"Trying to keep clear of the cops." With a grin, he ran his

eye down her frock, admiring the swell of her breasts beneath the dirty bodice, the narrow waist, the trim ankles under the muddy hem of her skirt. "Done that myself in my hobo days, riding the rails across America. Got a few tricks up my sleeve I'd be glad to teach you. I remember once in Reno, Nevada, back in '92—"

"Thank you for the meal." She stood. "Good-bye, now."

He caught at her wrist. "No, don't, please!" he said, and heard and was not ashamed of the pleading in his voice. "I've just found you. You *can't* go away."

"I can't?" Her eyes were on his, his fingers still tight on her wrist. "Why not?"

"Because." *Because I didn't know there were such women in the world,* he thought wildly. *Because you give wings to my imagination, and open great, luminous pages in books where heroes do heroic deeds for the sake of beautiful ladies. Because I am greedy for the feel of you.* "Because I can help you," he said humbly. "I want to help you."

"Help me? Why?" She pulled her arm away, but she sat back down.

"Because you need me," he said, his humility vanishing in a hero's boldness, which was abashed the very next moment by her throaty laugh.

"Need you?" She tossed her head, an amused smile on her lips. "Why in the world should I *need* you?"

"Because," he said, and leaned toward her, his eyes glinting with delight at the thought of the temptation he was offering her, his heart filled with the almost overpowering hope that she would accept. "Because I know a place where you can hide. A place where no one in the world would ever look for you."

CHAPTER TWENTY-TWO

*When bloody finger marks or impressions on clay, glass,
etc. exist, they may lead to the scientific identification of
criminals. If previously known, they would be much
more precise in value than the standard mole (informant)
of the penny novelists. . . . There can be no doubt as to
the advantage of having, besides their photographs, a
nature-copy of the forever-unchangeable finger furrows
of important criminals.*

Henry Faulds,
letter to *Nature* Magazine, 28 October 1880

At the Sibley House breakfast table on Tuesday morning, Kate was handed a telegram from Hodge, her
butler at Bishop's Keep. Patrick, the sixteen-year-old red-
haired boy whom she and Charles had taken as their own,
had arrived home the night before and was laid up with a
badly-sprained ankle.* The boy—a young man now,
nearly—had a marvelous gift for working with horses and
served as an apprentice to George Lambton at Newmarket,
one of the country's leading horse trainers. But he had suffered an accidental fall, and while he was not badly injured,

*Patrick's story is told in *Death at Rottingdean* and *Death at Epsom Downs*.

Mr. Lambton had thought it best that he go home for a week or two to recuperate.

Hodge's telegram assured Kate that the doctor felt Patrick to be in no danger, but she knew she wouldn't be easy in her mind until she saw him for herself, and if she went home, she could put the time to good use by working on her manuscript. Anyway, there was no purpose to her staying in the City, for it was clear that she could not find Charlotte Conway unless the girl wanted to be found. She could be anywhere in the vast city of London, and looking for her on the streets would be like looking for the proverbial needle in a haystack. Perhaps Charlotte would contact Nellie or Helen Rossetti or even Mrs. Conway, and Kate had made sure that each one of them knew how to get in touch with her. If Charlotte turned up, and if there was something she could do to help the girl, she could always go back to London.

O n Tuesday afternoon, Charles and Edward Savidge went to New Scotland Yard, to the newly-established fingerprint department. There, they met with Sergeant Collins, who had been appointed and trained by Assistant Commissioner Henry as the Yard's chief fingerprint expert. The evidence, now boxed and labeled with a caution against handling, had been moved from the evidence locker to Collins's office.

Sergeant Collins pulled on a pair of thin cotton gloves and opened the box. He took out a three-inch stack of Anarchist literature, all appearing to be copies of the same meeting notice, and several books, one by Prince Kropotkin, two others by Mikhail Bakunin. Next, he took out a much-folded sheet of cheap paper, clearly a letter, handwritten in French.

"Found in Mouffetard's pocket," he said, handing it to

Savidge. To Charles he said, "No point in testing for finger-prints, not on that rough paper."

Savidge unfolded the letter and read it. "I'd like to copy this," he said.

The sergeant nodded and took out a bottle of what appeared to be a clear, viscous liquid, bearing the label *Dr. Gabriel's Pure Medicinal Glycerine.* "Found in the newspaper office, on a shelf," he said, setting it on the table.

Finally, he took out three ginger-beer bottles, one at a time, very carefully. The long-necked, champagne-shaped bottles were made of stoneware (as was usual with ginger-beer bottles, which were meant to be returned and refilled), the neck colored brown, the rest of the bottle plain salt-glazed, with the manufacturer's name and bearded likeness impressed on the front. The bottles, each one capped with a screw-in stopper, appeared to be half full of a noxious-smelling liquid substance, identified by the Yard chemist, Sergeant Collins reported, as nitric acid. A square white evidence label had been applied to the back of each bottle. On it was written in ink the time and place the bottle was collected and the name *Finney,* the officer who had brought it in.

Savidge sat down to copy the letter into his pocket note-book. Charles watched as Collins dusted the four bottles with charcoal powder. A few prints showed quite clearly on the glazed surface, and these the sergeant photographed. Then he began to study the bottles, comparing the finger-prints on them to the inked prints of the jailed men, obtained from Holloway Prison.

"Any matches?" Charles asked, peering over the sergeant's shoulder. He had worked with Collins before, and had a great deal of respect for him. The man was, by now, the Yard's resident fingerprint expert.

"With your boys' prints?" Collins asked, putting down his magnifying glass. "No, I don't see any matches," he said slowly, then added, "But that doesn't mean they haven't handled these items, of course. The police who picked 'em up obviously didn't give a thought to preserving possible fingerprint evidence." He sighed heavily. "They never do, y'know. It'll take a couple of convictions and a great deal of training before anybody pays attention. The prints on the bottles probably belong to the officers who brought them in."

Savidge stood. "This means, of course," he said into Charles's ear, "that we'll ask for a continuance until after the Jackson trial." To Collins, he said, "I should like to finger-print all the officers who have handled the bottles. Can that be arranged?"

"No need, sir," Collins said cheerfully. "When Assistant Commissioner Henry took charge of CID, he ordered that every policeman's fingerprints be taken, for the purpose of exclusion. They're all on file. You and Lord Sheridan are welcome to come in and have a look."

"Splendid," Savidge said, "although it won't do much good for me to examine them. That's Lord Sheridan's baili-wick."

Charles, also wearing gloves, was taking another look at the four bottles, carefully turning them as they sat on the table, inspecting them from every angle to be sure that Collins had photographed all the prints. On the bottle that had been collected from Gould's room, he noticed half of a black-dusted print at the left edge of the label.

"This partial print here," he said. "Is the rest of it on, or under, the label, do you think?"

"On top, I'd guess," Collins said, glancing at it. "But the label has a matte surface. Doubt if it would take a print."

Charles took out his penknife, raised the left edge of the label and said, "Whiff a little of that dust here."

It took only a moment to see that the print extended under the label. Collins was about to remove the label to photograph the print when a fourth man walked in, thickset and wearing brown tweeds and a brown derby. Collins looked up. "Good afternoon, Inspector Ashcraft," he said.

Charles gave the man an appraising look. Charlotte Conway had said he was out to make a name for himself, Wells had called him a "rather obsessive fellow," and Rasnokov had suggested that he did not play straight. These were qualities that might well make him a valuable man to Special Branch.

"What's this?" the man demanded angrily. He threw his hat on the table and glared at Collins. "Why are you removing that label, Collins? That's police property you're tampering with! It should have stayed in the evidence locker."

"But, sir," Collins protested, "I was only going to——"

"I don't care *what* you were going to do. Those bottles are evidence in the Hyde Park case. They are not to be meddled with."

"Sir," Collins said quietly, "I very much need to——"

"Who gave you leave?" Ashcraft demanded, obviously in a foul temper. He looked at Savidge and Charles. "And who the blazes are these men? No one's applied to me for——"

"Assistant Commissioner Henry gave leave, sir," Collins replied, with the air of a man who knows when he's defeated. "This is Lord Charles Sheridan, who had the management of the fingerprint project at Dartmoor. And Edward Savidge, the barrister for the defendants——"

"I don't care who the devil they are," Ashcraft snapped, "they've no business messing about with evidence."

"We are hardly 'messing about,' Inspector," Savidge retorted. "As barrister for the defense, I have the right at any time to examine the evidence against my clients, and to submit it to expert analysis. Lord Sheridan, whose expertise in fingerprint analysis has already been recognized by the Home Office, is serving in that capacity."

"Fingerprints," Ashcraft said in a disdainful tone. He gave a loud snort. "See that those bottles are handled carefully, Sergeant. The contents must not be spilled on any account."

Savidge took out a notebook. In a measured voice, he said, "Please be so good, Inspector, as to give me the names of the officers who collected the bottles. They will testify for the Crown, I assume."

"Finney was in charge," Ashcraft replied sulkily. "He was assisted by Perry and Cummings."

"And yourself, I suppose," Charles said.

"Not I," Ashcraft replied.

Charles looked at him. "You've not handled the bottles, then?"

Ashcraft shook his head. "Nothing to do with them. Finney brought them in, along with the Anarchist literature. The glycerine was found in the newspaper office, and one of the Anarchists—Mouffetard, it was—was carrying the bomb-making instructions in his pocket." He looked at the stoneware bottles, which bore smudges of the black dust used to make the fingerprints visible, then scowled at Collins. "Those damned fingerprints of yours, Sergeant, are causing us no end of trouble, and to no purpose, none at all. When will you understand that they are *not* reliable evidence? They may be useful as a means of identifying certain criminals— *may*, I say—but they have never been used to achieve a conviction in a court of law. No jury will ever be persuaded by such scientific hocus-pocus."

"You are correct on the one point, Inspector," Savidge said, closing his notebook with a snap. "Fingerprints have not yet been used to obtain a conviction. In a fortnight, however, the case may have altered." He nodded at Collins. "Isn't that so, Sergeant?"

Ashcraft fixed the sergeant with a black look. "What's happening in a fortnight, Collins?"

"Why, the Jackson burglary case, of course, sir," Collins replied, as if he were amazed that Ashcraft did not know of it. "Haven't you heard talk of it? Jackson's to be tried at Old Bailey a fortnight hence. I'm to testify, since I made the fingerprint match. And there's a very good man—Richard Muir—standing for the Crown. Assistant Commissioner Henry chose him himself."

"Yes, Muir," Savidge said, in a tone of great satisfaction. "I don't know who's up for the defense, but in this case, my money is on the Crown. Muir is a workhorse, I'll tell you. Keeps all the facts and notes for a case on colored cards, one color for direct, another for cross, and so on. 'There's Muir at his card game,' people say. He—"

"The devil himself couldn't persuade a jury to convict a man on fingerprint evidence alone," Ashcraft said derisively. "Now, if you will excuse me, I have work to do. I haven't got the whole bloody day to stand around."

Charles watched the man depart, reflecting that there seemed to be some truth to what Miss Conway, Steven Wells, and the Russian had said. He turned to Collins.

"Could I have a look at that partial print, Sergeant?"

CHAPTER TWENTY-THREE

Jack felt increasingly frustrated with [his marriage to Bess]. During her pregnancy he had told Anna: "Just when freedom seems opening up for me I feel the bands tightening and the riveting of the gyves. I remember when I was free and there was no restraint and I did as the heart willed." Jack told male friends Bess was a gossip, mean-spirited, as cold as the Klondike.

Alex Kershaw,
Jack London: A Life

Lottie picked up the newspaper—*Freedom*, the only remaining Anarchist newspaper in London—and scrunched the pillow behind her back so she could sit more comfortably on the narrow bed, one of two in the chilly room. It was Thursday morning, and Jack was sitting at the table beside the window, typing away at his book, his back turned toward her, a cup of coffee at his elbow. That was how he spent most mornings, hunched obsessively over his typewriter, smoking and drinking coffee. He had to produce a thousand words a day, he said, or he would fall behind in the schedule he had set himself.

Lottie had been here only since Tuesday, but it had been long enough to know that Jack had been right about this place; in many respects, it was a perfect hideaway. No one would ever think to look for her in an upstairs room let to the American adventure writer Jack London, in the house of a policeman! What was more, Officer Palmer went out on his beat every morning and Mrs. Palmer and her two daughters were employed as seamstresses in a dress shop in New Bond Street, so the house was empty all day. And the Palmers lived on the first floor and Jack's room was on the second, at the rear; as long as they kept their voices down, there was little danger of discovery even when the family was at home. Jack's room even had its own private stair, so when Lottie needed to use the backyard privy, all she had to do was check to see that the coast was clear and make a dash for it. Even if she were seen, it would only be assumed that Jack was entertaining a female visitor, as he certainly had every right to do.

Of course, there were drawbacks, too, and one was so serious that it had almost prompted her to leave that very first day. Lottie had always held the unconventional belief that a woman's first responsibility was to herself, and that she had the moral obligation to be her very own person. To her, marriage seemed to compromise a woman's independence, without which she was nothing. She believed that love should be free, without constraint, and if one could not love freely, one should not love.

Lottie might be quite a few years ahead of her era in this belief, but she was certainly not alone, for several important women of her day also advocated free love. In England, more than a century before, Mary Wollstonecraft had attacked marriage as "legal prostitution." In the United States, the writer and self-trained physician Mary Gove Nichols spoke and wrote about the need for women's sexual emancipation, while Victoria Woodhull, a leader of both the free love and woman suffrage movements, led a determined campaign against marriage. As Lottie considered her position vis-à-vis relationships with men outside of the bounds of marriage, she was in the company of a substantial number of forward-looking feminist thinkers of her day.

So if Lottie had considered Jack London as a potential lover, she was making a choice that she herself would consider perfectly moral. He was quite the handsomest, manliest, most virile man she had ever seen, and she was enormously attracted to him, so much so that almost all thought of Adam Gould had flown from her mind. What's more, from the moment they met, Jack had made it abundantly, emphatically clear that he was attracted to her, as well. Considering that the two of them had been thrown together by fate (or so it seemed), Lottie saw no reason why she should not give herself to him eagerly, joyfully, without reservation. In fact, when he invited her to hide out in his room, she had assumed that they would become lovers. It all seemed very natural and, given her feelings against the restrictions of marriage and the prerogatives that women should claim outside of it, very right.

But that was before Lottie had found the photograph of Jack's wife and little girl, hidden under a pile of manuscript pages next to his typewriter, on the little table beside the window. Jack had gone out to get them some supper, and Lottie, curious to see what sort of writer he was and what he had written about the East End, had picked up the manuscript to take it to her bed and read it. The photograph—the picture of a smiling, voluptuous, raven-haired woman with a baby girl in her arms—fluttered to the floor, and when she picked it up, she read the inscription on the back: *To dearest Jack, from his devoted wife Bess and darling Joan.*

Lottie had stared at the photograph until the images blurred, then put the manuscript, unread, back on the table, the photograph safely concealed beneath it. Having seen it, though, she knew that she was in a corner. She was free to love, but Jack was not, and to give herself to him would be morally wrong. It would be to betray a woman she had never met—a woman who had given birth to Jack's child and to whom he had pledged his life—and Lottie could not in conscience bring herself to do this. In conscience, too, she had to condemn Jack for attempting to entice her into an adulterous relationship, and this new knowledge entirely changed her feelings toward him.

But what was she to do when he—as she knew he would—began to make love to her? Should she tell him she had found the photograph, and that it had changed the way she felt about him? Or push him away, letting him think what he might? Or simply leave, without explanation?

She'd told him, of course, that very first evening, when he'd come back with fish and chips and tea for their supper. She was too forthright, too honest and candid, to do anything else. For a moment he'd stared at her, his eyes dark, his lower lip thrusting sulkily, and then he'd laughed, a short, hard laugh that felt almost like a slap.

"Well, you're a straight-shooter," he said. "I'll give you that, damn it." He turned away from her and flung himself on his bed. "I don't love her, you know," he said gruffly. "She understood that when we got married."

"Then why in the world did you marry her?" Lottie asked wonderingly. It was a very real question. She could barely imagine marrying someone she thought she loved and accepting the restriction of her freedom that came with it. To marry someone she did not love was unthinkable.

"Because I wanted the restraint laid on me," Jack said sourly. "I was drifting, and when I'm drifting, it's hard to write. Bess was solid, solid as a rock. I thought she'd be a weight, holding me down, giving me a rule to live by, imposing some order on my life. And she does," he added bitterly, half to himself. "Entirely too much."

His answer almost dumbfounded Lottie. He married *because* he needed restraint, when marriage seemed to her to be entirely too restraining? Could the man not see that it was his obligation as a human being to restrain *himself?* And if he felt he was drifting, could he not find some anchor within himself to lay hold of, without looking for it in his wife, whose anchoring, restraining qualities he was bound, sooner or later, to bitterly resent?

But Lottie doubted that he was capable of answering these questions, so she merely shrugged and said, "Well, then, you got what you wanted, didn't you? A rule to live by. Order in your life." She could not quite keep the sarcasm out of her tone. "You should be happy."

"Well, I'm not," Jack said sulkily. "I want you, Lottie. We're meant for each other."

Ignoring the last sentence, with which she reluctantly had to agree, she rose and unfolded the newspaper wrappings from the fish and chips, sniffing appreciatively. "Smells good." She held out the package. "Here. Have some supper."

Jack regarded her sullenly. "Bess has a peasant's mind. She talks of nothing but the baby and the household. No imagination, none at all. She stifles me."

"No doubt," Lottie said, putting the package on the table and helping herself to a piece of fish. "But you're not being very consistent, are you? You want her to be an anchor, but you complain that she holds you down. Right?" In Lottie's view, it was dishonorable for a man to marry a woman to suit his own purposes and then condemn his wife when she fulfilled the role for which he had chosen her. Adam Gould would never think of doing such a thing.

"You don't need to be cruel about it," Jack said. He held out his hand with a seductive smile. "We can be friends, can't we? Come have a nice cuddle, Lottie."

"Not that kind of friends," Lottie said firmly. "And I'll only stay in this room on your guarantee that there will be no talk of cuddling or love. One word, and I'm out the door. Do you understand?"

"Yes," Jack said in a resigned tone. Then he flashed her a boyish grin. "But I'll bet a quid you'll change your mind."

"Don't have a quid," Lottie said.

"I'll loan it to you."

"Never a borrower nor a lender be," Lottie replied smartly, and ignoring his dark look, carried her feast of fish and chips to her own bed, where she made herself comfortable and ate hungrily until every crumb was gone.

In a way that she could not quite describe, Lottie felt relieved, as if the fates had kept her from mistakenly choosing the wrong path, which, once taken, might have led to enormous complications. And so she was able to sleep without difficulty in the same room with this very attractive man, and was easily able to ignore his glance, dark and passionate, which followed her as she moved around. Jack might be as sulky as a scolded child, but Lottie felt easy in herself. She had done what she felt right, without regret, and she was pragmatist enough to put aside what she couldn't or shouldn't do and focus instead on what she could.

So when Lottie saw the article on the front page of *Freedom* on Thursday morning, she began to get a glimmering idea of how she could help Adam, who was now much on her mind. After all, if he had not been at the *Clarion* to take her to lunch, the police would not have arrested him, so it was up to her to see that, somehow or another, he was rescued.

The article reported that at the request of counsel, the three Anarchists accused of bomb-making had been granted a continuance to the fourth of September, which was a fortnight away. They would be transported from Holloway Prison, where they were being held, to the Old Bailey, where they would stand trial. The article urged all London Anarchists to attend the trial and show, by their presence, their support for their comrades, who, whatever they had done, had done it out of their belief that all governments were oppressive, and that the only path toward freedom was to end the rule of tyranny.

Lottie had, of course, told Jack why she was hiding from the police, and what had happened at the newspaper office, and all about Yuri Messenko and Ivan Kopinski and Pierre Mouffetard and Adam. Now, she thought for a few minutes, shaping her idea. Then she looked over the top of her newspaper. "Listen to this, Jack."

"I'm working," Jack replied, around his cigarette.

"Then stop working and listen," she commanded, and read the article out loud. When she was finished, she put the newspaper down. "Something must be done, Jack," she said urgently. "Those men are innocent. They must be *freed*."

"Freed?" Jack turned around, a cigarette hanging from his lips. It was warm that morning; the window was open and he was wearing an undershirt that revealed his chiseled muscles—wearing it deliberately, Lottie suspected, hoping that the sight of his masculine torso might tempt her to change her mind. "You mean to infiltrate the jury, I take it," he remarked sarcastically. "And just how do you reckon to do that?"

Lottie tossed her head impatiently. "That's ridiculous. There's no way to infiltrate a jury. Our men will be found guilty, of course. I mean to find a way to free them from prison."

Jack's blue eyes glinted and he smiled, as if in spite of himself. "Anybody ever tell you that you're beautiful when you're passionate?"

She scowled. "Be serious, Jack. This is serious business."

"Serious? It sure as hell is," he agreed. He turned around and straddled his chair backward. "I've been in jail, and I know. And I'll tell you, Lottie, it ain't no easy thing to get a man out of jail, once he's behind bars."

"You've been in jail?" Lottie put her head on one side, regarding him thoughtfully. Jack had told her—endlessly, it seemed—about his adventures as a seaman, a gold-seeker, and a Socialist, but he had not mentioned jail.

"It happened in the Depression of '94," Jack said, launching into what Lottie had come to think of as his storytelling mode. "I was travelin' with Coxey's Army, a rabble-rousin' bunch of the unemployed who marched on Washington to try to get things changed. But I got fed up and deserted when we got to the Mississippi River. Hopped a freight headin' east. I ended up at Niagara Falls and got one good look at the river before John Law pinched me for vagrancy, along with a couple of other hoboes. They shoved us into a big iron cage and then hauled us off to a court-room, where the judge gave us thirty days apiece without allowin' any of us so much as a word in our defense." Jack's voice grew hard. "Trial was a farce. I was denied not only my right of trial by jury but my right to plead guilty or not guilty. Got my American blood up, I'll tell you."

Lottie stared at him. "I didn't think things like that happened in America."

"Neither did I," Jack said. "All I did was walk along their sidewalk and gawk at their picayune waterfall. What crime was there in that? Next thing I know, I'm rolled up snug as a bug in the Erie County Penitentiary." He paused. "I learned plenty from that experience, I'll tell you. It was like going to school. I learned how to pass the punk, pick a lock, pick a pocket—"

"Pick a pocket?" Lottie interrupted eagerly.

"Yeah." Jack grinned. "This old geezer shared my cell, Cardboard Clancy, his name was. They called him Card-board because that's where he liked to sleep on the road, in little houses he made out of cardboard boxes. Card, he was a masterful pickpocket." Jack lit a cigarette from the end of the one he was smoking and stubbed out the butt. His eyes were sparkling with the memory and the telling of it. "One day, in the mess-hall, ol' Card picked the keys clean out of the guard's pocket. Slick as a whistle, it was. Fella never even knew they were gone."

"And then what happened?" Lottie asked, regarding him curiously. The trouble with Jack was that you never knew how much of his tale to believe. He could recount a story so full of lively, real-life details that you felt you were actually there, then he'd laugh and tell you he'd made it all up and congratulate himself on having fooled you.

"What happened?" Jack shrugged. "Nothing happened. We were getting out the next week, so we didn't bother using the keys. Might as well get a few more prison meals under our belts." He grinned. "Anyway, Card just did it to show me how it was done. We had it all fixed up to go into partnership when we got out, y'see. Card thought I was a crook just like him, and I didn't see any merit in disabusing him of the notion. So I let him think I was the real goods, so to speak, and he spent a fair amount of time teaching me what he knew. Especially picking pockets. As I say, he was real good at it. We practiced on one another until I was real good at it, too."

"So you learned how to be a dipper," Lottie said in a speculative tone.

"A dipper?"

Lottie laughed. "That's what a pickpocket is called here. A buzzer, sometimes. A mobsman, if he's well-dressed."

"Well, I don't think they'd've called me a mobsman in those days." Jack chuckled briefly. "I was a tramp, pure and simple. And I wasn't doing it to pick up story material, or study human nature, either, the way I'm doing now. I did it because of the life that was in me, the wanderlust in my blood that wouldn't let me rest. But I hadn't the price of the railroad fare in my jeans, so I—"

"Did you practice dipping while you were a tramp?" Lottie interrupted. Jack's story was interesting, but he was taking a long time to tell it.

Jack gave her a shame-faced look. "Well, I wouldn't admit it to anybody but you, but I have to confess to giving it a shot a time or two. It's a useful trade, I've got to say. One time in Ogden, Utah, when I was dead broke and didn't know where my next meal was coming from, I passed this dandified dude on the street and—"

"I wonder," Lottie said, "if you'd mind showing me just how good a dipper you really are." She stood up. For a change from her gypsy costume, she was wearing a pair of Jack's spare trousers and one of his clean shirts. "Give me your wallet," she commanded. She tucked it into a rear pocket and turned her back on him. "Now, show me."

Without hesitation, Jack brushed against her. She felt nothing, not even the touch of his fingers, but when she reached for the wallet, it wasn't there.

He grinned at her mischievously, holding it up and reaching for her. "Is this what you're looking for, lady?"

She evaded his grasp. "So much for the wallet," she said. "How are you with keys?"

CHAPTER TWENTY-FOUR

Allow me here to give a word of caution about taking cold during the monthly period. It is very dangerous. I knew a young girl, who had not been instructed by her mother upon this subject, to be so afraid of being found with this show of blood upon her apparel which she did not know the meaning of, that she went to a brook and washed herself and her clothes—took cold, and immediately went insane.

Dr. Chase's Recipes; or
Information for Everybody, 1867

Nellie Lovelace sat in front of the mirror in her dressing room in the theater, staring at her reflection and fighting back tears. Tonight was the last time she would sit in the room that had become so dear to her in the past few months, with its big gold star on the door, its clever little costume closet, and its prettily-flounced dressing table littered with theatrical makeup, the mirror framed with photographs of herself in various theatrical roles. For tonight was the last time she would star as Princess Soo-Soo. She had been fired. The director, who had given her not just one warning but several, had finally told her that there was no longer any need of her services.

At the recollection of that terrible humiliation, Nellie stopping fighting, dropped her head on her arms, and gave way to bitter tears. It was an appalling thing to be fired from a role, especially such a plummy role as the Princess. The theatrical world was a close-knit society. By tomorrow, everyone in the cast would know what had happened, and by the following day, word of her disgrace would have rippled through every theater in London. Every director would know that she had been fired for missing cues and forgetting lines, and it would be next to impossible to get new work in a decent theater. If she was lucky, she might get a job as a chorus girl in the music halls, but likely not the Hippodrome or the Alhambra, the leading variety houses. The Paragon Theater of Varieties, maybe, in Mile End Road. She might even end up back in Whitechapel, at the Wonderland. At the thought, her heart sank. Given how far she had risen, such a thing would be a terrible come-down.

That wasn't all, of course. Working as a mere chorus girl or a bit-part player, she wouldn't be able to keep her beautiful little West End house, with its garden and piped-in hot water in the bathroom. She would have to sell her beautiful furniture and move back to the theatrical rooming house where she had lived before she became Princess Soo-Soo. And there were her debts. She didn't actually know how much she owed the dressmakers and jewelers in New Bond Street, but it must be hundreds and hundreds of pounds. Thinking that her stardom was ensured, she'd spent money far too freely on things that, she realized now, were not at all important.

And there was worse, much worse. Nellie had never read a medical book, and it probably wouldn't have profited her if she had, for most of the advice that was available to late Victorian and Edwardian women about their bodies was simply wrong. William Buchan, for instance, in his book *Domestic Medicine,* assumed that menstruation was a dangerous disease that required regulation and suggested the use of "corrective pills" to relieve its inevitable associated symptoms: "weakness, nervousness, giddiness, and hysteria." Other doctors taught that women should avoid all excitement during their menstrual periods, for intellectual stimulation, strong emotions, or intense physical exertion could obstruct the menstrual flow and lead to insanity and death.

But while Nellie might not have known what the learned doctors taught about the hazards of being female, she was not without experience where pregnancy (and its prevention) was concerned. From the 1830s on, newspapers had advertised "female syringes" designed to be used with various sperm-killing chemical douches, such as alum or sulphate of zinc and iron. Another commonly available contraceptive was the pessary, which Nellie's friends gigglingly called the "pisser." It was widely sold in chemists' shops to "correct a prolapsed uterus," but women knew that its real purpose was to prevent conception. They also fully understood the real and frightening implications of a missed menstrual period, and very few would have been silly enough to blame it on reading an intellectually-challenging book, or dancing at a ball for hours on end, or crying over a romance novel.

So when Nellie realized that she had missed the period that was due a week after her evening with Jack, it was certainly no wonder that she was upset, and no wonder that her anxiety caused her to miss a few more cues and bobble a few more lines, which only led to greater stress and more missed cues and bobbled lines, and to the final humiliation.

Perhaps Nellie should not be blamed for thinking that, even if by some miracle she wasn't pregnant, falling into bed with Jack London was the cause, pure and simple, of her professional downfall. Of course, she could not hold him solely responsible, for she knew she should have been more watchful, more on her guard against him. But Kate Sheridan was right, she thought with a weary anger. Jack had taken advantage of her naive eagerness to have a good time, and should she be indeed pregnant, he was going to find himself confronted with the responsibility of fatherhood. And if he felt no moral obligation to accept that responsibility, perhaps a letter to his wife in California might make him see the light.

But these thoughts provided cold comfort, and certainly offered no answer to her current dilemma. Nellie knew that she would have to start looking for work first thing in the morning. With a heavy sigh, she rose from her dressing table and began to pack her few belongings.

CHAPTER TWENTY-FIVE

⟳

BURGLAR SENTENCED TO 7 YEARS
FINGERPRINTS GET TRIAL BY JURY
NEW POLICE WEAPON AGAINST CRIME!

The Daily Telegraph, 3 September 1902

The Central Criminal Court was adjacent to Newgate Prison, in an old stone building that was called the Old Bailey after the name of the street on which it stood. In 1086, at the time the Domesday Book was compiled, this particular site was next to a gate in the stone wall, or bailey, around the City of London. In 1188, Henry II ordered that a prison be built adjacent to the wall; it was constructed by two carpenters and a smith for the cost of three pounds, six shillings, and eight pence. Over the following centuries, the gate and the prison (now called New Gate) were demolished and rebuilt several times. In 1539, a sessions house, or court, was built adjacent to the prison, and became known as the Old Bailey. Charles knew that both Newgate—probably the most notorious of English prisons—and the Old Bailey were soon to be razed, in order to make way for a grand new structure designed by E. W. Mountford, although he doubted that even a splendid new judicial building would

banish the tragic ghosts of the men, women, and children—
debtors and criminals alike—who had died or been executed
within Newgate's dark, dismal walls.

But the demolition was not scheduled to begin until the
following spring, and on Tuesday, the second of September,
Charles Sheridan and Edward Savidge presented themselves
in the covered yard between the prison and the Old Bailey,
some thirty minutes before the trial of Henry Jackson was
about to begin. They handed their admission cards to the
sheriff's usher and were directed up a stair, down a narrow
passage, and into seats in the spectators' section. The cham-
ber was unusually crowded with people, mostly off-duty
police officers, Charles suspected, since they had a significant stake in the outcome of the trial.

Charles and Savidge had scarcely taken their seats when
they heard the usher's cry. The crowd got to its feet as the
judge entered and took his place at the bench. A moment
later, Harry Jackson came in and stepped down to the front
of the dock, his head bowed.

The trial went swiftly. Richard Muir, black-robed and
white-wigged, outlined the Crown's case and called several
witnesses including Sergeant Collins, who told the impas-
sive jury how the evidence was obtained and what it meant.
Then Muir placed in evidence two photographic enlargements, comparing the single fingerprint that the burglar
had left at the scene of the crime with that of the print of
Harry Jackson's left thumb. Sergeant Collins demonstrated
the points of comparison between the two prints, and the
Crown rested.

The barrister for the defense was witheringly scornful of
both Sergeant Collins and the fingerprint evidence and dramatically passionate in his assertions of his client's innocence, pleading with the jury not to convict a poor laborer
on such intangible and untrustworthy evidence, "never
before offered in a court of law," he cried. But the jury,

unmoved by his passion, returned within the half-hour with a guilty verdict. Jackson was sentenced to seven years, the judge's gavel came down smartly, and the case was concluded.

"Well, that was one for the record books," Savidge said, as he and Charles repaired to a table in a nearby coffeehouse much frequented by barristers and court officials.

"Yes," Charles said, shaking his head. "Seven years for seven billiard balls. Hardly a fair sentence, if you ask me."

"It's not the sentence I'm talking about, and you know it," Savidge retorted. "Students of the law will be reading about the fingerprint evidence for years to come."

"And the police will have to learn how to deal with that kind of evidence," Charles said thoughtfully. "It will mean more training, greater care in the handling of evidence taken from the scene of the crime, and much more attention to the proper custody of evidence. Men like Ashcraft may have a difficult time of it."

"I doubt," Savidge said wryly, "that Ashcraft will ever learn. He's far too full of his own authority." He looked at Charles over the rim of his coffee cup. "What did you make of the fingerprint evidence in our case?"

"The question is," Charles said with a crooked grin, "what will the jury make of it? What's your prediction, Savidge?"

Savidge shook his head. "I never attempt to guess how a jury will react—especially not in a complicated case like this one, with three defendants. It will take a smart jury to sort through it all." He shrugged. "We'll find out soon enough—day after tomorrow, in fact."

Charles raised his cup in salute. "To success," he said. "May the innocent prevail."

Savidge gave a sarcastic laugh. "My word, Sheridan, you *are* an idealist."

CHAPTER TWENTY-SIX

ACCUSED ANARCHISTS ON TRIAL TODAY
3 IN BOMBING PACT
LINKED TO HYDE PARK EXPLOSION

Daily Mirror, 4 September 1902

With Patrick's ankle mended and her manuscript at last completed and ready to be delivered to her publisher, Kate came up to London early on Thursday, the fourth of September, the day of the trial. Charles had stayed in town during the intervening fortnight, busying himself with various investigations relating to the case, so they had little opportunity to discuss his work. Regarding the trial, he had left her a note at Sibley House saying that the preliminaries were scheduled to begin at ten o'clock in the morning. If she wished to attend, she should get there early, for it was likely that the spectators' box would be full.

Kate herself was not very interested in criminal trials and could think of several other productive ways to spend the day in London. But Beryl Bardwell was always fascinated by anything that smacked of the dramatic or presented narrative possibilities. *You never know,* she reminded Kate, *when we're going to have occasion to include a trial scene in one of our fictions. So we'd better take advantage of this opportunity.* Thinking it over, Kate had decided that Beryl was right. So that's why she was waiting in the spectators' line in the yard of the new Criminal Court Building in Old Bailey when the hearse-like horse-drawn van arrived, bringing the prisoners from Holloway Prison.

"Ooh, look!" crowed a stooped old lady to her companion, both standing in the line in front of Kate. " 'Tis the Black Maria. And them Anarchists, ain't they a sight?"

The companion, wearing an old-fashioned bonnet, snorted wrathfully. "Wantin' t' blow up the King, the newspaper sez. I 'opes they gets 'ung fer it."

Hung? Kate thought, startled, as catcalls and applause rippled through the line of waiting spectators. But surely the men were not accused of being accomplices in the Hyde Park bombing—were they? Had the police found evidence of that connection? She watched as the three men, dressed in ill-fitting dark jackets and trousers, their hands handcuffed in front of them, were roughly hauled out of the van and pushed through a door. They were being taken to holding cells, Kate knew from her reading of the newspapers, where they would be detained until they were to appear in the dock.

Kate was directed up a stair, down a hallway, and down another stair, and found a seat in the front row of the spectators' section, between a stout man whose breath reeked of garlic and onions and an old woman whose black knitted shawl smelt of a smoky chimney. The rest of the audience was a motley assortment of men and women, some fashionably attired, others (whom Kate took to be Anarchists or sympathizers) in the threadbare garb of the working poor, a few wearing black bands on their arms. Journalists with notebooks and artists from the illustrated periodicals, sketchpads in hand, were seated along one wall. Kate looked carefully, but if Lottie were in the audience, she did not see her, or anyone else she recognized—except for Charles, of course, who was sitting close behind the table reserved for the defense. The room was crowded, it was hot for September, and she felt very much as she imagined a *sardine à l'huile* might feel, jammed cheek-to-jowl with its oily, smelly neighbor.

At five minutes to ten, Edward Savidge and a younger assistant made their way to the defense table, which was arranged at right angles to the bench. Savidge, robed in black and wearing an incongruous-looking white wig, laid out his papers and notes and began to shuffle hastily through them as if he were looking for something he had lost. The prosecutor, a rather youngish man whose robe and wig gave him a dignity beyond his years, strode in confidently, followed by his assistant. The table in front of him was bare.

At five minutes after ten, the pretrial activities began. It happened that not a single juror who had been summoned had failed to respond, and twelve were soon seated in the jury box and sworn in. At half-ten, the prisoners were escorted into the dock, without their handcuffs but with their ankles shackled. The usher called sternly for silence, and everyone stood while one of the London aldermen entered through the door at the back of the court, followed by the High Court judge of the City of London, stooped and scholarly, with chiseled features and penetrating blue eyes. The alderman and the judge were seated, papers were rustled, volumes of law books rearranged, pens and pencils moved about with the flourish of a magician, and the trial began with the hearing of the pleas.

"Adam Gould, how do you plead?" asked the judge.

Kate watched as the first of the prisoners stood. He was blond, well-built, and good-looking, even in the ill-fitting clothing provided for the trial. "Not guilty, Your Honor," he said in a firm, ringing voice.

Pierre Mouffetard, the next to plead, did not present such a handsome appearance. His dark hair was raggedly cut, his face was set and hard, and his eyes blazed with radical fervor. He replied to the judge in a snarling, heavily-accented voice: "I do not recognize the authority of this court."

Savidge, getting to his feet, said calmly, "With Your Honor's permission, I enter a plea of not guilty on Mr. Mouffetard's behalf."

"Not guilty," the judge said, and rapped his gavel. With a glare at Savidge and a dark look at the judge, Pierre stepped back to his place.

"Ivan Kopinski," said the judge.

Ivan, his brown hair hanging in lank, dirty strings around his face, stood with his mouth closed, his eyes darting around the courtroom as if he were searching for someone. He wore, Kate thought, a look of stoic resignation, as if nothing that happened to him made a great deal of difference. After a moment, Savidge again said, "Not guilty, Your Honor," and the three pleas were entered. Kate settled back, avoiding the sharp elbow of the woman to her right. The trial was about to begin.

The Crown prosecutor, whose name was Sims, laid out the case for the jury with an elegant if rhetorical simplicity. The three defendants—two of them employees of the Anarchist newspaper, the *Clarion*, and the third a well-known trade-union organizer—were charged under the Explosive Substances Act of 1883 with the possession of explosives with intent to endanger life. He would not trouble the gentlemen of the jury with a lengthy and tedious presentation of the argument that would shortly be developed; he would simply note that he expected the jury—whose careful attention to and thoughtful consideration of the arguments he very earnestly and humbly solicited—would have no difficulty at all finding the defendants guilty of a most heinous crime against the persons of their fellow men, indeed (spoken in a hushed voice and with a wide flourish of his robed arms) against the very persons of the innocent members of the jury and the spectators assembled in this courtroom. For bombs were no respecter of persons, and a bomb would as gladly kill innocent men, women, and children as anyone else. There was a stir in the courtroom as Mr. Sims sat down, and many of the better-dressed spectators were seen to look nervously over their shoulders, as if fearing that a bomb might be tossed into their very midst.

Mr. Savidge then rose and reminded the jury that no man might be found guilty of a crime committed by an associate, except upon the evidence of relevant facts demonstrating his own guilt beyond a reasonable doubt. It was their duty as jurors to carefully sift the meaningful facts from the useless arguments and theories and discard as if it were chaff every meaningless rhetorical flourish. And with a sharp glance at the prosecution, he sat down. The spectators stirred with what seemed to be a restless disappointment, as if they had expected a more eloquent statement.

The counsel for the prosecution began by summoning Inspector Ashcraft, of Special Branch, Scotland Yard, to the witness box—the man, Kate recalled, whom Charlotte Conway accused of having her and the others followed. He was thickset and round-faced, and carried himself with an assertive confidence, standing firmly in the witness box. Having been sworn, he related how the Anarchist group— the Hampstead Road cell, as he called it—had originally come to his notice through the offices of a certain "reliable source" who had identified one of the defendants, Mr. Ivan Kopinski, as potentially dangerous. Thereby alerted, he had taken special pains to read each page of the *Clarion,* to determine whether it was printing seditious material.

The prosecutor then introduced into evidence an article taken from the *Clarion* and asked the inspector to read the marked paragraph. Putting on a pair of gold reading glasses,

Ashcraft read a paragraph urging all British Anarchists to support their foreign comrades "by any and all available means" and concluding, "Violence is the only thing the oppressors understand." He raised his eyes, looked around the packed courtroom, and rendered the final sentence with an excess of gravity. "An ounce of dynamite is worth a ton of paper."

There was another nervous stir, this one so prolonged that his lordship the judge was required to gavel it into silence. The prosecutor then inquired whether the inspector felt that the statement was seditious. Inspector Ashcraft was about to answer, but Savidge interrupted him, objecting on the grounds that the question called for an opinion.

The prosecutor looked down his nose. "May it please your lordship," he said to the judge, "this witness is an expert."

"Perhaps," Savidge said in a level tone, "learned counsel would care to submit the inspector's credentials for his lordship's examination. On what basis does Inspector Ashcraft qualify as an expert in the matter of determining what is seditious and what is not? In what capacity has the inspector previously served as an expert on this question? How—"

Sims threw up his hands with a great show of weariness and spoke to the judge. "I'll withdraw my question, my lord, rather than prolong these proceedings unnecessarily." He turned back to the witness and said snappishly, "Having read the article, Inspector, did you take any action?"

It had been his duty to act, the inspector replied with calm assurance. After the article appeared, each of the key members of the *Clarion* staff was placed under police surveillance. He himself had kept a close watch over the activities of the paper's editor, Miss Charlotte Conway, and had assigned experienced detectives to the others. Then one of the employees, a young Anarchist named Yuri Messenko, had died in a violent bomb explosion in Hyde Park on

Coronation Day. Fearing that the *Clarion* was the center of a dangerous bomb-making ring, the inspector had ordered a raid on the newspaper and taken the suspects into custody to prevent their flight to the Continent. When one of the suspects, Pierre Mouffetard, was searched, he was discovered to have on his person a letter containing certain bomb-making instructions.

"I show you Exhibit A," the prosecutor said. "Is this the letter?"

The inspector peered at it. "It is a translation of the letter, yes. And quite detailed, too. Anybody could make a bomb, following these instructions."

"Very well. Go on."

It was at that point, the inspector said, that he had perceived that the *Clarion* was an immediate danger to the safety and security of British citizens, and had ordered its type and equipment destroyed and the office closed. All the primary suspects had been placed under arrest, except (unfortunately) for Miss Conway herself, who had managed to escape and was now a fugitive from justice. Search warrants had been obtained for the living quarters of the accused men, each of the premises searched, and certain evidence retrieved, including three bombs that—

Sims held up his hand, his two gold rings flashing. "That will be all, Inspector Ashcraft." Turning to the jury, he remarked, with a rather paternalistic air, "You see, gentlemen, Inspector Ashcraft was not present when the searches were conducted. Only the officer who actually searched the defendants' quarters may testify to what he found."

Mr. Savidge rose to cross-examine the witness. Frowning, he said, "Your informant, Inspector, the one who originally brought Mr. Kopinski to your attention as a 'dangerous' man. What is his name?"

"I regret that I cannot say, sir," the inspector replied, in a tone that did not seem to Kate at all regretful. "This man continues to be useful to the police, and revealing his identity would jeopardize future investigations."

Savidge appealed to the judge to compel the witness to answer, but before he could rule, the prosecutor stood.

"Claim public-interest privilege," he said smugly. "Confidentiality in this matter is essential to the functioning of the police."

There was a momentary flurry in the courtroom. Furrowing his brow and pursing his lips, the judge deliberated for a moment or two, then ruled that the authorities' need to conceal a valuable source of information took precedence, in his opinion, over the accused's right to confront an accuser. Kate felt a quick stab of anger. Protecting informants could lead to all kinds of problems, couldn't it? What if the informant wasn't trustworthy? What if he were lying? She glanced at Charles and saw that he was frowning and writing something in a notebook. Mr. Savidge, clearly angry and disappointed, turned to the jury.

"It is my obligation to point out that Inspector Ashcraft is testifying only to his *belief* that the informant told him the truth. Since we are unable to question this so-called informant directly, we have no means of discerning whether—"

"I believe the jury quite understand the issue, Mr. Savidge," the judge interrupted. "Go on with your questions."

Scowling, Mr. Savidge complied. "Very well, Inspector," he said. "Tell us what charges have been made against Miss Conway."

"She is wanted as a material witness," the inspector replied. "A warrant has been issued for her arrest."

"But there are no criminal charges against her?" Mr. Savidge persisted. He glanced at the prosecutor. "She has not, for instance, been charged with sedition?"

The inspector colored. "Not at this time."

"Then it was judged by you or your superiors that the

article of seventeen July—the one you read out a few moments ago—was not sufficient grounds on which to pursue a charge of sedition?"

"I did not pursue a charge," the inspector said stiffly.

"Because the editor of the *Clarion* was merely exercising her right to speak freely?"

"May it please your lordship," Sims objected, "the witness has already answered."

"Sustained," the judge said, frowning at Savidge. "Counsel will refrain from badgering the witness."

Savidge's face tightened. "Thank you, Your Honor. Inspector, prior to the raid on the newspaper, you ordered the employees to be followed. You observed Miss Conway, you say?"

"I took it to be my duty to do so. And Yuri Messenko. The Hyde Park bomber," he added.

"Ah, yes." Savidge grinned bleakly. "You were there when the bomb exploded, I understand."

"I was. Some hundred paces behind. It happened at Hyde Park Corner, not far from Buckingham Palace," the inspector added helpfully.

"I see," Savidge said. "Messenko was carrying a satchel, was he not?"

"Yes."

Savidge leaned forward. "Well, then, Inspector, tell the jury why, if you knew this satchel-carrying Anarchist to pose a dangerous threat, you allowed him to approach Buckingham Palace. The King and Queen were arriving back from the Cathedral just at this time, were they not?"

The inspector frowned uncomfortably. "Messenko wasn't *that* close to the Palace. Quite a distance, actually."

"But you were not close enough to *him* to prevent him from exploding his bomb."

"Well, no, I—"

Savidge smiled tightly. "Just out of curiosity, Inspector,

how close to the Palace would you have allowed this dangerous bomber to approach?"

A titter went around the courtroom. Inspector Ashcraft
flushed. Sims jumped up. "Object, my lord! Calls for the
witness to speculate."

Savidge raised his eyebrows. "I wasn't asking the inspector to speculate, my lord. I quite naturally assumed that he
had some sort of plan to keep this dangerous man from
approaching too near the King and Queen. However, I do
not wish to embarrass him."

Kate smiled. The man next to her guffawed, and another
titter made the rounds.

"If Mr. Savidge is through with this witness," the judge
said, "the inspector may step down."

"Just one thing more, my lord," Savidge said. He was
shuffling the papers in front of him as if he were looking for
something. "It is true, Inspector, that you did not accom-
pany the officers who made the searches?"

"Yes," the inspector said, obviously relieved at the change
of subject. "I was otherwise engaged. On important police
business."

"I see," Savidge said. Still looking down at the table and
riffling papers, he said, "Then you have not handled any of
the evidence that the officers discovered?"

Inspector Ashcraft shook his head.

Savidge looked up. "I didn't quite hear you, Inspector.
Could you repeat your answer?"

"No," the inspector snapped, out of patience. "I did not
handle any of the evidence."

"Thank you," Savidge said absently, moving his papers
around again. "That will be all for the moment." As the
inspector stepped out of the box, Savidge added, "I reserve
the right, however, to recall this witness." He glanced at
Sims. "If my esteemed friend has no objection."

The prosecutor looked amused. "No objection at all," he

said in a supercilious tone, and called Detective Finney, who was sworn in. In a series of questions, Sims took the detective through the surveillance, the raid on the *Clarion,* and the subsequent searches of the living quarters of the men arrested at the newspaper, during which the bombs had been discovered, in each case hidden under the bed.

"And are these the bombs themselves?" the prosecutor inquired, gesturing at the three ginger-beer bottles he had placed in evidence as Exhibit B. The bottles, Kate saw, were quite ordinary stoneware bottles with what appeared to be screw-on caps. Kate saw that Charles was leaning forward, looking at them intently.

"Objection," Savidge said. "My honorable friend has not yet demonstrated that these so-called bombs are anything other than what they appear to be—that is, ginger-beer bottles."

"I will rephrase," Sims said with an upward roll of his eyes. "You collected these three pieces of evidence in the rooms of the defendants, did you not?"

"I did," Finney said.

"And did you assume, when you saw them, that they might . . . blow up?"

"Oh, yes, sir," said Finney earnestly. "They could've contained shock-sensitive explosives, y'see. Nitroglycerine, maybe."

"What did you do? I mean, how exactly did you handle these objects, which you assumed to be dangerous?"

"I labeled each bottle with the date and location. The bottle found in Mr. Mouffetard's room is labeled *one.* That found in Mr. Kopinski's room, *two.* In Mr. Gould's flat, *three.* Mouffetard and Kopinski live in the same rooming house, in Halsey Street," he added.

Sims indicated the bottles. "These are your labels?"

"Right, sir. Then I placed each bottle in a straw-lined crate and put the crate into a bomb box."

"A *bomb* box?" the prosecutor asked, widening his eyes dramatically. "Please tell the jury what you mean by that term."

"It's a box made of special, heavy-duty metal, designed to contain a possible explosion. The boxes were transported to the Yard, where an expert chemist examined the bottles and their contents, which turned out to be——"

"Thank you," Sims said, holding up his hand. "We'll let the chemist tell us what he found." He pointed to a stack of papers and several books. "This Anarchist literature, which I have entered as Exhibit C—you found it in Mr. Kopinski's room?"

"Yes. The papers advertise an Anarchist meeting. The books are by Anarchists named Kropotkin and Bakunin."

"Books advocating violence against the state?"

Finney nodded violently. "Oh, yes, indeed, sir. Very much so, sir."

"And one more found object." Sims pointed to another bottle. "Exhibit D. Please tell his lordship and the members of the jury what it is and where you found it."

"Bottle of glycerine, sir. Doctor Gabriel's Pure Medicinal Glycerine. I found it when I searched the newspaper office."

"Thank you," said Sims. "You may step down—unless, of course, my estimable friend Mr. Savidge has questions."

"I suppose I may have one or two," Savidge said, rising slowly. "Prior to the raid on the *Clarion*, the newspaper's employees were followed. How long did you say you followed the suspects, Detective Finney?"

Finney thought. "For about a fortnight, I'd say."

"A fortnight before the explosion in Hyde Park?"

"Yes. Maybe more."

"So you were following these persons for a fortnight or more for no other reason than that they wished to exercise *the right of the free press*?" As he spoke, his voice rose. The last few words were spoken with a flinty emphasis.

Finney looked uncomfortable. "I wouldn't put it that way."

"I would," Savidge said. "I certainly would. But never mind. Let's talk about these three ginger-beer bottles that have been entered into evidence. Did either of the officers with you handle the bottles?"

"No, sir." Finney squared his shoulders, assuming a brave look. "I was the only one. If something blew up, I didn't want them to get hurt."

"A commendable caution, I'm sure," Savidge remarked in a dry tone. "You testified that you applied the labels to the bottles. Where did you do this?"

Detective Finney smiled. "Right on the side, sir." The spectators tittered.

Savidge smiled. "Very good, Detective, very good, indeed. Where were you when you applied the labels?"

"In the defendants' rooms, sir. I labeled 'em as I found 'em."

"Thank you. You testified that you handled the bottles with care. How exactly did you handle them?"

Finney frowned. "Sir?"

"Did you pick them up by the base?" Savidge asked patiently. "By the neck? Did you cradle them in your hands? Did you wear gloves?"

"No gloves." Finney's grin was crooked. "But I was careful. Didn't want to get blown to pieces, y'see."

"I do see," Savidge said. He turned away as if to sit down, and the detective, obviously relieved, took a step backward preparatory to leaving the box. The prosecutor opened his mouth to call the next witness, but Savidge turned quickly, catching them both off their guard.

"And how about fingerprints, Detective Finney? Since fingerprint evidence prevailed in this very courtroom only two days ago, we must not neglect it. I don't suppose you made an effort to wipe the bottles clean of any fingerprints that may have been left by persons who handled them prior to your discovery?"

"Wipe them clean?" Finney darted a surprised look at the prosecutor. "No, I didn't see any reason to—"

"Very good, Detective. Now, then, did you make any effort to refrain from leaving your fingerprints on the bottles?"

Kate noticed that the judge seemed to be listening with a greater interest.

Finney frowned. "Well, no. I had to put on the labels, y'see, which means that—"

"So we are likely to find your fingerprints on all three of these bottles?"

"I suppose," Finney said, now quite clearly nettled. "But I don't know what you're—"

Sims had gotten to his feet. "I would like to ask my estimable friend what he—"

"Thank you, Detective," Savidge said. "That will be all."

The judge was leaning forward, a slight frown on his face. "Does counsel for the defense wish to explain to the jury what fingerprints are? I rather think that most of them are puzzled."

"I do indeed, but not at the present time, may it please your lordship," Savidge replied. "I expect to have occasion to do so later."

"Very well." The judge took out his gold watch and consulted. "Twenty minutes to the luncheon adjournment." He peered down at the prosecution. "Mr. Sims? Will that be sufficient time to present your next witness?"

"I believe so, Your Honor," Sims replied. With a sidelong glance at Savidge, he added, "Unless my honored colleague plans a lengthy cross-examination."

Savidge smiled.

"We'll risk it," the judge said, and tapped his gavel. "Proceed, Mr. Sims."

"Call Mr. George Baker," the prosecution said.

Mr. George Baker, sworn, identified himself as a chemist employed by Scotland Yard to conduct routine chemical analyses. He had, he testified, analyzed the contents of three ginger-beer bottles brought to him by Detective Finney.

"And what did your analysis reveal, Mr. Baker?" asked Sims.

Mr. Baker spoke with the precision that Kate might have expected from a chemist. "In the bottle labeled *one*, I found two hundred and ten milliliters of nitric acid. In the bottle labeled *two*, I found two hundred and fifty of the same substance. In the bottle labeled *three*, I found a hundred and seventy-five milliliters."

"A little over a pint, all told." Sims's face was somber. He seemed to suppress a small shudder. "And how might an Anarchist use nitric acid? As a weapon, I mean."

"In concentrated form, it can cause severe burns—thrown into a person's face, for instance. And it is an active ingredient of nitroglycerine, a well-known explosive."

"I see." Sims paused. "And to make nitroglycerine, you also need—"

"Glycerine, of course." At this elementary answer, Mr. Baker smiled in a self-deprecating way.

The courtroom buzzed. The judge rapped his gavel sharply. Sims raised his voice over the hubbub. "You've had an opportunity to analyze the contents of the bottle labeled Exhibit C, Mr. Baker?"

"Yes. It contains glycerine."

"So the Anarchists had, ready at hand, the ingredients of a powerful explosive. Is that not correct?"

"That's correct, sir. And nitroglycerine is the explosive compound in dynamite."

There was an audible gasp in the court, and several small squeals from the more fashionably-dressed of the ladies. One fanned herself, while another appeared to be searching in her reticule for her salts. The journalists and artists along the wall were scribbling and sketching madly. Kate looked at Charles and saw that he wore a faint smile.

The prosecutor cast a sympathetic glance at the spectators. "But there is nothing to fear from these bottles, I understand, since the substances are not in combination. The ladies in this court are safe, are they not?"

"Yes," Baker said dryly, "they are safe."

"However, since each of these four bottles contains an ingredient of an explosive, each therefore falls under the sanctions of the Explosives Act." He put on a pair of reading glasses, took a sheet of paper from his assistant, and read aloud, " 'Explosives are to be defined as any apparatus or substance used or adapted for causing, or aiding in causing, any explosion.' Is that correct?"

"That is correct."

Sims cast a triumphant glance in the direction of the defense. "Then, sir, we are justified in calling these containers of explosives 'bombs,' are we not?"

"I believe so, sir," Baker said.

"That will be all, Mr. Baker," Sims said conclusively, and swept to his seat.

Savidge rose. "I have several questions of the witness."

The judge pursed his lips. "You *will* be brief, won't you, Counsel?"

Savidge bowed. "I fear I cannot promise, my lord. However, I shall certainly try to—"

The judge gave an audible sigh. "Proceed."

"Very well. Mr. Baker, the nitric acid that you found in the bottles labeled *one, two,* and *three.* Does it have any purpose other than the manufacture of explosive?"

The chemist spoke somewhat reluctantly. "Nitric acid has many industrial uses related to metallurgy. It is also used to make certain fertilizers."

"It could be used to etch metal printing plates, could it not?"

Mr. Baker was wary. "So I understand."

"So it might not be surprising if nitric acid were found in the possession of a printer? And what about glycerine?"

"Glycerine," Mr. Baker acknowledged slowly, "has a number of applications related to medicine."

"It is used in soap, is it not? And in other cleaners? Could not Dr. Gabriel's Pure Medicinal Glycerine also be used to remove printers' ink from hands and equipment?"

"If you're suggesting that—"

"I am only suggesting, Mr. Baker, that these substances have many innocent uses. Wouldn't you agree?"

"I suppose. But in combination—"

"But the ingredients were *not* in combination," Savidge retorted sharply, "or so the learned counsel for the prosecution has assured us. That is correct, is it not?"

Mr. Baker sighed. "That is correct."

"Nor did any of one of the three defendants have in his possession all the ingredients required to concoct an explosive?"

"I . . . don't believe so."

"Very good," Savidge said, with the air of a man who is finally getting somewhere. "Now, tell us how you handled these bottles."

"Delicately. I had no way of knowing whether they might contain an unstable explosive compound." Baker paused. "However, once I unscrewed the stoppers of the ginger-beer bottles, there was little need to run an analysis. In fact, I was glad I was wearing rubber gloves."

Savidge looked puzzled. "What exactly do you mean by that?"

"Nitric acid fumes are very strong and quite distinctive. As I mentioned earlier, in concentrated form, the substance causes serious burns to the skin. It turns a bright yellow and begins to peel off after a little time."

Kate noticed that Charles, who had been watching the proceedings intently, was writing again in his notebook.

"So you never touched these bottles with your bare fingers?" Savidge asked.

"Absolutely not," Mr. Baker replied, with emphasis.

"Thank you." Savidge looked up at the bench. "That concludes my examination of this witness, if your lordship pleases."

"I am indeed pleased," the judge said, with obvious relief. "We will break for lunch, and return at two P.M." He banged his gavel sharply. "Court is in recess."

CHAPTER TWENTY-SEVEN

<hr/>

Until the opening of the first tea shops, there was nowhere a lady could have a meal by herself, nowhere for women to meet their friends outside their own homes; it was inconceivable for them to go to a public restaurant unescorted by husband or brother. . . . Roger Fulford in Votes for Women *contends that the tea shop was an integral part of the Women's Suffrage Movement.*

Alison Adburgham,
Shops and Shopping: 1800–1914

Kate had thought that she and Charles might have lunch together. He seemed, however, to be going off with Savidge, probably to talk over what had transpired that morning, and she did not like to intrude.

Still thinking about what she had heard that morning, she made her way out of the courtroom, left the Old Bailey, and walked the short distance to Ludgate Circus, where she chanced with pleasure upon a white-and-gold-fronted J. Lyons & Co. Ltd. tea shop, next door to Salmon & Gluckstein's tobacconist shop.

The coffeehouses that had proliferated so widely in London since the 1650s had always been an almost exclusively male preserve, while the tea shops that had begun to spring up during the 1880s were principally the domain of women, respectable places where they could meet their friends and enjoy a bite to eat while out shopping. The first Lyons shop had been built in Piccadilly in 1894 and had become immediately and enormously popular; this one, Kate saw as she entered, was new and much larger than it had looked from the street. It had a flower garden decor, with plants hanging from the ceilings and potted palms in the corners. Each table was covered with a white tablecloth and centered with a fresh bouquet of tiny roses. The place was quite crowded, the air filled with a medley of perfumes and the sound of light voices. Here and there were a few young men, probably from the newspapers along Fleet Street, but the tables were mostly filled with women. Kate saw an empty table against the far wall, in front of the lace-curtained front window, to which she made her way and sat down.

In a moment, the waitress brought her a menu. She ordered a salmon salad sandwich, a piece of marmalade cake, and a pot of Earl Grey tea, and leaned back to enjoy the sight of the busy street filled with pedestrians, omnibuses, and cabs, as well as quite a number of motor lorries. As she watched, she thought about the events of the morning. She was not an experienced trial-goer, but it seemed to her that the judge had favored the prosecution in his ruling, especially in that business about not naming the informant. It seemed terribly underhanded and tricky to her. What if this so-called informant were only a convenient fiction to ensure that certain persons became "suspects"? Or what if an informant had an ax to grind, and wanted, for his own reasons, to deliver the "suspects" into the hands of the police? If the defense couldn't question the informant, there was no way to ensure that the truth—

The waitress arrived with Kate's tea in a gold-trimmed white china teapot. And at that very moment Nellie Lovelace, looking quite forlorn, opened the door and entered, standing hesitantly just inside.

"Nellie!" Kate called, waving to catch her attention. "Nellie, over here!"

Nellie saw her and came toward her. "Hello, Kate." She seemed less than enthusiastic, or perhaps she was only weary. She did look tired, Kate thought—exhausted, in fact. Her face was gray and there were dark circles under her eyes. She was wearing a white shirtwaist blouse and a brown short jacket and brown skirt. The only color in her costume was a red tie and a red felt hat, its single feather hanging limply. She looked very young and vulnerable, almost like a schoolgirl.

"Do sit down and join me, Nellie," Kate said. "What a lucky chance, to run into you this way. You've been at the theater, I suppose." The Royal Strand was not far away, on Aldwych. She motioned to the waitress to bring another cup. "You'll have lunch, won't you? It will be my treat."

"Yes," Nellie said, sinking gratefully onto the chair. "How very kind of you to ask, Kate. I will have lunch. I know it's my turn to treat, but I'm afraid I'm a little short of funds." She asked Kate what she was having, and then repeated the order to the waitress. "What are you doing here, Kate?"

"I came for the trial," Kate said, and added, at Nellie's blank look, "the Anarchists' trial. You remember, the three men who were arrested at the *Clarion* the day Lottie escaped across the roof."

"Oh, yes, of course," Nellie said. "So much has gone on in my life in the past few weeks that I had quite forgot." She sighed heavily. "You haven't heard from Lottie, I don't suppose."

"No, I haven't," Kate said, and picked up the pot to pour Nellie a cup of tea. "I thought she might attend the trial. In disguise, of course," she added with a chuckle, "since the police have a warrant for her arrest. I didn't see anyone, male or female, who remotely resembled her, however. You've not heard, then?"

"Not a word." Nellie busied herself with lemon and sugar. "I've moved, though. I left an address, but she might not have bothered."

"You've moved?" Kate asked in surprise. "You've left your sweet little house? Where are you living?"

"At the Rehearsal Club, in Leicester Square." Nellie met Kate's eyes, her own lost and empty. "I've been replaced by my understudy, Kate. I'm not Princess Soo-Soo any longer." She shrugged her shoulders as if to say that it didn't matter, but the tone of her voice revealed otherwise. "I'm nobody, actually."

"Oh, dear," Kate said. "I'm so sorry." She wanted to ask what had happened, but felt awkward about it.

"Yes," Nellie said, picking up her teacup. "Well, I suppose it could have been helped, although I don't quite see how. I finally found some work at the Alhambra." She smiled bleakly. "In the chorus. But it's enough to pay for my room and board, and the women at the club are awfully nice, and so willing to help out someone who's in a spot of temporary trouble. I'm hoping that something better will come along."

"Well, then," Kate said with forced cheerfulness, lifting her teacup. "Here's to your new situation, and to the something better. I'm sure it's just around the corner."

"Cheers," Nellie said, raising her cup in salute. But her hand was trembling and the tea slopped down the front of her blouse. "Oh, drat!" she exclaimed. "Now I've gone and made a mess!" She snatched up a napkin and dabbed at her blouse, not making much headway. When she looked up, her eyes were filled with tears.

"My dear," Kate said quietly, "are you ill?"

Nellie put down the napkin. "No," she said, "at least I

don't think so. But I— But things—" She stopped, took a deep, ragged breath, and lowered her voice. "To speak frankly, Kate, I'm afraid I'm in . . . the family way."

Kate stared at Nellie in surprise, mentally counting the days since the last time they'd had dinner together at the Pioneer Club, when Nellie had told her what had happened between her and Jack London. "It's awfully soon, isn't it, Nellie?" she asked gently. "You can't be sure yet."

"Perhaps." Nellie colored deeply, biting her lip. "But I'm late. By nearly two weeks, now."

"Perhaps it's the strain of moving," Kate suggested. "And the new work. Too many changes all at once. I know from my own experience how we are affected by change."

"I suppose it's possible," Nellie said slowly. She lowered her glance, the color spreading from her cheeks to her throat. "Oh, I shouldn't have told you, Kate! You'll think I—"

"Fiddlesticks," Kate said, reaching across the table to take her hand. "Of course you must tell me what troubles you." She knew that Nellie must be uncertain and fearful, and she couldn't help feeling that she bore some of the responsibility for what had happened. If she had warned Nellie that Jack London was married, Nellie might have reconsidered her decision to accept the man's invitation to supper. She added, "I must know, so I can help."

Nellie's eyes were brimming. "Help?" she whispered. "If I'm truly—" She swallowed, and Kate felt that she could not bring herself to say the word *pregnant*. "If that's what it is, no one can help me. How can I work, Kate? How will I live? I can't support a child and care for it as well." She didn't say the word *workhouse*, but Kate knew that's what she must be thinking. That was where unmarried women went to give birth to their babies.

The waitress arrived with the sandwiches and cake and set their plates in front of them, giving Kate time to arrive at a swift decision. When she had gone, Kate said, in a practical tone, "If that's what it is, if you're pregnant, I mean, I'm sure I can help, in a great many ways. But we won't know anything for certain for a few more weeks. Maybe it's not true."

Nellie shook her head. "You're just trying to comfort me." She said it with a despairing sadness, as if comfort were a false commodity, something not to be trusted.

"Yes, that's exactly what I'm trying to do," Kate replied briskly. "Friends aren't good for much if they're not willing to comfort each other." With a decisive gesture, she picked up her sandwich. "Now, both of us must eat. I'm starving, and I know you'll feel better after you've had something."

The two women ate silently for a few minutes, and when they had finished their sandwiches and begun on their marmalade cake, Nellie said, in a very low voice, "Thank you, Kate. I do feel better."

"I hoped you would," Kate said. She leaned forward, feeling a deep compassion for this young woman, who might be facing the most difficult and dangerous period in a woman's life with no family to help and frighteningly few resources. "I want you to promise me that you won't worry about this, Nellie. Worrying doesn't accomplish anything. And I want you to keep in touch with me. I want to know what is happening." She paused and added, "I want to know *everything*."

"But if I . . . if I'm truly—" She gulped, her eyes large and frightened. "What will I do, Kate? Where will I go?"

Nellie looked as if she were once again slipping into despair, and Kate took charge. "If you are, truly, I have just the solution. You'll come to be with me at Bishop's Keep, for as long as you like. You can help Alice Byran with her matron's work at the school, and help me with my own work." She put her hand on Nellie's arm. "And in the meantime, you are *not* to worry. Do you hear?"

"Oh, Kate," Nellie whispered, blinking fast. "I feel just

as I did when you came to Miller's Court, to that awful, dirty alley where I was living, and offered me a new hope for the future—a hope that I could use my talent to help myself. How very long ago that seems!"

"Yes, it was long ago," Kate replied, thinking to herself that it could not be above four years. But four years was a very long time to a young woman who was scarcely twenty-one. How hard it had been for Nellie, then, to trust her, to believe that her help was offered freely, with love and respect and without condition. "And now you are grown into a lovely and quite talented young woman, with the whole world before you," she went on in an encouraging tone. "You've enjoyed a starring role in the theater, and you will again, once you've come through this sticky spot. You need to give yourself time, that's all."

"I wish I could believe you," Nellie said wistfully.

"Believe me," Kate replied, with emphasis. She drank the last of her tea. "Now, I have a request, Nellie. I need to go back to the courtroom, but I'm anxious for company. Won't you come with me? When the day is finished, we'll take a cab and I'll drop you at Leicester Square on my way back to Sibley House."

For a moment, Kate thought that Nellie was going to refuse. Then she managed a crooked smile. "I'd like to come with you, Kate. They say that court is sometimes as good as theater."

Kate put down her napkin and pushed back her chair. "Well, I don't know about that. But this trial is interesting, to say the least. And if you ask me, the chief villains may not be the defendants, but the prosecutor and the judge— and quite possibly a Scotland Yard inspector."

"That sounds like quite a cast," Nellie said, more cheerfully. She rose. "And a performance I don't want to miss."

CHAPTER TWENTY-EIGHT

"I must do my work in my own way," declared the Chief
Inspector. *"When it comes to that I would deal with the
devil himself, and take the consequences. There are
things not fit for everybody to know."*

Joseph Conrad,
The Secret Agent, 1907

During the luncheon interval, Charles and Savidge had
repaired to a nearby coffeehouse, where over steak-and-
kidney pie, they reviewed Charles's notes of the morning and
discussed the strategy for the afternoon, when the defense,
presumably, would present its witnesses. Savidge remarked
that the prosecution's case had gone very much as he had
expected. Sims had put forward no surprises, and if the afternoon went well, he was optimistic. "Although," he added,
"one never knows about a jury. They do strange things." And
he went on, over coffee and dessert, to several recent
cases in which juries had done the unexpected.

Charles agreed—one never knew about a jury. And the
defense hadn't been helped by the headlines in the morning
papers, announcing a new terrorist bombing threat, contained in a letter sent to the governments of both France and
Great Britain. It was within two days, as well, of the first

anniversary of the assassination of the American president, McKinley, and another article rehearsed that terrible event. Those members of the jury who had read the newspapers might find it difficult to separate the facts of this case from the growing national fear—and their own personal fears— of anarchy and revolution. And the situation certainly wasn't helped by the fact that Mouffetard was French and Kopinski Russian and that both of them looked the part of Anarchists. Worse, Savidge felt that neither could be put on the stand for fear that the prosecution might trap them in a damaging admission.

Back in the courtroom for the afternoon, Charles took a seat at the defense table, where he would be more readily available for consultation on the fingerprint evidence if Savidge needed him. He turned to look at the spectator sections, which seemed to include more working-class people this afternoon. He saw no one he knew, except for a rakish dark-haired man whose face looked vaguely familiar, although he could not place it. Charlotte Conway was nowhere in evidence, although he had half-expected that she might appear, perhaps disguised. Then he saw Kate, in the second row of the spectators' section, with Nellie Lovelace. He lifted his hand in a wave, feeling that the room—ill-lit and oppressively formal in its show of judicial authority—was somehow brightened by her presence. Odd, that, he thought. Kate could do nothing to affect the outcome of the trial, but her being there changed his feeling about what was to come, and he settled back into his seat with a greater cheerfulness. The prosecutor swept into the room with a confident step, the judge entered and took his place at the bench, and court was convened.

Sims called his final witness, who proved to be Mrs. Georgiana Battle, a green-grocer and the landlady of the Hampstead Road premises where the *Clarion* was located. Mrs. Battle—a gray-haired woman of late middle age with a smallpox-scarred face and a buxom figure nearly bursting the buttons of her rumpled navy serge—claimed to have overheard the defendants discussing the use of a bomb to kill King Edward and Queen Alexandra on Coronation Day. She had heard this conversation, she testified, through the wall that separated her shop from the newspaper.

" 'We mean to kill 'em,' wuz wot they said," she reported, in ringing tones. " 'We mean t' blow the Royal pair t' bits.' " She took out a dirty white handkerchief and applied it to her nose, which was liberally laced with broken red veins. "That's wot they said, egzacly, sir, 'orrible as it is t' 'ear."

"I'm sure it must have indeed been horrible," said Sims sympathetically. "But you kept your wits about you, didn't you, Mrs. Battle. You reported the conversatioin to the police, did you not?"

"I told 'em." Mrs. Battle nodded so emphatically that the stuffed robin on her black hat began to bob back and forth. "I sart'nly told 'em. I wud 'ate t' think—if the King an' Queen wuz blowed up—that I might've pervented it!"

"Thank you," Sims said. "I'm sure I speak for all of us when I commend you for doing your civic duty." He made a magnanimous gesture toward the defense counsel. "Your witness, Counselor."

Charles frowned, thinking that Sims must be confident of success, or he would not have been quite so careless with this witness. Savidge stood, hands in his pockets. "I don't recall your saying, Mrs. Battle," he remarked casually, "when this conversation took place. P'rhaps you would be so good as to tell us precisely when it was."

Mrs. Battle assumed a searching look, as if she were trying to remember. " 'Fraid I can't say for sartin'. Some time b'fore the King wuz crowned."

"I see. Do you recall when you told the police what you heard? Was it after Coronation Day?"

"Yes," she said definitively. "After that man blew 'imself up in the park."

"I see. So you heard this threatening conversation *before* Coronation Day, but you failed to tell the police until *after* Coronation Day?"

Mrs. Battle frowned. "I 'spose, but I—"

"Thank you. Now, then, perhaps you can tell us what these men looked like. You say there were three of them?"

"I couldn't see wot they looked like," she said.

"Oh? Why?"

" 'Cuz I can't see through the wall," she said, in scornful triumph. Several spectators laughed.

"Oh, of course," Savidge replied, in a chagrined tone. "I do apologize. I had forgotten that you were listening through the wall." He frowned. "On reflection, however, that seems a bit odd. Do you make a regular practice of applying your ear to the back wall of your shop?"

"Well, I does it sometimes," Mrs. Battle replied reluctantly.

"Sometimes. When you are paid to do so, perhaps?"

Mrs. Battle's glance went to the prosecutor, sitting at the table. He tented his fingers and glanced up at the ceiling. She looked back at Savidge. "Sometimes," she said, now very reluctantly.

"And did the police pay you on *this* occasion?"

Mrs. Battle now looked to the judge for rescue. "Does I 'ave t' answer?" she demanded.

The judge glanced at the prosecutor, frowned, and replied, "Yes," quite firmly. Apparently, Mrs. Battle was not deemed as important as the Yard's other informant, and was not to be protected.

"I wuz paid," she acknowledged sourly.

"Thank you." Savidge smiled. "I hope you feel that you were well paid for your trouble. Were you paid in advance, or when you provided the information?"

Mrs. Battle again glanced at the judge, who nodded curtly. "When I told 'em wot I 'eard," she said in a low voice.

"I see." Savidge paused. "And you are certain that these three men"—with a gesture to the defendants—"are the three you heard?"

"They are."

"Since you couldn't see them, I suppose you recognized their voices?"

Mrs. Battle nodded. "That's right. They've got an accent, not like you 'n' me. Furr'ners, all of 'em."

"And Mr. Gould—he was speaking with an accent?"

"Right again."

Savidge frowned. "But I don't believe Mr. Gould is a foreigner. He was born, I believe, here in the City, of British parents." He looked up at the box where the defendants were seated on wooden chairs. "Mr. Gould, say something, if you please, sir."

Gould rose and spoke the words of the Royal anthem, distinctly and in cultivated English. "God save our gracious King, long live our noble King, God save the King." He bowed and sat down again.

A wave of laughter swept the courtroom, and Kate heard several loud guffaws. Mr. Sims looked apoplectic. The judge banged his gavel. "Order!" he exclaimed angrily. "Mr. Savidge, you are not to try that trick again. This is not a theater."

Behind Charles, a man said, "You could have fooled me," and went on laughing.

"I apologize to your lordship," Savidge said with a bow. He turned to the witness. "Mr. Gould doesn't sound like a foreigner to me, Mrs. Battle," he said mildly. "He sounds very like a Londoner. Was his one of the *foreign* voices you heard and recognized?"

Mrs. Battle looked confused. "Well, maybe 'e wuzn't one of 'em, then. Or maybe 'e wuz there but wuzn't talkin'."

"I see. It does seem to me, though, that if Mr. Gould were silent, you could not know whether he was among the men—the *three* men—you claim to have overheard. But never mind. Let us focus on the others. You must have frequent contact with them—enough to know what their voices sound like. Are you on friendly terms with Mr. Mouffetard and Mr. Kopinski?"

Mrs. Battle bristled at this suggestion that she might be affiliated with Anarchists. "I sees them most ever' day. I'm sart'nly not *friends* with 'em."

"And do they make a practice of engaging you in conversation?"

Mrs. Battle considered. "No, they us'ally ignores me." She sniffed. "Hoity-toity like."

Savidge turned away from her and spoke in a low but audible voice. "How is it, then, that you are able to identify their voices?"

Mrs. Battle leaned forward, the robin bobbing frantically. "Wot's that ye said? Speak up, if ye please. I'm a little 'ard o' 'earin'."

The significance of Mrs. Battle's response was not lost on the audience, which chuckled. Members of the jury exchanged smiles and glances. The prosecutor was sitting quite still, his lips tight, his face set.

Savidge turned. "You couldn't hear my voice, Mrs. Battle, when it was perfectly audible to members of the jury and, I daresay, to his lordship. And yet you testify that you were able to identify voices you heard through a wall?" He stepped around to the front of the table, his expression fierce. "And that you heard the very words these voices were speaking, so that you could report the information to the police and be *paid* for it?"

Mrs. Battle reddened. "Well . . ."

"Justice may be blind," the judge remarked sternly, "but it is not hard of hearing. You can go to jail for perjury, Mrs. Battle. And giving false information to the police is a crime."

Mrs. Battle shrank back, her eyes growing large. "I . . ."

"Perhaps, now that you have had time to think about the matter," Savidge said, "you are not certain that these three men are the men you might have heard through the wall."

Mrs. Battle swallowed hard. "I . . . I guess maybe they're not," she said painfully. "It wuz hard t' tell. Through the wall an' all."

"And perhaps," Savidge persisted, "given your difficulty in hearing, you are now not positive that you heard anyone even mention the word *bomb*. Is that possible?"

Mrs. Battle's pockmarked face was dully mottled. She lowered her head. "It's possible, I 'spose," she said in a low voice. "S'pose I might've misunderstood."

"And perhaps it is even possible that you heard nothing at all through the wall?"

"I . . ." Mrs. Battle applied her handkerchief again. "Yes," she whispered.

Savidge, his lips tight pressed together, his eyes narrowed, glanced deliberately at the jury, as if to ask, *You do understand that this witness lied, don't you?* He turned back to the bench. "I have no more questions, my lord."

The judge's jaw was set, his expression angry. "The jury will disregard the testimony of this witness," he growled. "Mr. Sims, do you have any other witnesses?"

Sims rose and shook his head, his face nearly as red as Mrs. Battle's. "This completes the case for the prosecution, Your Honor," he said. Charles could almost feel sorry for him—but not quite.

"The defense may proceed," the judge said. "Call your first witness, Counsel."

"Call Adam Gould," Savidge said.

Adam, sworn and under Savidge's questioning, testifed that he had been employed by the Amalgamated Society of Railway Servants for five years. He was not an employee of the *Clarion,* but on the day of his arrest, he had come to the newspaper office in order to take Miss Conway to lunch. No, he was not an Anarchist, although he believed in the importance of social change. Yes, he was slightly acquainted with the man who had been killed in Hyde Park, but he knew nothing of any plot concerning bombs. He had absolutely no idea (said with great emphasis) how a ginger-beer bottle containing nitric acid came to be found in his flat.

In cross-examination, Sims inquired pointedly whether Mr. Gould's belief in social change included the use of the strike as a means to achieve it. "Yes, sir," Adam replied with great firmness, "as long as the strike is peaceful. I have never advocated violence." Adam was followed to the witness box by a union leader who testified to his character and hard work and his moderate position as an advocate for change. When he was finished, Charles thought that Adam Gould, at least, had appeared in a rather good light.

"Call Mrs. Sharp," Savidge said.

Mrs. Sharp, a tall woman with an uncompromising countenance, dressed in widow's black, was Adam Gould's landlady. She testified that Mr. Gould had occupied her second-floor flat for the past four years, and had always paid his rent on time. Unfortunately, however, his second-floor flat was not entirely secure, for the lock on the door was of the type that might be opened with a skeleton key. It would have been possible for some unknown person, unobserved, to have taken the back stair to the second floor and have entered the place, either to take something or to leave something.

Under the prosecutor's cross-examination, however, Mrs. Sharp had to admit that she could not say for a fact that anyone *had* entered Mr. Gould's flat. And when the landlord of the rooming house in Halsey Street had testified to the same effect—that neither Mr. Mouffetard's room nor Mr. Kopinski's was secure from entry and that any of the boarders in the house, or anyone from the outside for that matter, might have had access to the rooms—he, too, had to admit under Mr. Sim's severe cross-examination that he could not declare for a certainty that the rooms had been entered. Charles thought that while the testimony might have raised a question in the minds of the jury as to how the so-called bombs had turned up in the rooms, it had not gone far enough. He knew, however, that Savidge had another trick or two up his sleeve, and that it was time to go after the ginger-beer bottles.

"Call Sergeant Charles Stockley Collins," Savidge said.

Slowly, and with obvious discomfort, a pleasant-faced man of military bearing, wearing gray tweeds and neatly-trimmed gray chin whiskers, stepped into the witness box, was sworn, and gave his name. He was employed, he said, by New Scotland Yard, where he held the rank of sergeant. This announcement provoked a loud buzzing in the courtroom.

"Sergeant Collins," Savidge said, "does not wish to testify for the defense. We request leave of the Court, therefore, to treat him as an adverse witness."

The prosecutor rose to his feet, stood indecisively for a moment, then sat down again without saying anything. He leaned over to confer with his associate, who shook his head with apparent puzzlement. It appeared to Charles that Sims had not recognized Charles Collins's name, which had been properly entered into the witness list. Inspector Ashcraft, seated behind the prosecution's table, was staring darkly at Sergeant Collins, who seemed to be avoiding the inspector's glance. The judge rapped his gavel. "Let the record so show."

"Thank you, my lord," Savidge replied. "Now, then, Sergeant Collins, you are, I believe, an expert in dactaloscopy—in the forensic science of fingerprinting."

"I am," the sergeant said. "I am the head of the Yard's fingerprinting department." Collins appeared more comfortable now that he had been declared an adverse witness,

Charles thought, as if he could not be blamed for anything he might say. Charles hoped that were true, at any rate. He respected the sergeant and did not want him to suffer any professional disadvantage from his testimony today.

"Very good, Sergeant," Savidge said. "Earlier, his lordship suggested that members of the jury might appreciate an explanation of the term *fingerprint*. I should much appreciate it if you would be so good as to explain this science."

Sergeant Collins managed the explanation with skill and aplomb, explaining that the ridged lines that appeared in loops and whorls on the tips of the fingers, while they might be classified in a limited number of general patterns, were absolutely unique to each finger and, more importantly, to each individual, man, woman, and child. All people's fingertips carried a coating of perspiration and oils. When the fingers came into contact with any relatively smooth surface, they left a print of the fingertip ridges, much like that of an inked rubber stamp. When the surface was dusted lightly with a powder, the prints became visible. These could be photographed and the photograph enlarged for easier study. Charles noticed that as Sergeant Collins spoke, the jurors and spectators were holding up their hands, inspecting the tips of their fingers and whispering to one another.

The sergeant continued his explanation. Some fourteen years previously, Sir Francis Galton had developed a system for classifying and identifying fingerprints; the system had been recently improved upon by the Assistant Commissioner of London Police, Edward Henry, and was now in place. Many convicted prisoners had been fingerprinted; every suspect was fingerprinted upon his arrest; and the prints kept on file for possible future use.

Savidge nodded. "Thank you, Sergeant. That was enlightening. However, you have not mentioned the use of fingerprints in a court of law." He paused. "It is true, is it not, that fingerprint identification was recently validated—only two days ago, in fact, and in this very courtroom. Is that not the case?"

Collins nodded, speaking now with an eager pride. "Yes, indeed it is, sir. I am glad to say that Henry Jackson was convicted of burglary on the strength of his left thumb. Put it into paint that was not quite dry on the windowsill of a house he was trying to burgle." He grinned, straightening his shoulders. "I checked the print in the paint against Mr. Jackson's left thumb, which was taken when he was having a bit of a rest in Newgate last year, and it matched. Got seven years, he did, and deserved it, too." The spectators, enjoying Sergeant Collins's pleasure in the conviction of Mr. Jackson, broke into scattered applause.

Savidge chuckled. "Congratulations, Sergeant. You are to be commended for your careful investigation. Without your expertise, a dangerous thief might still be roaming the streets. Clearly, fingerprints deserve special attention in every police investigation." He paused for a moment to let the jury consider this, then went on. "Now, Sergeant, with regard to the defendants in this case. I have entered their fingerprint records as Exhibits E1, 2, and 3. You are familiar with these records?"

Collins became serious again. "Yes, sir. The prints were taken at Holloway Prison, sir."

"And you have examined the ginger-beer bottles entered as Exhibit B."

"I have."

"Since these bottles were discovered in the defendants' rooms, one would quite naturally expect that the defendants had handled them and left their fingerprints. Is that not the case?"

"It is, yes."

"Then tell us what you found, Sergeant. Did all three of the bottles show evidence of the defendants' fingerprints?"

"No, sir."

"No?" Savidge put on a show of being surprised. "Well, then, on which of the bottles *did* you find the defendants' fingerprints?"

"None, sir."

Members of the jury were seen to frown. Savidge appeared even more greatly surprised. "None, Sergeant Collins? None at all? How do you account for that fact?"

"Well, sir, they might have handled the bottles with gloves, or wiped them afterward to prevent leaving finger-prints."

"They might, I suppose, although that's not likely, since most persons do not even know of the existence of these prints. Is there another explanation for an absence of prints?"

"Yes, sir." The sergeant seemed perturbed. "They might not have handled the bottles at all."

"Thank you. Yes, I think we must consider that as a pos-sibility. Now, Sergeant, I should be most grateful if you would tell the jury whose prints you did find on these three bottles."

Sergeant Collins took a deep breath. "There were several of Detective Finney's finger- and thumbprints on each one, especially on the necks."

"Mr. Baker, who performed the chemical analysis, testi-fied that he wore gloves when he handled the bottles, to avoid possible burns from the nitric acid. I don't suppose you found his prints?"

"No, sir."

"Right. Well, then, were there any other fingerprints—other than those belonging to Detective Finney, I mean?"

"Yes, sir. There was a partial fingerprint on the bottle found in Mr. Gould's room."

"That would be Exhibit B3. And where on the bottle did you observe this partial print?"

"Adjacent to the identifying label."

"That would be the label that Detective Finney applied. In fact, it is possible to see only half of the print, is it not?"

"Yes."

"Where is the other half of the print to be found, then?"

"Under the label." The sergeant seemed to speak with increasing reluctance. Charles noticed that several members of the jury were sitting forward in their seats, their attention fastened on the witness.

"And how do you know this, Sergeant?"

"The label was loose enough at the edge to permit me to lift it with a knife blade and dust the surface of the bottle."

"If the print was under the label, that must mean—" Savidge broke off. "You're the expert, Sergeant Collins. Suppose you tell us what it means."

Collins's reluctance was clear. "That the print was on the bottle before Detective Finney applied the label."

"And Detective Finney testified that he applied the labels to the bottles as he found them in the defendants' rooms. This print, therefore, must have been made at some point before Detective Finney discovered the bottle."

"Yes."

"It is mostly likely the print of the person who placed the bottle under the bed, isn't it?"

"I suppose so," the sergeant said. "Yes, sir."

"And whose print is it?"

"I don't know, sir. I did not remove the label to see the entire print."

"You didn't?" Savidge arched his eyebrows. "And why didn't you remove the label?"

The sergeant dropped his glance. "I was instructed not to do so," he said in a low voice.

Savidge leaned forward. "You were instructed not to do so. By whom, Sergeant?"

"By . . . by Inspector Ashcraft, sir."

"By Inspector Ashcraft?" Savidge frowned. "I must say, I

find that puzzling, since one might imagine that the inspector would be anxious to learn whatever can be learned from the fingerprints on the bottles. However, we will leave that for the moment." He turned to the bench. "With your lordship's permission, I should like to ask Sergeant Collins to remove the label, study the fingerprint, and tell us, if he can, the identity of its maker."

Sims jumped angrily to his feet. "Objection! This is pure theatrical show, my lord. And most irregular."

The judge sighed. "Theatrical, yes. Irregular, perhaps. However, I see no reason why the fingerprint evidence should not be obtained, since it seems to be germane to the question of who handled the bottle. The defense may proceed."

Sulkily, Sims dropped back into his chair. Sergeant Collins left the witness box and went to the table where the exhibits were displayed. With a thin-bladed knife, he lifted the edge of the label and peeled it off. Taking a fingerprint kit out of his pocket, he dusted the print with a black powder, revealing it to be continuous under the label. Savidge handed him a magnifying glass.

"Now, Sergeant Collins," he said, "please study the print, and tell us anything you can about it."

Collins bent to the task. After a few moments, he straightened. "I would say that it is a right thumbprint. It is of a class we call a right loop. The ridges all tend to the right and close at the top, you see."

"I see. Well, then. Would you compare that print to Exhibits E1, E2, and E3—the fingerprints of the defendants, which were entered in evidence a few moments ago—and tell the jury whether it belongs to one of the men in the dock."

The spectators stirred restlessly while Sergeant Collins compared the card in his hand to the print on the bottle. At last, he looked up. "It does not belong to any of the defendants. I can say that definitely."

"I see." Savidge went back to the table and picked up another card. "Do you recognize this, Sergeant?" he asked, handing it to the witness. "If so, please identify it."

"It is a card used by Scotland Yard to register the fingerprints of all of the Yard's officers, for the purposes of excluding them."

"Very good. Please note," Savidge said to the jury, "that one side of the card contains ten fingerprints. The individual's name is on the other side of the card." To the clerk, he said. "Enter the card, please, as Exhibit F." He returned to the witness. "Now, then, Sergeant, I should like you to examine the right thumb print on this card and compare it to the one you just obtained from the bottle. Please do not turn the card over. You are not to see the name."

The process took several minutes. Intent on his work and oblivious to the stirrings and whisperings that filled the courtroom, Collins examined the Scotland Yard fingerprint card with a magnifying glass, then returned to the card to which he had transferred the print from the bottle. He repeated the process, then looked up, his brow deeply furrowed.

"Are you ready to tell us what you have learned, Sergeant?" Savidge asked.

"There are sufficient points of comparison to lead me to believe that these prints were made by the same person," the sergeant said slowly. He explained briefly that points of comparison occurred when certain ridges intersected or touched other ridges, and described six of these points on each of the two prints. "I am working under difficult conditions," he added. "Once the print is photographed and enlarged, and working with leisure and a microscope, I would likely discover additional points of comparison."

"We appreciate the difficulties, Sergeant," Savidge said. "You remain confident, do you not, that these two fingerprints belong to the same individual?"

"I do."

"Turn the card over, please, and read the name to the jury."

The spectators watched breathlessly as the sergeant reversed the card, gulped, and turned pale.

The judge leaned forward. "Whose print is it on the bottle, Sergeant?"

"It belongs to Inspector Earnest Ashcraft."

A loud murmur of voices rippled through the court. The prosecutor leaped to his feet, shouting objections. Ashcraft's face was curiously mottled. The judge pounded his gavel. "Order," he commanded. "I will have order in this court!"

"And what do you deduce from this evidence, Sergeant Collins?" Savidge asked, above the noise. The judge pounded his gavel again, and the spectators subsided.

"That Inspector Ashcraft handled the bottle at some point before Detective Finney applied the label."

"My lord, I object!" Sims cried, quite beside himself. "I most strenuously object! We have no assurance that the fingerprints on the card are those of Inspector Ashcraft. The card might have been substituted for or otherwise tampered with. It might—"

"If your lordship pleases," Savidge interjected smoothly, "Inspector Ashcraft might be asked to supply his right thumbprint, to ensure that there has been no tampering."

"I please," the judge said crisply. "I most certainly do please. Inspector Ashcraft, your thumb, if you will."

"But my lord," Sims said in a pleading tone, "this is most irregular. It smacks of—"

"Sit down, Mr. Sims," the judge said with a dark look. "The Court intends to get to the bottom of this matter. Inspector Ashcraft, *if* you please."

Sullenly and with obvious reluctance, Inspector Ashcraft came forward. Sergeant Collins produced a fingerprint kit, opened the inkpad, and rolled the inspector's right thumb, then printed it onto a card. Having examined it, he said, "It is the same print as that on both the bottle and the card."

"Recall Inspector Ashcraft," Savidge said promptly. Sims opened and shut his mouth several times, then sat down.

Sergeant Collins, his eyes averted from the inspector's angry glance, left the witness box, and Inspector Ashcraft resumed it.

"Now, Inspector," Savidge said. "You testified earlier that you did not handle any of the evidence in this case. Please explain to the jury how your thumbprint came to be found on the bottle in Mr. Gould's room. Did you put that bottle there, so that Detective Finney could later find it?"

Charles saw that Ashcraft's jaw muscles were working. "I must do my work as I see my duty," he said. "I would deal with the devil himself, when it comes to that."

The judge fixed cold eyes on the inspector. "Answer the question, Inspector. Did you put that bottle there?"

The inspector cleared his throat. "I claim privilege against self-incrimination," he said in a surly tone.

The courtroom became suddenly noisy again, and again the judge gaveled it into silence. "Order!" he commanded. "There will be order in this courtroom!"

"Very well." Savidge leaned forward. "Inspector Ashcraft, if you are not willing to speak, at least you may be able to hold up your right hand."

Frowning, Ashcraft held it up.

"I see, sir," Savidge said, "a faded yellow stain on your index finger, around where the skin appears to have peeled away. Mr. Baker told the jury that a nitric acid burn turns the skin yellow and causes it to peel. Did you burn your finger when you poured nitric acid into one of the bottles found by Detective Finney in the defendants' rooms?"

The inspector put his hand behind his back. "Privilege against self-incrimination," he growled.

With a heavy irony, Savidge said, "Thank you, Inspector Ashcraft. You have been most helpful."

The prosecutor, his youth and inexperience all too evident now, seemed to have lost confidence in his case—understandably, Charles thought. His summation was brief, faltering, and unconvincing. Savidge, however, spoke with a fierce resoluteness, pointing out that the case against all three of the defendants consisted of nothing more than guilt by association; that the informant who believed Mr. Kopinski was a "dangerous man" could not be questioned nor his veracity tested; that Mrs. Battle's testimony to an overheard conversation had been entirely discredited; and that the evidence of the ginger-beer bottles—the only direct evidence in the entire case—was seriously compromised. Inspector Ashcraft had testified that he had never touched any of the evidence, yet his thumbprint could clearly be seen on the bottle found in Adam Gould's flat, in such a way as to suggest that he had put the evidence where the police found it. He sought refuge in the claim of privilege against self-incrimination when asked to explain to the jury how this had occurred, and how his right index finger had come to exhibit the stain and peeling consistent with a nitric-acid burn.

By the time Savidge was finished with his passionate appeal, Charles thought, he had most of the spectators in his corner. It was then the judge's turn. His lordship spoke briefly (and fairly, Charles thought), laying before the jury the prosecution's arguments and those of the defense, and charging them to consider the case on the evidence only. Then he withdrew and the jury retired to its deliberations. It was four o'clock.

CHAPTER TWENTY-NINE

It is better that ten guilty persons escape than one innocent suffer.

Sir William Blackstone,
Commentaries on the Laws of England

It is better to execute a hundred innocent persons than to permit one guilty person to go free.

Vladimir Ilich Lenin

We must execute not only the guilty. Execution of the innocent will impress the masses.

Nikolai Kyrlenko,
Commissioner of Justice under Lenin

When the jury had retired, Kate and Nellie went out for a cup of tea. By the time they returned to the courtroom, the gas jets had been lighted, the spectators' section was half-empty, and the journalists were glancing uncertainly at their watches, as if wondering whether they might safely go out to a restaurant. The jury might agree at any moment; on the other hand, it might deliberate for hours if just one of their number differed in his opinion from the others.

At half-six, the usher came into the court and announced that the jury had reached a verdict. The spectators scrambled to return to their seats, and the prosecuting and defense counsels took their places. The defendants, still shackled, were returned to the dock, each one escorted by a warder, with a plain clothes officer standing guard. A dead silence fell upon the courtroom as the judge took his seat, and then the jury. The clerk called out their names, one by one, and then said: "Gentlemen of the jury, have you agreed upon your verdicts?"

"We have," the foreman answered in a stern voice. The verdicts were read out swiftly, a sibilant sigh, like the sound of ocean surf, washing through the room at each reading. Pierre Mouffetard, guilty. Ivan Kopinski, guilty. Adam Gould, not guilty. The three men stood, not moving, as still as stone.

"Not guilty!" Nellie exclaimed jubilantly. "They found Adam not guilty! Oh, I wish Lottie were here to see him go free. And surely the police cannot want her, now that the trial is over." Around Kate and Nellie, the crowd was exchanging excited whispers. "Guilty! Guilty! Not guilty!"

The judge pounded his gavel for order, and pronounced sentence: ten years of penal servitude for each of the two convicted men. "Ten years!" went the whispers around the courtroom, louder now, and awed. "Ten years!"

As Kate watched, the warder standing beside Adam bent down and removed his shackles. The warders beside Pierre and Ivan applied handcuffs. Then they were escorted out of the dock, leaving Adam standing alone and bewildered, looking after the departing prisoners, raising his hands and stepping toward them, as if to go with them. Perhaps he wanted to say goodbye, Kate thought, or to protest at the fate that released him and imprisoned them—or perhaps he had not yet realized that the jury had acquitted him, that he was unshackled and free to go.

Then Adam seemed to come to himself. He glanced once more over his shoulder at the others, then a great smile spread across his face, and with a leaping, jubilant step, he went down the steps and made for the defense table, where he seized the hands of both Charles and Edward Savidge, pumping them up and down.

"Ten years," Nellie said, suddenly sobered. "That's a very long time for . . . for what, Kate? For working at the *Clarion?* For being acquainted with the man who blew himself up?"

"I don't understand," Kate said angrily, "how the jury could find one innocent and the other two guilty. That awful old lady perjured herself, the inspector doctored the evidence, and the whole case was so flimsy that it took no more than a good puff of air to blow it all to pieces."

"It's because Mouffetard is French and Kopinski has a Russian name," Nellie said in a practical tone. "They let Adam Gould go free because he's English." She smiled crookedly. "Juries can do anything they like, I guess."

"I suppose," Kate sighed, gathering up her things. "It's late, Nellie, and we're both tired. Let's find a cab."

Feeling as if a terrible burden had been lifted from his shoulders, Adam Gould stood on the stone steps of the Old Bailey, a free man. He had thanked Lord Sheridan and Edward Savidge, and each member of the jury. In his excitement, he had even thanked the bailiff and the judge. It was all over now but the shouting, and there was plenty of that. Around him rose a stormy cacophony of voices, some people hailing him with jubilant congratulations, others hurling angry abuse. But Adam heard almost none of it, for he was too full of a turbulent storm of feelings. He was torn by anger and grief at the conviction of Pierre and Ivan, who were no more guilty than he of the crime with which they'd been charged. But he was also filled with a glad relief at the thought of his freedom. Now if only he could find Lottie. . . .

The twilight had been hastened into evening by a bank of lowering clouds, and a fine mist filled the darkening air. Eagerly, Adam searched the milling crowd on the sidewalks, under the gas lamps. Lottie. Where was the devil *was* she? He hadn't expected her to come to the prison to see him, but he had been both confident and afraid that she would come to his trial: confident, because he knew that she cared for him, afraid because he knew that if she showed her face in the courtroom, the police would grab her. He'd spent the whole day in the dock searching each face in the spectators' section, both hoping and fearing to see her and alternately jubilant and despairing that she was not there. And then, when the verdict was read out and he was acquitted, he hoped to see her come flying toward him, to fling his arms around her and hold her tight, hold her and hold her and never let her go. That would have been the real victory, he a free man and Lottie in his arms.

But she had not been in the courtroom and now, he saw, surveying the crowd with mounting despair, she was not outside, waiting for him in the street. Did that mean that something terrible had happened to her? That the police had caught her and were holding her somewhere? That she had been forced to leave the country, or—

And then he saw her. She was dressed in the garb of a Russian girl, in a white, full-sleeved blouse and dark skirt with an embroidered apron, a red *babushka* tied under her chin. But no matter what costume she had been wearing, Indian or Russian or Egyptian, Adam would have recognized that dear, familiar form and graceful motion anywhere in the world. He thrust up his arm and shouted against the clamor of shouting voices, the clatter of horses' hoofs, the confusion of noisy lorries in the street. "Lottie! Lottie!"

For a split second, she turned to look up at him, her face pale, her eyes wide and anxious and full, it seemed to him, of guilt. *Guilt? Not his Lottie! Never Lottie!* He thought her glance had met his and felt in his heart that she had seen him. But no, perhaps she had not, for she had already turned in the other direction. She was pushing swiftly against the current of moving people, away from him, toward the covered courtyard at the other end of the block, where the Black Maria waited to take the convicted Anarchists to the prison where they would begin their sentence. And she was not alone, or that was Adam's blurred impression. She seemed to be in the company of a strongly-built, dark-haired man in a dark jacket and green cloth cap. They moved side by side through the surging crowd with an easy, companionable familiarity and what seemed to be a common purpose. Who was the man? Was he one of her comrades? What was their object? What did they intend to do?

And then suddenly Adam's heart jumped into his throat and he knew (although he had no way of knowing) that Lottie and the dark-haired man, together, meant to free Ivan and Pierre. The two of them were bent on doing, outside the law, what Lord Sheridan and Edward Savidge had not been able to do within it. They intended to free the men who now faced ten years of penal servitude for a crime they had not committed, the innocent men who should have gone free, as he was free.

But how? Were Lottie and her companion armed? Were there other comrades with them, or others aiming to meet them in the yard? How did they mean to overpower the guards? Suddenly, he was struck by the almost paralyzing fear that their desperate plan would place Lottie in grave danger. Having lost one of their three Anarchists to the jury's acquittal, the warders and the police, who were armed with guns, would be in no mood to deal gently with anyone who attempted to interfere with them. At the worst, they might shoot her. At the least, they would capture her and take her immediately to jail. And if Lottie were innocent of everything else she might have been accused of, she would certainly be found guilty of attempting to free the prisoners.

Suddenly, Adam's paralysis vanished, and he sprinted after them. Whatever Lottie and her companion meant to do, he would join them. Freedom meant nothing at all to him if he could not share it with Lottie.

Adam Gould was not the only one who saw Lottie and recognized her. Nellie had emerged from the Old Bailey with Kate, and the two of them stood on the steps just outside the doors, looking through the gathering darkness for a cab.

"I'm afraid we'll have to walk to Ludgate Circus," Kate was saying, her voice concerned. "There's too large a crowd here, and half of them will be wanting a cab, just as we are. We might wait for Charles, but he may want to go off with Edward Savidge. I hope you're not too tired for a bit of a walk."

"I'm not, really," Nellie said, taking a deep breath of the misty air, which seemed almost sweet in contrast to the hot, heavy atmosphere of the courtroom, redolent of cigars and men's sweat. "I feel very well."

Nelie was grateful to Kate, in fact, for asking her to come to the Old Bailey. It had been much better for her to concern herself with the welfare of the three men on trial than to sit in her room at the Rehearsal Club, alternatively hating Jack London and feeling sorry for herself. If nothing else, the defendants' desperate plight had taken her mind off her own. Why, for three or four whole hours, she hadn't once thought about being pregnant, or wondered how she was going to manage. She—

"Oh, look, Nellie," Kate said, pointing to their right.

"There's Adam Gould, over there. Let's go congratulate him on his acquittal. I don't know him, but you do—you can introduce us."

Nellie looked where Kate was pointing, and just as she did, she saw Adam violently thrust up his arm. "Lottie!" he cried loudly, standing on his tiptoes and looking intently out over the crowd. "Lottie!"

Swiftly, Nellie turned in the direction of Adam's searching glance. She saw a dark-haired man in a green cap and a young Russian girl with a red *babushka* over her head and a basket on her arm. The pair was pushing against the jostling press of people, hurrying in the direction of the courtyard between Newgate Prison and the Old Bailey. Was the girl Lottie? Adam apparently thought so, although from this distance, Nellie couldn't be sure.

But then the pair, the man and the girl, passed under a gas street lamp, and with a sudden shocking jolt that almost seemed to knock the breath out of her, Nellie recognized the man.

"Kate," she gasped, pointing. "There! It's Jack London!"

Kate looked. "And that's Charlotte Conway with him, Nellie! I'm sure of it!"

As Kate spoke, Adam gave another loud cry and bolted down the stone steps. After that, it was all a wild confusion of shouting and pushing and scrambling as he attempted to shove his way through the crowd in pursuit of Lottie and Jack. Nellie would have gone after him, but Kate seized her arm.

"Let them go, Nellie," she said firmly. "Leave it to Adam to catch her."

"But what of him?" Nellie cried, desperately trying to pull away. "What of Jack London? I have to catch her, Kate. I have to warn her! I can't let him do to her what he did to me!"

"There's nothing you can do, Nellie," Kate said in a low

voice, putting a sisterly arm around her shoulders and pulling her apart from the press of people. "Perhaps it isn't what you're thinking, and there's nothing of that sort between them. Or perhaps, if Lottie has been with Jack for a time, the damage is already done. Either way, she won't welcome your interference. And you certainly don't want to confront *him,* do you?" She tipped up Nellie's chin, wiping the tears from her cheeks.

Nellie bit her lip, thinking distractedly. Kate was right about one thing—she couldn't push her way through the milling crowd to catch up with Jack and Lottie. And she suddenly realized that she didn't want to. Did she want to confront him? Perhaps, once she was sure she was carrying his child. But not yet, and certainly not now, in this public place, where she would be bitterly conscious of hundreds of eyes, watching, hundreds of ears, listening. She *had* to talk to Lottie, though—she could not allow her friend to be deceived and betrayed by that man, as she had been. But how would she find her to warn her? If not here and now, where and when?

There was nothing to be done for the moment. But Nellie suddenly realized, as she allowed her friend to lead her down the steps and into the darkening street, that she knew exactly how and where to find Jack London.

And with an anguished certainty, she knew where she would find Lottie, as well.

CHAPTER THIRTY

❖━━◉━━❖

Flight is lawful, when one flies from tyrants.

Racine,
Phaedra, 1677

Dmitri Tropov, alias Vladimir Rasnokov (among a great many other aliases), had not attended the Anarchists' trial, although he lingered near enough to Old Bailey to gain a clear idea of what was going on. He had felt that his presence in the courtroom might present an unpleasant complication, and from what he could gather from the bailiffs and barristers who wandered in and out of the Bell & Bailey, the pub nearest the court, his instinct had been entirely correct. If Charles Sheridan had noticed and recognized Vladimir Rasnokov among the spectators in the courtroom, the defense counsel might have attempted to summon him to the witness box, in spite of the Crown's pleading of public-interest privilege.

Tropov had no intention of revealing to an English court, however, the exact nature of his association with Ivan Kopinski. Besides, such proceedings were, in his experience, an utter waste of time. In Russia, when the police did their work properly, trials were unnecessary—unless, of course, the State wished to make some point or other, such as reminding the people who was in charge, or making an example of someone. To Tropov, the English notions of the jury of peers, presumption of innocence, and adversarial procedure seemed alien and unfamiliar—and foolishly utopian, especially when it came to dealing with crimes committed by the underclass. He had no doubt, however, that in the case of the Anarchists, the Crown would not hesitate to set aside such judicial abstractions as "justice" and "fairness" in favor of its own interests. And even though it appeared from all accounts that the defense was mounting a sharp assault on the prosecution's case, he was sure that the judge would find a way to resolve the matter as it should be resolved.

Tropov was astounded, therefore, when he heard the jury's verdict, which had spread through the Bell & Bailey like wildfire on the steppes. Only two of the Anarchists had been found guilty, while the third was declared innocent! Scarcely able to credit what he was hearing, Tropov left his mug of ale on the table, dashed across the street, and joined the milling crowd on the sidewalk, anxious to learn what had happened.

After a few breathless inquiries, however, he discovered that his fears were groundless. It was the Englishman Gould whom the jury had found innocent, a trade-union fellow and dangerous agitator, no doubt, but of no interest to Tropov. The penalty of ten years imposed on the other two, however—and particularly upon Ivan Kopinski—presented a new set of problems. Tropov had expected a shorter sentence, five years, perhaps, or seven at the most. It might be exceedingly difficult to lay hands upon a man when he finally emerged from a decade in an English prison. In the shifting landscape of European and Central Asian intrigue, ten years was an eternity. In ten years, Russia might well be at war with England.

Moving against the crowd, Tropov made his way around

to the yard between Newgate and the Old Bailey, where the Black Maria was waiting to return the condemned men to prison. He had no plan in mind, for he had to admit to being at a momentary loss as to what, exactly, to do next, with regard to Kopinski. He went simply to satisfy himself that the transport of the men was going as expected. It was not.

Tropov stood just inside the gate, along with perhaps thirty or forty people—some of them tipsy, others merely rowdy—which had gathered around the Black Maria. Night was falling and the gas lamps in the yard cast a misty glow across the cobbled pavement. As the door opened and the uniformed guards led the shuffling pair of shackled and handcuffed prisoners out to the waiting van, a slender young woman in a red *babushka* and embroidered apron flung herself wildly out of the crowd and ran the dozen yards toward them, screaming at Kopinski in an incoherent torrent of Russian.

Amused, Tropov smiled to himself. He couldn't quite catch the woman's words, but from her behavior and her gestures, it appeared that she had once been Kopinski's sweetheart—and was with child, it would seem, from the way she screamed and wept and pointed to her belly. Apparently, Kopinski had not practiced all the Anarchist tenets, especially that which discouraged relationships with women. The poor creature flew passionately at the handcuffed man, pummeling him with her fists and crying a few Russian words over and over again. This time, Tropov managed to catch them, or thought he had. *"Klyuchee!"* she screamed. *"Skreetm v'karmenye!"*

Kopinski appeared to be completely dumbfounded at this unexpected and highly emotional outburst, but he finally spoke a few surprised words in Russian. Hearing him, the girl threw up her arms, let out a long and heart-rending shriek of despair, and collapsed to the pavement in a huddled faint.

There was sudden pandemonium. The shouting crowd surged forward through the gathering darkness, completely surrounding the prisoners and the van. The horses whinnied and reared in their traces as the driver fought to hold them. The guards, the prisoners, and the people became a shouting, swirling, disorganized mass. It took a minute, perhaps longer, for the warders to regain control of the situation, push the crowd back, and hustle their prisoners into the van. It took a moment more for a dark-haired man in a green cap to push the crowd aside, revive the girl, and lift her to her feet. The bystanders parted, murmuring sympathetically, as he half-supported, half-carried the sobbing young woman out of the yard and into the street, where they disappeared from Tropov's sight.

"The prisoner's sweetheart, most like," said the old woman standing next to Tropov. She shook her head sadly. "Ten years is a long time. I pity 'er, raisin' the child 'erself."

"That's wot comes o' takin' up with th' crim'nal class," snapped her companion, a younger woman wrapped in a dark shawl. "She should've known better. Come along, Mum. It'll be rainin' afore we gets 'ome."

A guard stepped out from behind the van and raised and lowered his arm. The driver lifted his whip, the horses pulled, and the black, windowless van moved heavily out of the courtyard. Curiously, Tropov sauntered after it, watching as it turned into the dark street. On the other side of the pavement, just past the Bell & Bailey, a hansom cab pulled away from the curb, following the van at a little distance. A moment later, and the darkness had swallowed both.

Tropov took a cigarette out of his pocket, lit it, and considered this small but extremely entertaining bit of theater, for theater it was. Only two of the many persons in the crowded yard, it seemed—he, Tropov, and the prisoner, Kopinski—had understood what it was that the hysterical girl had actually said. Her Russian had been so abominably garbled as to be almost indecipherable, but Tropov had managed to make it out.

"The Frenchman has your keys," she had said. "Free yourselves. Get into the cab that follows the van."

Tropov's first impulse had been to cry a warning to the guards in order to prevent the escape of the two Anarchists, but he had quickly suppressed that urge. Now, he considered the situation, smiling, for it seemed that circumstances had turned, inexplicably but quite fortuitously, in his favor. Kopinski would shortly use the keys he had been so inventively provided to slip out of the embrace of the English judiciary and into the dark and gloomy night—an escape he would no doubt welcome. But under the circumstances, a fugitive Kopinski was far more available than an imprisoned Kopinski. Tropov's operatives were most efficient. They would very soon have the fellow.

CHAPTER THIRTY-ONE

ANARCHISTS ESCAPE PRISON VAN!
DANGEROUS PAIR AT LARGE IN LONDON
POLICE BAFFLED

The Times,
5 September 1902

Charles put down *The Times* and stood as Kate came into the breakfast room at Sibley House. She was already dressed to go out, in a plain blue tweed walking suit. Her auburn hair was pulled back so severely that she looked rather like a Salvation Army worker. "Good morning, my dear," he said, leaning forward to kiss her. "I hope I didn't wake you last night when I came home. It was very late."

"If you woke me, I must have gone straight back to sleep," Kate replied with a little laugh. "Yesterday was a very long day. I was exhausted." To Richards, she said, "Coffee, please." As the butler poured her coffee, she went to the sideboard to help herself to eggs, bacon, and a slice of toast. Over her shoulder, she added, "Savidge was wonderful yesterday, Charles. He showed up Inspector Ashcraft for exactly what he is, a conniving trickster." She turned. "You handled the fingerprints brilliantly."

"Apparently the jury weren't entirely impressed," Charles said dryly. "Two of the three men were found guilty."

Kate brought her plate back to the table and sat down, shaking her head. "It's such a pity, Charles. I'm glad that Adam Gould was spared, of course, but it's sad that the other two must suffer such a terrible injustice, and chiefly because they're foreigners. That seems to be the only reason they weren't acquitted. Isn't there anything that can be done? An appeal, perhaps?"

"Actually, something has been done," Charles said, with a chuckle. "A bit of escape artistry, worthy of the great Houdini." He held up the newspaper.

Kate scanned the headline and gasped incredulously. "They got away?" She threw back her head and laughed with delight. "Now, that's justice for you!"

"Poetic justice, if you ask me," Charles said, folding the paper and putting it beside his empty plate. He picked up his coffee cup. "The law wouldn't let them go, so they took the law into their own hands."

Kate attacked her eggs. "How did it happen?"

"According to *The Times*, the van was on its way back to Holloway Prison, when both men suddenly shed their handcuffs, overpowered the guard who had been locked in with them, and knocked him senseless. When the van reached the prison, the rear doors were unlatched, the guard was unconscious, and the prisoners were gone. The guard was not seriously injured, but he wasn't able, apparently, to provide any useful information about the escape. *The Times* says that the police are seeking a Russian girl."

Kate looked up, her eyes widening suddenly. "A Russian girl?"

Charles nodded. "It seems that she was involved in an odd commotion that occured in the yard outside the Old Bailey, when the men were being put into the van. The police are speculating that she managed somehow to get her hands on the keys and pass them to one of the prisoners. They're questioning the guards."

Kate leaned forward, her eyes intent. "Charles, that Russian girl—she was Charlotte Conway!"

Charles stared at her. He could feel his jaw dropping. "You saw what happened?"

"Not exactly." Kate sat back, picked up her toast, and began to spoon marmalade on it. "Nellie Lovelace and I were standing on the steps outside the courtroom after the verdict was announced, trying to hail a cab. Adam came out and stood on the steps, not far away. We saw him at the same moment that he saw a Russian girl in the crowd and began to call Lottie's name. Then he rushed down the steps after her. She was headed in the direction of the Old Bailey yard."

Charles's lips tightened. "You're saying that Adam Gould was involved in the escape?" If true, that was unfortunate. He could be charged with rendering aid to escaping convicts, and this time, Savidge probably wouldn't be able to get him off.

"Not Adam," Kate said, shaking her head. "He couldn't catch up to the girl. The sidewalk was very crowded, and she had a head start." She looked at him over the rim of her coffee cup, her eyes twinkling mischievously. "But someone else may have been involved in the escape—someone we both know."

Charles regarded her. He wished that Kate wouldn't play guessing games. "Who?"

Kate put down her cup. "Jack London."

"I don't believe it," Charles said firmly. "Why would Jack London be involved in an escape attempt? This matter has nothing to do with him."

"Oh, yes, it does," Kate said, half-smiling. She had the

air of someone who is deliberately spinning out a mystery and loving every moment of it. "He's in love with Charlotte Conway."

Sometimes his wife was almost maddening, Charles thought. He put his hand on her arm. "Enough, Kate," he said sternly. "Don't make things up. Tell me what you know. Tell me the *facts*."

She wrinkled her nose at him. "There aren't any facts, my dear. In something like this, there are only guesses and suppositions."

"Blast," Charles said softly. That's what he got for marrying a novelist. He sighed and capitulated. "All right, Kate. Tell me your suppositions."

"They aren't all mine—but I'll try. Nellie Lovelace supposes that she is carrying Jack London's child. Last night, as we stood on the steps, she saw Charlotte, dressed as a Russian girl, and London with her. She supposes that the two are staying together, in London's room in the East End. She also supposes that London is in love with Charlotte, because he spoke of her with great admiration. He seemed to be quite enchanted with her, according to Nellie." She paused. "Now, hearing your tale about the escape, I'm guessing that Charlotte Conway and Jack London somehow worked together to free those men." She smiled regretfully. "No facts, I'm afraid. Only suppositions and guesses."

Charles swallowed, hardly knowing where to begin. "Nellie Lovelace is carrying Jack London's *child*?"

"She's not sure," Kate said quickly. "And she told me in confidence, so perhaps I shouldn't have told you. But it does explain why she wants so *desperately* to talk to Lottie." She glanced down at the gold watch on her lapel, pushed back her chair, and stood up. "I must leave now, Charles. I promised to pick Nellie up in half an hour, so we can go to the East End and look for Lottie."

"The East End." Charles frowned. "Is that why you're dressed like a Salvation Army matron?"

"Exactly," Kate said. "And if I'm late, I'm afraid Nellie will go charging off on her own, without me." She bent over and kissed him. "I hope you have a good day, my very dear."

Charles stared at her departing back. "More coffee, Richards," he said at last. "Black, please."

Richards's sniff, he could have sworn, was sympathetic.

CHAPTER THIRTY-TWO

✦〓◎〓✦

And so it goes. I wander through life delivering hurts to all that know me . . . it is the woman who always pays.

Jack London,
letter to Anna Strunsky, 23 July 1904

Charlotte Conway had just finished tidying up the two beds when there was a quiet rap at the door. Frowning, she went to it and put her ear against it. Who could be knocking? No one but Jack knew she was here.

"Lottie," a voice whispered urgently. "It's Nellie Lovelace. I know you're in there, Lottie, so let me in!"

So surprised that she didn't take time to think, Lottie opened the door and stepped back. "Nellie, what are you—" She stopped, feeling herself go rigid with shock. "Lady Sheridan!"

"Hello, Miss Conway," Lady Sheridan said, entering the room. She was dressed in a very plain gray suit and wore no jewelry. She glanced around, her eyes lingering on Jack's typewriter. "What a cozy little room. I hope you won't mind if Nellie and I come in for a visit." Without waiting for an answer, she went on, in a light tone, "I always enjoy seeing other writers' work in progress. I'm sure that Mr. London won't mind if I have a look." She went over to the table and picked up the top pages of Jack's typescript, turning her back.

Lottie put her fists on her hips. "What can you possibly mean, coming here, Nellie?" she hissed. "Somebody might have seen you, or heard you walking up the stair. And if it's Jack you want to talk to—"

"I didn't come to talk to Mr. London," Nellie said loftily. "In fact, we—Lady Sheridan and I—lingered on the street to be sure he was gone. We saw the Palmers leave, as well," she added. "The house is empty. There's no risk of our being overheard."

Lady Sheridan put down the manuscript pages and turned around. "We know what happened last night, Charlotte," she said quietly. She pointed to the red *babushka* draped over the head of Lottie's bed. "You were wearing that, and an embroidered apron when you and Jack London went into the Old Bailey yard. Somehow, the two of you managed to slip a key to the prisoners. They freed themselves and—"

"They've escaped?" Lottie cried, nearly beside herself with relief. "Oh, I'm so *glad*! We weren't sure the plan would—" She stopped, suddenly suspicious. "How do you know about this?"

"Nellie and I, and Adam Gould, saw you on the street outside the Old Bailey," Lady Sheridan replied. "This morning, Lord Sheridan showed me the *Times* story. The two men bashed the guard on the head and went out the back of the van. It was unlocked when the driver arrived at the prison, and empty, except for the guard."

At the mention of Adam, Lottie's heart gave a little lurch. "Did Adam see what happened?"

"I don't think so," Lady Sheridan said. "He didn't seem able to get through the crowd. Or perhaps he saw that Mr. London was with you and gave it up."

Lottie felt suddenly anxious. "I hope you're not planning to turn us in. I—"

"Don't be silly, Lottie," Nellie said. "Of course we're not planning to turn you in. We came because I need to talk to you about Mr. London. I would have come sooner, if I had known you were here. It wasn't until last night, when we saw the two of you together, that I realized that you must be staying with . . . him."

Lottie colored. "Mr. London?" she asked defensively. "What do you want to talk about?"

"I'm sorry," Nellie said with a sigh. "I don't mean to embarrass you. But if you and he are . . . I mean, if he's promised you . . . if you have. . . ." She stopped, her cheeks glowing, her eyes suddenly brimming. Two enormous tears ran down her cheeks.

"What's wrong, Nellie?" Lottie asked urgently. She took Nellie's hands. They were very cold. "Why are you crying?"

"Oh, Lottie," Nellie burst out, "I hope you haven't let him make love to you. He's . . . he's *married*!"

"I know that, Nellie," Lottie said gently. "And I have *not* allowed him to make love to me. I am simply staying here until the police are no longer looking for me, and then I'll leave."

"Is that really true?" Nellie asked, searching her face. "You . . . didn't?"

"Of course it's true. I said so, didn't I?" Lottie dropped Nellie's hands, frowning. "But what does this have to do with you? Why—?"

And then an awful idea came to her, and she thought she understood why Nellie was crying. "I know that Jack took you to Earl's Court, because he told me," she whispered. "But did you allow him to—" She didn't have to finish the question, because Nellie's flaming face told her the truth.

"Nellie has had a difficult experience, Lottie," Lady

Sheridan said quietly. Her look was very straightfoward and direct. "Mr. London was not a gentleman. She has been concerned that he might have put you into a similar awkward and compromised position—perhaps even a precarious one."

Lottie lowered her head. "He might well have," she admitted. "But I found out that he was married and made it clear that I . . . wouldn't." She took a deep breath. "Since then, he's been . . . restrained. And helpful, I must say." She smiled crookedly. "He's a first-rate dipper."

"A dipper?" Lady Sheridan asked.

"A pickpocket," Lottie said. "He learned it when he was in jail. He picked the guard's pocket last night, while I was screaming Russian words at Ivan." She frowned at Lady Sheridan. "When you say that he wasn't a gentleman, do you mean—"

"He forced me, Lottie," Nellie broke in. "I think I'm . . . pregnant."

"Nellie isn't sure about that," Lady Sheridan said cautiously. "It's really too early to—"

"He *forced* you!" Lottie exclaimed, stunned. "Oh, Nellie, how awful! I would never have believed that he—"

"We'd both had quite a bit to drink," Nellie said, shamefacedly. "Part of the fault is mine, I know." She held out her hand in a pleading gesture. "But I tried to make him stop, honestly, I did, Lottie. I did! And then Lady Sheridan told me about his wife and child back in California. His wife is pregnant too."

"Oh, Nellie, I am so very sorry," Lottie cried, and opened her arms to her friend. How could Jack have done such a thing? But she did not doubt Nellie's word. There was something about Jack that allowed him to use vulnerable people to suit his own ends—and of course, when men took their pleasure, it was the woman who paid.

After a few minutes, Lady Sheridan cleared her throat.

"We must decide what to do," she said. "Miss Conway, now that the trial is over, you are safe from the police. You may wish to return home to Brantwood Street, or you could come back to Bishop's Keep with me."

Nellie wiped her eyes. "You could come and stay with me, Lottie. I lost my place at the Strand, but I'm working again, and living at the Rehearsal Club. The other bed in my room is empty just now. You'd be welcome."

Lottie squared her shoulders, thinking swiftly. If she left the City, she would not be able to help Ivan and Pierre, and her first obligation was to them. "I won't stay here any longer," she said at last. "That much is certain. Lady Sheridan, I'm grateful for your invitation, but I feel I had better remain in London. I've already made up my mind not to go back to Brantwood Street, so I'll accept Nellie's offer, at least for a few days." One thing, at least, she had decided over the past several days: She was no longer willing to be tied to her mother. The lodgers' rent ought to be enough to buy meat and potatoes, if not chocolates.

"I'm glad," Nellie said simply.

"Do you have anything to pack?" Lady Sheridan asked, glancing around the room. "Perhaps we had better leave, before—"

But it was too late. The door opened and Jack London, wearing his grimy slum costume, his camera bag slung over his shoulder, came into the room. At the sight of the visitors, his mouth dropped open. "What—?" His eyes went to Nellie, his brow furrowed, and a flush came into his cheeks.

"Hello, Mr. London," Nellie said, with a strained composure. "I—" She stopped, swallowing hard. "I think you should know—"

Lady Sheridan smiled and put her hand on Nellie's arm. "Good morning, Mr. London. Miss Conway, I think it's time we were going. Miss Lovelace and I will wait for you in the street."

"Thank you," Lottie replied, lifting her chin. "This won't take long." She gave Jack a pointed look. "Not long at all."

Out on the street, Kate put her arm around Nellie's shoulders. "You did very well, Nellie," she said quietly.

"I was afraid I was going to cry again," Nellie said. She gave Kate a grateful look. "Thank you for coming here with me. If I'd been alone with Lottie when he came in, I might have told him. About me, I mean." She flushed. "But it wouldn't have been a good idea."

Kate nodded, agreeing. A vendor's wagon at the corner caught her eye. "Let's have some hot tea while we're waiting for Lottie," she said. "It will make us both feel better."

They had just finished their tea when Lottie came around the back of the Palmers' house, carrying a paper bag. She was wearing a dark dress, with a shawl tied around her shoulders. Catching sight of Kate and Nellie, she waved and came toward them across the street.

"Well, then," Kate said, "shall we get a cab and go to the Rehearsal Club?"

Lottie handed the bag to Nellie. "I must ask you to take this and go on without me," she said. "I'll come to the club later this evening, or perhaps tomorrow. I must do an errand right now."

Nellie took the bag, which Kate saw was full of clothing. "Do you know where to come?"

"It's in Leicester Square, isn't it?" Lottie replied. "If you could leave my name at the desk, with a spare key, I could let myself in even if you aren't there." She paused, frowning. "No, don't use my real name, Nellie. Leave the key for . . . for Hazel Lovelace. I'll be your sister. And I have a little money. I can pay for my share of the room."

Kate regarded her steadily. "This errand," she said. "Does it have to do with the escaped men?"

A wagon filled with vegetables clattered past on the cobbled street. Down the way, a newspaper boy was crying the headlines. "Anarchists escape from prison van! Getcher news here!"

Lottie looked as if she did not want to answer, but after a moment, she said, in a guarded tone, "I suppose I owe you the truth, since you and Lord Sheridan have been so kind. Yes, my errand has to do with the escape. Getting the men out of the van was only the first step. They're safe now, in a hiding place in the Russian area of the East End. I am meeting a comrade this morning to make arrangements for getting them out of the country." She turned back to Nellie. "That's why I can't go with you now, Nellie. And if I'm caught, I don't want you involved."

Nellie shook her head. "Lottie, you are so *brave*."

Lottie laughed. "Brave? Foolhardy is more like it. Smuggling them out won't be easy, since the Yard is probably looking everywhere for them. But we have to try."

Kate remembered the anger she had felt when the jury's verdict was announced, and her feeling that justice had not been served.

"Yes," she said firmly. "You have to try." She bent forward and kissed Lottie's cheek. "Good luck, Lottie. We'll be thinking of you and wishing you well."

CHAPTER THIRTY-THREE

*There is no denying the aesthetic satisfaction, the sense
of poetic justice, that pleasures us when evil-doers get
the comeuppance they deserve. . . . The satisfaction is
heightened when it becomes possible to measure out
punishment in exact proportion to the size and shape of
the wrong that has been done.*

Arthur Lelyvekl,
Punishment: For and Against

Former Inspector Ashcraft was in a mood as black as the
coffee he was stirring. From his seat in the corner booth,
he was keeping one eye on the entry to the Little Moscow
Café, although he was not sure that his message had been
received—or if it had, that his contact would respond.

Early that morning, Assistant Commissioner Henry had
called both Ashcraft and Chief Inspector Mattingly into his
office. He was obviously angered not only by the debacle of
the trial but also by the Anarchists' escape, the news of
which had stunned Ashcraft into a bewildered disbelief.
How had the wardens been so lax as to allow their keys to be
stolen and the men to escape? The Anarchists were known to
be dangerous—why had there not been a larger guard, more
effective security procedures? Who was responsible for—

But the inspector had not been able to give voice to any of the questions and doubts that stirred like a storm within him. He was required to stand at attention and listen as the assistant commissioner made it plain that he had only two choices: He could resign his position and leave Special Branch quietly, without any fanfare; or he could stay and face an internal investigation and, quite possibly, a public trial. The decision had been wrenching, for Ashcraft had wanted to proclaim to the world that he had done what he did only because it was his *duty* to keep the streets of London safe from Anarchists. His duty had required him to stretch the law, and justified him in stepping outside of its bounds when necessary. But the assistant commissioner did not want to hear any explanations or justifications; he only wanted to castigate him for breaking the law and embarrassing the Yard. And of course, Chief Inspector Mattingly could never acknowledge that he had encouraged Ashcraft to do what he had to do to bring the Anarchists to justice, and especially Kopinski, whom the Russians badly wanted. The inspector had taken the easiest way, and resigned.

But there was something else, too, that had figured in Ashcraft's decision, something that he feared might come to light if he were swept up in an investigation. He knew, in the deepest recesses of his heart, that it was Charlotte Conway who had been his undoing. Even now, and even to himself, he was not prepared to admit how desperately he had wanted the girl. The more he had watched her through that lighted bedroom window, or tripping down the street, or bending over her desk in the newspaper loft, the stronger his desire had grown. And since he could not have her, something inside him—some fiercely passionate part of him that he could barely recognize as himself—had determined that no other man would have her, either.

It was this determination that had led to his fundamental error, for when the raid had inadvertently netted Charlotte

Conway's lover along with Kopinski and Mouffetard, Ashcraft had decided to take advantage of the situation. He should, of course, have released Adam Gould and been done with it. There was no question of finding evidence against the man, since Ashcraft knew he was not involved with the Anarchists. But since he had determined to ensure the conviction of Kopinski and Mouffetard—and especially of Kopinski—it seemed a small matter to make up another bottle and put it under Gould's bed. He could not have known that the young man was a friend of some overly-enthusiastic lord who thought he knew something about fingerprints and wanted to meddle in police matters. If Sheridan had not organized the defense, it was likely that the whole thing would have come out exactly as he had anticipated, with guilty verdicts for all three.

"I received your message from Petrovich," a voice said. There was a tone of deep disdain in it. "You wanted to see me?"

Ashcraft had become so deeply absorbed in his thoughts that he had not seen the tall, stooped-shouldered man enter the café. The man slipped into the booth on the opposite side of the table and regarded him with watchful eyes. There was nothing inside the man, Ashcraft thought drearily, no devotion to duty, no humanity, only that cold, uncaring, never-ending vigilance. Didn't these Russians ever stop *watching*?

Tropov rested his elbows on the table. "What is it you want?" he asked finally. Ashcraft knew, by the tone of his voice, patronizing and contemptuous, that he had heard about the trial and guessed, no doubt, that he had been dismissed.

"I have something for you," Ashcraft said stolidly. "Something that might be of value in your work." Reaching into his coat pocket, he took out a small black notebook. His eyes lingered on it as he placed it carefully in the center of the table. Offering it to Tropov—was it a betrayal of his duty? Was he somehow giving aid to an enemy he did not fully understand?

No, his notes on the Hyde Park affair and the lists of names of the men and women who had served the Yard as informants—this was not evidence, but merely his own personal jottings. And since Assistant Commissioner Henry himself had made it clear that Ashcraft's services were no longer required and the Hyde Park matter was closed, Ashcraft felt himself at liberty to do what he liked with his personal records. Moreover, it did not matter that Tropov served the Russian secret police. They were both on the same side, ultimately: the side of law and order, opposed to the death against lawlessness, chaos, and disorder.

Sitting across the table, Dmitri Tropov picked up the notebook and thumbed the pages. If he felt anything at all, it was something like contempt. He saw little that was new to him, and nothing that was of any particular interest. However, since the notebook contained Ashcraft's personal notes, a closer reading might reveal something of the strange workings of the English, and for that reason might have some marginal value. This was his last meeting with Ashcraft, but there would no doubt be other policemen with whom he would have to deal. He tossed the notebook on the table in front of him.

"And why is it that you want me to have this?" he asked. It was an idle question, for nothing that Ashcraft had to tell him could be of any interest to him now.

Ashcraft turned away, appearing to be absorbed in the graceful movements of the balalaika player who was taking his seat on a stool in the corner. In a muffled voice, he said, "I assume that you have heard what transpired at the trial yesterday. You must know, as well, about the escape."

"Right on both counts," Tropov said carelessly. "And if you're asking if I know where Kopinski and Mouffetard have got to, the answer is no. I have no idea." He clicked his tongue scoldingly against the back of his teeth. "Careless of you, that business about the ginger-beer bottles. But it would have come out just the same in the end. They would all three have escaped. In Russia, of course, we would not have let that happen."

Ashcraft turned back. A dullness seemed to have settled in his eyes, and his shoulders slumped as if he had suddenly become very weary. "My superiors have determined that my services are no longer required." His voice was flat, without depth or resonance. "I was sacked this morning."

Tropov pursed his lips, considering the matter. When he had heard the verdict and the report of what happened at the trial, he had known that Ashcraft was finished at the Yard. Did the notebook, and this meeting, constitute a request for employment? Did this fool think he had something of value to offer the Ochrana, something that might be of some conceivable use to them? Or might this be a trap, laid by someone with more brains than Ashcraft?

For a moment, Tropov studied the man's hopeless eyes, his defeated expression, the dejection in his shoulders. Deciding that it was neither a trap nor a request for employment, he picked up the notebook and slipped it carelessly into his pocket. Ashcraft was a buffoon and this, whatever else it might be, was his final blunder. One must never give an enemy a weapon that might be used to destroy oneself—and that was what Ashcraft had just done.

Tropov smiled to himself. How could Ashcraft possibly explain the possession of his personal notes by a foreign agent? The man was obviously past ruination, and this was just another piece of evidence of his unforgivable errors of judgment. Tropov was quite certain that it was for similar errors of judgment and not a violation of some high-minded principle that Ashcraft's superiors had turned him out. The man could count himself lucky. Had he been a Russian agent and brought so public a disgrace on the State, he would have lost not only his job but certainly his liberty and probably his life.

"So what will you do now?" he asked. Another idle question, since it hardly mattered to Tropov whether the man lived or died.

"My family and I will be leaving England," the other replied dully. He shrugged his defeated shoulders. "Canada, New Zealand, Australia—who knows? Somewhere, anywhere." He glanced at the pocket into which Tropov had dropped the notebook, his eyes as hungry as if he were searching for emeralds. "I trust you will put my information to good use. Some of those listed there—especially a man named Nicholas Petrovich, a very useful man, by the way—might know where the escaped Anarchists are hiding." A light flickered briefly in his eyes and then went out. "Perhaps you will be better at catching and keeping them than the Yard."

"Yes, of course," Tropov said reassuringly, although he wasn't sure why he bothered. He thought of the multiple ironies here. Much of the information in Ashcraft's notebook was pure rubbish, and Nicholas Petrovich was the double agent who had fed it to him. The real truth about what had transpired in Hyde Park, and how and why, of course, Petrovich had not supplied.

Tropov slid out of the booth and stood, looking down at the man. "I wish you well," he said, the phrase a meaningless formality. He touched his cap and turned to leave. Behind him, the balalaika player began to sing. The mournful notes followed him out the door.

CHAPTER THIRTY-FOUR

decorative divider

Freedom is the will to be responsible to ourselves.

Friedrich Nietzsche,
Twilight of the Idols, 1888

Ivan Kopinski sat cross-legged on the dirty floor of the tiny room at the back of the cigar shop in Church Lane, staring into the musty darkness. He could smell the familiar odor of strong Russian tobacco and hear the murmur of male Russian voices from the meeting room at the back of the Russian Free Library, on the floor above. The booming Slavic voice of the cigar shop proprietor, a ham-fisted brute of a man called Boris, could be heard occasionally, punctuating the murmur with bursts of raucous laughter, along with Petrovich's nervous, high-pitched giggle. He and Pierre were among friends here, and safer from discovery than they would be anywhere in London.

But they had been hiding in this cramped space since the hansom driver had delivered them here the night before, with little opportunity to stretch their legs or move about. Petrovich had brought them packets of fish and chips from a nearby shop, and Boris had brought them a couple of bottles of beer and some tea. While Ivan had been able to tolerate the slow monotony of the passing hours by reviewing in his mind all of the things he would do once he was entirely free, Pierre had early on shown the strain, rolling his eyes, slapping his hands against his legs, and muttering incoherent French curses under his breath.

But while Ivan might be physically uncomfortable and Pierre fidgety, at least they were no longer handcuffed or shackled. They had rid themselves of the cuffs with the keys that had turned up in Pierre's pocket after the fracas in the Old Bailey yard. Unfortunately, there were no keys to the shackles, so they had literally flung themselves out of the swift-moving van onto the pavement, hoping they wouldn't break their necks. Fortunately, the hansom cab that Lottie had promised was close behind and the driver, a hulk of a man, had hauled them on board and driven them swiftly into the East End. The hacksaw Petrovich had provided had made short work of their leg irons, and they were free. *Free!* Ivan exulted, and in the next dazed breath wondered, *Free to do what? Go where? How?* But no matter. The answers to these practical questions would emerge when Lottie came, as the hansom driver said, to give them their instructions. For now, it was enough to know that they were free, and responsible to themselves.

It was night again now, Friday night, and the darkness pressed ominously against the pane of the single window high up in the wall. Even Ivan was beginning to find the long wait trying. That Special Branch inspector, Ashcraft, he would be turning over every rock trying to find them, of course, and there were betrayers everywhere—even upstairs, in the Russian Free Library, where information about those unfortunate enough to be fugitives from the Ochrana was passed quietly and sympathetically from mouth to mouth. One could not know who among the comrades could be trusted with one's life, and who was ready to sell valuable information for the price of a family member's freedom, or even for a hot meal and a bed.

There was a soft tap at the door, then two more in quick succession—the signal. In a fluid motion, Pierre rose from his crouch against the opposite wall and went to the door, opening it a crack. "It's me," came a whisper, and Pierre opened the door and stood back.

Ivan scrambled to his feet, blinking stupidly at the candle Lottie was holding shoulder-high. She cast a quick glance over her shoulder and slipped into the room. Pierre closed the door behind her.

Ivan watched as Lottie set the candle on the shelf beside the door and glanced around. Her hair had tumbled loose onto her shoulders and her eyes glinted like stars, he thought, in the oppressive darkness of the room. He stepped forward, suddenly aware of how hungry he had been for the sight of her.

She turned to him, smiling, a smile that seemed to banish the shadows. "Hello, Ivan," she said, stepping toward him. "I'm sorry that this has taken so long. I came as soon as I could, but there were so many details to manage—"

"Never mind that," Pierre growled savagely. "Is it arranged?"

Lottie turned to look at him, a furrow appearing between her eyes. "Yes," she said.

Ivan found his voice. "When? How?"

"Tonight," Lottie replied. "Very soon. A comrade who drives a freight wagon will take you to Dover, to a place where you will be safe. On Sunday morning, you will take passage to Ostende on a fishing boat. It is all taken care of. That's what took so long, you see. We had to wait on a telegram confirming the details."

"And after that?" Pierre demanded, his voice rising. "What after that?"

"Once in Belgium," Lottie said, "you are to contact a man named Friedrich Witthaus. He will help you find lodging in Brussels, or see you on your way to Switzerland." She looked from Pierre to Ivan, managing a small smile. "You are ready to leave?"

Ivan suppressed a dry chuckle. It was not as if he and Pierre had anything to pack. They had nothing but the clothes on their backs and a few toilet articles—a comb, a razor, soap, and a toothbrush—in their pockets. Pierre had also managed to obtain a small derringer, which was now in the pocket of his canvas coat. He had convinced Petrovich to get it for him, telling the man that he did not intend to be taken alive. Ivan didn't like the idea that Pierre was armed; the Frenchman was impulsive and hot-headed and it was hard to predict what he might do. But Ivan's protests went by the way. Pierre was resolute, determined. A man in his position must have a gun.

Lottie was speaking. "Since this is likely to be our last time together, there is something I have to know. Which of you put Yuri up to that business in Hyde Park? He could not have made the bomb himself."

Ivan braced himself against the thought that he would not see Lottie again. "I wish I knew," he said sadly. "Whoever it was signed poor Yuri's death warrant."

Lottie fastened her glance on Pierre, and he shifted uneasily. "I had nothing to do with it, if that's what you're thinking. I am no bomb-maker, regardless of what that fool of an inspector claimed. I could not have manufactured that device—and if I had, I would not have entrusted it to Yuri. He was incapable of carrying out a complicated and perilous task such as that."

Lottie frowned, her face shadowed in the flicker of the candle. "Then where did he get it?" she persisted. "Who could have given it to him?"

Pierre shrugged. "Scotland Yard. That bulldog Ashcraft, or one of his agents. They would know Yuri would fail. They used him to discredit our cause—and to create an excuse to seize Ivan and me." His eyes narrowed dangerously and he jabbed his thumb into his chest. "But not Ivan, no. *C'est moi*, Pierre, they were after. I am the one they were afraid of."

Ivan shook his head, thinking it was just like Pierre to imagine that he was the center of the Yard's attention. "It was not the English police," he said. "Ashcraft is not very smart, but even he would not give a bomb to a half-witted boy to throw at your King and Queen. The boy might by some chance succeed, and even if he failed, other Englishmen might die. It is only the greatest chance that no one was nearby when the bomb went off." He shook his head again. "No, no. The English are too sentimental for such things."

Lottie looked at him intently. "Then who?" she demanded, and her voice took on an even greater urgency. "Who gave Yuri the bomb?"

Over the days in Holloway Prison, Ivan had applied himself to this question. He had thought at first that Yuri himself had conceived and carried out the action, one last splendid sunburst of anarchistic glory, one final heroic deed. But the more he had reflected, the more he had remembered of the details of the weeks before that fatal day in Hyde Park, and the more convinced he was that Yuri had not been a hero, but rather the unknowing pawn of a dangerous man.

"It was the Russian secret police, Lottie, the Ochrana." He heard her little gasp of horror but did not stop to comfort her. She liked to play at being an Anarchist—it was time she knew the real truth of things. "The Ochrana are ruthless. They would not care who died, the King, the Queen, one or two Englishmen, a dozen. But they would have the same motive—to discredit our cause. And to provoke the English police into closing down the *Clarion* and making arrests." He paused and added, in a lower voice, "They would do all this to have me arrested and sent back to Russia. A member of the Ochrana was following me, watching me." *He* was the cause of Yuri's death. Ivan knew this now, as certainly as he knew his own name. And he would have to live with the knowledge for the rest of his life, however long or short that might be.

Lottie's eyes widened. "You, Ivan? But what have *you* done to make them come after you?"

Pierre laughed. "Yes, Ivan," he said mockingly. "Tell us what you have done that has made you such a dangerous man that you must be hunted down and hauled back to Russia."

Ivan took a deep breath. He would not have answered Lottie, but Pierre's mocking tone pricked his pride. "When I escaped from prison in Russia," he said, "I caused the death of a high official, the son of a princess and a favorite of the Czar. The Ochrana——"

There was a noise and Ivan stopped. The door was open several inches. Lottie stepped forward. "It is the wagon driver," she said, "the man who has come to take you to Dover. He——"

"Wait," Pierre commanded. His hand had gone to his coat pocket, where Ivan had seen him put the gun. "Let us see who it is."

The door swung open and the candlelight glinted on the barrel of a revolver. Ivan sucked in his breath. The tall, thin Russian holding the gun was the same man who had followed him prior to his arrest.

"Frenchman," the man said, "I will have that gun in your pocket." His voice was cold and hard as steel.

Pierre hesitated, his eyes going to the man, then to Lottie. Ivan saw his jaw clench, saw him consider whether to seize her as a shield, then abandon the idea.

"Come, come now." The man's voice took on an edge. "No harm will befall you or the woman. I have no quarrel with either of you." His eyes went to Ivan. His gun was trained on Ivan's belly. "I am here for the murderer Kopinski." He held out his left hand. "Give the gun to the woman, Mouffetard. It is of no use, anyway. There is no powder in the cartridge."

No powder in the cartridge? The meaning of that came to Ivan at the same moment it came to Pierre. The other slowly lifted his hand out of his pocket, and Ivan saw that he was holding the derringer. He handed it to Lottie.

"Now to me," the Russian said, still holding out his left hand. "Do it," he said, more harshly. "I am losing patience."

Reluctantly, Lottie put the gun in the man's hand. "Who are you?" she whispered. "You're not from Scotland Yard. What do you want with Ivan?"

"I heard your friend telling you all about it when I opened the door." The man chuckled. "Do you not believe him?"

"You're from the Russian secret police?"

"That is correct. I am Dmitri Tropov."

With pain, Ivan saw that Lottie was breathing in short, irregular breaths, and her face had gone very pale. "How did you find us?" she whispered.

Tropov smiled. "One of your comrades is in my employ. I shall leave it to you to discover which one. You are clever— you should enjoy the sport. It will be like the game you call hide and seek."

Lottie took a step forward. "And you are the one who gave the bomb to Yuri?"

"Who else?" Tropov shrugged. "Of course, he was not expected to get anywhere near your King and Queen, although if he had, it might have proved interesting. You can appreciate that, can you not? You are an Anarchist, or so you say. Had he succeeded, he would have been a hero, would he not?"

Lottie sounded incredulous. "But you expected Yuri to blow himself up on the street, where he would kill innocent people?"

"What of it?" Tropov asked. His voice grew sharp. "We

are done with talk. You and your French friend may go. I want only the Russian."

Lottie turned to look at Ivan, her eyes large and luminous and very frightened. "Ivan," she whispered imploringly, "I can't let you—"

"Go, Lottie," Ivan said. The pain slashed through him like a sword. "You can do nothing to help me." He raised his voice. "Pierre, take her out of here."

Pierre held out his hand to Ivan. "Farewell, comrade." His smile was crooked and there was a bright glint in his eyes. "We shall meet again."

"I think not," Ivan said, hopelessness enveloping him. "Just get her out, before Tropov changes his mind."

Pierre pushed Lottie past the Russian. Stumbling, she put both hands on the knob and began to open the door. Lifting his chin as if in defiance, Pierre thrust both hands into his pockets and made as if to follow her. Then, so swiftly that Ivan could not be sure what he was seeing, the Frenchman whirled, his hand flashing in a lightning-fast slash across Tropov's throat.

"*Viva l'anarchie!*" Pierre cried triumphantly, and held up the bloody razor. "Death to all police!"

Tropov's left hand went up to his throat with a lazy, languid gesture, as if he were brushing away an insect that had stung him. He leaned backward against the wall, his eyes going wide, his mouth gaping in a soundless cry, blood spurting from the slashed artery in his neck. His fingers loosened and the revolver clattered to the floor. His knees failed him and he slid down the wall.

He died where he sat, in a puddle of blood.

CHAPTER THIRTY-FIVE

The Revolution looms large and the bourgeoisie will not see it.

Jack London,
letter to Anna Strunsky, 15 October 1902

Charles dedicated several days of the week following the trial to the drafting of his report to the King. Kate typed it for him on Thursday, and he delivered it to Ponsonby on Friday, the twelfth of September. In it, he wrote that the bombing in Hyde Park was an isolated event instigated by a Russian secret agent named Dmitri Tropov, who had been discovered murdered at the rear of a cigar shop in Church Lane, a victim, no doubt, of one of the many Russians who bore the Ochrana a passionate hatred. The young man who had carried the bomb was dead, the Anarchist newspaper for which he had worked was closed, the Anarchist cell in Hampstead Road had been disbanded, and two of the Anarchists had been brought to trial. What had happened in Hyde Park, he concluded, was not likely to happen again. Their Majesties faced no continuing threat.

The report was fairly brief, for Charles had intentionally omitted certain important elements of the affair. He did not, for instance, describe the details of Tropov's murder or Kopinski's and Mouffetard's escape from the country, which Charlotte Conway had recounted to him and Kate when she visited them at Sibley House on the Saturday following the trial. Where the two fugitives had gone was none of his affair, and certainly none of the Crown's. They were apparently beyond the reach of English justice, and when Charles discussed the possibility of their pursuit with Assistant Commissioner Edward Henry, he did not sense that Henry had an urgent interest in going after them. Henry seemed to feel, in fact, that Inspector Ashcraft's illegal acts—the acts of *former* Inspector Ashcraft, that is, for the man had been sacked—had tainted the convictions to the point where he could not justify pursuit of the fugitives. And while numerous crimes had been committed, including two homicides, they had in effect cancelled each other out. Justice, it seemed, had been roughly served.

Moreover, Charles saw no reason to include in his report any description of the part played by Charlotte Conway and Jack London in the escape of Kopinski and Mouffetard. Nor did he say anything of his discussion with Captain Steven Wells, of the Intelligence Branch of the War Office, and specifically excluded what Captain Wells had said (which might have offended the Royal ears) when Wells learned that his Russian contact, Rasnokov, had also been in the employ of Ochrana, and that he had recently died a violent death. These omissions notwithstanding, Charles felt that he had fulfilled his commission, and he was glad to see an end to it.

There were a few other related matters in which the Crown could have no interest, and which were resolved over the next several weeks. Following his acquittal, Adam Gould returned to his position at the Amalgamated Society of Railway Servants, and was busy hammering out the details of a new contract with the Metropolitan Railway that gave the workers higher pay and shorter hours. Recognizing that Charlotte Conway needed work and confident in her valuable skills, Adam had found a position for her at the union's office. Charlotte had stayed with Nellie Lovelace at the Rehearsal Club for a fortnight, but when she received her first week's pay, she and Nellie pooled their resources and found a flat together. Nellie had discovered, much to her relief, that she was not pregnant; she was still working at the Alhambra, but had moved from the chorus line to a minor role and was understudy for the female lead. Nellie hoped that, over time, her disgraceful lapse would be forgotten and her talent would allow her to recover her reputation.

As for Jack London, he had completed the research for *People of the Abyss* and returned to America by way of the Continent—or so he had written to Kate in a letter that he hoped she would forward to Lottie. In it, he had humorously outlined his adventures with a group of rowdy Continental revolutionists:

> On the train I met a Frenchman named Pierre. We grew chummy. At Spezzio we were delayed by a train-wreck. We went sailing in the harbor, & on an Italian man-of-war became acquainted with a boatswain. The latter got shore liberty and proceeded to show us the town. Both he and the Frenchman were revolutionists. Birds of a feather, you know—and by three in the morning there were a dozen of us, singing the Marseillaize (spl?) and clashing with the police.

Kate had debated whether to show the letter to Lottie and did, finally. Lottie, however, declined Jack's urgent request to correspond with him, and (as far as Kate knew, anyway) that was an end to the matter.

* * *

Before they left London for East Anglia, Kate and Charles accepted a dinner invitation from Bradford and Edith Marsden. It was Kate's first visit to the Marsdens' elegant home, which was newly purchased and freshly furnished in the latest decorative style. Edith, too, was stylishly up-to-date in a low-cut gold-colored gown. Her bosom was adorned with a cascade of delicate lace, her hair was elaborately dressed and sparkling with diamond pins, and she wore a diamond-and-pearl choker at her throat. Kate, who did not often wear jewelry, felt very plain indeed in comparison to this brilliance, and briefly regretted that she had not worn something more elegant than her green dress.

Bradford was in excellent spirits, Edith was her usual playful self, and the drawing-room conversation was sprightly. When the gong sounded and they went into the dining room, the cut-glass chandelier was filled with lighted candles, casting a warm, flickering light over the elegant table, laid with the best crystal, china, and silver and centered with an enormous bowl of hot-house flowers. The dinner, of course, was splendid: two soups and two entrées; for the second course, Chicken à la Richmond, sirloin of beef with horseradish sauce, and vegetables; and for the third course, roast partridges, Charlotte Russe, and Cabinet pudding. As they sat at the table over dessert, an imposing Apples à la Parisienne, Kate reflected that the food that had appeared on the table that night might easily feed an East End family for several weeks. She was turning over this troubling thought when Bradford remarked to Charles, in an offhand way, "I say, old chap, that trial you were involved in—it was a queer business, wasn't it? And unfortunate."

"Yes, very queer," Edith put in brightly. "Bradford told me all about it, Charles. One of the Anarchists was acquitted, wasn't he, and the others ran away? Such dreadful, filthy creatures, Anarchists." She smiled at her husband. "But Bradford assures me that they can do us no serious harm." Edith had worked as a secretary to Cecil Rhodes before her marriage to Bradford, and Kate had rather liked her. Now, she wasn't so sure, for Edith seemed shallow, and more interested in fashion and opulent living than in anything else. Kate wasn't sure about Bradford, either.

"Don't know what the world's coming to," Bradford said, as the butler refilled his champagne glass. "Anarchists everywhere, assassination in America, revolution on the Continent, whole thing's going to hell in a handbasket. Don't know why the jury acquitted that trade-unionist, either. He—"

"He was acquitted because he was innocent," Kate put in hotly. "Because the policeman put the evidence in his room—and in the rooms of the other two men, as well."

Edith's eyes widened. "Oh, no," she said. "That *can't* be true, Kate! Not a policeman!" She turned with a coquettish smile to Charles. "Tell me, Charles, that it's not true. The police would never do such a thing!"

"I'm afraid it's rather sordid," Charles said. "I don't think the details would be of much interest." He smiled at Kate, and she read the message in his eyes. Edith would neither understand nor believe what had happened, and as for Bradford—

Bradford frowned. "What that fellow Ashcraft did might have been technically illegal, but in my opinion, he was morally justified. The function of the police is to keep us safe from dangerous men. They must use whatever means are necessary to ferret out terrorists and lock them away."

Charles said nothing. Kate opened her mouth to object, but closed it. Charles was right. The Marsdens were among those who feared social change because it might threaten their way of life. Argument would not persuade them otherwise. She might as well save her breath—here, at least. There would be other, more productive opportunities to speak out.

"I heartily agree with you, my dear," Edith said in a sensible tone. "They must use whatever means are necessary. Society must be protected at all costs."

Bradford smiled and his tone lightened. "As long as law and order are maintained, the country will prosper—as we have prospered, my dear." He cast an approving look down the length of the table, his glance lingering on the magnificent choker Edith wore around her neck. "And if they want revolution," he added almost carelessly, "they shall have to face the consequences. That's all I have to say."

Edith smiled at Kate and signalled to the footman to pull back her chair. "Shall we, Kate? I'm sure the men are going to talk about politics. We'll go to the drawing room for coffee and our own little chat. I've a new silver coffee set I'd like you to see, and I'd very much like your opinion on the draperies. They were quite expensive, but I'm not sure that the color is exactly right."

Suddenly Kate had had enough. "I'm so sorry," she lied, "but I have the most terrible headache. I do hope you'll forgive us if we say good night now."

A few moments later, Kate and Charles were in a cab, on their way back to Sibley House. "I trust your headache is better," Charles said, looking at her with a grave smile.

"It was a silver-coffee-set-and-expensive-draperies headache," Kate confessed. "I did not think I could tolerate another minute."

There was a longish silence. At last, Charles said, "I heard from Hardwicke Rawnsley today, Kate. He's just back from taking a look at the land I propose to give to the Trust, and is entirely in favor of the transaction."

"Well, I should think so," Kate said with a little laugh. "Canon Rawnsley did not strike me as the kind of man who would look a gift horse in the mouth—especially when there are more magnificent horses to be had in a few years."

Charles reached for her hand. "You're sure that you approve of my giving Somersworth to the Trust? It's not the sort of thing that Bradford or Edith Marsden would understand, and I'm sure there will be others who feel I am letting down the side by giving it up. Shirking my duty, as it were."

"Shirking your duty?" Kate put her hand in his. "I should say you are *doing* your duty, my dear. The Trust will be here long after you and I are gone, and perhaps a way will be found to make Somersworth available to all the people."

"Perhaps." Charles's eyes lightened. "And we might look on it as a small gesture in support of the revolution."

AUTHORS' NOTES

I prefer living to writing.

Jack London
letter to Alice Lyndon, 1909

Susan Albert writes about Jack London

When Bill and I learned that Jack London, the noted American adventure writer, had visited the British capital at the time of the coronation of Edward VII, we decided that he would play a major part in the book that we had in mind. We had read and enjoyed many of his stories; we knew that he was a self-avowed Socialist; and we knew that his book, *People of the Abyss* (written during the months of August, September, and October 1902), was a scathing critique of the slum conditions in the East End. Although we didn't know much else about him, he seemed to be a perfect character for our novel—a major American writer, in the right place at the right time, with strong political sentiments of the right sort.

But as we began to read about London's life, other aspects of his character began to overshadow his writing and his radical political beliefs. The man brimmed with exuberant life and sexual energy. He was greedy for experience, for fame, for money and all the things money could buy. He was the center of the universe for himself and for those who loved or desired him, often to their detriment. On the train trip from California to New York, a few weeks before the beginning of our novel, he fell into a railway-car sexual affair with a "sweet woman" with whom "nothing remained when our three days and nights were over." He claimed never to have loved Bess (the woman to whom he was married at the time of this novel, the mother of his two daughters) and walked out on her in July 1903, claiming that she was turning him into a "house animal" and his home into a "prison." He had already begun an ardent affair with Charmian Kittredge, who learned to sail, box, decipher Jack's handwriting, offer judicious stylistic suggestions, and corrected and retyped his typescripts—all the prerequisites, one imagines, for a successful relationship with Jack London. But when Bess filed for divorce, she named another woman, Anna Strunsky, whom Jack had also loved (and quite as passionately as he now loved Charmian) in 1902. Bess's error was corrected, and (despite several miscellaneous new affairs) Jack and Charmian were married in November 1905.

As Jack's enormously energetic life went on, many other conflicts emerged within this complex and self-destructive man. But at the time he appears in our novel, his greatest energies (outside of his writing) seem to have been devoted to finding the love of his life, his "mate woman," and that is the way we have portrayed him. While his sexual relationship with Nellie and his romantic attraction to Lottie are entirely fictional, we believe they are an accurate portrayal of Jack London's uses of women, and that they show him as he was, at once passionate and manipulative.

London loved hard, lived large, and died early, before his fortieth birthday, his life a study in contradictions. As a Radical Socialist, he was eager for the revolution, but he pursued the capitalist dream to the last day of his life, accruing as much as he could and spending far more than he earned. As a writer, he had a stunning and disciplined talent, but his other appetites pulled him away from his work; as he said himself, he preferred living to writing, and while his readers gobbled up his stories, his critics felt that the more he wrote, the less memorable was his writing. As an adventurer, he genuinely loved the wilderness of the sea and the frozen North; as a skilled self-promoter, he knew that to sell his books, he had to sell his adventurous life. (Unlike other writers of his era, he would be very much at home in our time.) But it is these complexities and contradictions that made Jack London large, large as the world, larger than life, and that is the way he will be remembered.

Bill Albert writes about Anarchism

> *The liberty of man consists solely in this: that he obeys natural laws because he has himself recognized them as such, and not because they have been externally imposed upon him by any will whatever, divine or human, collective or individual.*

Mikhail Bakunin,
Father of Anarchism, 1814–1876

When I was growing up, my knowledge of the Edwardian period was embodied by a single large English penny in my small coin collection. On the back, Britannia was serenely seated with shield and trident on a throne, as she had been on other English pennies for the century before this coin was struck. On the well-worn front was the massive head of a man, in profile, with an impressive beard and high forehead: Edward VII. I was aware that this king had ruled for only ten years and I was convinced that nothing of importance could have happened during his reign.

I was, of course, wrong. The first decade of the twentieth

century in England was a period of radical change, in several senses of the word. At the beginning of the decade, the landed elite still had a firm if nervous grip on power. Against them were arrayed a multifarious assortment of liberals, radicals, and reformers: Chartists, Fabians, Socialists, nihilists, Communists, Bolsheviks, home rulers, trade unionists, and suffragists. And on the extreme fringe of these left-wing factions were the Anarchists.

Unlike the others, the Anarchists had no real plan for social change, only a dream. In fact, their basic philosophy more or less prohibited the formation of a plan, for a plan would require organization and the Anarchist creed insisted that all forms of organization, even those as basic as the family, had to be abolished. The dream went something like this: One day the revolution would come, the state would be swept away, the people would be free from oppression, and all would be well. Man's darker nature (which was the result of oppressive government) would be brightened, and evil would vanish. There was no point in attempts at reform; indeed, reform merely postponed the inevitable revolution.

Anarchists sought to hasten the revolution in two ways: by propaganda of the word (education), and by propaganda of the deed (violence). English Anarchists seem to have contented themselves mostly with the former: countless meetings, lectures, marches, banners, leaflets, and of course, newspapers. They could adopt this milder approach because England had pursued a relatively tolerant course in dealing with political dissent, while in Spain, Russia, and elsewhere, protest was rewarded with the garrote and firing squad. The Continental Anarchist turned terrorist and resorted to bombs and assassinations, while Britannia watched nervously.

In England, ultimately, it was the more moderate forces that swept away the monopoly of power held by the upper class. Unions were organized and strikes provided the workers with real economic power. The franchise was extended. Liberal and even radical politicians gained seats in the House of Commons, at first a few seats, and then a great many. For a few years, their programs were frustrated by the hereditary House of Lords, but finally, under the threat of the creation of massive numbers of liberal peerages by the King, the Lords allowed passage of the Reform Bill and ceased to exist as a significant political power. The social revolution had come, almost without bloodshed, and the Anarchists, left without a cause, slowly faded away.